# APOTHEOSIS OF THE IMMORTAL

## BOOK I

JOSHUA A. CHAUDRY

Published in the United States by Adakyn Press, 2014

http://www.adakynpress.com

E-Book ISBN: 978-0-9915617-1-1

Paperback ISBN: 978-0-9915617-0-4:

Cover art by Damonza.com

Printed in the United States of America

# Dedication

*This book is dedicated in its entirety to my son, Caleb Chaudry, as a small way to thank him for his patience, support, and the sacrifices he has made so this dream of mine could be fulfilled. He gives me the drive and determination to keep trying, even when my shoulders are heavy with disappointment and my outlook is bleak.*

# Acknowledgements

There are so many wonderful people who have helped me along this arduous yet thrilling journey. So many people I would like to thank, however to name them all would be something like a page of genealogical listings in the book of Genesis—I would be saying so much without truly saying anything at all. Therefore, I have chosen to reserve this page for those few special people whose support and dedication to my life in general have been so huge that I consider them soul mates—people who have directly affected the course of my life in one way or another, and have made me better for it.

I would have to recognize my parents and grandparents, who fight at every turn to get my life on track, yet are always there for me either way; my brother and sister, who have always loved me unconditionally; my niece and nephew, whom I love like my own; my late friend Mathew Rickett, who, during his last weeks of battling cancer, actually comforted me instead of the other way around; and my son, who inspires me to rise from my couch every morning—with his damn alarm clock!

*"To write is human, to edit is divine."*

– Steven King

I would have never understood this quote if not for my editor Faith Freewoman. She has the gift to take my words and transform them into art. Faith has changed me as a writer, giving me the perfect mixture of support and reprieve to allow tremendous growth as a novelist. She picks and prods, asking me the perfect questions, questions poignant enough to bring me to my own solutions. The knowledge I have gained from working with her is absolutely priceless, as it will be with me and show in my writing forever. The most wonderful thing about working with Faith is that she allows you to create a product all your own, brought forth by your imagination and creativity, yet you couldn't have done it without her. It is, she is, an amazing and beautiful paradox.

I would like to thank Teresa Reasor, an author, and another great artist in the field. She has helped with my edits and her insights are sometimes nearly magical. She has been with me from the beginning and continues to be there for me whenever I need guidance; her help gave me my first big breakthroughs as a writer, and without her graceful interjections I would not have been able to reach my destination.

I would also like to thank Ellen Fox, who has supported me in many ways since the beginning of this project. She is a brilliant writer and has somehow been able to inspire the same in me from time to time.

I would like to thank my father, Dr. Khalid R. Chaudry M.D. for all of his emotional and financial support; without his faith and unconditional love this would certainly have never happened.

Lastly, I would like to thank *You & Me Coffee & Tea* for providing great coffee and a wonderful working environment.

# ELIJAH 2014

H E WENT TO sleep next to his little brother Malaki—boys in a castle, exchanging gallant tales of Solomon, the older brother they idolized, and dreaming about the brave knights they might one day become. But the sinister night had abruptly crucified that age of innocence and Elijah emerged a man—full of hate and intent on vengeance.

It seemed like an eternity had gone by, but he remembered every detail, every moment like an hour… the fear and confusion on Malaki's face, his murderer's stench and cold stare. He remembered his mother's dead eyes desperately calling for help. The puddles and splashes of blood covering the walls and floor. The merciless destruction of Sara, the girl he'd loved his whole life.

Revenge was all he had lived for in the hundreds of years since he opened his eyes and raised his head from the cold stone floor of Rothber Castle. Some time during that terrible night he had been baptized in blood and birthed into immortality. His mind and body had solidified with clear and immutable purpose, though his soul had been crushed in its wake. His soulless geste was cold and cynical; everything pure and sacred was dead. All that remained was a hard and implacable shell, an unyielding carapace—immortal, and fully sustained by hate. Nearly a millennium of blood, lust, and dreams of revenge hadn't been enough to sway his purpose or dull his passion.

A great abyss separated Elijah from his human capacity for love, respect, and peace of mind. The mortals with whom he interacted were mere keys on a piano, striking the strings that dulled his senses and eased his pain.

He was a dead man walking.

# ELIJAH – THE ABYSS
# 1190 AD

*"He who fights with monsters should look to it that he himself does not become a monster. And when you gaze long into an abyss the abyss also gazes into you."*

*"Beyond Good and Evil,"*
*Aphorism 146 (1886). Friedrich Nietzsche*

# CHAPTER 1

"NOOOO! ELIJAH, HELP meeeee!"

Elijah was jolted from his dream of playing childhood games with his beloved Sara by his little brother's shrill cries. His pulse thundered as Malaki continued screaming his name.

Lunging to his feet, his eyes still bleary with sleep, he sprinted to the stairwell. Beneath the faint, flickering yellow light of the rushes on the wall, Elijah watched in horror as a burly man descended the stairs with little Malaki thrown carelessly over his massive shoulder.

Elijah was disoriented from his sudden trepidation, and the dim light was making it worse. Rushing forward, he didn't notice until it was too late that the usually cold, dry floor was now warm and wet. And just as a horrible stench made him gag, his bare feet skidded on the steps, and in the flicker of rushlight Elijah saw they were saturated with a blanket of red.

His shoulder struck the edge of the wooden banister and numbed his arm, making it impossible to catch himself when he tumbled backwards and hit the whetted edge of every stair as he fell to the bottom.

He landed on his aching back, and his eyes fell on a gruesome sight only inches from his face, one so dreadful his mind refused to accept what his eyes were seeing. A surge of horror exploded in his chest.

His mother's body lay on the stone floor next to him. She was naked, and nearly every inch of her was covered in blood. Her dead eyes were still crying out for help; her face was frozen and distorted with terror. Her chest had been completely ripped open, the wound too hideous to comprehend, and Elijah's stomach roiled as he gagged again on the stench of blood and death.

"Elijah!" Malaki's shriek jerked Elijah's attention up and away from the horror lying beside him.

The stranger handed his little brother over to a second man. Dressed in dark robes, the second man's silver hair hung unkempt from his forehead to his jaw, and a ragged beard covered the lower half of his face. He looked like he hadn't bathed in months, and his putrid stench clouded the room. But when he turned with a struggling Malaki in his arms, Elijah recognized him immediately.

"Father!" The word was torn from his throat in accusation. His long-lost father's arms were wrapped tightly around Malaki's small body, holding him still almost effortlessly.

As soon as he heard Elijah's exclamation, Malaki suddenly went limp. Elijah saw a flicker of hope in his little brother's eyes. Until this moment, Malaki hadn't known it was his father whose grasp was now so strong around his chest.

Malaki's fear vanished as he realized he was right where he had longed to be, wrapped tightly in his father's arms.

Elijah shot him a fiercely warning glance. This was not the father they had known all those years ago, and he didn't want Malaki to give in to that seductive fiction, to believe this man meant him no harm.

Catching the powerful warning in his brother's gaze, Malaki

was brought back to reality. This man's embrace was different. It wasn't one of a loving father, but of a vicious stranger bent on causing harm.

*What is happening? Where is Solomon?* Elijah's thoughts careened around his brain. He watched with utter disgust as the filthy man lifted Malaki's head and pressed his lips against the soft warmth of the boy's cheek. Malaki was innocent; he was sacred, and this defilement was too much. An unholy rage stirred within Elijah; he must end this now.

"Stop this debauchery. I will *not* let it continue." Elijah's voice was quietly, intently venomous.

His father didn't say a word. He just looked directly into Elijah's eyes for a long moment. Then, without hesitation, he shrugged his shoulders indifferently, bit Malaki on the shoulder, and then snapped his neck.

Elijah's mind and body blanked, frozen in disbelief. Then he was ripped back to painful awareness when he heard his little brother's body hit the cold stone floor.

"No!" The word ripped from Elijah's very soul. The pain nearly crippled him. "What are you doing?" Elijah shoved to his feet, bruised and bloody from the fall, his body protesting every movement. He searched his father's eyes, but found no reason for this devastation, and saw no remorse.

Suddenly Solomon appeared in the doorway between Elijah and their father, and Elijah's heart leapt with relief. Solomon's enormous strength could certainly settle this score. Malaki had meant just as much to him, if not more. Elijah's heart was still wrenched with sorrow over the loss of his little brother, but he found a bit of solace in knowing Solomon would surely make their father pay long and painfully.

He watched his big brother, waiting for him to act, but slowly realized he wasn't looking at the great man he grew up admiring. The Solomon he knew would never have tolerated this and would not have hesitated to kill in restitution for what had just been done to their little brother.

But now Solomon's face was sheepish, his eyes apologetic. Far from ferocious, his big brother looked broken—and *afraid*!

"He's killed Mother and Malaki!" Elijah shouted, trying to yank Solomon out of his trance. But his older brother just stood there frozen; he did nothing.

Realizing Solomon's many years at his father's side must have made it impossible for him to act, Elijah quickly decided he would relieve his brother of this burden. Solomon had been older than he and Malaki when their father left, and their bond had been strong. Elijah had also loved their father, but the man before them now was not the man Elijah remembered. He was no longer their father.

A thought leapt into his mind. Solomon had just gone to see Sara. "Solomon! Solomon!" He yelled frantically, but his brother wouldn't even look up. "Just tell me Sara is safe," Elijah begged.

The evil his father had become laughed, but Solomon remained silent, hanging his head.

Panic sank in even deeper now. "Solomon!" he shouted again. "Tell me!"

Solomon barely looked up and shook his head slowly to the left and then to the right. Shame was smeared all over his face.

"What have you done, Brother?" Elijah screamed, overcome with grief.

Looking again towards Malaki's frail, lifeless body sprawled at the feet of the monster, Elijah's resolve hardened and his mind filled with rage.

His father stood silent; the look on his face was condescending. None of tonight's events had disturbed him in the slightest.

"Why?" Elijah cried.

His father fished out a small pistachio nut from the satchel draped around his shoulder and pried it apart with his teeth.

The cracked shell spewed from his mouth and landed in a pool of saliva just inches away from Malaki's body. He still didn't say a word.

Elijah glanced again at Solomon, who was still hanging his head, looking defeated, even submissive.

Anger and frustration stormed through Elijah, building rapidly to an explosion. He understood why it would be so difficult for Solomon to stand against their father, and he wouldn't blame his brother.

This was his father's doing. His father's silence and impiety fed his anger as he stalked forward. "I'm going to kill you!" he shouted.

The need for retribution narrowed his focus to the man standing proudly over his little brother's broken body. He could already feel his father's neck crushing beneath his hands; he pictured it in his mind. As he continued forward, he glimpsed a large log hanging from Solomon's capable hand and was elated and relieved to see Sol had finally regained his composure and was ready to help him.

Lunging for his father, Elijah spotted movement out of the corner of his eye. It was Solomon; he was swinging the piece of wood like a club. It wasn't until the wood crashed against his own temple and the cracking pain of the blow dropped him to his back that he grasped his brother's betrayal.

As he lay on the ground, the liquid heat of blood and pain surged from his head and through his neck. He was more confused than ever. What had just happened?

*Why? Why?* The single word echoed through his mind while everything went black.

## CHAPTER 2

ELIJAH AWOKE TO the unusual feeling of cold stone on his back. Confused, he raised his head and wiped the sleep from his eyes. Then he sat up and slowly looked to his right and then to his left, his neck and back stiff and aching.

He could tell it was morning. The corner of the kitchen table glowed, as it did every morning, from sunlight shining through a small round window in the wall where he now rested his back. It looked almost like the sun had burned a small hole right through the wall.

His hands, which were still rubbing his face awake, suddenly became rigid as the horrible smell of guts and rotting flesh assaulted his nose.

A deep pain lanced through his heart as a hazy memory of his mother's broken flesh flashed into his mind. After a moment of confusion, he slammed his hands hard against the floor and shot to his feet. Already spotting his mother's legs on the other side of the table, he hurled himself forward, hoping that what he had seen was a nightmare.

But it was not a dream. The revolting stench of death and a sickening sense of betrayal swallowed him whole and dropped him to his knees. He looked again at his mother's chest. She had been gutted, ripped wide from her bellybutton to her neck.

Why had they done this? Why the defilement and mutilation? *Why leave me alive? Better to die than have to live the rest of my life haunted by this terrible sight.*

*Did they mean to leave me alive? Maybe they think I'm dead like Mali...* Elijah suddenly remembered how his father's strong hands had snapped his little brother's neck. He quickly scrambled to his feet and began to search. But he couldn't find Malaki anywhere. There was no lifeless little boy lying on the stone floor. A surge of hope gripped him. Could Malaki be alive?

"Malaki!" he shouted, racing through the corridors, through the servants' quarters, and the storage room. "Malaki!" There was no reply, but he refused to give up hope, not yet. When he threw open the kitchen door, the cool morning breeze lashed against his cheeks. "Malaki, can you hear me?" Still no response. He was losing hope by the moment, but there was still one place to look.

*Of course*, he thought, racing back through the kitchen. Guilt raked at his spine as he leapt over his mother's corpse like she was just another obstacle blocking his path, but he quickly pushed the feeling aside. There was no time to pay niceties to a corpse—Malaki could be lying hurt somewhere, and his mother would want Elijah to make that his first priority.

Continuing up the stairwell, he hoped with every step he would find his brother playing in one of the upstairs rooms. For a moment his mind flooded with a beautiful vision. He saw Malaki, as he had so many times before, hunkered down on the floor with a bit of charcoal and a tiny piece of parchment between his knees.

As he burst through the doorway at the end of the corridor, and into their empty bedroom, the last bit of hope and tenderness drained from his body. Falling to his knees, a crushing hopelessness squeezed his chest. He opened a dresser, pulled out a thin blade, and jammed its sharp point hard into his neck.

As the blade pierced agonizingly through his flesh, on the verge of delivering a mortal wound, he thought about what little effort it would take to penetrate his jugular and ease the throbbing in his throat and the unbearable pain in his belly. He wanted so much to shove just a little harder and thrust the blade through to the other side of his neck. His soul was dead and his will was broken. All he wanted was an end.

Just as he was about to set the blade to its bloody purpose, Elijah thought of his mother lying dead and bloodied at the bottom of the stairs. He thought of Malaki, his body no doubt lying broken in some gulley. And Sara. He didn't want to imagine what horrors she had faced. If he died now, who would avenge this savagery? Who would exact the retribution his loved ones deserved? From where would vindication find its way?

As these questions rolled round in his head, his spirit was vexed. As much as he longed for death, there was no one else to deal out the vengeance and punishment that were owed. Avenging his family was his responsibility, and he knew he must see it through before reaching after the eternal peace he longed for.

Dropping the small and bloodied blade to the floor, he rose to his feet a different man—one with purpose, a single purpose. All he could feel now was rage, an unfamiliar feeling, but one he would come to know all too well. It would stay with him for ages to come.

Elijah couldn't imagine why his betrayers had murdered his family, their family. The family they lived with and loved for so long. The children they had protected, their cherished wife and dear mother. But it no longer mattered. From this day forward, the hope of vengeance would be his only respite.

# CHAPTER 3

ELIJAH RUMMAGED THROUGH his mother's room. He was looking for a decent piece of cloth to wrap her body. It didn't make much difference at this point, but she deserved at least that much effort and much more. Eager to catch up to his father and brother, he moved quickly into his bedroom and grabbed the blanket his mother had made when Malaki was just born. It wasn't the nicest piece, but it seemed fitting.

Elijah stretched out the woolen cloth on the kitchen floor. Sliding his arms beneath his mother's shoulders and hips, he gently lifted her. The foul and musty odor of rotting flesh nearly knocked him over as he pulled her close to his chest and then laid her carefully in the middle of the outstretched fabric. He was horrified by her weight; she was far too easy to lift.

*Did they remove all of her insides?* The thought sickened him. *What were they doing here last night? What did I miss? Why?* The questions went on and on, but he knew they were pointless; there were no answers available, at least not right now.

As he wrapped her, he noticed a glint at her neck. It was the small, round metal pendant she had worn on a chain for as long as he could remember.

It was etched with a tiny inscription which read, *Everything begins and ends with a will, and a purpose is only as strong as the will that propels it.* Now spattered with blood, the pendant dangled just off her right shoulder. He gently pulled it from around her neck and gazed thoughtfully at it for a moment before fastening it around his own neck.

An elderly lady named Lilith lived just across the valley, in the old cottage Elijah had once called home. She had been the hand-maiden of Lord Jeffrey's mother. Having been Jeffrey's wet nurse, his nanny, and his teacher, she had practically raised the man. She loved him as her own and greatly appreciated the help Elijah's family had given in caring for him during his final months.

Once Jeffrey had sent William away, Lilith had been the only servant left to care for Jeffrey. Elijah's mother had decided to give their old land and cottage to her when they moved into the castle.

Elijah carried his mother's body along the worn path that wound alongside the stream and eventually led to the small patch of trees hiding Lilith's tiny cottage from the main path. The famil-iar smell of pine greeted him as he cut between the trees. The old cottage appeared in the clearing, and his memories stirred at all the familiar sights and smells of his youth.

His mother's small herb garden had grown ragged, but he could still detect the fresh thyme, dill, and basil tangled amidst the weeds. Nostalgia warmed his soul, but he had no tears left to cry. Elijah laid his mother's wrapped body on a soft patch of grass next to the old garden. His body was surprisingly strong; the trip hadn't strained his muscles, but his mind was weak with anguish.

Hearing him approach, the elderly woman came out to meet him.

"What in God's name has happened, child?"

Elijah silently kneeled at his mother's side and dropped for-ward, pressing his forehead into her shoulder.

"Is this Esmeralda?" The old lady's body was strong and her

senses were sharp, but any fool could see Elijah was wracked with grief.

"There, there, child, everything's gonna be all right. Some wounds never fully heal, and some losses will always be near to us, but it does get a little easier with time—you learn how to deal with it, how to move on."

The old woman had suffered much loss of her own and Elijah knew it, but that knowledge didn't help him right now.

"What happened, son? Where's the rest—where are your brothers, I mean?" As she asked, the old lady gently touched Elijah on the shoulder.

He remained silent; he had no idea what to say or where to begin. The entire night seemed surreal.

"Well, bring her on in. I'll put a blanket on the hearth and light some candles. You can lay her down and take whatever time you need to mourn your loss." Her tone was inviting; she was a kind and gentle soul.

Although he still couldn't bring himself to speak, he was a bit comforted by Lilith's kindness and warmth. He was grateful not to be alone. Picking up his mother's body, Elijah followed the old woman through the open doorway and waited while she retrieved a thick woolen blanket from a small cupboard and carefully covered the hearth. He laid his mother's corpse on the blanket while Lilith lit a few candles and placed them around her. The strong smell of incense filled the small room as she waved the smoke across Esmeralda's body.

"Sit down for a moment." Both her voice and hands were shaky as she pulled over a small wooden stool and shoved it towards Elijah. He dropped hard onto the stool and, putting his head into his hands, he rubbed his eyes vigorously.

"Oh! Are you hurt son?" Lilith quickly wet a rag and began rubbing vigorously at Elijah's neck. "There's no wound, so it must have been your mother's blood."

*What?* Elijah rubbed his fingers across his neck where he had jabbed the thin blade. Lilith was right, there was no wound. *How is this possible?* But his thoughts were quickly buried by the stench of his mother's corpse that penetrated his nostrils and swamped his mind.

"It was my father, and Solomon." Elijah finally offered hoarsely, after a long silence.

"What do you mean? Are they okay?" Lilith didn't understand.

"They killed her, and Malaki." Elijah declared while staring blankly at the floor.

"Your father, William, and Solomon did this?" Her voice rose sharply with shock. "How? Why? Are you sure?" She was staring at Elijah in disbelief.

"I don't know. Father just showed up last night, after I had gone to bed. I must have somehow slept through it when they killed Mother. Malaki's screams woke me up. A large man was carrying him tossed over his shoulder and was running down the stairwell. I tried to rush down to help him, but the stairwell was covered with Mother's blood. Before I could make it to the bottom step, I hit the banister and tumbled down the steps, ending up next to Mother's mutilated corpse." He paused for a moment, overcome.

"I stood up just in time to see Father break Malaki's neck with his bare hands, like it was nothing, like *he* was nothing." Elijah's voice was steady now. Tears were streaming down his face, but he didn't notice. "I tried to get to Father. I wanted to kill him for what he had done, but Solomon cracked me on the head with a log and I must have been unconscious before I hit the floor." Elijah spoke while gently rubbing his neck in disbelief.

"Your father and Solomon... well, I just can't believe that. Your father is such a gentle man. And Solomon, well he's just as fine a boy as I've ever met." Her tone was somewhat challenging. Elijah was sure she knew he was no liar, but he also knew his story didn't make any sense. Still, she couldn't ignore the lifeless body lying on her hearth.

Elijah rubbed his head and stared down at the floor. He didn't say a word. He wasn't even listening; he was lost.

"We don't have much time before your mother starts to stink. You'll have to get her in the ground soon." She was being kind; the stench of dead flesh was already overtaking the sweet smell of burning incense and making it hard for Elijah to breathe.

"There's a large stone just up the hill," he said. "It's where we played as children and mother used to tell us stories." The old lady was already nodding before Elijah had finished speaking.

"Yes, I think that would be perfect. You go put your mother to rest, and I'll put on some supper. After you've eaten, I'll help you clean off the rest of that blood, make you a bit more presentable."

"No, thank you. I'll be fine." Elijah didn't feel hungry; he was still too upset to keep anything down. Besides, the old lady had done enough.

"What'll you do?" she asked, seeming more curious than concerned.

"I'm going to find them, and I need to hurry." Elijah gently swept his mother's wrapped body up in his arms and headed for the door.

"What'll you do when you find them?" she shouted as Elijah walked out the door.

"I'm going to kill them." His grit and determination were growing by the moment. His hate grew with every step he took carrying his mother up the steep hill. He was no longer a man. He was a purpose, a cause; he had nothing else, and nothing else mattered.

# CHAPTER 4

H E DUG A deep grave next to the stone and placed his mother inside as gently as he could. The smell of sod and wet dirt was comfortingly familiar. When he looked over at the huge pile of dirt, it seemed to be climbing its way to the top of the stone, the way he and his brothers used to. Their mother would sit on the stone and tell stories or sing songs while he and his brothers climbed all over her.

She told them wonderful tales of courage and love, heroes and villains, stories that had fired his imagination. He realized now they hadn't just been stories. Now Elijah had seen villainy and known the deepest of evils, but he was no hero, nor did he want to be. He had no desire for justice or peace. He would not seek recompense or to balance the scales. Nothing could restore what had been taken. So he would bring punishment; he would bring balance; he would bring death.

*A nice enough place. She loved it here.* He knew his mother would have approved of her eternal home.

After filling in the grave, he said his tearful goodbyes and started walking. He knew he would never see this place again, nor did he want to. It was too late in the day to make it very far before dark, but he didn't want to stay another night in this place, and oddly, he wasn't at all tired from the digging.

A small stream stretched both east and west of the small cottage where he grew up. Sara still lived with her parents in a cottage much like the one he had known for so long. It was only about an hour's walk through the dense forest, following the stream to the east. His steps were quick and light. He wasn't running, but he moved with an ease and speed that astonished him.

He initially dismissed it as excitement, but he couldn't explain it away when he saw the small cottage off in the distance in barely half the time it should have taken him to get there.

He could tell it was dark, but he could see with a startling acuity, much deeper into the night than ever before. Staring once again towards the cottage, he noticed something was different. Curiosity and concern set his feet in motion, and he took off at a full sprint. His feet pushed from the ground as if he were weightless; he launched himself forward with every step.

*What is going on? How can I be moving this fast?* He made it up the steep hill to the cottage with amazingly little effort; he wasn't even breathing hard. He was barely even breathing at all, actually. Still, his body was stronger than ever! *Am I losing my mind? Am I dying?* He was frightened and exhilarated at the same time.

The far end of the cottage had been destroyed. The roof and logs were all in ashes, and only a pile of rocks remained. The smell of burnt wood and thatching filled the small clearing. There was also another smell, one Elijah didn't recognize, but the sickening feeling that stole over him filled him with dread. When he rushed over to look at the destruction left behind, seared flesh and bone sticking from the ashes confirmed his horrified suspicion.

"Sara!" he exclaimed. "Sara!" There was no response. Dead silence. Though it had been buried deep, he had hoped his brother might somehow have been wrong, and she might still be alive. That hope was now completely crushed. Clearly she had died with the rest of her family.

Slumping to the ground, he leaned his back against what was left of the stone foundation and wept. *Why would they do this to Sara and her family? It makes no sense!*

He didn't know how he could keep going after this, but as his thoughts drifted away from his precious Sara and towards his father and Solomon, hate drove him to his feet. Yes, hate would keep him moving towards his purpose.

He thought briefly about burying what he could find of the bodies in the house, but decided it wouldn't make any difference. It would only slow him down. The only difference he could make now, for anyone, was to find and kill the ones responsible, those who remained of his family.

# CHAPTER 5

ELIJAH HAD NEVER been far from home. He knew there was a small town somewhere on the river to the east; he had been there with his father when he was younger. He couldn't remember exactly how far the town was, only that it hadn't taken more than a few days to get there. He didn't know how yet, but he needed to stock up on some supplies.

Pushing himself up from the broken cottage wall Elijah thought he noticed movement coming from within, beneath the ash and rubble. Maneuvering closer, he spotted a foot sticking out from beneath some thatching. *Sara?* Could she be alive? His heart leapt as he climbed inside to investigate.

As he lifted the thatching he was aghast at what lay revealed at his feet. Sara wasn't moving; her withered body looked like a corpse. Elijah kneeled down beside her and wiped the blood and ash-stained hair from her face. She was still beautiful.

Suddenly, a cloud of ash flew into the air as Sara's body convulsed furiously. She heaved and coughed, and then her body became still once more. *How can she still be alive?* The thought sent Elijah into a panic; he had to keep her alive, but didn't know how. Sliding his arms under her, he shoved to his feet, cradling her frail body as he rushed to the riverbank.

Desperate and unprepared, he tilted her head back and poured a handful of water down her throat. There was no response. Elijah searched for signs of life, but found none. She wasn't breathing, and he couldn't feel her heart beating.

Unsure of what to do next, he decided to carry her to town, hoping someone there would know what to do for her. It was dark, but Elijah felt there wasn't much time. He still wasn't tired, and he urgently needed to get help for Sara.

He ran as hard as he could, never getting tired or weak. He was impossibly fast. What had happened to him? What was the source of this new power? How long would he have it? He didn't know, but thought his father might.

Elijah was still running towards town when Sara's body suddenly convulsed again, jerking against his arms as she gasped for air. Looking down, he saw her eyes open for just a moment. His heart practically leapt out of his chest with joy. It was the first time he had seen her beautiful eyes in nearly three years, the first time since his father had decreed that Solomon would be the one to marry her.

He rushed to the nearest tree and placed her gently on the ground beneath it. He propped her head and back against a large, protruding knot. Her breathing was shallow, but pressing the side of his face against her chest, he could feel it gently rise and fall with each gasp for air. Thrilled, he ran back down the path and retrieved another handful of water from the river. This time, as he poured it into her mouth she gagged violently and spewed it back out. That worried him, and he found himself praying for the first time in years, and to gods he no longer believed in. Then he stopped, reminding himself that if the gods did exist, they had already forsaken him.

"Sara. Sara." He spoke softly, but received no response.

Although he was still unsure what to do, each breath she took was cause for hope. Elijah decided to let her rest awhile beneath the thick canopy of leaves that provided a bastion against the breaking dawn.

Hopefully she would regain consciousness soon. Elijah was anxious to learn exactly what had happened to her and how she was still alive. As the hours passed, he discovered that, although his body was now stronger than ever, his mind was beginning to drift and lose focus.

Perhaps it was a reaction to the tragedies of the past night and day, or something else he didn't understand, but his mind was somehow undone. He decided to lie down next to Sara. The idea of getting some sleep comforted him, although he knew his gripping concern for Sara would probably make sleep impossible.

He lay there with his eyes closed for what seemed like hours. He thought about his entire life. But brutal images of his mother and Malaki continued to surface, even when he tried to concentrate on something pleasant. There were moments when the clouds seemed to part and he could see his mother's beautiful face and hear her voice, but those images would soon fade and be replaced by the gruesome scene that had confronted him at the bottom of his stairwell.

Elijah had no idea how much time had gone by when he began to hear voices. Sitting up, he saw five men walking along the river path from the east. His only thought was to hide Sara; he feared what they might do to her.

But there was no time to conceal her, so he decided to try to draw them away. One of the men caught sight of him just as he stepped into the road.

"Hey you, boy, what are you doing over there?" As the man spoke, he lurched closer, lifting his chin belligerently and narrowing his eyes. The other men followed; they were all approaching fast. Elijah could now tell from their look and manner that their intentions were as vile as their stench.

"Just headed to town for some supplies." Elijah smiled awkwardly, quickly shifting his eyes away from the man's menacing stare.

"Are you alone, boy?" As the man spoke, he looked around, as if to see for himself.

"Yes, I am." Elijah knew they were dangerous, but he didn't have many options, and his anguish over all that had happened made him feel like he had little to lose.

"Well, go ahead, empty your pockets. Hand over your silver." The man stepped closer and the others circled around Elijah. The leader was about Elijah's height and was wearing all leather, except for a wool tunic.

His speech revealed a nasty set of teeth, some yellow, mostly black. He was perhaps the ugliest man Elijah had ever seen. His fat nose bulged inches from his face, and his long, greasy hair was knotted into patches. His men weren't as ugly, but shared the same putrid stench.

"I don't think I will." Elijah's voice was nearly a whisper. He had no silver, but his anger and frustration had reached a boiling point, driving him to taunt the small drove of bandits. Elijah carried no bag, and his clothes were nearly rags. What could they possibly expect to find?

"You are on your way to get supplies, so you must have some silver. Now give it to me, boy!" He hauled out a knife as the two men behind Elijah grabbed him by the arms and pressed firmly against his shoulders. Elijah didn't resist. "I'll just gut you and take it myself." Spittle flew into Elijah's eyes and mouth as the man bawled out his threats.

The men surrounding him now smelled even worse than their leader looked. Elijah could barely force himself to breathe. He thought he might be killed if he struggled, and worried what would become of Sara if he did. Still, his hate drove him on, and he decided to fight anyway. It was selfish and baneful men like these who had just ruined his life. As the man in front thrust his knife forward, Elijah instinctively jerked his right arm free. The man who had been holding it was flung into a tree rooted a few feet from the path.

Elijah's power still surprised him and, what was even more surprising, these men now seemed to be moving in slow motion. It took little effort to quickly redirect the thug's knife and shove it straight through his throat. The two men standing beside the knifed man drew swords.

Elijah grabbed the man to his left by the throat and crushed it with ease. Then, as Elijah threw him forward, his flailing body knocked over the man who still stood before him. That man fell hard on his back as the dead man crashed against his chest.

Elijah remembered there was a fifth man behind him and turned quickly, but was met with a sword. The bandit thrust hard, and the sword sank deep into Elijah's abdomen. The other two men had risen to their feet and stood proudly above the seemingly defeated Elijah.

The three men watched and laughed as Elijah fell to his knees groaning. The men stood there jeering as one man spat on him and another kicked him in the side. Elijah was sure he was dead, but then, after the initial shock wore off, he began to feel strong again and struggled back up onto his knees. *What have I become?* he thought.

Their faces immediately turned to shock as they watched Elijah clasp the sword by its blade and pull it slowly out from beneath his sternum. Throwing the sword to the ground, Elijah climbed to his feet and glared at the wide-eyed trio. He began walking towards them, his only goal to crush them utterly. After seeing his power and the look in his eyes, the three men turned and ran away as fast as they could. Elijah thought about letting them go, but the anger burning within him overruled the impulse.

He was at their backs in a flash, snapping the first man's neck midflight. He hammered his palms into the other two from the back and they both fell headfirst onto the path before them. Without hesitation, Elijah walked over and smashed in one man's head with his heel. He watched as the last man crawled backwards. He enjoyed seeing him wriggle like a worm on a hook as he begged for his life.

"You would have me give to you the life you were so eagerly and callously going to steal from me?" Elijah was furious. He knelt down beside the man, who was now crying and begging.

"Shhh." Elijah's calm voice and demeanor quieted the man while Elijah gently held his head still, framing his face with both hands. He looked deep into the man's eyes. He didn't know what he'd hoped to find there, perhaps a reason for all this, for evil, something he could recognize and put his finger on. He found nothing, no reasons, just the desperate eyes of a man who wanted nothing more than to see another day.

*People are just evil; it pervades us all,* he decided. He snapped the man's neck and gently lowered him back to the ground. *Even me.* He looked back, examining the carnage left in his wake, and a guilty satisfaction broke across his chest. The entire experience had been bittersweet, but mostly bitter.

He suddenly noticed one of the bodies lying on the ground was still moving. As he quickly moved closer, he saw it was Sara! Elijah blinked and rubbed his eyes. His mind was reeling. When he left her, she was barely breathing. How could she have dragged her nearly lifeless body from under the tree and all the way to the road? And why?

She was now lying atop one of the men Elijah had just killed. Elijah was baffled, and he walked closer, only to be frozen with shock and disgust at what he saw. The girl was sucking at the dead man's neck, at first gently, but then more and more vigorously as her strength seemed to grow. Soon she was viciously rending the man's dead flesh, spitting out tissue and bone as she went.

Confused and appalled, Elijah decided to pry her away from the nearly-decapitated body. He bent down to pull her off, but, as he placed a hand on her shoulder, she threw her head up and hissed like one possessed. This creature resembled Sara, but was crucially different.

The whites of her eyes were a dark crimson, and the veins around them were pulsating and bloated with life. Long, sharp, bloody teeth tore through the edges of her widely parted lips. Startled, Elijah jumped to his feet and tripped backwards over a corpse. Pouncing like a cat, the Sara-creature was on top of him before his back hit the ground.

Unlike the men now lying dead around him, she was not moving in slow motion. Her tired, lifeless body had been transformed; her strength was superhuman. Grabbing him by the wrists, she forced his arms outwards and pinned them hard against the ground before she sank her teeth deep into his jugular.

Elijah was taken completely by surprise. Just moments ago she had barely been able move!

*What is happening? What is wrong with her?* Gathering his wits, he slowly pushed his hands from the ground to her shoulders. Thrusting his arms forward with all of his might, he pried her head away from his neck. When he looked into her eyes, he could no longer see Sara at all; this thing attacking him was a monster, void of all its former humanity.

Launching her into the air and across the path, he knew what he needed to do, but also knew, without any doubt, he could never do it. Killing had become easier than he ever imagined. He even enjoyed it, but, despite the ghoulish vision before him, he believed somewhere inside this monster was the woman he had loved his entire life. He decided to subdue her.

He shoved to his feet and hurried over to where she had landed hard against a large rock. She lay unconscious, but she was still breathing. He was relieved, since it might buy him enough time to figure out how to help her.

He moved closer, checking carefully to be sure she was truly unconscious, a bit worried that this was a ploy. But as he stood over her bloody mess of a body, he noticed her face once again looked human. She had been restored to the beautiful girl he had known and loved for as long as he could remember. Cradling her in his arms, he was blanketed with the love he had always held for her, and full of joy to have her back. Perhaps there might still be hope for the wonderful girl he had known, as well as the monster she had become.

# CHAPTER 6

"Elijah?" A soft, familiar voice vibrated against his chest as he trudged along the road toward civilization. He stopped immediately, worried about what might happen now that Sara had regained consciousness, about what she might do. He walked over to a tree not far from the path.

Her face and clothes were still covered in blood, but her expression was now soft and heavy as Elijah knelt down and gently leaned her back against the tree. She seemed weak once again, broken, as if she were conscious but wished she weren't. She just stared up at him blankly; he thought she must be in pain.

"Yes, it's me, Sara. I'm here." Elijah broke her stare and shifted his eyes to the ground. He was utterly confused; he had no idea what to do or say.

"Thank you." She sobbed and then burst into tears as she pulled Elijah close and laid her head on his shoulder. "I have missed you so much," she sobbed, as she wiped her tears on his shoulder. "Why did you leave me? I've waited for so long." She was squeezing him tighter and tighter. "I'm so sorry." She spoke between sobs. Though it was mostly healed, she could see the mark where she had bitten and sucked at his neck. She squeezed him tighter and clenched his tunic firmly in her fists.

"I'm sorry, too, but I didn't think I had a choice. I couldn't have borne seeing you with him. I couldn't." Elijah was also in tears, holding her close, realizing what a terrible mistake he had made.

"Of course there was a choice. I loved *you*, Elijah, and I would never have married your brother. If you had talked to me even once, you would have known that. I was yours; I wouldn't even speak to Solomon for the first two years after I found out. I was waiting for you, but you never came; you never came." She was still weeping, but her tone was sharper.

"Shhhh, I'm here now. Tell me, what happened to you, Sara?" He gently pushed her away and looked into her eyes. "Why were you trying to eat me?" Narrowing his eyes and furrowing his brow, he swallowed hard; he was afraid of what she might say.

"I don't know." Releasing Elijah from her tight grip, she sniffled and wiped the corners of her eyes with her knuckle. "The last thing I remember from before I blacked out is William chewing on my neck. Chewing! Like some animal." She squinted and lowered her head. "Solomon just stood there watching," Sara mumbled with teary eyes. "Your father must have sucked out nearly all of my blood before I fainted. That's all I remember." Her eyes were soft and apologetic as she looked up again at Elijah.

"What about your family?" he asked.

A deep sorrow eclipsed her face, and immediately he was sorry he had asked. He could almost see the painful memories rushing through her mind. She squinted against the horrors until her eyes closed completely.

"I remember all of it, even the smell of my parents' burning flesh." She just dropped forward and cried out.

Elijah couldn't bring himself to press any further. He stared into space, baffled. *What was going on? What awful thing happened to spur this madness?*

"After that," she continued after a while, "all I remember is the smell of blood. The dead men on the road, the smell of their blood stirred something inside of me, a hunger… I couldn't stop myself. Blood was all I could think about, and once I started I couldn't stop, I just wanted more and more." She had stopped crying now and was speaking more quickly, with enthusiasm, as if it had been terrible and wonderful all at the same time.

Strangely, Elijah could relate. He had experienced something similar when he took the lives of the thieves on the road. Still, this seemed different; it was so strange. He didn't want to be a bigot, but Sara's actions just seemed more perverse than his straightforward killing. Still, how could he judge her after what he had done?

"How did you kill all those men on your own Elijah?" Her thoughts mirrored his own.

"This dreadful experience has changed us somehow, Sara. Like you, I am much stronger and faster, but I have no desire for blood." Elijah looked up and saw her embarrassment and remorse. "No, I wasn't trying to say you are bad, or I'm better than you, only that I haven't experienced that, at least not yet." Elijah was worried, not just for Sara, but for himself as well. There were too many similarities between their circumstances. How long before he experienced the urge to tear through someone's flesh?

"Anyway, when I saw you on the road, I could hear your heart beating beneath your chest and the fresh blood pulsing through your veins. I tried to stop myself, but I couldn't; I lost control. It was like something else took over and was driving me on, forcing me. Nothing else mattered; I just wanted your blood." Her eyes seemed to glaze; the excitement faded from her voice, changing to remorse and embarrassment.

"What have they done to me, Elijah?" She was weeping uncontrollably as she pulled Elijah into another tight embrace. "If you hadn't left me, this might never have happened." She sighed as she spoke, and her voice lost its fervor, as though her admission had released something.

Elijah had never looked at his actions in that way before, that he had left her, but now it seemed obvious, and his heart seemed to sink into his stomach.

"What are we going to do?" she asked, resting her head gently against his shoulder again. It seemed she was at least as concerned and perplexed as he was by their current situation.

"I don't understand what's going on, Sara," he whispered in her ear as he held her. What had they done to her? What had they done to him? He placed his hand on the back of her head and gently stroked her hair. Maybe her madness was over. He knew he could never kill her, but wasn't so sure about what she might do to him.

"But I know who does know." His resolve hardened and his vision focused back to the beginning, back to William. "We have to find Solomon and my father," he declared, glaring into the distance. They were out there somewhere, and he was determined to find them.

"What? What are you going to do when you find them?" Her voice sharpened with fear as she tugged at a lock of his hair.

"I'm going to get answers. I'll find a way to help you, and then I'll kill them. I'll kill them all—Solomon, Father, and that ugly bastard who was with them." The fire and strength in his voice seemed to quiet her fears.

"I guess you will always be my prince." The words danced from her lips in a lovely melody and flooded him with new strength as he met her gaze. After a moment she smiled and shifted her eyes down to her stained garments.

Elijah shook his head and tried to focus on what needed to be done right now. "First, we need to clean you up. We are almost to town, and you shouldn't be seen like this." Elijah opened the large satchel he had retrieved from one of the dead men on the road, figuring the thief no longer had need of it. He had filled the satchel with everything he thought might be of use, including a few garments and a leather sack of water.

Ripping off a scrap of his tunic, he poured the water over it and dabbed at her face and neck. The blood rubbed off to reveal the beautiful and innocent girl he had dreamed about so many times.

Though he'd never had the courage to officially make his affections known, she knew he had been in love with her then, but did she know he still was?

She giggled as he poured the water over her head and hands and rubbed until she was spotless. Rubbing the last speck of blood from around her mouth, he recalled how she had always captivated him, and he knew he was comforted to have her with him now, in the midst of this madness. He suddenly realized he had lost himself in his imagination and had been gently rubbing her face for far too long.

"That's got it." Blushing, he quickly pulled away and looked at the ground. After a moment he looked back up toward the soft curves of her face and saw she was still gazing back at him. His embarrassment at showing affection didn't seem to have bothered her; she just smiled, warming his heart. Maybe she was simply happy to have him here, or perhaps she too still had some measure of feelings for him.

"You'd better put this on." His eyes were shifting from embarrassment as he handed her the freshest tunic he could find. Taking it from his hand, she waited for a moment and then smiled again, perhaps glad that this strong man now seemed more like the nervous boy she remembered.

"Would you care to turn around?" she asked.

"Oh, of course." His face burned with even more embarrassment at his ineptness, and he quickly turned his back to her.

# CHAPTER 7

SARA AND ELIJAH hid in the forest just outside of town. They had decided to wait until nightfall to enter, hoping the darkness would help conceal their presence. They were no longer covered in blood, but Elijah's guilt over the events of the previous night wasn't as easy to wash off. It was as if the world would be able to see right through his façade of youth and beauty to the monster he had become.

Darkness, he had decided, would be his ally. This is where he would live, away from the piercing light that would expose him for what he really was. Besides, if his father and Solomon were there, it would be much better if Elijah spotted them first.

"Elijah, I am starving. I'm beginning to feel weak." He looked over to see her eyes were closed. Her voice was cracking as if she were scared.

He didn't understand her problem. "Don't worry Sara. I lifted quite a bit of silver from the rogues I killed last night. We will be able to buy enough supplies to last us quite a while." Lying beside her on the ground, he rolled over and brushed her cheek gently.

"You don't understand, Elijah. I can hear the blood pumping through your veins like a drum. I can smell it. It's not regular supplies I am hungry for." She rolled away from Elijah as she spoke, and he saw her wipe away a tear.

"Everything will be okay." For Sara's sake, Elijah hid his discouragement. He'd been almost convinced the incident from the night before had been a one-time occurrence, triggered by her closeness to death.

"It's going to be all right, Sara; we will figure this out. Let's try you on some real food and see if that helps. Just please be strong and don't hurt anyone." He pulled at her shoulder as he spoke. She lifted her face and he was horrified to see blood beginning to pool in the veins around her eyes; even the whites of her eyes were beginning to turn red.

"Sara, what's happening? What can I do?" He wanted to help, but didn't know how.

Seeing his horrified grimace, she hid her face once again in embarrassment. "I'll be fine; let's just hurry." Her voice was muffled as she spoke from behind her hands.

"Don't be embarrassed, Sara. I know this isn't your fault. Just stay close to me and keep your distance from everyone else." He took her hand and helped her to her feet. In minutes, they emerged from the forest at the town gates. Elijah wished it was closer to full dark, but he knew the shops would close if they waited much longer.

As they walked into town, Elijah stared everywhere, completely amazed by the sights. He had only been about five years old when he'd last been here, and now it was like seeing it for the first time. It was just a small town, but it didn't seem small to him.

He had never seen so many buildings in one place, or so many people. Even this late in the evening, the place was buzzing with life. Sara was pressed firmly against him and was squeezing his arm ferociously as they walked through the town. He could tell she was fighting to keep her wits about her and hoped to god she didn't lose control.

"The first thing we need to do is get some new clothes so we don't look so out of place in these filthy rags, and then we will get some food for you." He whispered over his right shoulder to Sara who was now attached to him like a leech as she hung her head awkwardly. He searched down the row of buildings and signs until he saw one that read *Gondal's Tailoring and Linens*.

"There it is; stay with me, and remember to keep your head down." He pulled her close and kissed her on the side of the head, ineffectually trying to ease her obvious misery. As they walked through the door of the tailor's shop they saw a number of fancy dresses and all sorts of men's clothes.

"Can I help you?" A small voice piped up from across the room.

"Yes, my wife and I need to purchase some new clothes." As he spoke, he could see the man behind the counter eyeing Sara and pushed her further behind him. "We were raided on the way here. We barely made it out with our lives." Elijah spoke to ease the man's obvious curiosity. The man stood up and squinted; he was either suspicious or he couldn't see well.

"Okay, I'll just need to get your measurements." The man turned around and rifled through some things looking for his equipment.

"No, we don't really have time. I just need a tunic, leggings, and a surcoat with sleeves and a hood; my wife, only a simple gown and a surcoat. Anything will do." He spoke quickly, knowing he needed to get Sara out of there as quickly as possible.

"Well, everything I have is there in front of you; just pick out what you'd like." The man pointed to the back wall and sat back down, never taking his eyes off of the pair. Elijah quickly grabbed everything they needed and walked to the counter.

"What is this?" Elijah frowned as he pointed to a small hat lying on the counter.

"That is called a beret; you have never seen one?" The man

seemed surprised, and he held it out to Elijah. "Here, try it on. I'll sell you this entire lot for seven billon obole." Elijah tried on the beret and looked down at Sara, who was still staring at the floor.

"Very well, I'll take it, but all I have are silver deneros." Elijah took them out of his pouch.

"All right, five denero." The man slapped the counter and smiled as he shouted, obviously his way of concluding a sale.

"Do you have a room where we can put on these fine new clothes?" Elijah asked while handing him the silver.

"Yes, there is a room in the back." The man nodded towards a corridor connected to the adjacent wall.

Elijah was glad to get away from him; he could feel Sara's grip tightening around his arm and was worried she wouldn't be able to control herself much longer.

As they entered the room in the back, Elijah noticed her face looked much worse; the whites of her eyes were now bright red and she was beginning to resemble the monster he had seen last night.

"It's okay, Sara, just try to stay calm; we are almost finished. After this we'll get something to eat." He handed her the gown and surcoat and then turned around to change. "Damn, this is a lot of layers; I can't believe people actually dress like this, can you?" Sara didn't reply so he turned around and found her leaning against the wall, nearly unconscious. "Sara, Sara, wake up." He shook her gently as he pleaded.

After a few seconds, her eyes opened and she hissed, revealing two sharp fangs.

"Sara, calm down." He held her firmly against the wall. After a minute she began to look more human and Elijah let her go. "Here, put these on." Elijah handed her the clothes again.

In a matter of moments she had changed, and once again attached herself to Elijah as they walked back through the store and out the door.

"Look over there," Elijah pointed across the street to a tavern. "I'll go in and get some food for us. You just stay out here and keep your hood up." He opened his eyes wide and held her by the shoulders as he stared into her bright red eyes.

"No, I need to stay with you," she pleaded, trembling with fear.

"I think it's safer for you to stay out here. There are a lot of people in there; you might lose control. You'll be better off out here. Just stay in the shadows where no one can see you. I'll only be a minute." He led her to the side of the tavern and reminded her again to stay there while he went inside for supplies.

Walking into the tavern, Elijah was overwhelmed by the smell of sweaty men and barley ale. The place was loud and rowdy. He looked to his left and saw a man pulling a working woman into his lap; she quickly jumped to her feet and slapped him across the face. The man stood up, and, for a minute, Elijah thought he might slap her back, but he just sat back down and took another swig of his ale.

"What can I do for you?" The man behind the bar was put together well and had a pleasant manner.

"I just need some food, whatever you've got will be fine," Elijah's eyes were wide as he gazed around the room while drumming his fingers on the bar.

"Well, we mostly serve alcohol here, but we do have some bread and maybe some turkey bits." The man smiled and laughed.

"Thank you. I'd like to have one loaf of bread and the bits. And please hurry." Elijah kept tapping his fingers on the bar as his worry for Sara continued to escalate.

A few minutes later the man brought out a bag. As he handed it to Elijah, a loud scream blasted into the tavern from outside. Everyone in the bar dashed out to investigate.

Elijah expected the worst, and he was right. As he walked out of the bar, he saw a circle of men standing around Sara as she dropped the blood-drained body of a young man to the ground. Her hood had flown back, exposing her still-red eyes and distorted face.

"She is a demon! We must kill her," voices shouted throughout the crowd.

Elijah watched as they came at her with swords and pitchforks. "We need to burn her. It's the only way to make sure she stays dead," another voice harangued from somewhere in the crowd.

Sara was hissing and clawing at her attackers, but she was surrounded by a large horde and couldn't watch them all. A few men slashed at her from the front as another man sneaked up behind her. He pulled back his sword, ready to thrust it through her heart.

Elijah hadn't wanted to kill anyone else, but he had no choice at this point. He raced forward and snapped the man's neck before he could strike. Seeing his speed and power left the crowd awestruck, and everyone took a few steps back. Seizing the opportunity, Elijah cradled Sara in his arms and ran as hard as he could out of town. It would have been impossible for the townspeople to keep up with him. He could feel Sara gnawing viciously at his neck as he ran, but it didn't slow him down.

He didn't know how long he ran, but he finally began to feel weak from the blood loss, although she was no longer sucking at his neck. Stopping for a minute to rest, he laid Sara on a hillside. Her eyes were closed as he lay beside her. She looked human once again.

He lay beside her quietly, wondering what he was going to do with her, if he could help her at all.

# CHAPTER 8

W*HY COULDN'T HE sleep?* Elijah's eyes were heavy and his mind was weak; he couldn't understand why he didn't drop off to sleep immediately.

"Elijah, my prince." Sara rolled over and was now lying on her side with her head propped on her hand. Her dark hair fell down her back and gently caressed the ground. As he looked at her, she filled his soul with love; in spite of all he had seen her do, he saw nothing but beauty.

"You rescued me again!" She smiled and crawled closer to him as she spoke.

Before he knew it, she was on top of him, straddling his waist. She slowly leaned forward. What was she about to do? Elijah needed to be wary; she was very fast and strong.

All of a sudden she went for his neck again, mouth open. But did she want to kill him or kiss him? Elijah's instinct was to throw her off. He was strong enough, but he couldn't bring himself to do it. He worried he might have made the worst decision of his life. Giving her the upper hand like this could get him killed... but then, where she had been gnawing just minutes ago, her soft lips and wet tongue stroked over the mending wound like healing rains.

Her mouth moved across his neck and then down to his collarbone. Elijah couldn't move. He was frozen in ecstasy. Once again her lips caressed his skin, and her soft hair cascaded down around her face, tickling him a bit.

After taking a moment to regain his composure, he wrapped his arms around her and flipped her onto her back. Now he was on top; he was in control, and he continued to kiss her on the mouth and neck and then lower. Slowly, he ran his hand up under her gown, along the thigh of her bent leg.

They continued kissing passionately as he pushed her gown further up and she pulled at his tunic. In just moments, their clothes were off. As they began making love, Sara moaned out in pain and ecstasy, as it was her first time. Elijah moved to retreat, but she grabbed him, urging him on; her fingernails raked hard against his back. Elijah was inside of her as they rolled over once again and continued making love; her hands were now pressed firmly against his chest. Before that night they had both been virgins, together they had become something much different.

Once more she went for his neck, and once again her soft lips flowed against his skin. As need to once again feel her tongue on his neck built inside him, he was surprised by a sharp pain as she was once again sucking at his neck. It hurt, but he enjoyed it, and putting his hand on the back of her head, he pressed her face against his neck to let her know it was okay. It wasn't the pain he enjoyed, but the closeness, and he realized then, due to his new condition, he was as able as he was happy to be her life-giving source.

Grabbing a handful of her hair, he pulled her away from his neck and pushed her mouth to his. As he kissed her, he could barely taste the blood on her tongue.

As the night lingered, her tenacious grip around his chest

lost not a bit of fervor. He thought for a moment how drastically different his life had become overnight. He also decided that, until he could find a way to help her, until he could discover a more permanent solution for her hunger, she should use him as her only source of blood, and no more innocent people would have to die.

Neither of them could sleep. Curled up in each other's arms, the two talked about many things. Despite the recent atrocities that had changed their lives, they were both finally where they had longed to be for years.

"We'll need to go soon." Elijah swept the hair from her cheek.

"Where are we going?" She looked up into his eyes.

"You've heard of Jaen; that is where we need to go. It's to the south." Elijah spoke with confidence as he laid his head back on the ground. "No more eating people, either. If you need blood, you will take mine, understood?" he stared into her eyes to emphasize his point.

"Understood." She closed her eyes and ran her fingers down his face; she seemed happy.

Elijah knew, despite everything they had been through and the horrors they had witnessed, they were still the same people at heart. There were differences; they were no longer innocent children playing together, as they had years ago. Their childhood had vanished long ago, but only now had their innocence been taken from them.

# CHAPTER 9

WHEN THEY PASSED other travelers on the road south, Elijah would pull Sara close to him. He lived with the constant fear that she would lose control.

The sun had just broken over the horizon when they first saw the city of Jaen. Just outside the city, he took her far from the path and removed his tunic.

"Here, eat." He turned his head and gestured toward his neck.

"I'm not even hungry. I'll be fine." As she turned to walk back to the path, he caught her arm.

"Please, Sara, feed yourself. I don't want to risk any more lives." He pulled her close and kissed her before he turned his head and closed his eyes. He still wasn't used to watching her feed; her distorted face made her look like a stranger.

After she was finished, he waited the moment it took for his wound to heal, then wiped off the blood and replaced his tunic and surcoat.

"I've got a good idea where to start looking. I know Solomon, and he couldn't come to a place like this without visiting the temple."

She nodded. She, too, knew of Solomon's love for all things holy, which now seemed ironic, if not bizarre.

Elijah was mesmerized when they walked through the city gates. "I didn't know men could build such things!" He stared wide-eyed at all the buildings within the city walls.

"That must be it." Sara pointed towards the most beautiful and elaborate building Elijah had ever seen, and he knew she must be right. As they walked through the entrance of the building, Elijah saw a large group of men who all seemed to be moving and speaking as one. The language they were speaking was very similar to his own, but not exactly the same; still, he could tell they were praying.

A tall man with a thick beard immediately noticed them and began to speak as he walked towards them, although Elijah could only make out a small bit of what he was saying. He was obviously agitated and seemed to be directing Sara into a different room as he motioned for them to remove their shoes.

Elijah instructed Sara to wait outside while he quickly looked around for Solomon. He removed his shoes and sat them against the wall while she walked outside. This seemed to appease the man, because he quit talking and left Elijah alone.

"You are from the north." Elijah turned to look at a man speaking in his own tongue.

"Yes, my name is Elijah, and I am here looking for someone." Elijah went on to describe Solomon. The man immediately began to nod. He claimed to have seen such a man there just two days ago, but had no idea where he had gone.

"He came in and watched the men doing their prayers. He watched for quite a while. He seemed to be carrying a great burden and it looked as if he wanted to pray, but perhaps didn't know how, so I walked over to speak with him. As soon as I reached him he politely excused himself and left, and I haven't seen him here since. Excuse me a moment." After speaking with

Elijah, the man turned and began shouting at a couple of young boys who were wrestling.

Elijah recalled the pitiful, self-loathing look on Solomon's face just after they had both watched their father murder their youngest brother, Malaki. He imagined that was the burdensome look the man had seen on his face a couple days ago, and it infuriated him. Solomon had *no right* to feel sorry for himself!

Elijah quickly left the mosque, feeling an urgent need to find Sara, worried about what she might do. He looked around outside the mosque, but didn't see her or her hooded surcoat anywhere. He immediately thought the worst and a surge of nerves began to crash around in his chest. He didn't want anyone to be hurt, but mostly he was worried about what might happen to Sara if she couldn't control herself.

"Sara!" He shouted again and again as he searched frantically, looking in every dark corner he could find. Hopefully he would find her in time. As he rushed through the market square he spied a petite, hooded figure stepping out from one of the shops. He was filled with relief as the figure turned to reveal Sara's beautiful—and still human-looking—face. He rushed over to her as he wiped sweat from his forehead.

"What's the matter?" Sara's smiling face quickly turned serious as she looked up at him.

He reached out and grasped her left arm.

"Oh, I see, you were worried I had run off to kill someone. You don't have to watch me every second, Elijah. I'm not the monster you see every time you look at me." She rubbed what seemed like a tear from the corner of her left eye as she spoke and then looked down at something she held in her hand.

Elijah began to feel raindrops, first only one or two on his hand, and then pelting down everywhere. As rain began to pour from the sky, he could hear people scurrying about, trying to escape it. In seconds it seemed as if they were alone in the square.

"I was worried about you!" Elijah shouted over the rain. "I don't care about these people. It's you; you are everything I have left and everything I care about. I know what these people will do if you lose control and they catch you... and I need to be there if that happens."

He was now gripping both of her arms and staring intently into her eyes. "I love you! I always have, and I would do anything to protect you from them—not the other way around." He pulled her into his chest and kissed her on the forehead.

"Always my prince," she said softly as she wiped a wisp of hair from his cheek. "Give me your arm," she said, smiling shyly.

"What's this?" he asked as she tied something around his wrist.

"The man in the store said that if you turn it, it becomes the Arabic symbol for the number eight, but as it is, it's the sign of a horse tether." She grinned at the look of confusion on Elijah's face.

"Why do you want me to wear a hor—" he began, but was quickly interrupted.

"I love you too, Elijah." She finished tying the bracelet around his wrist and then folded his big hand inside of hers. "The past years of my life were miserable without you. I can't be apart from you again, and this will ensure that." She shifted her eyes up to his face, and then looked back down at the bracelet.

"We will be tethered together for all of eternity, as long as we wear these bracelets; so don't lose yours! The man said that the strength of two tethered horses was far more than just the sum of their independent strengths. So, the way I see it, as long as we wear these bracelets, we remain tethered together... and as long as we remain tethered, there is no burden we can't bear. And no one, not even your father, will ever be able to harm us again."

Letting go of his hand, she fell into his embrace and gently propped her chin on his rain-soaked shoulder. "I don't know if anything that man said is true, Elijah, but I do know that nothing makes me feel safer or stronger than being with you." She had pressed her face against his ear as she whispered through the pouring rain.

Elijah gently pushed her back and placed a hand on each side of her face as he gently kissed her lips. He loved her more than life, and he knew she was right. Together they could do anything, perhaps even move on and leave this mess behind them. Feelings of hope and peace moved freely through his mind and body for the first time since his family was butchered.

He had no idea why Sara believed in him so strongly, but it filled him with strength and courage. He realized he had much more than just hate and revenge to live for. He had Sara. He had love, and he would protect her at all costs.

With her eyes closed, Sara stood breathless for a moment. Slowly opening her eyes, she caught Elijah's gaze and smiled. Then she took a couple steps back and threw her arms in the air as she began to spin.

"Dance with me, Elijah!" She shouted. It had been years since he had danced. He had been with Sara then, too, and it had been raining just as hard. After a still moment of quiet reflection, Elijah took her hand and the pair danced beneath the rain.

# CHAPTER 10

"THAT WAS A lot of fun." The shower had finally subsided, and the sun hovered directly overhead. The two sat under a tree just outside of the city. Elijah was peeling an orange.

"That looks good. I miss real food." Sara scrunched her nose and poked a stick into the ground.

"Here, try it." Holding what was left of the orange, Elijah reached out his hand.

"No. Even the smell makes me sick." She pushed his hand back as she spoke. Taking the last bite, he threw what was left of the peel on the ground and wiped his hands together.

"How far did you say it was to Granada?" He was still chewing his food. He knew the distance, but was trying to get her to think about something else.

"Well, it would usually take at least a few days, but I think we could be there before nightfall." She grinned broadly. Since finding peace in each other, they were both having fun exploring the extent of their new powers.

"I hope you can keep up, because I'm going to be leaping across the tree tops!" Elijah pushed to his feet and off the ground in one swift motion. He landed on a large tree limb several yards above where he had been sitting. "Come on up. The view is great." He extended his hand.

"Not right now." Rising up from the rock where she had been sitting, she stood and crossed her arms. Elijah noticed she was no longer smiling.

"What's wrong, Sara?" Elijah dropped from his position on the tree to stand right in front of her with his hand resting on the side of her neck.

"Elijah." She lifted her head and looked him in the eye. "What if we can't find a way to fix me? What if there is no way? What if I have to remain a monster forever?" She spoke with her eyes closed as a single tear rolled down her cheek.

"Sara, you are not a monster. You just need blood, and you can get that from me. Even if we can't find a way to change you, you won't have to hurt anyone anymore. You are not a monster." He stopped speaking for a moment and wiped the tear from her face. "If you were really a monster you couldn't control your hunger the way you do; you wouldn't care to." As he finished speaking he pulled her to him and held her for a few moments.

"Better now?" he asked, gently easing her away.

"You don't need blood; why do you not need blood?" She looked and sounded frustrated. "Perhaps it has something to do with who we were before all of this." She looked down for a moment and then stared directly into his eyes.

"Sara, you are not evil, and this is not your fault. I don't understand the differences between us either, but if it was as you suggest, then everything would be reversed." He gently rubbed the hair above her ear. "You have always been a good person, better than me." Elijah smiled. "Are you okay now? Can we go?"

"Yes, I'm fine." She leaned in to hug him once more. "I guess we should go if we are to have any chance of finding William." She was still pressed against him while she spoke.

"All right; come on." He took her arm and gently tugged her towards the path. They ran hard, hoping they might find William and Solomon in Granada. They ran through the forest, taking care to stay a good distance from the road. They couldn't risk being seen.

# CHAPTER 11

THEY STEPPED THROUGH the city gates just as night fell. Since there was no one in sight, it was obvious that something wasn't right.

"My father must be close," Elijah whispered as his eyes scanned their surroundings. It wasn't hard to spot the mosque; it was even larger and more elaborate than the one in Jaen.

"Wait here." Elijah turned to Sara as they reached the foot of the stairs leading up to the mosque. "I'll be right back." He kissed her cheek and tucked her into a crevice beside the stairwell before starting up the steps.

"No!" Elijah heard someone cry out from the other side of the city.

"Did you hear that?" He peered down at Sara from the top of the stairwell.

"Yes, and I smell it too!" She quickly looked back down at the ground.

"What do you mean?" He was back at her side in an instant.

"I smell the blood; lots of it." She pointed in the direction of the scream.

"Is that what that smell is?" Elijah had noticed an unusually strong stench, but hadn't realized what it was.

"Maybe we should just go." Sara was still staring at the ground.

"Why would we do that? Our answers are here, and we might be able to help those people. Come on." He tugged at her arm, but she wouldn't budge. "Don't be afraid, Sara; I won't let them hurt you again."

She still didn't move. "It's not that Elijah; I just want to leave… please." Her voice was quiet but insistent.

"Why? What is wrong? Look at me, Sara." He could feel the change as soon as he touched her face. Tensed muscle and bulging veins had replaced the usual soft curves. "Sara." He spoke softly as he cupped her chin in his hand and slowly forced it up. The moonlight revealed everything.

"You are not going to hurt anyone, Sara," he reassured her. "You are not like them."

"I'm afraid, Elijah!" She stepped closer and pressed her face against his chest. "You don't know what it's like."

"Maybe not." He wrapped his arms around her. "But I do know you, Sara. Please trust me. You can handle it. We need to do this." He cradled her face with his hands and stared down into her crimson, pulsating eyes.

"Okay," she whispered.

Elijah could still sense her fear; he could hear the reluctance in her voice, but he believed she was strong enough to get through it. Besides, this was the only chance they had to find a cure for what ailed her.

As the two grew closer to the stench they began to see more and more signs of William's malevolence and ferocity. Bodies and bits of bodies littered the streets.

"There!" Elijah pointed as he saw movement in the distance. "Did you see that?" He received only silence. "Sara?" He looked back to see her standing immobile, seeming to be in a trance as she stared down at the bodies and blood. "Sara!" He shook her and her head snapped up quickly, her teeth bared.

"Sorry." She closed her mouth.

"You have no need to apologize; come on." He took her hand and they rushed forward. A monstrous figure resembling William was revealed as a body fell to the ground in front of them. His face was disfigured like Sara's.

Elijah closed his eyes for a moment and took a deep breath. Visions of William snapping Malaki's neck flashed vividly and relentlessly in his mind; hatred and rage began to stir once again in his gut.

"Father!" he roared as William looked up.

"What? How is it that you are here, Son?" Elijah could see his father's new eyes flickering with a mixture of excitement and confusion, almost as if Elijah was the last person in the world he had expected to see. His father's eyes were bright, almost glowing, but not in the same way as Sara's. They radiated a rich, sweltering light that burned in small blue circles around his pupils. Elijah turned his attention to the burly man standing beside William, but Solomon was nowhere in sight.

"Let her go." Elijah stalked forward as William grabbed a small girl from the other man's arms.

"Why? You want her?" William held his arm under the girl's neck and cocked his head, pressing his chin against the side of her head. He looked at Elijah and then at Sara, who was trying to hide her face. "I can see that *she* does, but you? You are controlling yourself quite well. Don't fight it, Son."

William cut the girl's neck slightly with his claw as he shoved her to the ground. Elijah helped her up from where she'd fallen and moved her to safety behind him, keeping himself between her and William.

"What is it you want?" William threw his hands in the air.

"What I *want* is to rip the spine from your back, but I will settle for answers. I need to know how to help Sara, how to cure her. If you help her, I will let you live; I will forget about you." Elijah cracked his neck and rolled his shoulders back. The frenzy of emotion erupting within him was expanding, moving outward to his fingertips as he stretched his fingers before clenching them into fists.

"You are going to make demands of me?" William laughed raucously. "You always were such an arrogant little shit." Spittle flew from his mouth as he shouted.

"Tell me, Father," Elijah repeated.

"I have already helped her. I have transformed her into a goddess, and there is no cure for that." William stepped backwards, towards the side of a building. "I know you are angry with me, Son, but we are the same now, you and I, and I am delighted to see you are alive." Again, Elijah could see an awestruck confusion in his eyes.

"Angry?" Elijah forced a laugh. "We are not the same; we are nothing alike."

"Ahh!" Elijah looked back towards the sound to see Sara chewing and sucking on the child's neck.

"No!" Elijah rushed over, grabbed Sara by the arm, and jerked her away from the girl. She whirled and jumped on Elijah, nearly knocking him to the ground. He grabbed her by the neck and slammed her head against the brick wall beside them, again and again, until she fell unconscious.

"I have no answers for you, Son," William continued lazily, as if nothing had just happened, "but I will let you live. Come with me, and I will show you a whole new world. I have great plans, and I will let the two of you be a part of it. You are one of us, now, and if you do not indulge, you will not survive."

The bright glow in his father's eyes pushed Elijah further into the storm of rage threatening to consume him. Those eyes weren't like Sara's; they were actually glowing bright blue. He looked over at the big man standing beside his father; his eyes suddenly filled with blue sparks that grew together and burned as one, just as bright as William's.

He could feel his mother's pendant resting against his chest, and it triggered visions of her mutilated corpse that flashed through his mind. He closed his eyes; his pulse began to race faster and faster. All of this was his father's fault; Sara was his father's fault.

Even with his eyes closed he could feel William watching his every move, the wringing of his hands, the grinding of his teeth... waiting.

"Don't be foolish, Son," William warned. "You have made it this far, don't test your luck. It will not end well for you."

Elijah opened his eyes and launched himself at William. In an instant, his right arm was wrapped tightly around William's waist and his shoulder rammed hard against his abdomen. He lifted his father's feet off of the ground as he continued to push forward until they crashed into the wall at William's back. Part of the wall crumbled around William as Elijah quickly pulled away and kicked his father the rest of the way through.

William pushed himself up and fastidiously tugged at the sleeves of his tunic. Moving like lightning, he pulled a dagger from his belt and swung it at Elijah's throat. Elijah leaned back to avoid the blow, but was met with a hard backhand to the face as William quickly spun. Elijah slammed his right heel into William's side, forcing him to crash into the wall once again.

"I'm impressed." William smiled and turned back to him, pointing at Elijah with his dagger. "You must have fed!"

"I told you, I am *nothing* like you." Elijah turned his head slightly and spat blood on the ground.

"Liar!" William lunged at Elijah's chest with his dagger.

Elijah twisted to his left and grabbed William's wrist as the dagger grazed him just beneath the collarbone. With his other hand, Elijah tightened his fingers around William's neck and lifted him off the ground.

Elijah's grip tightened as he leaned forward and slammed William's head and back hard against the ground while continuing to squeeze his neck. His anger once again narrowed his view as he kept his eyes focused on William's, waiting to see the life extinguish within them.

Taking advantage of Elijah's rage, William struck him hard with his left fist, first against his ribs and then his jaw. The second blow rattled Elijah and knocked him off balance, causing him to loosen his grip around William's throat. William quickly jumped to his feet and kicked Elijah in the face, knocking him from his knees to his back.

William fell on top of him with his blade, forcing it into his stomach and then jabbing it through the side of his neck, where he held it.

"I'm not that impressed," William whispered into Elijah's ear, keeping his weight on his chest. He used the blade in Elijah's neck to twist his head to the side, bringing Sara into view. "I'm not going to kill you," he said cheerfully, "not this time, but I can't help what happens to her."

Elijah struggled to move, but was pinned down hard. He had lost a lot of blood and his father was simply too strong.

Sara was awake now, and clutched tightly in the burly man's grip.

"No, please," Elijah begged.

"I'm sorry, Son, but I have to teach you a lesson." William nodded towards the big man, who pulled a large knife from the leather strap on his side.

"Elijah!" He heard Sara shriek his name in agony as the man began carving her with his knife. Suddenly, a sharp pain in Elijah's neck caused the world to disappear around him.

# CHAPTER 12

A STINGING PAIN RADIATED throughout Elijah's neck and he thought his head might explode. Pushing to his feet, Elijah suddenly remembered where he was and what had happened.

"Sara!" he yelled at the top of his lungs, but heard no response. He looked all around. He didn't see her anywhere, but he saw the little girl. Dead. Elijah knelt down and closed her eyes.

"Elijah." He heard a faint call from the other side of the building. Elijah ran past the ruined wall and saw Sara lying a few yards away. Her body had been carved up everywhere. There was an especially deep gash in her neck, but she was scarcely bleeding. His heart sank as he realized she must already have bled out.

Her eyes opened as he dropped to his knees next to her. *I can still save her! I must.* Tears sprang to his eyes as he tore his teeth through his wrist and gently lifted her head to drink.

"No." Her voice was barely a whisper, and she didn't seem to have much strength left, but Elijah could feel her pulling away.

"You have to drink, Sara!" Elijah pressed his wrist to her mouth again.

"No, Elijah." She turned her head and spit out the small amount of blood that had trickled into her mouth. "I don't want to live if I have to be like this. Please, Elijah." She tried to spit again, but barely had the strength to lift her head.

"This isn't your fault, love; you can learn to control it." Elijah gently lifted her head onto his lap. "Let me help you."

"You already have, Elijah, so many times."

He wiped his own tears from her cheek.

"I waited for you to come." She opened her hand. "I want you to take this." It was her bracelet. "I need you to know that it's not your job to avenge me, or your family."

Elijah stifled a sob and looked away.

"Promise me you will leave all of this behind you, that you will forget about revenge. Don't let this turn you into someone you are not. Promise me you will remain the prince you have always been."

Tears continued to streak down his face as he once again looked away. How could he promise her such things?

"Please, Elijah." Her hand brushed softly against his face. "Give this to her when you find her."

He could see the bracelet hanging from her thumb, and he reluctantly took it.

"Give it to who?" Elijah sobbed.

"Promise me, Elijah! Promise me you will find your princess and you will give the bracelet to her."

"No. I won't. There will not be anyone if you don't stay." He could feel her getting weaker.

"Promise me, Elijah; find her." Her eyelids dropped shut, as though just the effort of keeping them open had exhausted her.

It finally sank in, she was going to leave him; he was going to lose her.

"I promise, then! Do you hear me? I promise!" Elijah shook

her and her eyes opened for another moment. He couldn't let her die without her last wish.

"Always my prince." She smiled. "Is the little girl still alive? Were you able to save her?" Elijah could see the pain in her eyes.

"Yes, she is fine." He would say anything to help her be at peace.

"Thank you." He saw a look of remorse lift from her eyes before she closed them again, for the last time.

Rain began to fall and he sat there beneath it, holding her, as he allowed the waters to hide his pain. The rain poured from a cloudless sky as if it were her last gift to him. He held her as he carefully recalled every beautiful moment they had shared, and regretted every moment they should have. It rained only long enough to hide his last tear, and then it stopped.

Elijah carried her into the forest outside of the city. He built a small pyre of found wood, an altar, and kissed her one last time. Before burning her body, Elijah pulled two silver deneros from his pouch and placed them in her mouth. This was not a custom of his ancestors, but his mother had once told him a story about the great love between Psyche and Cupid.

In the story, Psyche carried two coins with her into the underworld to pay the ferryman for a ride back across the River Styx and back into this world, so she could be with her true love. Elijah thought Sara must have been planning to find a way back to this world, because that was the only way he could ever find his princess, as she had made him promise he would do.

A deep, stinging pain set in at the center of his chest as he faced the fact that he had just lost the last person in this world he cared about, and who cared about him.

Despite what he had promised Sara, he knew that at least for the moment, revenge was the only thing he had left to live for.

He would find William and he would kill him, even if it took a thousand lifetimes.

# Hassan of Alamut
# 1195 AD

*"You must let go of your hate, it is the only way you will ever reach your full potential, and to do that you must be firmly grounded in hope. Hope will make you resolute; it will allow you to be steadfast and unshakable in your will. A tree with deep enough roots can grow tall in the most miserable of terrains."*

# CHAPTER 13

ELIJAH SCOURED EVERY city to the east and to the north, relentlessly hunting the men who had brutally murdered his loved ones, travelling until he reached the ocean on each side.

He learned much about the world beyond his narrow peasant existence as he traveled. He watched armies with men numbering in the thousands ruthlessly crush through much smaller forces, with not an ounce of mercy.

He learned how men fought over gods and religion, bringing war into his homeland and claiming it was their god's will. Elijah no longer believed in the gods, not even Janus, the god of beginnings and endings. During times of war, the Romans would open the door to Janus's temple as a symbolic gesture, and his image was worshipped at a small shrine not far from Elijah's old home. He learned that men would use any excuse to take what they wanted.

He had seen much fighting, but had been careful not to get involved. On his way back north, he arrived at a city called Cordoba, where he saw a great force gathering and heard the people in the city cheering.

The Almohad caliph Yaqub al-Mansur was leading an army to retake the lands to the north; they would be marching towards Toledo in the morning. Elijah knew his father would stay as far away from the toils of men as he could, so Elijah decided to get ahead of the army and leave right away, since he was also headed toward Toledo.

When he reached the pass of Muradal, he saw a large group of men, most of them on foot, surrounding a handful of heavily armored men on horses. The armored men, who were now being forced to dismount, had crosses on the mantles covering their breastplates. The men on foot were also armored, but mostly in silk.

As Elijah approached, it occurred to him he was about to witness an execution. He watched as the men on horseback were shoved off their horses to the ground. He was reminded how much he hated wicked men who took lives without cause or mercy.

The landscape was narrow and cavernous. The Christian knights had clearly surrendered because they had no choice; there was nowhere to run. They had allowed themselves to be blocked in on both sides. Elijah thought it was a very stupid move for a group of mounted knights, or any group of soldiers for that matter, to take this route.

"What have these men done?" Elijah spoke in fluent Arabic. A few men pulled their swords, shocked at how silently he had appeared before them. They relaxed when they perceived an unarmed peasant, probably a local farmer.

"This is the business of the caliph. Now run along, boy." The big man who seemed to be in charge sheathed his sword and turned back to his captives.

"Are you going to kill them?" Elijah pressed closer as he spoke.

"They are enemy spies; they deserve execution. Now leave

this place, or I'll count you among them." The man had clearly styled himself as the one in charge. Elijah didn't know what to do. He wanted to simply kill the man, but decided to give him a chance.

"Leave these men now, for they only serve loyally, as you do." Elijah took another step forward.

"These men are criminals and will be executed," he turned to his fellow soldiers. "Get this boy out of here." Two men came at Elijah with swords. He countered in two swift moves, forcing their swords into each other's chests; they dropped immediately. The leader turned and stared at the carnage, then at Elijah.

"Who are you?" The man's eyes were still wide.

"I make you the same offer. Let them go or die."

The large man tugged on his beard for a moment, as if to consider all that had just transpired. There were hints of awe, but there was no fear in his eyes. Suddenly one of the men who had been tied up on the ground broke his bindings and leapt towards the big man facing Elijah, his face disfigured as Sara's had been, his mouth wide open to free his fangs.

Elijah jerked the two swords from the men who'd first attacked him and leapt to intercept the monster. He shoved one sword in the monster's belly and sliced off its head with the other.

"Allah be merciful." The big man now stood behind Elijah with his company of soldiers. The five other men who had been tied up also broke their bindings and rose to their feet, revealing their true nature. Elijah had made a grave mistake.

"This is a trap; you and your men need to get out of here *now*!" The monsters were all moving in to attack.

"I don't think so. If it is God's will for us to die here today, then so be it." As the big man spoke, the men behind him all rushed into line without hesitation.

*Are these men crazy?* Elijah knew they stood no chance

against these monsters. He turned for just a second to see the big man grin at his bewildered look.

Taking his time, the man bent over and scooped a handful of dry dirt into his hands. "It helps with the grip." Just as he spoke, another vampire leapt forward. When the monster was nearly upon him, the man rose and pulled his sword in one quick and fluid motion. The vampire was parted from his head before he hit the ground. The other vampires began hurling themselves at Elijah and the men behind him.

Two of them came at Elijah. The vampire on his right swung his sword at Elijah's neck, but Elijah caught the blade and yanked it from the monster's grip. It then jumped on him but was barely able to bite through the flesh on his neck before Elijah grabbed his face and pushed him away, twisting and pulling on the monster's chin until his neck ripped in two.

*No mercy, then.* The bite on his neck had reminded him of Sara. No one would ever drink his blood again.

The vampire to Elijah's left was smiling and hissing as he twirled his blade and thrust it forward. Elijah's mind was still consumed with hatred and grief over Sara, but then he realized these vampires might know something about William. Without flinching, he allowed the monster's sword to puncture his abdomen. Grabbing the vampire's wrist, he pulled him closer, forcing the sword deeper. As the two came face to face, Elijah could see fear in the monster's eyes.

"What are you?" Confusion eclipsed the vampire's face.

Elijah smiled. He glanced behind him to note that his companions had sustained few losses; his big friend's men had fared well. Now the only vampire left alive was the one holding the blade that pierced Elijah's stomach.

"What do you know of a vampire named William?" Elijah demanded. The vampire tried to turn his head but couldn't; his chin was now firmly in Elijah's right hand. He tried to free his hand from the sword, but Elijah held tight. The vampire remained silent. "Talk! Now!" Elijah shouted as he twisted its head nearly off.

"His eyes glow blue," Elijah shouted.

"As do all vampire lords'," the monster replied. Elijah twisted a bit further.

"Yes, yes, I have heard that name when others speak of a master vampire, a vampire lord. I hear he is vicious and has much ambition. I heard he was going east towards Mesopotamia."

The monster speaking to Elijah had diminished to a man once again. "What are you?" he asked again, almost pleading.

"What is a vampire lord?" Elijah pressed his thumb and fingers inward, between the vampire's teeth, forcing its mouth to open. It finally nodded as blood flooded its throat, forcing it to gag.

"A vampire lord is born; he is made by God himself. He is not bitten."

Elijah's eyes widened, as he seemed to look straight through the now frail-looking being before him. The fog of rage dissipated, and his brows bent in disgust as he once again focused on the pitifully reduced monster in front of him.

"God," he whispered as his eyes closed, opening again only narrowly.

"Yes, God. Now, tell me who you are, what you are." The vampire spoke between clenched teeth.

"I am the reckoning." Elijah pulled the sword from his own gut and threw the vampire to the ground.

The men surrounding him stood there with mouths agape and furrowed brows.

"You're going to let him go?" The big man beside Elijah was wiping his blade clean with a piece of cloth as the vampire ran off into the desert.

"He's not your enemy in this war; he is an enemy to us all.

I can only hope he might lead my father to me. You don't seem entirely surprised by what happened," Elijah said as he watched the wound on his stomach heal.

"I have seen many things in my years as an Assassin. I have been sent from my home at Alamut to the corners of the earth to perform my duties." The man was still wiping his blade as he spoke.

"Have you seen these things before?" Elijah asked, swinging his chin toward the vampire bodies.

"A few times; they are hard to kill. I have never seen one fight against the others as you do." The man looked up from his blade and stared at Elijah.

"I am not one of them. I am something else. My name is Elijah." The man seemed satisfied and did not press. "How is it that a mere man can kill such things?" Elijah picked up a sword at his feet.

"With that." The man pointed to the sword in Elijah's hand. "As an Assassin, I have trained since I was just a boy to master many weapons."

At that moment Elijah realized he needed to become skilled in the use of weapons if he was to beat his father when they next met.

"Now, you tell me, how could one so blessed by God twinge and scoff at the sound of His name?" The man returned his blade to its scabbard and faced Elijah squarely.

"You tell me this, my learned and God-fearing Moor, how could a man who knows so much of the ways of God be so easily deceived? To see a blessing in the hollow eyes of a man who is cursed at his core is to have the eyes of a fool."

The two stood face to face. A single spark could have ignited bloodshed.

"Teach me the sword." Elijah spoke after a long silence; his expression was fierce.

"I have no time to teach you anything, and besides, it looks like you have all the tools you need." The man looked down at the slain bodies lying at Elijah's feet.

"Not where I'm going. I have a sworn duty, and without those skills, I might not be able to see it to its proper end." Elijah held the big man's stare.

"Very well." The man looked around for a brief moment and then back at Elijah. "It seems you may have saved my life; assist me with my task tonight and I will train you to wield the short sword of an Assassin. With your natural abilities, it shouldn't be as difficult."

Elijah considered his words for a moment and then nodded.

"My name is Hassan. I am named for the great Lord of Alamut, Hassan-i Sabbah. Put these on." Hassan pointed to the dead man's clothes that lay at Elijah's feet. "They will allow you to move freely while giving you a certain amount of protection."

Elijah bent down and disrobed the dead Muslim soldier. "Where are we going?" Elijah frowned as he donned the dead man's garbs.

"We are going to send a message." Hassan instructed the other men to continue scouting the area for spies while he and Elijah rode towards Toledo on horseback.

"What about the rest of your men?" Elijah shouted as they galloped.

Hassan quickly halted and turned to Elijah. "Those are not my men." Hassan's tone was firm, if not agitated. "I am an Assassin; I work alone. I broke my journey to speak with the caliph before performing my mission, and he asked me to help these men catch a group of spies that had been seen roaming the paths outside of Cordoba." Hassan stared at Elijah for a moment, as if he were reconsidering their arrangement, before putting heel to flank and thundering forward.

# CHAPTER 14

I T WAS NIGHT by the time the city came into view, illuminated by the faint glow of a crescent moon. Hassan said the moonlight made them vulnerable and insisted they leave their horses behind. Stealth and speed would be their primary weapons as they crawled toward the city wall.

Elijah watched from a distance while Hassan dispatched a lookout by sneaking up behind him and slicing his throat. He then motioned for Elijah to move forward. Elijah could hear roars coming from within the city walls.

"I can't get to these lookouts without the sentries on the wall seeing me. I need you to take care of them. Leave your sword; just a dagger to the throat and then let them fall outside the wall."

Elijah thought it sounded easy enough, but his mind was elsewhere.

"Hassan." Elijah grabbed him hard by the arm to keep him from disappearing into the night. "Do you hear the cheers?" Elijah looked at Hassan and then at the wall.

"Of course I do. They are preparing for battle, to fight and die if necessary for their God." Hassan jerked his arm free as

Elijah's grip loosened. "Now get to the wall!" Hassan pointed with his dagger.

"Those are the same sounds that were rising from Cordoba as I fled the city. A different language of course, but it sounded the same." Elijah looked back towards Hassan.

"What is your point, Elijah?" Hassan was growing anxious; they didn't have much time.

"How much land and wealth do these two gods need? What makes it worth sacrificing thousands of innocent lives, as well as the lives of the dedicated soldiers, who risk everything when they fight and bleed on the battlefield?" Elijah narrowed his eyes but continued to hold Hassan's gaze.

"Elijah, you are a naïve boy; you know nothing of this. To die in the service of God is the greatest honor one can hope to achieve." Hassan glanced down. "Now, we have to move!"

"When your side wins, will your God work the land, the limitless acres soaked with the blood of innocent farmers? Will he tend to the livestock he stole from the starving children of innocent herdsmen? Christian, Muslim, there is no difference," Elijah growled, willing the Assassin to listen. "These wars are fought to steal from those who are too weak to guard their own goods, and to kill anyone and everyone who stands in the way of what their leaders want—leaders who are not gods nor devils, but mere men, men who want far more than they need and infinitely more than they deserve."

Elijah looked back towards the city wall. "I am going to help you with this assignment," he continued, "but I want something to be clear. I am neither on your side nor on the side of your God. If the gods truly exist, they only bless you in the morning so they can curse you at night. I am not a good man, but I am obviously more blessed than you are when it comes to imagination, because I can think of many things worth far more than dying for a selfish god." Elijah quietly pulled the dagger from his belt and disappeared into the darkness.

He raced towards the wall and scaled it effortlessly. He approached the first sentry with blinding speed and accidentally sliced off the man's head. Luckily, he caught it just before it fell into the city. He was more careful as he sliced the throats of his next two victims, dropped them off the far side of the wall, and then jumped back down.

Scanning the scene, he saw Hassan had already taken care of all but one lookout. Excitement burst into his chest. Every life he took was a poor substitute for the lives he wanted to take; still, it helped to relieve some of his frustration.

Elijah looked at the dagger in his hand for a moment before sliding it into his belt. Rushing forward, he wrapped his arms around the last lookout's chest and pulled his chin backwards until his head was separated from his body. Tension and frustration once again escaped Elijah's body. His burning passion dulled as a slight calm flowed over him. He needed this.

Elijah saw shock and disdain on Hassan's face as he approached.

"What now?" Elijah rolled his head back to further relieve the tension already building again in his shoulders.

"There, in that tower." Hassan pointed to the only tower in the city. "Alfonzo is there, and we are charged with delivering a message to him."

Elijah watched Hassan climb the city wall; he did it with ease, obviously agile and strong. Elijah took off after him and then waited for him at the top. Elijah offered a hand to Hassan as he neared the top, but the proud Assassin swatted it away.

"Stay here; this part only needs one man." Hassan climbed to his feet and looked towards the tower. It stood more than six feet from the wall. He took a running start and leapt across the gap.

Elijah watched. He was stunned to see the Assassin stick to the tower wall like a lizard and begin climbing towards the window near the top. Ignoring Hassan's instructions, Elijah followed, and the pair slowly made their way up. Hassan quickly pulled himself through the window and, after looking around, shrugged and motioned for Elijah to follow.

Elijah's heart was racing. He was eager to kill again as he jumped through the window and saw a lone figure lying in a large bed. Hassan unfolded a letter and laid it on the ground next to the bed. He pulled his dagger and flung it down; the blade tore through the paper and stuck into the wooden floorboard.

"Let's go." Hassan pointed to the window.

"What? We're not going to kill him?" Elijah was disappointed; tension knotted his body. His jaw clenched and he began to grind his teeth, making the muscles in his face tight and rigid.

"No! I told you, we came here to send a message. Now, let's go." Hassan spoke sternly. Elijah's frustration continued to grow until he reached down and grabbed the dagger and the note. The note instructed Alfonzo to stop his campaign or he would be killed. Elijah held the dagger over Alfonzo's chest for a moment and looked back at Hassan.

"No." Hassan mouthed, shaking his head as he motioned for Elijah to follow him out. Swinging the dagger with his right hand, Elijah slapped the note against the bed's headboard and jammed the knife through to hold it in place. Alfonzo snapped up in his bed, startled.

"Who's there?" he shouted before calling for his guards.

Elijah rushed towards the window. He grabbed Hassan and leapt to the wall, glancing once over his shoulder before he fell from the wall and hit the ground running. They were out of sight in no time and Elijah stopped.

Hassan was shaken up and angry. "What was that about? I

told you to stay on the wall. You nearly sabotaged my mission with your lust for bloodshed," he shouted.

"Your mission is over; now train me." Elijah pinned him with a stare.

Hassan huffed and turned his back, running his fingers through his hair and taking a deep breath. "I can't train you here; we must go back to Alamut. It is a long journey." His eyes had softened, and Elijah could see he was getting tired. "We have to cross the sea."

## CHAPTER 15

ELIJAH HAD NEVER been on a ship before, and the trip was miserable. It seemed to last forever, especially since he was nauseous most of the time. After finally arriving on shore near Antioch, it didn't take them long to steal a pair of horses and make their way to Qadmus, the nearest Assassin stronghold. They were welcomed there, given food and a bath.

The next morning they left for Alamut. After another arduous journey, they finally arrived at a fortress near the Caspian Sea. The fortress was located at the end of an almost vertical path near the top of a two thousand meter-high ridge in the Elburz Mountains. This fortress, where Elijah would learn the art of weaponry, seemed nearly impenetrable.

Hassan began his lessons right away. The first weapon Elijah learned was the short sword. Elijah proved to be a keen student of the martial arts and Hassan agreed to further his training. He soon learned the dagger and then the sword and dagger in combination. Along with poison, paranoia, fear, and the art of a well-polished tongue, these were the most common weapons of the Assassins of Alamut; every soldier was trained extensively in these arts.

Elijah trained night and day, never sleeping. When Hassan was away on a mission, Elijah worked tirelessly to master the most recent techniques that had been shown to him. Soon he began to study on his own and even develop his own style of fighting.

He was given his own bedchamber, which he rarely entered; the sands of the training grounds had become his new home. When he wasn't there, he was poring over the wealth of knowledge in Alamut's famous library. Quickly surpassing his mother's sporadic lessons in reading and writing, he practically inhaled the library's vast array of contents, easily absorbing new languages and arcane subjects. He read all the books on warfare, fighting techniques, and weapons training first. From there, he moved to history, religion, alchemy, astronomy and the seven liberal arts.

Once he had bled those sections dry he moved on to the mechanical arts. He studied agriculture, hunting, navigation, weaving, and medicine before he found a section on blacksmithing. He studied metalworking extensively, determined to make his own weapons. Then he practiced constantly, until satisfied he was proficient enough to cast the weapon he believed shamed all others, a weapon that seemed to have been forgotten by time.

Many of the old books he had read cataloged weapons that had been used in different ages and cultures around the world. There was one that seemed to leap from the page every time to catch his eye. It was a thick, curved iron sword with a single edge; it could be used to thrust like a straight sword, but it could also be used to hack with nearly the strength of an axe. It was called a *kopis*.

The *kopis* was a one-handed sword used by the ancient Spartans, and a truly vicious-looking weapon. "…the quintessential adornment of a truly bad man." The book read like King Leonidas was the devil himself, commanding a legion of three hundred demonic minions. The book was written by a Roman, so the hateful aspect vexed Elijah. Throughout his studies of history, the Greeks seemed to have been the only peoples who ever gained and held Rome's respect.

Still, he knew every sword was only a fashioned hunk of metal; the truth of its virtue and vice lay only in the strength of its molding and composition, the character of the forge, the sharpness of the edge—and the distribution of the weight, which was key to the weapon's balance and to the fierceness of its blow. The only other virtue held by any weapon was merely an expression of the man wielding it.

The *kopis* was forged out of one solid piece of metal from hilt to tip, which made it very sturdy. Elijah fashioned two of them, identical in every respect, except for size. The blade of the larger *kopis* was nearly seventy centimeters long, much longer than the classical weapon. The shorter blade was only thirty centimeters.

Elijah was satisfied with his creations; the two weapons were nearly perfectly proportionate in size and weight. The smaller *kopis*, or "dagger" as Elijah called it, hung beneath his right arm from a leather strap of his design and making. The larger one hung from his right hip in a scabbard he had fashioned to hold it in perfect position to strike quickly.

## CHAPTER 16

THOUGHTS OF THE past kept Elijah focused. He needed to be the ultimate weapon when he finally had another chance to face his father, and a first chance to face his brother, on the field of battle. As Elijah grew stronger and more fierce, the Assassins decided to make use of his deadly potential.

He was sent on many missions throughout Asia, Eastern Europe and the Middle East. He always searched out the local temples, hoping to find his brother, but he was never successful. As his frustration grew, he relished bloodshed more and more. Soon he grew tired of killing only targets; single kills no longer soothed the frustration, anger, and guilt that were festering inside him.

He became reckless, killing when he didn't need to kill. He earned a bad reputation at the fortress and was shunned by nearly everyone except Hassan, who had always tried to fashion Elijah's character along with his skill. Now their training sessions were often interrupted by Hassan's long lectures.

Elijah was growing tired of his constant berating about self-control, and about loyalty to the code of discipline and leadership he claimed had held the Assassin order together for so long.

# CHAPTER 17

"HASSAN, YOU KNOW as well as I do that he must go; he is not an Assassin." The imam gently squinted his eyes and patted Hassan comfortingly on the shoulder. "He has been here for years and still keeps to himself. He doesn't sleep; he makes the other men uncomfortable." The imam turned and faced Hassan squarely. "We don't even know what he is, for God's sake."

"He completes every mission efficiently, does he not?" Hassan jumped to Elijah's defense.

"Yes." The feeble imam stared at the ground. "But you know as well as anyone that we live by a code here; we hold certain beliefs and values that he does not. Our missions are a byproduct of our beliefs, that is all."

"He is a good man; he showed that to me the first day we met. He just needs time to find his way." Hassan stood up from his seat at the imam's side and paced the floor.

"He is not one of us, Hassan, and honestly, I am disappointed that you of all people can't see that." The imam looked up and watched Hassan as he paced. "Why does this sit so uneasy with you?"

"Because he saved my life, and because he refuses to compromise; he is the most passionately committed man I have ever met. He is searching for something, and when he finds it, he will become something the world has never seen... someone who could end this madness and bring peace, not only to the Holy Land, but to the world."

"I must warn you Hassan, you flirt with blasphemy; you make him out to be some kind of god."

Hassan suddenly paused and stared at the imam. "We judge him because he is different, because we don't understand him. But his bravery, his fearless refusal to follow codes or creeds or anything but his own passions and beliefs, will one day lead him to a freedom like we will never know. If we help him to find it, he will able to make a real difference in this world." Hassan sat back down and leaned in close to the imam, deciding to try another approach. "Give me more time to work with him, to guide him. He has boundless potential, and we cannot afford to make an enemy of him."

"Enough! I concede." The imam threw his hands into the air. "I have a very important mission for you. And although I was hoping your student would be gone by now, I'm sure his particular set of skills will be of use to you. Understand, however, this will be his last chance."

"I understand," Hassan smiled.

# CHAPTER 18

"ELIJAH, THE IMAM has given us a mission." Hassan stepped down from the main archway leading into the fortress and onto the sands of the training grounds. The grounds were located on a cliff side that fell more than two thousand meters to the rocks below.

"Us?" Elijah retorted in a sharp tone, his brows bent and his eyes sharply narrowed. "Are you to watch me now?"

"Someone needs to." Hassan glared at him fiercely.

"Watch yourself, Hassan." Elijah raised his right arm, pointing at him with his *kopis*.

"Elijah, in all of your years here with us, you have never explained why you are here, why you train so hard, study so endlessly. What you are working towards?" Hassan's fierce gaze dissipated as he squinted and threw up his hands.

"That is my business." Elijah lowered his sword and looked at the ground.

"Tell me Elijah, what are you doing here?" Hassan had asked before, but he had never pressed like this. "It is widely known amongst the members of the order that you visit temples of all kinds as you travel. What, or whom, is it that you seek?" Elijah twirled the blade in his hand and then slowly lifted his eyes towards Hassan.

"As I said, that is my business." He spoke firmly.

"Very well, if you insist." Hassan ran his fingers through his hair. "Just tell me, then, who is William?" Elijah's eyes widened; Hassan could see the storm brewing within.

"He is a vampire, a vampire I am going to kill." Hassan had turned around, but was once again facing Elijah.

"What is so special about this vampire?" He lifted up his head and met Elijah's cold stare. He held his stare for a moment and then shifted his eyes to the sands below as he considered Elijah's fate. Elijah didn't say a word.

"I have taught you all I can, Elijah. You are better now with your sword than anyone else, but I fear I have failed to teach you the most important of lessons. I have failed to help you unlock your truest potential, your greatest strengths."

Elijah's jaws clenched; he was tired of Hassan's rebukes.

He had become the best swordsman in this elite order. Even when he moved slowly, with the speed of a mortal, no one could best him. He had even managed to beat Hassan in this manner the last few times they had trained. He believed that to be the true reason Hassan refused to acknowledge his mastery.

"Elijah, you can practice beneath the sun and the moon, and in the darkness when no light avails itself, but, until you learn to be steadfast and control your emotions, you will never be more than a man swinging a sword." Hassan turned back towards the stairs.

"What do you mean?" Elijah fumed.

"Elijah, the dirt beneath my feet is not always going to be dry, but that doesn't mean I'm going to allow my sword to slip from my hands. Similarly, I am not going to act against my nature, against what I know in my heart to be right, merely because my passion throws me in another direction." He took a step closer.

"Every time you give in to your emotions and go against what you believe, you are doing the worst thing a man can do. You are betraying yourself. You are giving up control of your mind and body. You allow yourself to become merely a reaction, when it is proper to be an action."

Elijah ground his teeth; he despised speeches. Still, despite the distance that had grown between them, Elijah had great respect for Hassan; he owed him much.

"Elijah, you must stop allowing what happens around you, what happens on the outside, to control who you are on the inside. Rather, be steadfast and allow who you are on the inside to dictate what happens on the outside—your actions."

Elijah squeezed the back of his neck hard, trying to relieve some of his escalating tension. "I have heard this all before, Hassan, and I don't need any more of your babbling. You are right; you have taught me all you can. I am the best; there is nothing more for me here." Elijah began to walk towards the fortress archway.

"Wait, Elijah, please, just let me get this out, and I promise I won't bother you with it again." Hassan waited for a moment, gauging Elijah's receptivity, and when he looked back, Hassan continued.

"When you allow another person's actions—whether they be in the past, present, or perceived as likely in the future—to cause you to act out of character, then you have allowed that person to control you. Allowing hate to fester inside you is the easiest way to give up control of your actions and of who you are as an individual." Hassan took a few steps closer.

"You must let go of your hate, it is the only way you will ever reach your full potential, and to do that you must be firmly grounded in hope. Hope will make you resolute; it will allow you to be steadfast and unshakable in your will. A tree with deep enough roots can grow tall in the most miserable of terrains.

"In addition, when you become able to put aside your emotions, to use your intellect to decide what is right for you, and to proceed unwavering towards that end, you will be unstoppable. But remember, you must rely on a foundation of hope, not hate." After speaking, Hassan waited patiently for a response; he still believed Elijah might come to see the truth of what had raised Hassan from his humble beginnings to the man he was today. He knew that same foundation could ground Elijah, and save him.

After a long moment of silence Elijah began to speak. "And just what do I have to hope for? Death, to end this miserable existence?" Elijah's stare challenged Hassan to reply.

"Every man can hope for peace, even if you believe peace can only be found in death." Hassan held Elijah's stare unflinchingly.

"I appreciate the skills you have taught me, but leave this matter alone. Hate is what sustains me; it drives me on. Everything has been taken from me; hate is all I have left. Hate alone will see me through to my ending, and to William's. Hate is my strength, my truest ally." Elijah started again for the archway.

"You are wrong." Hassan spoke in a low tone.

Elijah stopped and remained frozen for a few moments, trying his best to remain composed in spite of the tension and frustration that threatened to consume him. He took a deep breath and looked up again at Hassan. He made his stare like ice, and Hassan got the point.

"Agreed. I will not speak of this again, but this mission is very important. I will be much more likely to succeed if I have you by my side, but it needs to be handled delicately. Do you understand?" He stared at Elijah, who finally nodded.

"Kayqubad II, the youngest of the three brothers, the three

Sultans of Rum, is on his way to Karakorum to meet with the Great Khan. The Sultanate of Rum has resisted 'requests' from the Khan for an alliance on numerous occasions. Right now, our spies tell us the young sultan has advised his brothers to meet the Khan's demands. We cannot allow this alliance to be forged. With the sultanate under his wing, the Great Khan would surely move against us. His forces are vast in number, and with the sultanate's soldiers at his disposal, the Order of Asasiyun might finally meet its end."

"You want to kill him?" Elijah interrupted.

"No, no, no, we cannot kill him. That would only push his brothers towards an alliance with the Khan, if only for the sake of seeing our order destroyed." Hassan's tone was uncompromising. "Our intelligence tells us he travels with a company of forty soldiers and his slaves. He is traveling along the Silk Road; we should be able to intercept him before he gets to Bukhara."

"Go it alone, then. You don't need me." Elijah interrupted again as he sheathed his sword and stalked past Hassan.

"Yes, I do." Hassan grabbed Elijah by the shoulder and spun him around. The two men stood face to face. "Hear this; he will be in a tent in the middle of the desert surrounded by more than forty guards and lookouts. It is probable that there will be no cover. I need someone who can get in and out of there fast enough that no one will notice him, or at least no one will be able to catch him. All you need to do is dagger this note to the floor beside his bed." The note said the same thing as so many others Elijah had delivered, the same as the first note he ever delivered for the order. It was meant to spark paranoia in the target, letting him know the truth, that he could never be safe, never far enough from an assassin's blade, forcing him into submission.

## CHAPTER 19

ELIJAH AND HASSAN waited in the desert for the sun to go down. They were just out of sight of the sultan's lookouts.

"Remember brother, no bloodshed tonight; the very existence of our brotherhood depends on it." Hassan took the note from a small pouch hanging from his waist and handed it to Elijah.

*Brother.* Elijah pondered that for a moment as he looked at the note in his hand and then up again at Hassan.

"Do you understand, Elijah?" Hassan pressed. Elijah closed his eyes and took a deep breath. Hassan's words had run right through him. He could feel frustration and hate building with the tension in his back and shoulders. He rolled his head backwards trying to relieve it but it had little effect. Elijah was growing very tired of these mortals who gave him instructions as if he were some kind of subordinate.

*Brother.* He thought about Hassan's words once more and then took off towards the tent with blinding speed. He could see well enough in the dark to stay as far as possible from the guards and lookouts stationed around the tent.

Standing in the dark, just fifty paces from the front of the tent, Elijah saw he needed to create a distraction to help him slide by the two men guarding the entrance. He grabbed a small stone from the desert floor and threw it towards the left side of the tent, hoping the guards would investigate, but it failed to get their attention.

When the ruse failed, Elijah's pulse began to race in anticipation of the coming release. He rushed toward a lookout standing about thirty paces from the front right corner of the tent. He approached from behind and plunged his dagger into the lower right side of the man's back causing him to cry out in pain, and then sliced through his windpipe so he couldn't continue.

A bit of tension lifted from Elijah's shoulders, but only enough to leave him aching for a stronger release. He plunged the blade twice more into the lookout's side and twisted it, relishing the man's grunts and moans.

He could hear the other guards calling out; he heard them running towards him. Elijah plunged the blade into his prey's heart once, twice, three times, but his frustration and tension were now only growing. Killing this man hadn't provided the release he had expected.

He wanted to continue stabbing, but as the running footsteps grew louder, he realized this was his only chance. He raced around the back of the tent to the front entrance, and slipped in.

To his surprise, the sultan was asleep. Elijah wondered for a moment how a man could sleep through this commotion, but then he noticed the opium pipe next to the bed. A woman sat up in bed beside the sultan and looked straight at Elijah. She didn't scream; she appeared to be frozen with fear.

Elijah's tension continued to escalate; he wanted so badly to kill this pathetic worm who called himself a sultan, but he could not allow himself the pleasure. He had orders, and he didn't want to let Hassan down. Elijah laid the note down on the ground next to the sultan's bed and raised the dagger to plunge it through. He could hear footsteps and voices now; he needed to hurry.

Elijah paused with his the knife raised and thought once more about Hassan's words.

*Brother.* He thought. *Orders.* He thought. He no longer cared to take orders from mortal men. He would do as he pleased.

A rush of peace and freedom flooded his mind and soul as he rammed the dagger down into the sultan's gut, and while the sultan's screams rang out Elijah was awash in a bloody calm. He pulled the blade from the man's belly and slit his throat wide open.

As guards came rushing into the tent, Elijah spun from his kneeling position and thrust the small *kopis* through the first man's heart with his right hand. At the same time he pulled his sword loose with his left and swung it at the man coming in behind him, severing his head. He plowed through the rest of the men like a sandstorm.

With each swing of his blades he saw William's face and his cold, callous eyes at the moment he twisted Malaki's small neck. Every slice of his sword dulled his pain, his anger and his guilt; with every thrust of his dagger he tried desperately to kill his sensitivity, his memories, his old life, himself.

The only surcease he could find was in the battlefield. He could lose himself in the blood, the killing, and the screams. But when the fighting was over, once all the screams had died down and there was no more blood to shed, everything he had fought to escape came rushing back into his soul—all the pain, all the anger, all the guilt.

Elijah saw Hassan standing a few yards away. He approached him, his body stained red with the blood he had spilled. Hassan's expression was grim; his eyes wandered. He wouldn't meet Elijah's gaze.

"Do you realize what you have done, Elijah?" He rubbed his fingertips hard against his temples.

"I have opened the gates to the temple of Janus; let the war begin." In that moment, Elijah knew war would be his peace. The battlefield would be his holy of holies, his solace, his only sanctuary.

# CHAPTER 20

As THE WEEKS and months passed back in Alamut, Elijah became increasingly isolated. Despite his formal apology, most of the members of the order blamed him for the increasing Mongol attacks on Assassin strongholds, as well as their recent advance towards the Alamut valley, even though the Sultanate of Rum hadn't been involved.

In fact, the Assassins' best intelligence sources asserted that the sultanate blamed the Great Khan for the slaughter. The scene had looked much more like the vicious and merciless work of the Mongol hordes rather than the targeted slayings typical of the Assassins.

Still, Elijah realized, whether or not his actions had directly hurt the order, he had put them at risk and betrayed their trust. He knew it was time to move on. Even Hassan had seemed to lose his conviction that Elijah could be helped… or even trusted. He seemed to finally understand that Elijah's hate was what he held closest to him, his most dear mistress of malady.

"Elijah, I need to speak with you." Elijah wasn't surprised to finally hear from Hassan. He knew Hassan would be the one. He was the only one with the fortitude to do what was necessary.

"I've been waiting for you, my friend. I thought you would have come much sooner." Elijah raised his brows and smiled gently.

"I have been putting it off because I know your potential is vast. I still believe you will realize that potential one day, Elijah, just not here, not with us. There is nothing left for you here." Elijah knew Hassan was right. He was ready, and leaving this place would allow him more time to search for his father and brother.

"I will be gone by morning." Elijah smiled in a friendly way and reached out his hand to Hassan in a polite gesture. Hassan grabbed his hand and then pulled him into a tight embrace.

"Never give up on finding hope and peace, my stubborn student," Hassan whispered into his ear. He gently pulled away, his eyes red and wet with tears. He pinned Elijah with his gaze. "I have heard men say that if you take away a man's family he truly has no reason left to live. I always hoped they were wrong, my friend, and I still do." Hassan smiled broadly as he quickly wiped his right eye. On the way back from their last mission, Elijah had finally told Hassan a bit of the truth about his family.

"Please, travel with me one last time. We must go to the fortress at Maymundiz. I have something for you there, and I want you to see the imam and request his permission for and acknowledgement of your departure from the order. I know you do not need his permission; it is simply a display of respect for all he has allowed of you. I hope you will do it, for me." Hassan gazed at him expectantly.

A quick rush of anger burned through Elijah's body. *All he has allowed of me? What about all of the missions I have accomplished for the self-righteous bastard?* He looked to the ground and swallowed everything he wanted to say, then looked back up at Hassan and nodded.

"I agree." He softly spoke in agreement for the sake of

Hassan alone. He respected the big man, and had grown to care for him. "When do we leave?"

"Right away. Get your things and meet me at the gate." Hassan spoke quickly, then hurried back into the fortress. Elijah didn't have many things, nothing more than his weapons and clothes. He had an extra set of silk robes that fit into a small bag; his matching blades were both on his person at all times.

Hassan had Elijah's horse waiting for him when he arrived at the gate just minutes later. There were also five other men waiting with him. Elijah recognized them; they were five of the most skilled assassins in the order. He was immediately suspicious.

"Why are they here, Hassan?" Elijah hitched his chin in their direction, a scowl narrowing his eyes.

"We have started traveling in packs ever since the Mongols began invading the valley." Hassan's eyes widened and he broke Elijah's gaze as he spoke. Elijah wasn't buying it; Hassan knew Elijah alone could easily handle any raiding or scouting party they might encounter.

Was Hassan really going to try to kill him? Surely he wasn't that stupid. Elijah did not want to kill Hassan; however, killing the others would be a pleasure. He was sure this plan was not Hassan's, but orders from higher up. Hassan was just a good soldier who was now being ordered to clean up his own mess, or so it seemed.

"Okay, let's go." Elijah mounted and led the way. He hoped his exposed back might encourage them to get on with their plan; he would see it unfolded as quickly as possible.

Elijah waited and waited, and before he knew it they were nearly at the fortress and still nothing had transpired. Had he been wrong? Had his own guilt led him to misinterpret Hassan's demeanor back at Alamut? Even so, what could explain his blatant lie about traveling in packs?

Soon, Elijah could see the fortress in the distance. As it came into focus, so did Hassan's plan and the reason for his lies and uneasiness. A huge Mongol force was approaching the fortress at Maymundiz.

Elijah immediately halted his mount and Hassan stopped right beside him. He turned to look at Hassan; there was no apology in his eyes. He was loyal to the bone, and did what he was commanded to do. "I knew you wanted me to leave, but it never occurred to me that you wanted me to accomplish that task by trying to fight off this invasion."

Hassan looked at the ground for a moment and then back at Elijah.

"I know you thirst for blood to fill the loss that consumes you. Right now you are not a man, simply a pit of lust; your only desire is to kill." Hassan paused for a moment and shifted his gaze to the fortress, then once again back to Elijah.

"These men knocking at our gates are not men at all. They bring a horde of monsters, monsters like the ones we encountered the day we met and the one that killed your family." Hassan paused again, waiting for Elijah to say something, but he remained silent, so Hassan continued.

"Although you refuse it, I know how much you long for death, and there before you is what you long for." Hassan extended his hand and pointed at the horde gathering below the fortress.

"I have tried to teach you to control the darkness within you so you can unlock peace and your true potential, but today, my brother, I concede. The power before us is pure evil. It is an army of demons, and they threaten to overwhelm us, to annihilate us." Hassan paused for a moment and took a deep breath.

"I have seen the darkness that lurks just beneath the surface of your thoughts, and that darkness could consume the devil himself. I know it is wrong, and selfish, and it goes against everything I believe in and have tried to teach to you, but I am asking you this one time, in order to save our brothers and our imam, please give in to that darkness which pervades you. Relish the bloodshed; fill your cup until it is overflowing. Unleash hell upon them, Brother!"

Hassan stared intently at Elijah, who sat quietly on his horse, thinking over all that his teacher had just done and said. Hassan had tricked him into coming here, and the Assassins were using him to ensure their survival, but none of that mattered.

If the army before him was truly an army of vampires, the same villainy that had taken everything dear to him, then he had no choice. He could feel his chest tighten and his heart begin to race as he jumped down off of his horse and strode toward the fortress.

"Elijah! One more thing." Hassan was fiddling with something around his waist. "I said I had something for you. I have seen your affinity for the ancient Spartan *kopis*. This sword is the finest weapon I have ever seen. I acquired it early in my association with the Assassins. It belonged to the greatest Khan of them all, Genghis Khan." Hassan threw the sword and sheath to Elijah.

"And before that," Hassan's smile stretched all the way across his face, "to King Leonidas himself. It is fitting, don't you agree?"

Elijah was speechless as he removed the sword from its leather guard to admire it. He examined it at arm's length. It was exquisite; the weight, the balance, the length and detail, a weapon created by a true artist.

"Leave your dagger beneath your arm, brother. I think you will need both your swords this day." Hassan smiled and laughed.

Elijah drew his other sword and held them both out in front of him before twirling them as he knelt and laid them side by side on the ground. He washed his hands in the dry dirt and retrieved his weapons before rising to his feet..

"What are you doing?" Hassan asked, when Elijah threw the leather encasing on the ground.

"I won't have need of that, not today." Hassan smiled and nodded as he drew another sword from his saddle.

Elijah led the other men into battle on foot. As his excitement grew he moved faster and faster, soon leaving the horsemen far behind. The fortress was highly elevated, and the channel that wound its way to the fortress gate was narrow and steep enough to make the siege extremely difficult. It was in such a position that the Mongol army was unable to surround it; they were forced to fight on one front.

Still, the landscape was grim. Rows of Mongol archers on horseback were raining arrows down on the fortress. Huge ladders were propped up against the wall. Hordes of men were climbing the ladders, while numerous vampires climbed up the wall itself.

Assassin archers were stationed on the high wall, picking off hundreds of Mongols. They threw buckets of hot oil on some of the ladders and set them ablaze. The Assassins also poured oil on the vampires who scaled the wall and attempted to hit them with flaming arrows. However, most of the vampires were too fast and were up the wall in seconds. Mongol catapults were bombarding the city wall and setting fire to many Assassin archers.

Noting that the vampires who made it to the top of the wall were doing the most damage, Elijah looked back at Hassan. Pointing with a sword, he instructed Hassan and his men to take to the wall. Elijah charged the horde from the right side, using his swords to deflect numerous arrows.

He dodged a spear as one arrow lodged in his thigh; he yanked it out without missing a step. As he grew closer, he could see the soldiers' faces more clearly. Hassan was right; there was a huge company of vampires.

One vampire lunged for him with a spear. Elijah was barely

able to maneuver away, and in one quick motion spun around and drove a sword directly into the back of the vampire's head.

Elijah jerked the blade, swinging it outward as he turned and quickly decapitated a vampire to his right. Another vampire grabbed Elijah's swinging arm and held it. Elijah quickly leapt into the air and drove his other sword straight down through the vampire's throat, nearly severing him at the neck.

There were so many of these monsters, he didn't seem to be making any headway. Their preternatural speed and strength reminded him these were not mere men, and with their vastly superior numbers, it seemed as if he would soon be over whelmed.

Still he hacked and slashed his way through them, making his way into the center of the battle outside of the wall. At this point, it seemed every vampire on the battlefield was aiming for him. Elijah deflected two more swords and he spun around and decapitated the vampires wielding them with one blow. He quickly glanced behind him and spotted an arrow honing in on him only a few yards away. He bent to slip the arrow and at the same time drove the sword he had crafted himself into the ground. Drawing the dagger from beneath his arm, he hurled it at the archer and nailed him in his left eye.

As the archer fell, Elijah could see Hassan behind him. He pulled his sword from the ground and quickly raced to Hassan's side. Retrieving his dagger, he could see the archer had been human. Elijah couldn't understand why the khan would send hundreds of men to certain death.

Rolling past Hassan's side, he positioned himself so they now stood back to back.

"Even knowing your strength and skill as I do, I am impressed! You drew the vampires away from the wall in a matter of seconds. I will never doubt your abilities again." Hassan deflected a lunging blow just to the side of his abdomen and stabbed the ensuing vampire through the side of the head with his dagger.

"What do you mean, 'again'?" Elijah looked over his shoulder and quickly noticed Hassan's smile. "Well, I did learn from the best. But listen to me, Hassan; you are going to have to be quick out here." Elijah smiled through the blood covering his face.

"I can see that." He quickly rolled behind Elijah to dodge an arrow.

"Ouch! That was not exactly what I meant." They both smiled as Elijah jerked the arrow from his abdomen.

Elijah's adrenaline was racing. Every deformed face he saw reminded him of Sara and his father, and his fury grew to the point of mindlessness. It drove him on, made him even faster, stronger. He was now cutting through the vampire horde as if they were merely human, only occasionally having to yank an arrow or a blade from his flesh. His fury had stirred fear among the vampires, making it easier to chop them down.

Soon the invading Mongol force began to withdraw, but Elijah was consumed, possessed by a deepening darkness as he continued to harry the retreating Mongols, relishing their screams. Elijah came so close to the hill where the enemy was retreating that he was met with a blanket of arrows. He was hit in five places but continued on.

"Elijah, come on," Hassan yelled from just out of range of the bombardment. The second round of arrows knocked Elijah to the ground and Hassan tried to grab him, but Elijah pushed away. He flicked off a dozen or more arrows and began to push himself to his feet when the third volley hit and nailed him to the ground. Hassan and two of his men quickly retrieved him and dragged him out of the archers' range. Hassan's men removed countless arrows from all over his body as he lay motionless, still gripping his swords.

"Come on Elijah!" Hassan knelt at his side.

"It is time for us to leave, sir. He is gone. He's not even healing." The two men grabbed Hassan and tried to force him up.

"Go on! Leave me!" Hassan shouted. "I'm staying right here; you don't know this man like I do. He is too damn stubborn to die." His voice was uncompromising. "I brought him here, and I am not going to leave him." Hassan's eyes were wide with anger as he reared back and slapped Elijah on the face with all of his strength.

Elijah didn't move or make a sound. Hassan reared back to hit him again, but stopped when one of his men noticed Elijah's wounds beginning to heal. A few seconds later, he opened his eyes, took a deep breath, and rose to his feet, his overwhelming rage unabated.

# HULAGU, THE KHAN
# 1256 AD

*"You fight for me. Now do what needs to be done! Whether with your bow or your sword, move swiftly, set death on its course and get out of the way. Remove yourself from the consequences. Now get on the horse!"*

# CHAPTER 21

"THANK GOD! WE must get back to the fortress." Hassan tugged at Elijah's right arm.

"Go." Elijah's tone was implacable as he stared into Hassan's eyes. "Go, *now!*" he shouted.

Hassan finally submitted and led his men back to the shelter of the fortress. He couldn't risk their safety just because of Elijah's stubbornness.

Only Elijah remained outside. He stalked back and forth, just out of range of the Mongol archers, increasingly anxious for more battle, more carnage. His muscles were knotted from holding himself in check; he ached for bloodshed.

After several minutes, Elijah dropped one of his swords to the ground, pried a spear from the dead hands of a Mongol soldier and ran nearly a quarter of the way back to the fortress before he turned and scanned the hilltop, searching for a target. Selecting a soldier at the edge of the Mongol camp, he took three long strides and launched the spear as hard as he could. It soared up the hill with tremendous speed, finally crashing through the chest of the onlooking soldier and pinning an unsuspecting vampire to a tree behind him.

Elijah paced for a moment to give them time to respond, but quickly grew impatient and reached down for another spear. As he was prying the fingers open from around the spear, he was caught off guard by an unexpected feeling of empathy.

The hands of the vampire and human corpses that lay beneath him were undistinguishable now. The vampires had reverted to their original form when they died. Still, each pair of hands was distinct. He found himself musing about how distinction and uniqueness were such human qualities. The hand he was touching was cold and lifeless now, and before that it had belonged to a monster.

Elijah's thoughts sank deeper. There was a time when those hands were warm and human, he thought. He remembered his father, the father he had known as a child. He imagined, ages ago, before lifetimes long spent, the hands on the corpses around him had held someone close to provide safety from the cold or protection from the night. He imagined they had brought comfort to broken hearts as they wiped single teardrops from soft, small faces. All of the lives lost on this bloodstained battlefield were just a fraction of the lives he had taken, and the lives he would have to take if he were to continue on this path.

Suddenly the blast of a trumpet rolled down from the Mongol camp and interrupted his thoughts. He straightened and closed his eyes for a moment to gather his wits. When he opened them again, his geste was like stone once more. Readying his swords, one in each hand, he stared up the hill. He was ready for more battle, to spill whatever amount of blood was needed to satiate his lust—though he feared there would never be enough—and to end this.

He didn't see hordes of Mongol vampires descending upon him as his eyes carefully combed the hillside; he saw one lonely figure descending from the camp. A woman emerged from the darkness of the shadowed hillside and into the faint white light of a crescent moon. She appeared to be human, but Elijah couldn't be sure.

She was truly beautiful, but she was definitely not a Mongol. Her eyes were wide and round. Nearly black, they matched the color of her hair, which flowed like silk past her shoulders and fell just below her breasts. Her olive skin was dark and smooth. Her stride was steady as she approached.

"Are you foolish enough to think I will not kill a woman?" Elijah knelt and laid both swords on the ground.

"My Khan only wishes me to escort you to his tent; he wishes to speak with you. He would like to find out what it is you want." The woman stood straight with her hands clasped at her waist.

"I only wish to continue the battle." Elijah stared at her fiercely as he reached down, grabbed a handful of sand, and rubbed it between his hands.

"Why do you do that?" The woman's eyes were narrowed as if she was straining to see, but she wasn't.

"So the swing of my sword will be vicious and true when I take the head of your Khan." Elijah's eyes widened as he clasped his swords and stood up straight. The woman didn't flinch.

"You have made a name for yourself. My Khan is aware of who you are." The woman pushed the hair flowing over her chest behind her shoulders.

"And what is it that you know?" Elijah gripped his swords and stepped closer.

"I know he fears you. He believes he cannot win this battle while you stand in his way."

Elijah smiled. "Then I have got him right where I want him. Why would I waste my time with words?" Elijah tapped the dull edge of the sword in his right hand against his shoulder.

"Because I know other things, important things." Her gaze never left his.

"Go on." Elijah rested both swords against his shoulders.

"You are the immortal who drinks no blood; you are the vampire slayer."

"My name is Elijah, and I slay much more than vampires." Elijah walked closer until their faces nearly touched. "What else do you know?"

"I know one of those swords is a true *kopis*. By its look, it must have belonged to a very important Spartan." The wind was blowing hard; it blew wisps of hair around her face and she again tucked it quickly behind her.

"So you know weapons." Elijah sheathed his old sword and lifted the Spartan sword, admiring it. "My friend, the man who gave me this, told me such things find their way to deserving hands. Do you believe that?"

"Actually I do, but sometimes it takes a while; sometimes it has to pass through much filth to reach its destination." Elijah dropped the sword to his side and circled around to her back.

"What would it prove to kill a woman?" Her voice was calm and steady.

"I have nothing to prove. What does it prove to kill anything?" Elijah whispered in her ear as he pressed the point of his sword gently against her back.

"The Khan wants to make you an offer." The woman turned and gently pushed Elijah's sword to the side.

"What could he possibly offer me?" Elijah laughed.

"I told you; the Khan has heard of you. He believes he knows what you seek. He offers to take you to William." Elijah quickly raised the *kopis* to her neck with one hand and grabbed the back of her head with the other.

"What did you say?" he growled.

"I told you. My Khan wishes to speak with you in person."

Elijah let go of the girl and began racing up the hill. Halfway up he stopped and turned back to her. "What is your name?" He couldn't deny his interest; she was beautiful, and her courage was admirable.

"My name is Ayda." Her voice was gentle and soothing. The moonlight limned the curves of her body as she climbed towards him. For the first time in ages his body burned with a lust not grounded in hate nor satisfied by blood.

"Know this, Ayda. If you are lying, you will die as well. Your head will fall immediately after your Khan's." As she reached him, he extended his arm and turned up the palm of his hand, beckoning for hers. Her palm was soft, and her long nails raked slightly against his wrist as she surrendered her hand fearlessly.

Elijah stared into her eyes and took a moment to feel the stroke of her fingers before he slid his hand forward and clamped his powerful fingers around her arm.

He turned and continued up the hill, holding the girl closely at his side, until he reached the perimeter of the camp. There he was met by a person who appeared suddenly. Elijah knew he was too quick to be anything but a vampire. Elijah's sword was at its neck before he could speak.

"You have no need of that here; the Khan has given orders that you not be harmed. Follow me." The vampire turned and headed into the camp after Elijah pulled his sword away from his throat. Elijah followed him through the camp, which was lit with torches standing every few yards.

Every monster they passed glared at Elijah threateningly. They passed tent after tent of blood-guzzling vampires until they finally arrived at a huge tent standing at the edge of camp, just behind a large tree. The vampire leading them stopped by the tree and asked that Elijah set aside his swords before entering the Khan's tent.

"If these are not here when I get back, I will find you, and I will kill you." Elijah let go of Ayda's arm and laid both of his swords at the base of the tree.

"Her, too." The vampire pointed to Ayda.

"She is one of yours, you mule! Why would you be worried about her?" Elijah grabbed her once more and walked towards the tent.

"I have some ideas." The large vampire smiled as he stepped into their path, blocking their way to the Khan's tent. "You are not going anywhere with her until she has been searched."

"Are you certain you want to pick this wretched night to be your last?" Elijah asked.

"I am just doing my job," the vampire replied.

"Okay." Elijah smiled and stepped backwards; he instructed Ayda to back up against the tree.

"This is outrageous! I am a personal servant to the Khan. If you touch me, he will have you killed." This was the first time Elijah had seen her lose patience, although he wasn't sure if she was scared or disgusted.

"Shut up and spread your arms and legs. Just let him get this over with." Elijah stepped forward and kicked her feet apart. She narrowed her eyes and glared at him.

"I'm just doing my job." The vampire was only slightly taller than Elijah, but his size was reminiscent of some beast of burden. "Although I will enjoy this just a little." The beast smiled as he leaned in close to snuffle along Ayda's neck, gently rubbing his nose against her jaw. Elijah watched as she cringed.

"I change my mind." Elijah grabbed his old *kopis* from the tree and held it just under the vampire's throat. "Back up." Elijah's tone was low, but commanding.

"Eric, take care of this idiot. I have had more than enough of him! If you ever try to touch one of my servants again, I will kill you myself." The voice came from a tall and somewhat pudgy, but strong looking richly dressed man standing in the opening of the Khan's tent. A human, much smaller than the vampire, walked from the pudgy man's side and smacked the vampire hard across the face.

"Elijah, I presume?" The pudgy man turned his attention to Elijah, who nodded as he laid the *kopis* back against the tree. "These fucking vampires, you can't do anything with them. Ayda, bring him in." He turned and disappeared into the tent. Ayda stepped forward and motioned for Elijah to go with her.

"This isn't over." The vampire whispered to Ayda. His voice grated on Elijah's nerves.

"Thank you for reminding me." Elijah turned to face the monster. Without any hesitation, he grabbed the dagger hanging beneath his right arm.

"Ohhh!" The vampire bellowed as Elijah wiped the blood from his blade and placed it back beneath his robes. Everyone around the Khan's tent took to their feet and retrieved their weapons just as the vampire's nose bounced off of the tree and fell to the ground.

"Stop!" The pudgy man spoke from the tent entrance. "Everyone return to your tasks. Elijah is my guest, and we have much to discuss."

"My pound of flesh." Elijah leaned over and retrieved the vampire's nose; he looked at it for a moment before tossing it to the ground. He noticed a faint smile on Ayda's face as she pulled back the tent opening and ushered him in.

The inside of the Khan's tent seemed smaller than the exterior implied. The air was permeated with smoke and the strong sent of lilac. Elijah quickly found their source in a pile of burning incense on a small wooden stool near the rear of the tent.

Most of the space was dark, and Elijah wondered if that was intentional. A few small lanterns hanging about the tent dimly lit the center of the small room, revealing a rectangular wooden table and four chairs.

"Come in, come in, please, and have a seat." The large, richly dressed man, flanked on each side by armed guards, gestured towards a chair with a fluffy silk cushion positioned directly across the table from him. "Leave us," his host, obviously the Khan, commanded the guards.

Elijah sat down and the armed men quickly left the tent.

"You, too." The Khan motioned for Ayda to leave.

"She stays." Elijah then noticed what had evaded him before; in the darkness behind the Khan was an overlay in the cloth which he had mistaken as a seam. The room he was in seemed so small because there was at least one more behind the overlay. Elijah imagined what could be hiding behind the overlay, how many people. He knew he was exposed without his weapons, but was confident he could get his hands on one quickly enough if he needed to.

"Whatever you want." The man forced a smile. "I am Hulagu Khan, brother to the great Khan."

"Wait." Elijah interrupted. He turned and beckoned Ayda to the table as he grabbed another chair and positioned it at his side. "Go on." Elijah instructed, as he watched Ayda take her seat.

"As you will." The Khan cocked his head to the side and took a deep breath. "As I attempted to explain, my brother, at the behest of William, the one you seek, has charged me with conquering these hashish-smoking Ismaili Assassins. If I don't take their fortresses, he will not be happy, especially the fortress at Alamut." The Khan lowered his chin and smiled.

"Please get on with it. What is it you are offering me, exactly?" Elijah took a piece of fruit from the wooden bowl at his elbow.

"When rumors first started circling about the vampire-hunting Assassin who could not be killed, I immediately told William, and he told us about you. Now, what is it you want with William?" The Khan leaned back and took a gulp of wine before pushing the chalice across the table to Elijah, who swept it aside.

"What, precisely, did he tell you about me?" Elijah stared blank-faced at the Khan.

"He just said that he might have encountered the person I described a few years earlier, but he didn't seem certain. He ordered us to kill you or bring you to him." The Khan took a deep breath and reached across the table to retrieve his cup.

"A Khan taking orders from a vampire." Elijah smiled.

"Just tell me what you want with him." The Khan drummed his fingers on the table and took another sip.

"I'm going to kill him." Elijah's voice was monotone and his face was again expressionless. Wine spewed from the Khan's lips, and he leaned forward to keep from choking as he cackled. He cleared his throat and sat in silence for a moment.

"I will give you that opportunity, if you help me first." The man's brow furrowed and he took another swallow of wine.

"How can I help you?" Elijah's eyes narrowed.

"You can allow me to complete my charge." The Khan pulled a jug of wine from beneath the table and filled his goblet again before maneuvering into a more comfortable position.

"Allow you to take this fortress, you mean." Elijah spoke bluntly.

"Not just this one, but Alamut as well. There is a library there, correct?" Elijah didn't speak. "Ever since William has taken his place at my brother's right hand, he has set our forces to raid every library known to man. I don't know what he is looking for, but I would have it finished." The Khan grabbed the jug and began to drink directly from it.

"I would have you kill him... William, I mean. I would have you kill them all." The Khan looked up at Elijah, who made sure he remained expressionless. "William has my brother's ear, and he whispers into it, pulling his strings like a puppet master." The

Khan paused momentarily and wiped wine from the corner of his mouth. "Well, what do you say?"

Elijah rubbed the thick bristles on his chin as he considered the Khan's offer. He thought about Hassan and all he had learned at Alamut... but then his thoughts turned to Sara and his family, and then to William and Solomon. *This might be his only chance to find the murderers.*

"You will allow everyone who surrenders to leave unharmed, and you will take no prisoners." Elijah watched the Khan as he shifted nervously in his seat; obviously he was not used to taking orders.

"Very well, I give you my word." The Khan extended his hand to Elijah.

"If you don't do as you say, I will cut down your entire army, your family, and I will burn everything you love to the ground." The Khan's eyes widened with shock as he raised his brow. Elijah rose from his table and walked towards the exit.

"And her, I want her." Elijah turned around and pointed at Ayda just before he reached the opening.

"I am not a slave." Ayda jump from her seat and looked at Elijah with disgust.

"I'm sorry Elijah, she is my best servant, and, as she made very clear, she is not a slave." The Khan leaned his head to the side and scratched the right side of his head. Elijah looked at him and then at Ayda, who was staring back at him, the grin on her face a boast.

"Please, for the sake of you own men, take time tonight, as you are sitting with your generals and planning out your strategies, to consider one basic fact, one deadly certainty." Elijah took a couple steps back towards the Khan.

"There is only one way to that fortress. You have to climb down that hillside. Just remember, whenever and however you decide to come down, nothing will change the fact that I will be waiting at the bottom, and I don't sleep." Elijah glanced over at Ayda and smiled before turning to leave.

"Wait." The Khan's voice sounded defeated. Elijah's smile widened as he turned to face the Khan. "Take her; she's yours."

"What?" Ayda shouted in protest.

"I'm sorry, Ayda; I have no choice. Have we reached an agreement, then?" The Khan ran fingers through his dark hair as he looked up at Elijah.

"I will be back in the morning. Make sure there is a tent ready for me. I'll need a bed, and a table with a bowl of fresh fruit. And make sure I have an extra room in the back as you have." Elijah nodded toward the overlay in the cloth behind him.

"Is that all; are you sure there is nothing else?" Hulagu Khan rose from his chair and shrugged his shoulders.

"Just wine, a few jugs of that wine. Chain her in my tent until I get back." Elijah watched as Ayda dropped her chin to her chest; her beautiful dark hair hung like a silk blanket over her face as she folded her arms.

"Leave someone there to tend to her needs, a woman. Make sure she gets whatever she requests, and make certain your men know, no matter what happens, they are not to touch her." Elijah walked to the edge of the tent and disappeared into the camp.

# CHAPTER 22

AFTER LEAVING THE Khan's tent, Elijah spent a few hours in solitude. He knew how much Hassan depended on him, how high Hassan's hopes would be now that they had forced the Mongol horde to retreat, and how upset he would be when Elijah informed him of the new direction he must take.

Hassan was a proud and stubborn man. He believed in planning and preparation, numbers, thick walls, and in the art of intelligent warfare. But beyond that, once he had done all he could, Hassan slept peacefully, foolishly believing everything was and would always be as God willed it. This was exactly why Elijah believed neither Hassan nor any of his men would surrender; they would die in that fortress when the sun came up.

Elijah had never met a more intelligent man, which made it all the more confusing for him, how a thoughtful philosopher of sorts could find his peace in answers that only created larger and more complex questions. There was no reasoning with the man; he was too stubborn when it came to his convictions.

Still, Elijah had to try.

On his way back to the fortress, Elijah was still wrestling with what he had just done to Hassan and his men. He told himself he didn't have a choice. He had to find his father and avenge his family, and this was the only glimmer of hope he had found since he last saw his father.

This was his life. Besides, Hassan and his men had already forced him out. He was under no obligation to them, and he wasn't a fool; he had no illusions about who he was. He knew he wasn't a good man, not anymore.

So why couldn't he rid himself of this miserable feeling? Why did he feel guilty about betraying a man who had just betrayed him? Perhaps it was because he knew if he couldn't convince the big man to leave, then Elijah would be consigning him to death. Perhaps it was because Hassan had been Elijah's only friend since he had lost Sara. Perhaps it was because Hassan had probably saved his life earlier that day.

Elijah didn't know… perhaps it was because he understood the reasons for Hassan's betrayal. Elijah knew Hassan had done everything he could to help him, not just with weapons, but also with his soul. He had tried to help Elijah find peace, and when that didn't work, he had tried hard to make the brotherhood find a place for him, to allow him to stay.

It was only after Elijah had burned down every bridge Hassan had built for him that Hassan was forced to deceive him, to bring him here, perhaps still hoping Elijah might prove himself indispensable to the leaders and be allowed to stay. It seemed Hassan was still looking out for him, as he had since the beginning.

But Elijah had to find his father; he couldn't renege on his deal with the Khan, not now that hope lingered just beyond the horizon.

He would have to find a way to force Hassan to surrender. Elijah swallowed hard and took a deep breath before entering the fortress.

# CHAPTER 23

HASSAN AND ELIJAH argued for hours. "We have their backs against a wall. If you would just continue with us, we can win." Hassan pleaded.

"This is the only chance I've had, after so many years of searching, to confront the man who killed everyone I loved, nearly everyone I knew." Elijah slammed his hands down on the table where Hassan was sitting. "If I don't take this chance, there might never be another; I cannot risk that." Elijah rocked back onto his feet and continued pacing back and forth across the stone floor. "If you surrender, he has promised me that no harm will come to any of you; you can all go free." Elijah stopped pacing and turned to face Hassan.

"We will not surrender." The imam shouted from his seat at Hassan's side.

"I am speaking to my friend!" Elijah was growing more and more frustrated. "Hassan! Look at me!" Hassan raised his head from his hands and looked Elijah in the eye. "Please don't listen to this old fool." Elijah motioned to the imam.

"That is quite enough Elijah." Hassan rose from his chair and stared down into Elijah's eyes. "You are speaking out of turn, my friend." Hassan held his stare for a few moments more before turning around and walking to the front window of the high tower. For a moment he just stood, gazing out at the huge force resting below him on a rise in the valley floor.

"Have you ever seen such an army, Elijah?" Hassan seemed mesmerized by the sheer size of the force. "I want you to know that I do not blame you for this. This is not one man's fight, and I apologize for the way I brought you here." Hassan didn't give Elijah time to speak. "Your path is away from here, and our path together seems to have come to an end. Go now, Brother and find the answers you seek." Hassan closed the shutters and stepped away from the window. He took a deep breath and sighed before turning towards Elijah.

His strong body had aged since he and Elijah had first met. He wondered why he hadn't noticed it before; it seemed so obvious now. Shades of silver and white streaked just above Hassan's temples and threaded through his beard. The skin around his eyes looked thin and sagged gently; wrinkles spread from the outer corners of his eyes like rivers flowing into the sea. He looked weary.

As he raised his eyes from the floor, Elijah saw something in them he had never before seen there; still, he recognized it. In that instant it seemed as if all the labors of Hassan's body had finally caught up with his mind and he was tired. It seemed he was now longing for death, the way Elijah had longed for it for as long as he could remember. And it was not longing in the way a religious man joyfully embraces death in greedy anticipation of receiving all he has been promised. It was the simple desire to close one's eyes in hopes that it would be for the last time. Elijah finally saw what Hassan had become; despite his speed and strength on the battlefield, he was an old man.

"Hassan, don't stop fighting yet, not yet!" Elijah begged urgently.

"I will not stop fighting, not until they break through those walls and put me down. That I promise you." Hassan walked back to the table and took his seat once more.

"No, Hassan! You are stopping, giving up, quitting. Men like you and I have nothing. We know nothing but war and death; we love nothing, except the way the iron feels in our hands and the perfect balance and curve of a well-forged sword." Elijah walked over and knelt beside the big man. "This comes easy to us, as does dying," he whispered.

"What would you have of me?" Hassan spoke in a low voice; his fingers began wrenching the edge of the table as he turned to Elijah.

"I would have you survive, to fight the real fight, the painful one; fight to live. Save your people; save them for a better death, at least." Elijah stood and walked away from the table.

"We will not surrender!" The imam stared intently at Elijah, but his eyes were full of fear. Elijah understood the conflict between the man's words and what he saw in the man's eyes. Elijah had known fear each time he stood before his father, but his soul wouldn't allow him an escape.

"Then you will surely die." Elijah walked through the archway leading to the gate.

"Elijah." Hassan shouted.

Elijah turned to face him.

"I truly hope you find what you are looking for, and much more."

Elijah nodded and was gone.

# CHAPTER 24

"YOU ARE REALLY going to betray your friends so easily?" Ayda looked up from the floor. Her ankle was chained to an iron ring that had been hammered into the side of a thick wooden slab that was part of Elijah's bed.

"I only have one friend." Elijah sat on a thick cushion which was layered in silk and topping the wooden slab. Ayda retreated slightly as he reached for her leg.

"I'm only trying to help you, girl. Besides, you are no use to me chained up." Elijah grabbed the chain and began dragging her towards him. As she slid forward on the ground, her gown was forced up, exposing the smooth skin on her legs to above her knees. Elijah was caught off guard for a moment; his eyes followed from her ankles, to her knees, and further. He leaned forward, hovering over her as if her legs were the steps to Mount Olympus and he had just climbed to the heavens.

"Please don't." Her lips trembled.

"Shhh." Elijah quickly hushed her as he pulled her dress down to cover her thighs. He fumbled with the cuff around her ankle for a minute before leaning back and pulling the chain loose from his bed. "Here." Elijah handed her the loose end of the chain. "Take that to the Khan and have it removed."

Elijah walked to the tent opening and called to a guard standing outside. When the guard entered, Elijah instructed him to take Ayda to the Khan and have the chain removed.

"I have the key here, sir." The guard pulled a small key from his pocket and handed it to Elijah.

"Thank you." Elijah knelt and removed the cuff from Ayda's ankle, handing it and the chain to the guard, who quickly exited the tent.

"What do you want with me?" the girl asked as she picked herself up from the floor and sat on the bed.

"Well." Elijah remained on the floor, but leaned back against the bed. He didn't know what to say. He didn't even know why he had asked for her, other than he had wanted to wreak some small revenge on the Khan for putting him in an impossible position.

Still, he couldn't deny that the girl intrigued him. She had courage; she was beautiful. She was one of the very few things that had distracted Elijah from his blinding rage and driving need to avenge his family's slaughter. "I just want to talk." Elijah bent his right leg and wrapped his arm around his knee.

"Talk?" Ayda shook her head in confusion. "What do you want to talk about?"

"We could start with you; tell me about your family." Elijah stared up at her from the floor.

"My family is none of your business." Ayda raised her voice, but her eyes dimmed and the muscles in her face loosened as she dropped her head slightly and rubbed the side of her neck.

"Why don't you tell me about William?" Ayda raised her head and looked at Elijah, the fire back in her eyes.

Elijah held her stare for a moment and then looked away.

"I'll be back. I don't need to chain you up again, do I?"

Elijah got to his feet and smiled. He selected an apricot from the bowl sitting on the table and turned back towards her. "This is excellent. Now, please inform the Khan I need some pineapple." Elijah turned and walked out of the tent.

"Is that it?" Ayda followed him out.

"Yes, that is all." Elijah took the last bite of his apricot and threw the pit on the ground.

"I am here only to fill your bowl?" She bumped into Elijah and took a step back when he stopped walking and turned towards her.

"Yes, and to talk." He stared at her in awkward silence. "You seem disappointed. I can give you more chores if that's what you really want." Elijah stepped forward and gently placed his hand on her hip. The gown she was wearing followed her curves, as did his eyes, from her hips up to her breasts.

"No." She spoke softly.

"No?" Elijah leaned forward until their faces were only inches apart. He looked down at her lips and then back up at her eyes; he watched them as they shifted down towards his lips and then quickly back up.

He leaned in closer; his hand moved from her hip to the small of her back. Just as their lips were about to touch, Elijah turned his head slightly to the side and pressed his head against hers. "Then get to work," he whispered into her ear, and quickly walked away, marching to the edge of the camp. He stood on the hillside, looking down at the Assassin fortress.

# CHAPTER 25

THE SUN HAD been up now for a couple of hours. Due to Elijah's insistence, the Khan had waited, giving the Assassins more time to consider surrendering the fortress. At this point, Elijah believed there was no more reason to wait, no reason to drag out the inevitable; it seemed Hassan was not going to change his mind.

Elijah stood with the Khan on the hillside and watched as the Mongols moved their siege engines into position. The fortress was strong and well positioned, but the Khan had collected the best engineers, weapons, and techniques from around the world. It wouldn't be long before the walls fell around Elijah's big friend. He instructed the Khan to send in soldiers once the walls fell, to fight the Assassins hand-to-hand. Elijah knew it wouldn't be the Khan's smartest move, but it would give Hassan a good death, one he deserved.

There weren't many other options; the only way into the fortress was up a narrow ravine. The Khan agreed, but had one stipulation. He would not waste his human soldiers; he would only send in vampires. Elijah agreed, and just before the Khan gave orders to begin the bombardment, the Assassins, led by Hassan and the imam, walked out unarmed. The Khan ordered for the two leaders to be brought to his tent. He and Elijah were waiting just outside the tent when the pair arrived.

"Get on your knees before the Khan you Hashishiyun dogs," barked one of the guards. Hassan's hands were bound at his back, and the man standing beside him kicked the back of his right knee and pressed on his right shoulder, forcing him to the ground.

Elijah quickly stepped forward and smacked the man with his open hand. The man fell to the ground, unconscious, as Elijah knelt at Hassan's side. The other officers and guards standing near them backed away and pulled their swords. A couple of other men stepped forward and carried the unconscious man away.

"Elijah! Please, relax," the Khan shouted as he motioned for the men around them to stand down.

"I did!" Elijah jerked the small *kopis* from beneath his arm.

"Elijah, you need to stop for a minute and think about what you want. Is this man more important than finding William?" The Khan waved his hand over his head as if he were summoning someone.

Elijah cut the ties binding the two men's hands and then slid the *kopis* back under his arm. As he stood up and pulled the two men to their feet, a huge man seemed to appear from out of nowhere.

Elijah took a moment to examine the giant standing before him. The darkly painted wooden mask covering the man's face took him aback, but it was the man's burning blue eyes that commanded Elijah's attention. He was a vampire lord, but was too big to be his father.

"That is a lovely mask." Elijah turned to the Khan. "Instruct your giant that if he doesn't want to lose his fancy mask, along with his head, he needs to get out of my way, right now!" Elijah pressed the palm of his hand against the hilt of the old *kopis* on his hip—he had left the other one in his tent—and gently stroked it with his fingertips.

"Elijah, I think it is time we establish a few ground rules; please come." Elijah watched the Khan as he gestured invitingly towards his tent.

Elijah glanced once more at the masked giant and then turned his attention to Hassan. "Are you unharmed?"

"I'm fine." He was rubbing his wrists.

"Elijah!" The Khan shouted from the entrance of his tent. Elijah quickly pulled the *kopis* from its scabbard. Everyone took a step back, except for the man in the mask, who stepped forward.

"Here." Elijah threw the sword to Hassan. "If that man takes another step towards this tent, make sure I don't have to look up at him when I come back out." Hassan nodded to him before Elijah turned and followed the Khan into his tent.

"Sit down." Hulagu Khan pulled out Elijah's chair as he walked past it to the other side of the table and sat down. "We have an agreement. You need to remember, you need me as much as I need you."

He stared at Elijah for some form of acknowledgment, but Elijah didn't move; he didn't say a word. Seeing Hassan tied up had made him regret his decision, but what could he do now? His mind raced as he considered his options and chose his next words with great care. Elijah knew Hassan would be safe for now; they wouldn't risk hurting him while Elijah was alone with the Khan.

"The man you nearly killed out there is one of my generals; his name is Baiju. I'm sure you can understand why I can't allow you to disrespect one of my generals." The Khan narrowed his eyes as he stared at Elijah. "Especially in front of my men." He leaned his head back and rubbed his temples. Elijah remained silent. "Do you understand?" He slammed his hands on the table.

Fury erupted in Elijah's mind and erased his caution. The answer was obvious; he could use the Khan for leverage as he walked Hassan to safety, but he would have to be willing to give up finding William, at least for now.

"And I won't tolerate anyone beating my friend while he is tied up!" Elijah shouted as he leaned over the table. "Leave him untied, and you may beat on him all you like, or you and your generals can at least attempt to do so." Elijah sat back in his chair and slightly lowered his head, holding the Khan's stare. The Khan smiled.

"The man in the mask is named Roman. He was sent here by William, for my protection. He will also be charged with making sure you behave." The Khan's smile widened as he wagged his finger at Elijah.

"Then you'd better hope *he*'s behaving, or we'll find him a few inches shorter when we step out of this tent." Elijah pushed his chair back and stood up.

"You really think your friend out there would stand a chance against the vampire William sent to protect me from you? I don't even know if you could fare well in a battle with Roman. I have been assured he is strong enough to protect me. Among the vampires in this army, he is second only to William." The Khan pulled out a jug of wine and poured two cups.

"You don't know my friend." Elijah lifted his eyebrows and pushed his now empty cup against the table as he considered the Khan's words. "What about Solomon? Is he not second to William?"

Elijah narrowed his eyes as he leaned against the table. He tried to imagine why his father would trust someone above Solomon, or why Solomon might not be as strong. Perhaps William had killed Solomon; Solomon hadn't been there the last time Elijah had seen William.

"Do you know of Solomon?" Elijah asked, narrowing his eyes further. The Khan seemed disinterested.

"I have heard William speak of him, but I don't know where

he stands among them. I have never met him." The Khan quickly blinked his eyes; he seemed to be trying to gather himself.

"But he is alive?" Elijah asked.

"Yes, as far as I know. How, exactly, do you know so much?" He gulped down one cup of wine as he offered the other to Elijah; Elijah quickly shook his head and the Khan sat it on the table. "How are you connected to them?"

"That is not of concern. What is of concern is what I am to do now that I know you cannot be trusted to honor the terms of or arrangement." Elijah walked to the side of the table. He wasn't sure there was a way out his situation that left both Hassan and the Khan alive.

"Elijah, this doesn't have to be difficult. We can get along and make this as pleasant as possible, but I will not allow you, or anyone, to question my authority by disobeying or challenging my generals."

Elijah nodded; perhaps the Khan hadn't ordered that Hassan be bound and treated badly. "But it wasn't I who went back on my word. You agreed they would not be prisoners, and then you marched my friends up here like common slaves. We have an agreement, but if you expect me to keep my word, then you had better do the same." Elijah grabbed an apricot from the Khan's table, and then a few more.

"You are correct. I apologize; I will speak with all of my generals tonight. This kind of mistake will not occur again, I assure you." The Khan lifted the other cup from the table and downed its contents.

"Then you didn't order that they be bound and humiliated?" Elijah asked, sounding disinterested, before taking a bite of apricot.

"Of course not. I had no idea." The Khan's brows furrowed as he stood up and poured another drink. Elijah watched him for a moment. Maybe there was a way out of this. He nodded as he turned and left the tent.

"Here." Elijah handed an apricot to Hassan and one to the imam.

"Elijah!" The Khan rushed out behind him. "I need to speak to your imam." The Khan stepped towards the imam while Elijah kept his eyes on the man in the mask. Those eyes were haunting him. They weren't William's, but could they be those of the burly man who had carried Malaki down the stairs and delivered him to his death?

*Roman.* He mused. The name didn't bring anything to mind. *Why the mask? What else could they be hiding?*

Elijah wasn't afraid of the giant, but he couldn't shake the uneasy feeling of familiarity that seemed to crawl up his spine every time he saw the man's eyes begin to burn as William's had. The conspicuous change in the Khan's confidence and demeanor when the masked monster was around convinced Elijah that Roman wasn't just another vampire lord; he was definitely something more.

"I need you to send a message to Alamut and instruct them to surrender peacefully." The Khan extended the bowl of fruit in his hand towards the imam, who retrieved an orange. "Then, when we arrive, I will be able to keep my word to our friend here," the Khan gestured towards Elijah, "and allow them to leave unharmed."

The imam looked to Hassan as if for guidance, or approval. Hassan nodded.

"Writing that letter will save our brothers' lives. It is the right thing to do." Hassan accepted the parchment from the Khan and handed it to the imam. "Will you find him a place to sit?" Hassan asked the Khan.

"Of course, come with me." The Khan pulled back the opening to his tent and guided the imam to a table, where another man laid ink and a quill pen. The imam wrote the letter dictated by the Khan and sent it to Alamut with Hassan.

Elijah stayed with The Khan as he prepared his army to move.

# CHAPTER 26

E LIJAH SAT ALONE just outside the Mongol encampment. Once again, he struggled with what he had done. Tears fell from his chin as he mourned the man he had become, as he realized he was willing to stop at nothing, to stoop to any treachery, to achieve his revenge. Most men, even the worst of them, lived by a set of guidelines; some men had a lot of lines and some had only a few. The longer Elijah lived and the closer he came to a confrontation with his father, the more he realized his lines were just a fiction.

They were a necessary fiction, one that allowed him to maintain the illusion that he was still a decent man. It was ironic that losing those lines, realizing they no longer existed, made him feel freer and more lost at the same time. It now seemed illusions were all he had left of his old self.

"It appears there may be a soul in there after all." Ayda sat down next to him.

"What are you doing? Where did you come from?" Elijah turned his head away from her and swiped at his eyes with his arm.

"I saw you sitting here. I yelled first." She wrapped her arms around her knees and looked at him.

"You really shouldn't pry." Elijah leaned forward and pulled his hair back on the side of his face opposite Ayda; he tucked it behind his ear and tugged on a curl that fell just below his jawline.

"I'm sorry; I didn't mean to pry. I just wanted you to know I found your pineapple. I'll leave you alone." Ayda stood up and looked down at the wavy locks of hair hiding Elijah's face.

"Ha." Elijah laughed as he pushed the hair from his face and looked up at her.

"What is it?" Her brow furrowed as she narrowed her eyes.

"I don't even like pineapple." Elijah laughed again.

"What? Why did you ask me to get it?" Her expression was rigid and remote.

"I'm sorry," Elijah couldn't stop laughing. "I never thought you would be able to find one, not out here."

Ayda's expression slowly softened until Elijah noticed a hint of a smile spring up on her face. "What would you require of me now?" She bowed sarcastically.

"Find me a papaya," Elijah grinned. She stared at him for a moment with a wide smile.

"I will be in your tent, when you would like to talk." She leaned over and pulled the hair from behind his ear. "You're not so bad." She looked into his eyes for a moment before turning around and walking back into the camp.

Elijah enjoyed watching her. It was a temporary escape from the hell that filled and surrounded him; she was like a single drop of color on a solid black canvas.

He was about to get up when Elijah noticed a Mongol bow lying a few feet away, propped against a small tent at the edge of camp. Elijah reached for the bow and examined it. This bow was nothing like the ones used by Assassins; it looked more like a work of art than a weapon.

"The key is in the construction." Hulagu Khan emerged from opposite the tent and noticed Elijah admiring the bow. "Our bows are layered with boiled horn and sinew; it makes them much stronger and more accurate. Our best archers can hit a bird's wing in midflight." The Khan smiled proudly. "Do you know the bow? It seems you are nearly unmatched with the sword." The Khan motioned for a soldier. He took the soldier's quiver and threw it to Elijah.

"I have no use for a bow." Elijah caught the quiver and immediately held it out to the soldier.

"A person can learn a lot about himself from the bow. It can lead one to perfection." The Khan looked at Elijah and then again at the quiver. "If you really plan to kill William, you need all the perfection you can get." The Khan pushed the quiver back towards Elijah and walked away. Elijah eyed the weapon as he considered the Khan's words.

"How hard could it be?" Elijah pulled out an arrow and picked up the bow. He took a look around as he nocked the arrow onto the bowstring. Finding a large tree about fifty paces off, he raised the bow and pulled back on the string. He took his time, carefully lining up the arrow with the middle of the tree trunk. Remaining as steady as he could, he loosed the arrow... and it lodged in the middle of a smaller tree a couple yards back and to the left of where he had aimed.

"You got one! Let's just hope he was in league with that big bastard, because otherwise you could have just killed one of your own men."

Elijah turned around to discover the Khan standing just behind him.

"What? I knew you would give it a try, and I didn't want to

miss it when the great Elijah fell on his face." The Khan smiled as he stepped forward and reached for the bow.

"Well, they should wear uniforms if they don't want to fall by friendly fire." Elijah handed the Khan the bow with a small, sardonic bow.

"Ha!" The Khan stretched back the bowstring and closed one eye. "Did this curmudgeon actually make a joke? You are an old man, are you not? Despite your youthful appearance." The Khan took an arrow and fitted it to the string. He looked over at Elijah, anticipating a response, but Elijah remained silent.

"How do you know William?" The Khan pulled back the string as he raised the bow towards the large tree Elijah had attempted to hit. "Even more curious, how do you know Solomon?" The Khan released the arrow; in an instant it was lodged in the very middle of the tree Elijah had chosen. "Very well, if you don't wish to discuss that, then tell me how you learned to survive without blood." The Khan retrieved another arrow and nocked it.

"I'm not vampire." Elijah sat back down with his wrists on his knees.

"If that is true, then what are you?" The Khan held the bow at his side as he turned towards him.

"He slaughtered my family; that is why I need to find him." Elijah picked up a small pebble from beneath his right knee and tossed it towards the Khan.

"Do you want some advice?" The Khan turned back towards the tree. "Forget about William; he is too strong. You will only get yourself killed." The Khan raised his bow and loosed another arrow.

"Do you know how many kids there are out there just like you? Children left orphaned because of William and beings like him? They all dream of revenge, but the smart ones eventually learn to appreciate that they escaped death and they move on with their lives." The Khan turned towards Elijah.

"The ones who can't move on die," he continued. "I truly am sorry about what happened to your family, but if you don't move on while you can, you will probably die, too." The Khan propped one end of the bow on the ground and twirled it with his fingers. "Don't misunderstand me. You are a gifted warrior, but even if you kill him, what then?"

"I didn't ask for your advice, and I don't want it." Elijah stood and brushed off his knees.

"Listen to me, Elijah; I knew a man just like you once." The Khan sat down on the ground and motioned for Elijah to sit beside him. "I was just a boy, but I still remember his face. He was the leader of a nearby tribe. He was such a strong man; I'd heard stories about him. They say when my grandfather's men went into his village, he killed at least ten of them by himself before his own people handed over his wife and two children to appease the Great Khan." Finding interest in the story, Elijah slowly walked over and sat down beside the Khan.

"A week before, my grandfather and his men had entered another village and slaughtered every last man, woman, and child. You see, he knew the story would spread quickly, and the next time he entered a village the people would be too afraid to resist." The Khan took a deep breath and continued.

"The great Genghis Khan sliced the throats of this man's family. I suppose it was another show of power, letting the villagers know *he* was their new leader. That was the first tribe that joined his growing empire." Elijah looked at the Khan, who had dropped his head to his knees.

"That is a nice history lesson, but what does it have to do with me ?"

The Khan remained silent for a moment longer before lifting his head and turning towards Elijah. "Just listen." He continued the story then. "I didn't know the man until years later. Grandfather spared him to help solidify the union of the tribes. He even made the man one of his generals, but even then the man couldn't let it go." The Khan shook his head.

"You see, he didn't have your strength; he couldn't come at his enemy straight on. Instead, he spent decades earning the Khan's trust, until he eventually became part of the Khan's inner-most circle of advisors." The Khan took another deep breath and exhaled slowly.

"I was eight years old, and my grandfather had just returned from a long conquest. He had invited his closest companions over to stay and celebrate the victory. Everyone was drinking wine, even the guards, everyone except the man who had finally become my grandfather's most trusted friend." The Khan's eyes were shut as if he were seeing it all over again in his mind.

"That night, I was in the hallway when the door to my grandfather's bedroom chamber broke open and my grandfather nearly fell out onto the floor, followed by three young girls. They couldn't have been more than a few years older than I was. I thought one of them was the most beautiful creature I had ever seen. Anyway, I had never seen my grandfather so drunk; he sent the girls away with the guards and told them to have fun. Less than an hour later I heard light footsteps outside of my door. Hoping it was the girl I had seen earlier, I stepped outside to take a peek. My bedchamber wasn't far from the Great Khan's."

The Khan turned to Elijah; his eyes seemed to droop with guilt or regret.

"Needless to say, it wasn't the girl. It was the man who had fought so hard for his village, and as he walked towards me his surcoat swung open, and I saw a blade. I know it doesn't seem like much, but that part of the palace was strictly for family, and even the few guards who were allowed to stand outside my grandfather's chambers were not permitted to be armed. I knew something was wrong, so I asked him what he was doing. He said there was an emergency and he needed to speak with the Khan. I walked beside him as he made his way to my grandfather's room. I told him Grandfather was asleep and then asked why he was armed. He quickly replied that there was no time, he had to speak to my grandfather right away. He told me to go back to bed.

"I told him I would get my grandfather for him, and as I tried to run past him, he grabbed me and shoved me against the wall. 'Go back to bed, now!' I could tell he was nervous. 'Grandfather!' I yelled. The man pulled out his dagger and pressed it to my throat. 'Don't say another word,' he whispered.

"A moment later I heard my grandfather fumbling around in his room. He asked what was going on, but when no one answered, he yelled for the guards, who weren't around.

"The general yelled, 'I've got your grandson out here and I will kill him if you don't come out and face me.' The next thing I heard was the large iron bolt inside my grandfather's door slam shut; he was going to leave me there to die.

"'You should have checked the door first!' I heard my grandfather chuckle before he yelled once more for the guards.

It wasn't long before two of them came racing around the corner. The man whispered into my ear and then pushed me away; by the time I turned around he had slit his own throat and blood was pouring out everywhere. I had never seen so much blood, not back then; he was the first man to ever die before my eyes."

Hulagu rubbed his eyes and nose before turning once again towards Elijah.

"Well!" Elijah exclaimed after a long silence.

"Well, what?" The Khan's eyes widened and he gently shook his head.

"What did he say, what did he tell you before he killed

himself?" The Khan exhaled loudly and leaned his head to the right.

"Did you miss the entire point of the story?" The Khan looked at Elijah, who just stared back without saying a word. Then he shrugged. "He simply said he was sorry." The Khan's expression dimmed, his eyes glazed.

"You see, Elijah, if that man could have just let it go, relinquished his anger and need for revenge, he could have had a new life, a great life. The Khan had placed him in a position of great power and wealth. Most important, he wouldn't have died before his time." The Khan stood up and started to walk back towards his tent.

"Hulagu." Elijah picked up the bow and stood. "I understand the intention of your story, but what you don't understand is that there is more than one way to die. Days and years mean nothing to a man who is already dead on the inside. There are some things more important than being alive, and for such a man, living a few extra years would have been a duty, a torture, a prison, not a privilege." Elijah picked up another arrow from the quiver lying on the ground.

"You truly are hopeless." The Khan walked over and grasped Elijah's shoulder, squeezing tightly. "So, if you refuse to listen, then I have no choice but to help. I would love to see them all dead, and you are the only person I know who might possibly accomplish that, but you are not yet ready." Elijah pulled back on the bowstring.

"Pull it back to your chin and then exhale as you release."

Elijah dropped the bow to his side and turned to the Khan. "Are you finished?"

The Khan shrugged.

"Quiet, then. I need to concentrate." Elijah raised the bow and aimed once again at the big tree.

*Tap, tap, tap.* The Khan rapped the tip of an arrow against a rock lying at his feet.

Elijah rubbed the sweat from his brow with the arm of his tunic as he tried to shut out the Khan's annoying distractions.

"You must be fully in the moment," the Khan continued, as if Elijah had not spoken. "You cannot allow yourself to be distracted; not by anything. When a true archer is about to take his shot, the entire world around him disappears, as does the distance between him and his target." The Khan stopped tapping.

"I don't want your help, Hulagu." Elijah quickly pulled the bow and arrow down and tossed them up and towards the Khan. "Show me what you can do," he dared.

The Khan watched the bow and arrow climb higher and higher into the air before falling towards his hands. He turned his head slightly to glance at the arrow Elijah had buried into the smaller tree and then looked back at the bow.

As the bow and arrow fell closer, the Khan reached out and latched his left thumb around the bowstring; his middle finger curled around his thumb to reinforce his grip while his index finger held the still-laced arrow in place. At the same time, he curled his other thumb and fingers around the grip. Pulling back as he quickly twisted to his right, he released the arrow just as the smaller tree fell into his sight.

Elijah heard a short whooshing sound and then a thud as the arrow lodged into the tree, leaving no distance between it and the arrow Elijah had accidentally shot into the tree. He could feel his eyebrows lift as his mind boggled; that had been truly an amazing feat.

"Now will you let me help you?" The Khan was smiling proudly.

After gathering himself, Elijah reached over and grabbed the bow from the Khan's hand. He turned back towards the camp and took a couple steps before the Khan stopped him. "Well, do you have nothing to say?"

Elijah stood silent for a moment before dropping the bow; he spun back towards the tree, retrieved the small *kopis* from beneath his right arm and launched it in one fluid motion. The blade tore into the trunk just between the two arrows, causing them to fall from the tree.

"Very nice !" The Khan applauded. "You know, however, that I am right-handed. If you had thrown me the bow from the other side I would have split your arrow in two." The Khan continued to clap for Elijah's performance. He bowed and then walked through the brush to retrieve Elijah's blade. "You are a man of great skill." The Khan spoke as he handed Elijah his small *kopis*.

"As are you, and it seems from your display that you might be an adequate instructor." Elijah smiled as he tucked the *kopis* into the leather holster under his arm.

# CHAPTER 27

I N THE HOURS it took the army to prepare for the march, Hulagu Khan worked with Elijah, giving him basic instruction in the use of the bow.

"Think of the bow as an extension of yourself; don't try so hard. Allow everything to flow naturally." The Khan waved his hand through the air in a fluid motion. This was the same kind of nonsense Hassan had preached at him about the sword. It had helped, especially at the beginning, but as time passed, Elijah began to learn and develop on his own, in his own way. He expected the same would be true with the bow.

"When you pull back the string, hold your breath, and then exhale just as you release."

The Khan repeated the same phrases over and over again. He was reminding Elijah more and more of Hassan, and it began to irritate him.

"And remember, don't try so hard to line up your shot; don't think about it; don't *try* to do it, just do it." The Khan instructed as Elijah nocked another arrow on the bowstring.

*Instinct*, he thought. *Don't think about it, just do it.* He quickly raised the bow and loosed an arrow without thinking about it and the arrow landed even further away from the target. Elijah huffed and looked to Hulagu for an explanation.

"You'll get it; the bow takes much time. It will teach you patience, if nothing else." The Khan laughed as he mounted his horse. "Come, we will practice more when we set up camp at Alamut." He motioned toward a second horse.

"I'll catch up; I need to collect a few things first." Elijah threw the quiver over his shoulder and turned toward his tent.

"Elijah, your tent has been packed up; it will be waiting for you at Alamut." Elijah looked towards the Khan and the waiting horse, then back at the nearly-deserted hillside. It seemed only moments ago the place had been buzzing with life.

"She'll be waiting there for you as well." The Khan smiled as he nudged his horse forward.

"Who?" Elijah thought of Ayda just after he spoke.

"Ha!" The Khan cackled as he heeled his horse's flanks and galloped ahead.

Elijah collected his weapons and tied a small satchel to the saddle's cinch strap, then spurred his mount to the Khan's side. As they climbed the hill just to the right of the Maymundiz fortress, Elijah dismounted to pick up the encasing he had dropped the night before.

Remounting his horse, Elijah noticed the Khan's face; he tried to quickly conceal the hint of recognition in his eyes, but Elijah caught it.

The Khan stared for another moment and then smiled, motioning for Elijah to continue on. Elijah had never moved with an army before. It was a slow process, all the more so because he was anxious to get Alamut out of the way and finally face his father again.

The army marched through the night, the next morning, and into the evening. Elijah was relieved when Alamut finally came into view.

"Let's set up camp here." The Khan turned and spoke to Elijah as he raised his arm in the air and twirled his finger. The entire army set to work immediately, and the camp was ready in less than an hour.

# CHAPTER 28

ELIJAH WAS SITTING on the edge of the bed polishing one of his blades when Ayda walked into his tent.

"You summoned me?" Ayda stood just inside the tent with her hands clasped behind her back.

"You look disappointed." Elijah wiped his last blade clean before inserting it into its scabbard and setting it aside. "Please come in and sit down." Elijah motioned to a stool a few feet in front of him.

"Of course I am not disappointed. I truly enjoy wasting my time on your pointless errands." Following his direction, Ayda sat on the stool and waited for further instruction.

"I thought you would be used to taking orders and running errands, for the Khan, I mean." Elijah leaned forward on the bed, placing his forearms on his knees. "Oh yes, that reminds me, did you find me that papaya?" He asked with a slight grin on his face.

"What is it you really want of me?" Ayda swiveled on her stool and crossed her legs as she propped her elbows on the table behind her. The lantern inside the tent cast shadows, highlighting every curve beneath her silk gown. Elijah watched the hollows behind her knees expand and contract as her lean muscles tightened and released with every move.

"I want you to distract me." Elijah sighed as he leaned back. "Tell me about your family?" Elijah rubbed his hand across his face.

"Tell me about yours." Ayda walked over and sat on the bed beside him.

"I really don't want to bore you." Elijah leaned forward again and propped his elbows on his knees.

"I see." Ayda stood up and started back towards the stool.

"Wait. Please, sit." Elijah took her wrist gently. Ayda turned around and looked down at his tired eyes.

"If you insist." She hesitantly sat back down beside him.

"As a child I lived on a small farm; my family worked a tiny parcel of land for the local lord." Elijah smiled as he lay back in his bed and his mind drifted away.

# CHAPTER 29

"MALAKI! ELIJAH! GET in here. I need that water for your supper." The sharp sting of onions stung Elijah's nostrils as he pushed through the heavy wooden door just ahead of his brother Malaki and held it open.

Their mother, Esmeralda, always spent hours preparing their meals, cooking and cleaning, chopping and peeling. She had always been an attentive mother, making sure her boys had everything they needed. Making them happy made her happy, but since their father had been away she had become even more attached. Her boys were her life.

"Sorry, Mother." Malaki rushed forward and, lifting the pail of water from over his shoulder, shoved it onto the large wooden butcher block. The water momentarily danced around the edge of the pail, threatening a spill, but soon calmed. "Elijah was teaching me to fight. He said I could be a knight now that we live in a castle." Malaki's voice vibrated with excitement as he skimmed his fingers along the rim of the bucket.

He had experienced challenges in his life, but under his mother's care and his brothers' love and protection, he had been able to remain a child, excited, carefree, and a bit spoiled. In the midst of *their arduous day-to-day struggle, he was the bright focus that kept the darkness at bay for the rest of his family. His carefree and loving spirit brought life to them all, and they all would gladly shoulder extra burdens to keep him untainted by the rigors of life.*

*"Very good, Malaki." Esmeralda tried to hide her true sentiment; she knew her youngest son wanted nothing more than to be strong and brave like the big brothers he loved and idolized. Turning from Malaki, she shot Elijah a momentary frown. He grinned and shrugged. Every boy learned to fight through play, but since their father had been away, their mother had become fiercely overprotective of Malaki.*

*Elijah thought her overwrought and overbearing behavior would not serve Malaki if he were ever called upon to defend their homeland. He needed to learn a man's skills and responsibilities, and Elijah was glad to help him with that—when they were out from beneath their mother's ever-watchful eye.*

*Besides, there were no other children around, and Malaki enjoyed the playful instruction of his big brother. Elijah was just glad his little brother had finally grown out of playing toddler games. Nowadays, an adventure through the forest and a good walloping kept Malaki happy.*

*"But remember, there is a big difference between being a knight and being knightly." Esmeralda's voice was stern but loving. She had said those words many times since they had taken lordship of Rothber castle. Her sentiment was true; she valued loyalty, honor, and courage far more than gold and renown, but her deepest concern was for her boys. She would have them innocent—far from the horrors of war.*

*Esmeralda had grown up surrounded by war, and most of the men in her family had died at war during her childhood. She knew its true form, that it held little glory. War was far from the glamorous undertaking young boys dreamed about.*

*"Is Papa coming home?" Malaki asked.*

*Elijah's little brother still worshipped the man he barely knew. He hadn't seen him in over three years, which was more than a third of the boy's life. All sharp knees and elbows, Malaki's thin frame appeared frail compared to Elijah's own muscular bulk. Remembering how scrawny he had been at that age, Elijah had no doubt the little runt would soon grow into a man as strong as he, or perhaps even Solomon.*

*For now, though, he was still a child, and Elijah hated to see him disappointed. The longer their father stayed away, the more Malaki grew. It was becoming harder to dance around his incessant questions about the long-absent man, especially with the growing possibility that their father might never make it home.*

*"Of course he'll come home, Mali."* *Elijah splashed Malaki with some water from the pail as he tried to distract his little brother.*

*"Stop it, boys,"* *their mother snapped.* *"Of course Malaki; he'll be back soon."* *The subject made her uneasy, so she always tried to quell these questions before they grew into conversations that would leave her trying to explain what she could not.*

*"What is he doing, anyway?"* *Malaki pressed.*

*What, indeed? It had been nearly two years since they received the one vague letter that mentioned he was nearing the end of his journey and promised a swift return. Since then, they had heard not even a rumor of his whereabouts.*

*"What he must, so you can become a knight."* *Elijah smiled and winked playfully, even though he, too, knew nothing of his father's actions or whereabouts and was also growing increasingly anxious.*

# CHAPTER 30

THEIR FATHER HAD disappeared into the night more than three years ago, sent to perform a secret errand for Lord Jeffrey. He had never kept secrets from the family, so they knew the situation must be dire. He explained only that he wouldn't be gone for more than a season and the family would surely prosper from his endeavor.

Before he left, he had kissed each of his sons, each once on the side of the face, as he had done so many times before... even with Solomon, who stood nearly a head taller than his father ... and told them to take care of their mother while he was away. Grasping tiny Malaki in his strong arms, he smiled and admonished him to get into as little trouble as possible.

A few months later, when Lord Jeffrey died, his priest had brought Esmeralda the deeds to all of Jeffrey's lands and castle; they amounted to nothing more than a few scrolls tucked in a leather satchel.

Elijah was tilling the field, trying his best to ease some of the heavy burden that had been thrust upon his older brother, when he first saw the priest riding towards their cottage with another horse in tow. As he watched the priest ride past, he'd thought someone must have died, perhaps their father! He had only seen one other *priest in his entire life, on a trip with his father to a small town far from home.*

*The smell of fresh soil followed the priest as the two enormous horses kicked up soft tufts of grass and chunks of earth. They were huffing and snorting wildly, and their manes whipped through the air as they nodded and shook their heads to protest the strain. Once they were tied, their sweat-soaked coats gleamed when sunbeams shot through overhanging limbs of the tree. Both horses were strong animals, but they had been pushed too hard. They had obviously traveled a long way, and in a great hurry.*

*Grabbing a bucket, Elijah secured it to the rope and pulley and lowered it into the well tucked between the cottage and the small field he had been working when he spotted the priest. Elijah listened for the familiar slosh as water met the open bucket and poured in. Then the pulley squeaked as he tugged at the rope to bring the now-heavy bucket slowly up from the depths of the well. He was so distracted by the horses, he hauled on the rope carelessly, then winced, more from surprise than pain, as the frayed edges jabbed his hands.*

*Hauling a pail of water from the well, he lifted it to the horses' muzzles one at a time to give them each a quick drink, and then sat it down within their reach. The horse that had been in tow nudged at Elijah's hand with its large head as if to say thank you. The skin on its nose and mouth were softer than anything Elijah had ever felt. And it was tall and bulky, very different from the scrawny animals Elijah was used to seeing. It was a beautiful creature, the stark white on its forehead and forelegs contrasting sharply with its black body.*

*Then he hurried to their cottage, where he and the other two boys listened from a safe distance while the priest explained to Esmeralda that Lord Jeffrey had written a will just months before his death, and it left everything to them. The priest seemed as surprised as they were to learn Lord Jeffrey, having no living heir, had given complete and untethered rights to all of his properties, possessions, and titles* to their father. Lord Jeffrey had further instructed that they should move into the castle immediately, and had asked the priest to bring them one of their newly-acquired horses to help with the move.

Elijah was thrilled to learn the beautiful black and white beast now belonged to him. The entire family was overjoyed to have the new home and land, but mostly they were relieved. They knew what this meant; their father must have completed his task and would surely be returning soon.

Esmeralda instructed the boys to gather all of their belongings and pile them into the back of a small wagon Solomon and his father had built years ago. Elijah and Solomon attached the old wagon to the horse as best they could; it had been built to be pulled by oxen, but they made it work. Esmeralda was especially anxious to have everything in order when their father returned. Her husband had a kind and cheerful nature, and would surely be pleased to see the work she had done and the effort she had made to demonstrate her appreciation.

Their eager anticipation of his return lasted for months, but slowly waned as seasons came and went with still no sign of their husband and father.

For several seasons, Elijah had been beating back the dreadful feeling his father was dead, but he had finally succumbed. He believed only death or something much worse could have kept their father away for this long. He was most deeply concerned for Malaki, who was so young yet. He didn't want his little brother's youthful innocence to be corrupted by the loss of his father, so Elijah did his best to maintain a façade of optimism.

He was sorry his father would never get to see and experience the new life he had earned for their family. They had a much nicer home, but little else had changed. They had more land than they could work and no one to help. Still, it was a huge step up and the possibilities seemed limitless.

# CHAPTER 31

"WHERE'S SOL?" MALAKI asked, blinking away tears from the sting of the freshly chopped onions. Lest Elijah think him a baby, he quickly lowered his head and wiped the tears from his rosy cheeks.

"He's chopping wood," Esmeralda said as she cut up the last of the carrots and gently dropped them into the bubbling pot steaming upon the stove.

"He is all finished." A welcome breeze sneaked around Solomon's back and drifted in through the open doorway. Leaning into the foyer, Solomon tossed a piece of wood to Malaki. "Put that in the stove." He spoke in a loud, friendly voice. Elijah was glad to see him so relaxed; he knew his older brother still carried the biggest part of the responsibility for the family's well-being.

Solomon's cheerful smile lit up the kitchen as he walked back in the door carrying a heavy load of wood, bringing with him the smells of freshly split pieces and sweat from his labors.

He stacked the fuel as neatly as he could against the wall next to the stove, trying to avoid the very vocal scolding that would be handed down if he made a mess of it. Esmeralda kept a tidy home; everything was in its place, and she had a keen eye for offenses. She even watched carefully while Solomon fed two large pieces of lumber into the huge iron stove.

All the boys had been forced to take on added responsibilities to help compensate for the absence of their father. Still, no one had borne the burden more than Solomon, who had immediately taken it upon himself to lessen the blow of their father's absence as much as possible. He seemed determined to assure his younger brothers had time to enjoy their youth, and the freedom to roam and play.

Though Solomon was only three years older, Elijah recognized the way his older brother had changed in the years since their father had left. Solomon had quickly grown into his adulthood, both in size and demeanor. He was a father figure to both of his younger brothers now, but especially to Malaki , and Malaki practically worshipped him.

Solomon also worked hard to assure the extra burdens not fall to their mother. Esmeralda already worked too hard, many times laboring alongside the boys in the field. Besides, taking care of a family was a man's work and Solomon had shouldered the burden with gallantry.

The smell of fresh beef and vegetable stew filled the small kitchen and floated into the dining hall. The boys were huddled at one corner of a huge banquet table, their stomachs growling at the tempting smells, making them even more anxious for their supper.

"Get your bowls!" Esmeralda shouted and smiled; she knew the boys were already waiting, bowls in hand. They raced into the kitchen and lined up in front of the stove. Elijah had made it in first, but Malaki quickly shoved his way to the front.

Elijah smiled and laughed as the small boy nearly knocked him into the butcher block. Malaki almost always got his way; everyone in the family had a soft spot for him. Esmeralda dipped a large ladle into the pot and filled each boy's bowl. After retrieving their supper, the three boys, along with their mother, trooped back into the dining room to sit at the lonely corner of the large and intricately carved mahogany table.

Elijah had never been comfortable eating there. His eyes were always drawn along the surface of the table away to a vast emptiness that seemed to swallow it whole. It made him feel empty and sorrowful. It reminded him of how alone they really were, especially with their father gone. Elijah often longed for a world beyond this lonely castle, a world full of life and laughter—a world full of adventure.

Besides Malaki, there seemed to be no joy or hope left in any of them; Elijah imagined that was the reason they all clung to the tiny boy so tightly. If not for his dedication to his family, Elijah would leave this dreary castle behind and go live in a town or a city. He would find a girl and he would dance. He had only danced once, a long time ago, and he remembered it as one of the most joyful moments of his life. But he knew those things were not possible for him, not when he was needed here, and the long emptiness of that table was a constant reminder of that.

Glancing across the table, Elijah could only see Solomon's angled and muscular jawline and profile, because his brother was also staring down towards the lonely end of the table. His jaw muscles were clenching and rippling as if he was grinding his teeth. Moments earlier he had been cheerful and smiling; Elijah wondered why he now looked so distressed.

Does the empty table trouble him, too? he wondered. Did it stir in Solomon the same loneliness that tore at Elijah's very soul? But that could not be so; Solomon had someone. He had a future here; he would most likely have his own family soon.

Elijah was happy for his brother, but envied him greatly. He harbored no ill will towards him; how could he? It wasn't Solomon's fault, and he had even spoken out against the decision out of concern for Elijah, but they had been able to do nothing to sway their father's purpose.

Solomon was the oldest, so he should be married first. That's *all there was to it. Elijah tried hard to understand his father's rea-sons. Proximity was the problem; there were hardly any eligible girls nearer than a weeks travel.*

*The look on Solomon's face shouldn't have worried Elijah now. Ever since their father left, Solomon's brow had seemed forever fur-rowed. He struggled long and hard to achieve the best for his family. But then Elijah realized this expression was different; Solomon was eating faster than usual and he didn't say a word, which was not like him.*

*He looked over at Elijah and tried his best to muster a convinc-ing smile, but Elijah didn't buy it; he saw something completely dif-ferent in his brother's eyes. He saw fear! Elijah had never seen him afraid, not even when their father left. Now Elijah was nervous, too, and intrigued; what was going on? Solomon's silence told Elijah it would be better to pry into this matter tonight, when his brother came upstairs for bed.*

*

"We lived in the middle of nowhere, days from the nearest town. My brothers and I used to play games together in the forest by my house."

"So you were close to your brothers?" Ayda interrupted. She gently placed her hand on the bed beside Elijah's leg as she turned to look at him. Elijah lay motionless for a moment, con-templating the question.

"Yes." He looked up at her and smiled after a long silence. "We were definitely close. My father would take us for long walks into the forest; we would walk so far we would have to camp for the night and come home the next morning." Elijah turned his head when the bed jiggled and saw that Ayda now lay beside him.

"He never planned for us to stay out there all night—at least that's what I believed back then—but my younger brother,

Malaki, would keep pushing. 'Just a little farther,' he would say, and my father always had supplies, so we would just end up staying." Elijah looked back up at the top of the tent, adrift in thought.

"That sounds nice. Your father sounds like a good man." Ayda rubbed the back of her hand across Elijah's rough and prickly beard.

"Yes, he was." Elijah's voice was low and monotone.

"Tell me more about your brothers." Ayda pressed.

"Malaki was smart and witty. He could get you to do anything, and he always wanted to play; we used to swordfight with sticks until he was tuckered out." Elijah smiled and laughed. He enjoyed those good memories, but over the years they came to him less and less often.

"And your other brother, tell me about him." Ayda's voice was soft and low; her eyes were closed. Elijah hoped she would fall asleep soon. He wanted her to stay.

"My older brother was more like another father to me and Malaki. He took good care of us; when Father was hurt, he took up the slack and worked his hands raw every day so Malaki and I could play like he believed children should, even though I was only a few years younger than he was." Elijah remained still; he kept his focus on the flapping tent, trying to hide the emotion in his voice.

"What was his name?" Her voice was just a whisper now; she would be asleep soon.

"Sol—uh—Solomon." Elijah's voice rattled and his throat choked as he coughed up Solomon's name.

"That's a good name; a strong name." Ayda opened her eyes wide and then blinked hard, like she was trying to wake up. "What about your mother?"

Elijah turned his head hard to crack his neck; he didn't know if he could speak about his mother without baring his soul. He hadn't spoken of her to anyone.

"Her name was Esmeralda, and she was beautiful. She used to sing to us. I still hear her singing, sometimes, when I lie down." Elijah looked over at Ayda and her eyes were closed; he grabbed the chain around his neck and pulled it until a small pendant worked its way out of his tunic. Elijah read the inscription aloud, as he had a thousand times, "'Everything begins and ends with a will, and a purpose is only as strong as the will that propels it.'"

"That is beautiful; was it hers?"

Elijah jerked his head around; he was shocked and jolted by Ayda's voice, which was now coming from just over his shoulder.

"Yes. Yes, it is, I mean was." He tucked the pendant back into his tunic and looked up at her as he rested his head back on the bed. "I'm sorry, I thought you were asleep."

"No, I'm sorry; I shouldn't have been so pushy. Your family sounds wonderful. I can see now why you want so badly to find William."

Elijah closed his eyes for a moment and considered telling her the entire truth, but decided it would be pointless. "What? How do you know about William and my family?" He looked up at her once again, feeling frustrated and uncertain.

"I apologize. I overheard you tell the Khan." Her eyes quickly shifted away from Elijah. He had paid attention to who was around when he spoke of his family to the Khan. He had been confident no one else was close enough to hear, but decided to let it go for now.

"Tell me one more thing." Ayda sat up on the bed. "How did you get to be... what you are?"

"I really don't know." Elijah's eyes widened and he took a deep breath. "I woke up on the floor after seeing William butcher my family and I slowly discovered I was faster, stronger;

I could see and hear better and farther. I even had better reflexes, better balance." He sat up beside her.

"I fought my first vampire that day. It was very difficult, but I won, obviously, and I have become faster and stronger every day since. Now, even most vampires seem to move in slow motion." Elijah looked down at his personally crafted *kopis* and then at Ayda.

"So, you believe, given the chance, you could take William's head with your *kopis*." Ayda leaned closer and shifted her eyes to the ancient *kopis* and back to Elijah.

"That is exactly what I think—his and Solomon's, at the same time!" Elijah could feel the blood rushing through his veins. He took another deep breath and tried to calm himself.

"Solomon? Your brother Solomon?" Ayda's eyebrows rose what seemed to be a full inch, and her forehead crinkled as her eyes opened wide.

"Of course not." Elijah stared at her hard so not to reveal his lie. "You need to go; I'm getting tired," he lied again.

"As you wish, but only after tell me why you choose to carry the *kopis*." Ayda moved back to the stool.

"I don't know; I was just looking through a book of weapons and that one seemed... right. Why do you ask?"

"I was just wondering if it said anything about you. I mean, it is an ancient weapon."

"I know that."

"There are far superior weapons; the *kopis* was the Spartan warrior's alternate second weapon. His primary weapon was a spear, and his secondary weapon was a sword, usually a double-edged short sword called a *xiphos*." Ayda paused for a moment.

"What is your point?" Elijah asked as he leaned forward and gently shook his head.

"My point is, although you can thrust with the *kopis*, it was primarily used as a hacking weapon. The *xiphos* proved to provide a much cleaner kill. Those Spartans who chose the *kopis* did so because they didn't care if the kill was clean, and they wanted to inspire fear. The *kopis* is and will forever be remembered as a bad man's weapon. Are you a bad man?" she asked, seemingly in earnest.

Elijah reached forward and picked up his ancient *kopis*. He examined it as if for the first time. "I did read that in the library at Alamut; that might have been part of the reason, I don't know. This one was carried by King Leonidas when he and his three hundred men died fighting the Persians." Elijah's eyes were unfocused, as if he had journeyed somewhere far away in his mind. "I am definitely not a good man, but then I have been alive for a while now and have only found one truly good man. They are rare creatures." He spoke again after a moment of silence, as he laid the *kopis* back on the floor. "How do you know so much about weapons?"

"I have..." She paused and looked at him and then at the ancient *kopis*. "I have spent a lot of time in libraries. May I touch it?"

Elijah picked up the sword and handed it to her.

"Was this really Leonidas's sword?" Ayda smiled and her eyes seemed to glow as she examined it. She looked up at Elijah, who nodded. "I wouldn't have imagined him carrying a *kopis*. How did you get this?" she asked.

"I am an Assassin... or I was," he boasted. "How do you think?" Elijah smiled as he retrieved the *kopis* from Ayda's outstretched hands. "It was a gift from Hassan." He was reminded of his big friend every time he saw the sword. As he placed it back on the floor next to his bed, he wondered what might come of Hassan now that the entire Assassin network had taken such a huge blow.

"Very well, we will leave it at that." Ayda smiled. "I know a good man, also. Actually, he is a great man. He is my brother.

His name is Khalid. He is stubborn and proud, but, when it counts, he always does what he believes is right for those he loves. I think that makes him a great man." Ayda moved back to the bed. She pushed Elijah's hair away from his face and looked into his eyes.

"You remind me of him. You don't look like him; you just seem similar. That is why I cannot believe you are all bad." A few moments later, she stood up and walked towards the exit.

"Where is he now? Why are you not with him?" Elijah leaned back on the bed and put his hands under his head.

"He had a family, a wife and a daughter." She turned back to face him. "When they died, he ran as far away as he could." She paused. "He wanders in the desert from time to time, but he always comes back to me eventually. Before he made a family, I was all he had, and he was all I had." When she finished speaking, she quickly turned and exited Elijah's tent.

## THE BEGINNING:
# WILLIAM 1186 AD

*His chest flooded with the thrill of power as he held the heart up in the air like a trophy. Not wasting any more time, he sat down on the floor next to the mutilated corpse and began to eat. He devoured the entire thing in minutes and then waited patiently to receive his gift.*

## CHAPTER 32

"THE TIME IS fast approaching, William. This year will have great significance in the future. We are on the verge of a discovery that will forever change our stations in life and reserve for us a place in history esteemed beyond all others." The old man spoke slowly, his words interspersed with dry coughs and small gasps for air.

His voice was raspy and low, muffled by the cloth he held forever over his mouth in an attempt to keep this terrible plague from escaping his already mutilated body. His caretaker knew it was merely a politeness, unlikely to make any real difference. It was like barricading the front door in an attempt to stop the devil himself from making his way inside, while leaving the windows wide open. Regardless, William appreciated the effort.

"This discovery will tear open our minds and with it the very fabric with which this world has been held together." The old man continued his oratory with great effort, now gasping for breath after every second or third word.

William had been at his lord's side every day for the last fifteen years, ever since he had been trampled by oxen while working in the fields, and had become unable to work the parcel of land allotted to him by his feudal lord.

Fifteen years later, Lord Jeffrey now lay nearly lifeless before him. William remembered the day after his accident, how he had feared his family would starve. William only had two boys back then, and only one old or strong enough to help in the fields.

Normally, Jeffrey would have taken whatever wealth a family possessed as a final payment for taxes owed and thrown the entire family off of his land. William had been quite relieved to find his situation was a bit special, since William's mother had grown up with Lord Jeffrey.

She, like her mother before her, had been a servant to the family. Since she was about the same age as Jeffrey, they had become close playmates and Jeffrey had eventually fallen in love with her.

The Castle of Rothber, if you could call it a castle, was nothing more than a rock cellar beneath one small but sturdy tower. It was connected by a small corridor to a large room which had been divided on the inside into a dining hall, a kitchen, a small storage room and the servants' quarters, where only one servant was permitted to stay each night.

Jeffrey himself was no stranger to hardship; he had spent much time out in the mud and the muck with his servants. His family lived more like peasants than lords, as was quite common among small rural lordships of the time. Jeffrey himself was indifferent to the intricacies of titles and status, so he had been broken-hearted when his parents told him he must marry someone other than William's mother.

All the money in the world wouldn't have changed his mind, but it wasn't his to change. Jeffrey's mother had come from a wealthier land to the north and could not endure allowing her eldest son to marry a peasant girl, and a personal servant at that.

She had been married away to Jeffrey's father when she was only fourteen, bartered for a return of loyalty, which wasn't needed, or even of any consequence.

However, she was the youngest of seven sisters and quite homely, so the fact that fate had brought her to this dreadful place did not surprise her in the least. Still, she would do what she could to see her son climb out of it.

"What exactly do you mean, sir?" William asked, uncertain of whether the old man was dreaming or had finally gone mad.

"My journal," Jeffrey croaked, pointing a bent, arthritic finger toward the chest lying beside his bed. "Bring it to me."

William opened the chest, paying scant attention to the familiar creaks and musty smell.

Almost daily, since Jeffrey had been sick, he had asked William to retrieve his journal, or a quill, or some other obscure item from the chest. He pulled out the old leather journal with both hands and heaved it onto the bed beside Jeffrey. Pawing at the leather covering, Jeffrey flipped it open and took out an old letter.

"Read it." His voice was a raspy whisper as he carefully stretched out his arm towards William. William carefully unfolded the letter and read the short message.

"'It is real' –Roman."

William was mystified, but he had learned a great deal of patience while caring for this old man. The name was familiar. Over the last few months Lord Jeffrey had spent much of his time recounting to William stories about a mysterious island, Jeffrey's own grandfather, and a man named Roman.

*The two couldn't be connected, could they?* William thought. Roman had died more than eighty years ago, and this letter wasn't nearly that old. Besides, William knew Jeffrey's stories were just that, stories and fanciful tales. Jeffrey had told him Roman died on one of his expeditions with Jeffrey's grandfather while they searched a secret island that supposedly held "untold power" and "immortality".

"My grandfather received this letter just months before he died." Jeffrey began; no doubt able to see William's confusion as he scratched at his beard. "I am a dead man, William. I was already bedridden by the time I discovered this message in some of my father's old things. Nothing can save me now, nor do I want to be saved." His voice was growing forceful.

"I have no children or family of my own. You are the closest thing I have to a son," he said simply. Jeffrey's late wife had lost three children during childbirth and one to fever a few months after. "Whether you believe it or not, I loved your mother, and that is the reason I have been telling you about the island and about my grandfather. It *is* real, all of it. It is the answer for you and your family; it's the answer to this plague that has ravaged me. If you can find the island, you can save your family from the deadly curses of life," Jeffrey said with desperation.

"Wait, wait, Lord Jeffrey. With all due respect, sir, you are talking nonsense; magic islands, powers, freedom from plagues, this can't be real. You told me yourself that your grandfather saw Roman die. How could this letter be from him?" William's curiosity was growing, but he was still hesitant to believe such a far-fetched tale.

"Listen, my son," Jeffrey's voice was weakening with exhaustion, but he continued to press; his tired voice relentless. "My father wasn't very old when my grandfather died. He remembered my grandfather went mad about a week before he died, just after a middle-aged man came to the castle with a message for Grandfather. They spoke privately for only a moment, and the stranger left quickly. For the next week, until he died, my grandfather insisted the man who had visited him was Roman. It never occurred to me it could have been true until I found that letter."

"Even if you are right, what would you have me do?" *Had Jeffrey gone mad?* William was just a simple peasant; what could he do? Still, he respected the old man enough to wish him to feel at ease in his final days, even if William privately thought him mad.

"I want you to find the island, or find Roman, and save your family from this curse. I will pass land and title to you to this end alone. You must promise me. Your family will never again want for anything. Promise me." His old frame had hardened and he was speaking with a newfound strength, as if he was mustering all he had for this final act. He stretched out his arm and opened his hand to William.

"I will do as you wish," William said, although still not convinced. He could not believe in such fairy tales, but if granting this final request from his lord would help his family, he knew he must. William clasped the old man's bony hand in his own. "I promise," he said, completely unprepared for the trials and horrors that lay ahead.

# CHAPTER 33

WILLIAM WAS A simple man. He was not easily given to adventures or throes of passion and imagination. He had never been absent from his family for very long, either. The only time he had been separated from them was while he was busy caring for Lord Jeffrey.

His body was ripe with motion sickness when he stepped off the small ship onto a rocky shore. He vowed to never leave home again—if he ever made it back. He thought this entire quest was a joke, but if it meant a better life for his family, as Jeffrey had promised, then he would stay the course. This was the fifteenth island he had scoured in the Mediterranean. He found nothing on the others, and he was sure this one would be no different.

As he watched the small vessel push back out to sea, he thought of his family and how much he loved them. Mostly, he thought of his lovely wife Esmeralda. He could count the days and hours since he had last seen her warm smile, and even if he could see it again tomorrow, it wouldn't be soon enough. She meant the world to him.

For a moment he thought about just getting back on the boat and sailing home. Jeffrey was probably dead by now and the castle his; no one would be the wiser. Still, he was a man of his word, and he owed it to Jeffrey to finish the task.

Jeffrey had told William that Roman and his grandfather, Caius, had been exploring a small island they called Shiria in the Mediterranean Sea, off the coast of Turkey. His grandfather had told him of the monolithic stones the ancients had placed in intricate designs, stones so large they could not have been carved or carried by mortal men. He had also left Jeffrey a map, which seemed useless to William.

Caius and Roman had believed the natives on this island had a secret that could free men from death and give them unimaginable power. There were stories of the island passed down from ancient times, but they were scarce now. It was said the island was guarded by a dense fog and illusionary magic. There were also stories of men who had lived hundreds of years, men who had gathered those monoliths single-handedly, and even men who could turn into ferocious beasts at will. Most people who had heard of the island steered clear of the area; they believed it to be cursed.

Some said it was the home of the gods. Then there were those like Caius and Roman, who didn't care. They just wanted power, at any cost. Caius had said they had been exploring one of the ancient sites, a circle of huge, freestanding stones on the edge of a giant cliff. He said Roman had stumbled and fallen over the edge of the cliff onto the jagged rocks below. Caius took Roman's death as a bad omen and gave up the search. He left the island that same day—never to return.

*And here I am,* William grumbled to himself, *following in the footsteps of two old fools.* He looked around, but the island seemed deserted. About a hundred yards down the beach he spied a small path disappearing behind the tree line and decided to see where it led. After walking for hours, he finally came to a small hut tucked discreetly off the path.

He walked through a thicket of trees and bushes before finally arriving at what seemed like a small dirt moat surrounding the hut. His curiosity was piqued when he heard the steady clank of chisel against rock. The clanking stopped when he walked a few steps around the hut.

William was shocked to see a huge man with nearly solid-black skin. He was carrying a massive stone, at least twice as long as a man and nearly half that in width and depth. William was dumbfounded. The stories were actually true! He watched as the man laid the enormous, unfinished stone down, next to another that had been chiseled with astonishing precision to create a perfectly rectangular monolith, larger than anything William had imagined possible.

# CHAPTER 34

"TELL ME, WHAT is it that you want?" The man spoke in a very unusual dialect, never turning to look at William behind him. William was silent. He was completely mesmerized.

*Clank, clank, clank.* The man went back to work on the huge stone.

"I want to be like you." William had finally pulled himself together and surprised himself with how forcefully he spoke.

"You want to be like me? You don't even know me." The black giant still didn't look up from his work.

"I want your power." William was tired of playing games. The man put down his tools and looked at William for the first time.

"And just what power would that be? Do you want to carry around big rocks? Do you want immortality? Are those the furthest reaches of your ambition?"

His words made William feel small and foolish.

"Don't feel bad," the giant continued. "Everyone wants power, but the greatest of powers have to be earned. They can't just be given away. Power only comes through sacrifice, in one way or another." As he listened, William noticed the giant's eyes were solid white

"Teach me." William's voice was stern. The man looked at him for a long minute.

"Very well. My name is Odam. If you can handle it, I will teach you to wield true power." There was solemnity and strength in his voice. William's excitement grew with every breath; he was going to be powerful!

"Let's start with this rock." Odam gestured to the monolith he had been carrying just moments ago.

"I can't lift that." William believed the man was making fun at his expense.

"How do you know? You haven't even tried." Odam's voice was hollow and monotone. "If you're not up to it, you are welcome to leave." William could tell the giant was completely serious.

William thought it was useless, stupid, in fact, to even attempt it, but this man was persistent. He stretched his arms, preparing them for a big lift. He squatted in front of the massive stone and reached his arms as far around it as he could. Clenching tightly, he thrust his legs and back upward with all his might.

The stone didn't budge. He'd known he wouldn't be able to lift it, so his feeling of disappointment seemed strange. He burned with humiliation, sure this man was mocking him.

William looked up at Odam, who was busy picking at the apricot in his hand.

"I don't know, maybe it's too big," Odam said, his face expressionless. William knew Odam had never expected him to be able to lift the rock. He was growing frustrated. "Here." As he spoke, Odam handed him a chisel and a stone. "Cut one centimeter off of each side and make sure the edges are smooth."

*What game is this man playing?* William thought. *He knows as well as I do one centimeter won't make any difference at all.*

"Or you're always free to leave," Odam said, probably sensing William was questioning his instruction. William thought it was ridiculous, but he wanted to impress the man; he wanted to learn real power. So he went to work chiseling the huge gray stone in front of him.

## CHAPTER 35

W ILLIAM HAD CHISELED relentlessly for days. He was exhausted. Finally deciding his work was complete, he called for Odam. He waited and waited.

After nearly an hour, Odam came slowly strolling out of his hut.

"I'm finished," William said proudly. Odam walked slowly around the stone and carefully looked over every inch.

"Good work. Did you lift it yet?" He was staring expressionlessly into William's face.

*Of course not,* William thought. His frustration with this man was escalating rapidly. "Well, I haven't tried, but I don't see how I could. It's barely smaller than it was a few days ago." William knew his tone of voice revealed his frustration.

"You haven't tried? Then you certainly could not." Odam stared into William's eyes again as he spoke.

William couldn't tell if Odam was trying to teach him some mystical secret or if he was just toying with him, but he thought it was worth staying a few more days to find out. So, once more, William bent down in front of this monolithic stone and tried with all his might to lift it, but, once again, it didn't budge.

"It must still be too large." Odam spoke as if he was a bit surprised.

William searched his face for a hint of humor or sarcasm, but found nothing. The man himself was a stone—a monolith.

"Take off another centimeter," the giant ordered.

William was furious. It wasn't going to do any good, and the work had peeled the skin right off his hands—he had worked them nearly to the bone.

William swallowed hard and went back to work. He worked diligently, but his progress was much slower; he could barely hold the chisel now, or the stone. Finally, more than a week later, he finished his task.

Before he called for Odam, he reached down and tried to lift the stone, but still couldn't budge it. He called for Odam and sat down, lying back on the huge stone, nearly too exhausted to sit up. He didn't know how much time had passed before the tremors of the large man's footsteps roused him.

"I still couldn't lift it," William exclaimed as he noticed Odam's presence just above him.

"At least you tried this time." Odam's voice was slightly condescending. "Cut it again," his voice thundered. Without waiting for a response, he through William an orange and walked back into his hut. On the outside, he was emotionless, but Odam deeply hoped this man could renew his faith in mankind and muster the strength to find what true power really was.

"Cut it again! Cut it again! This is useless, and this man is insane!" William shouted inside his head. Still, he had no choice. He had seen true power and he wanted it. He wanted it so much he was even willing to continue with this ridiculous exercise. Grabbing his tools, he pulled himself up and began banging away at the unforgiving stone.

# CHAPTER 36

OUT OF THE corner of William's eye, he saw a middle-aged looking man, very tall, with a thick build, vault over a downed tree and maneuver through the dense brush with ease.

"I have been watching you hammer that thing for days. I thought you would have given up by now. You are starting to remind me of that crazy bastard inside the hut," the man spoke articulately. "Whatever you're after, you are wasting your time. He's not going to teach you anything; he just wants to see how long he can make you kill yourself banging that damn stone. I've seen it happen before." The man widened his eyes and grinned slightly as he spoke, making William feel even more like a fool.

"No, he has real power. I've seen it, and I'll do whatever it takes to get it." As William spoke, the man's grin turned into a wide smile.

"You're right, he's got power, but he'll never share it with you. He thinks you're an imbecile, out here pounding rocks all day while he sits comfortably inside. But I can show you how to get real power. Just come with me." The man spoke like a silver-tongued devil as he lifted the huge monolith up in his arms.

"I won't give you games or riddles; I'll take you right to the source." Seeing the man's display of power and listening to his sales pitch was all William needed. He was tired of pounding rocks and believed it wasn't getting him anywhere.

"The name's Roman." The oddly large man reached out his hand.

"Roman, you say? I've heard that name before. My name is William. It's very good to meet you." William was tingling with enthusiasm, and after this encounter with the infamous Roman, his desire for power was growing by leaps and bounds.

Odam overheard the men's conversation from inside his hut and was terribly disappointed the man had been so easily led away. He had been the first person to seek Odam out in nearly a century.

It had been millennia since he had made an immortal or even met a human with the will and desire to find true power. Something about this man had given him hope. There was strength in him, however misguided.

"What do I need to do?" William asked Roman, increasingly anxious.

"That depends on how much power you want. I could give you power right now with just one bite... strength and immortality... but for even more power, you need to go to the source. He's just on the other side of the island." A faint smile lit Roman's face.

"Just a bite?" William asked with a frown.

"Yes, just a bite, and then death will never harm you. Instead, death will be your ally," Roman stared at William intently as he spoke.

William didn't like the idea of being bitten; besides, it sounded too insignificant.

"Take me to the source." As soon as William had finished speaking, Roman took off through the jungle with amazing speed and agility. It was an awesome sight, and it was impossible for William to keep up. After tripping a few times over vines and branches, and fumbling through a briar patch, William finally emerged from the forest onto a rocky cliff.

He was amazed to see Roman standing atop one of six monoliths sitting upright in a circle, each of which was more than twice as tall as a man. It was just as Jeffrey's grandfather had described.

"The secret is over the edge." Roman hopped down from the huge stone and pointed over the edge of the cliff.

*Over the cliff? Is this man crazy?* William crept across the large flat rock constituting the top of the cliff and slowly made his way to the edge. Being afraid of heights, he nearly fainted when he looked over and saw the jagged rocks below.

"Not afraid of heights, are you?" Roman was laughing. "Oh, come on, it's not that far." He was now roaring with laughter.

"Are you asking me to jump off of this cliff? I'll die." William was shocked and frightened.

"Not always." Roman seemed to be speaking from experience. "Well, there is another way. You can just take the path that leads around the cliff. It will also take you to the bottom." Roman was grinning once more as he pointed across the cliff to a small, trampled path cutting through the dense underbrush.

William ran over to the path, filled with relief. For a moment he'd wondered if he had made a terrible decision, following this crazy man. The path through the jungle wasn't a cliff that fell over onto jagged rocks that seemed something like tearing teeth as the waves crashed against them, but it wasn't a stroll through the valley around Rothber Castle, either. William was beginning to despise the way this crazy man pressed through the thick jungle like it was nothing, going over and under, but mostly just straight through.

Stinging sensations raked across his body as he tore his way through more than one nasty thorn bush. This trail was barely a trail at all. Ducking under a large, overhanging tree limb, he was glad to see Roman had finally stopped. He was resting against a large tree growing on the side of a ledge. The tree was so close to the edge, its roots were hanging out.

"Where to now?" William was tired and he was beyond ready to acquire his promised power.

Roman said nothing, he just pointed over the ledge.

"Is this another joke?" William was tired of this man's jokes.

"No joke. That is the only way down from here." He grinned obnoxiously.

William took another look over the ledge. It wasn't so bad. The fall would be roughly twice the length of a man, and the dirt at the bottom looked soft enough.

Desperate to find an end to this tiresome journey, William leapt over without another word. His feet hit the ground first, followed instantaneously by a loud cracking sound. William collapsed, grasping his left ankle and moaning wildly.

"Stop crying, boy!" William looked up in time to see Roman leap over the edge and land on his feet with ease; he seemed just to glide through the air. "Lord Adol is just inside, and if he hears you, you won't have a chance. So muster some grit and let's get moving." The man moved on without giving William even a moment to catch his breath and get used to the pain.

William wanted to scream at the condescendingly clever bastard, but knew it would only hurt his cause. Grabbing a nearby limb, he pulled himself to his feet, and, placing nearly all his weight on his right leg, he hobbled after Roman.

For the first time in a few days, he thought about home and how much he would love to feel Esmeralda's warm embrace. His son, Elijah, had broken his arm once falling out of a tree. He had been so brave. The thought heartened William and gave him a new strength.

"It's just up ahead." William could see the sharp, teeth-like rocks, but nothing else except the side of a cliff. *What now?* he thought.

"There is nothing here." William exclaimed as they reached the very bottom of the cliff.

"Is that so?" Roman walked to the cliff face as he spoke and slammed his fist mightily against the rocky surface. A large, square piece of the cliff side slid back nearly two paces, leaving openings on either side.

William followed Roman through the crack on the right.

# CHAPTER 37

WILLIAM COULDN'T SEE much. There were a few torches along the wall that seemed to cast more shadows than light. They seemed to be in a cave. Roman took down one of the torches and touched the flame to a small gutter that jutted out from the cave wall.

The gutter quickly caught fire, racing in both directions around the space. The fire revealed the true nature of the cavern, and William gaped. The space around them was nothing like the caves or caverns he'd seen before.

It didn't even smell like a cave. The air was fresh and dry. The cavern was completely lit now, and it was huge. There was no dust or dirt; the place was immaculate.

They were standing on a foyer of sorts, a landing atop a large staircase hewn from rock. It was spectacular. William had never seen anything that compared. At the four corners of the staircase were enormous columns. Each was different; each had a unique shape and different carvings.

The carvings were beautiful and intricate, portraying all sorts of horned and vicious-looking creatures—most of which William had never seen or heard of. The rest of the cavern, if you could call it that, was no less amazing. On the floor were carvings and statues that seemed part human and part beast. Intricately designed patterns and pictures covered the walls and ceiling.

"Impressive, isn't it?" Roman muttered, seeming pleased with himself, though William doubted he had much to do with any of it.

"It certainly is." William was still astounded; he took time to examine each piece.

"Come on, we don't have time for all of this right now." Roman's voice was stern as he strode to the back of the cavern. William quickly fell in behind him; if there was more to this place, he definitely wanted to see it.

There was a huge archway at the back, opposite the stairs. It opened up into a large corridor. There were similar archways on each side of the corridor, but each was sealed with a large stone. It actually appeared as if the archways were just carved into the wall.

At the end of the corridor was another archway. It was also sealed, but it was different from the others. It was covered in etchings of symbols William didn't recognize, and was beautifully designed. Roman slammed his fist hard against the stone, and it slid backwards, just like the other one had.

William could see light flooding in from both sides of the recessed rock.

"Come in." The voice coming from behind the stone was deep and loud, and it seemed to make the walls around him shake. He feared the place might collapse on top of him as he followed Roman past the stone and into another opening, not quite as large as the main hall. To William's surprise, it was a library of sorts.

Every wall was carved out to make bookcases at least fifteen feet high. The shelves were completely filled. Much like the main hall, this room was filled with odd but beautiful artwork. Near the back center of the room was a huge, throne-like chair carved out of stone.

In the chair towered a man, much like Odam, except he had pale skin and light gray eyes. He wore a silk robe that left most of his body visible, and his skin was covered with some of the same symbols and markings William had seen in different places throughout the cavern. They seemed to have been carved into his body. At his feet were two naked women with olive skin and long, dark hair. The women were on their knees at either side of him. Bent over, they were massaging olive oil into his feet with their hair.

"What do you ask of me?" his voice thundered. William couldn't speak; he stood frozen, in awe. His entire belief system had been turned upside down. It seemed everything he thought was real was a fiction and everything he had never imagined could ever be was right in front of him, here and now.

William had been raised to believe in the Roman gods, but he never really believed. Now, in the last few days, he had met two gods and had no idea what else might be out there. He was overwhelmed.

"I am Adol. Why have you come? Speak!" The towering being's voice grew even louder and fiercer.

"Forgive me, please. It's just that I recently met a man much like you, but his skin was solid black and eyes snow white." William was almost trembling as he spoke.

"He is no man!" Adol shouted. "He is my brother, Odam. My brothers and I appear in this world as we see ourselves." He was speaking now in a more gentle tone. "I believe you have come to me to acquire what you could not from my brother. I might be offended by that, but I know my brother can be a bit difficult with his ideals and philosophies." As he spoke, Adol scratched at the stone arm of his throne.

"Yes, you are right. I want power." William's eagerness now outweighed his fear, and he spoke boldly to the giant before him.

"And what would I receive in return, if I gave you this power you are searching for?" Adol's voice was a deep, resonant whisper.

"I am sorry, sir, but I have nothing," William replied, burning with fear.

"You come to me with nothing and expect me to give you priceless gifts?" His tone was patronizing, if not condemning. "Surely you have something. Do you have a family?" The question struck fear in William's heart.

"Yes, but you could not possibly be interested in such ordinary people?" William's voice was shaking.

"That all depends on how much you want this power you speak of." Adol laughed, a deep, hollow laugh that chilled William to the bone. "Sacrifice, that is how power is unleashed upon mortal men." Adol's tone was now deeper and more serious.

William shivered as a deep foreboding overcame him and he suddenly wished he had never come here. He wanted more than ever to simply be home with his wife and sons.

"Are you saying I have to kill my family before I can be like you?" William feared the answer to his question.

"Be like me? You are just a man; you could never be like me, but you can become very powerful. You wouldn't have to kill your *entire* family, just the one you love the most. That will be sacrifice enough." Adol's voice was taunting; he was obviously enjoying this very much.

"I could never do that; there must be another way!"

"There might be one other way. Many centuries past, my brother created a nasty race of immortals. They are truly vicious and fearsome creatures. He only created a handful, and they are difficult to locate. The creatures are both man and beast, changing from one form to the other at will. Find one of these rare bloodlines, beast or beast kin, and eat its heart. Know this is an impossible challenge, but if you accomplish it, I will surely imbue you with even greater power." Adol smiled as he continued clawing at his throne.

"Is that it, just find and kill a powerful immortal or his kin and eat his heart?" William's tone was sarcastic, but a flicker of hope lit deep within him. William had knowledge this god obviously did not. He could find a bloodline; he was certain of it.

"Yes, that is all. I am Adol, God of Death, and Lord of Endings. I give you my word, if you kill one of my brother's immortals or its kin and eat its heart, you will be more powerful than you have ever imagined. But, as I said, it is an impossible task. You should just kill the one you love most, your wife or child, perhaps, and eat their heart. That would be much easier, and I would be just as satisfied." The big god smiled and laughed another deep and hollow laugh.

"You mean this is all just a test to see if I'm worthy? You could give me the power right now if you wanted?" William was appalled as the words leapt from his lips.

"This is no test." Adol snapped back as he loomed up from his chair and stared threateningly at William. "Who are you to question me? You are pitiful creations, unworthy of anything from me. This is for my amusement, and I only make you this offer because, if you succeed, I will use you as I see fit. You will be mine. Now go; leave this place and don't come back until you are an immortal." His voice was dark and vicious.

William turned and headed for the opening in the stone. He was more than happy to flee this place. Adol's presence was awesome, but terrifying.

"Wait! There is one more thing." William turned back around to face Adol. "Have you ever killed a man?" Adol asked as he gently rubbed the side of his scarred face.

"No, I have not," William answered honestly.

"For some reason, it seems to be a trying task for most men, but I hear it gets easier." He now spoke in a monotone voice, his face expressionless. "I'm going to help you get started." He pushed his left foot forward as he spoke, and catapulted a girl onto the ground in front of William. "Kill her." The god's sinister voice was demanding.

# CHAPTER 38

H E SAW THE naked girl at his feet was very young, probably not more than fifteen years old.

"I can't kill her!" The words burst forth; William was horrified.

"Oh, I think you can. You do want power, don't you? Roman, give him your blade." He turned and gestured to Roman as he spoke. Roman appeared from behind William holding out a small dagger. William had forgotten Roman was even there.

"Here, take it." Roman extended his hand, holding the dagger by the blade. William took it from his hand and looked down at the girl. She looked scared, but she didn't make a sound. She looked up and met his gaze as she pushed herself off the floor and onto her knees.

The girl was beautiful, young, and innocent. For a moment, their souls seemed to merge into one. He thought about his children at home, about the power he could have, and about how killing this young girl would change him forever. He might receive all the power in the world, but his soul would surely be forever damned.

"This is the only way?" He looked back up at Adol. His voice was now steady; he was composed.

"It is." Adol was uncompromising. William looked back down at the girl, catching her gaze once again. She looked at him for only a second and then closed her eyes as if she knew what was coming. A small tear welled in the corner of her left eye and rolled down her cheek.

William was now consumed with the desire for power; nothing else seemed to matter anymore. He took one step towards the girl and thrust the blade forward with his right hand, first through her chest and then her neck. The girl's screams were both thrilling and chilling at the same time. Now William knew power; what could be more powerful than the power over life and death? It was beautiful, and he wouldn't stop; his hunger for more would rage on.

The girl fell to her back; her screams were only whimpers and gurgles now as blood flowed from her wounds and spilled from her mouth.

William was overcome with an exhilaration such as he had never known. He fell on top of the girl and continued stabbing through her flesh with the bloodied blade as Adol laughed uncontrollably. He stabbed her over and over again, in the chest, stomach, neck and face until she was completely unrecognizable.

When he had finished, he could barely lift his right arm. He collapsed on the floor beside her. He was exhausted; he was reborn. He had been more alive in the last five minutes than in his entire life before. He was a new man.

"Now you can go." Adol smiled a grim, knowing smile.

William picked himself up. Although covered in blood, he was eager to move on. He knew what he needed to do and was more than ready to get started.

For years he had heard stories of immortal men who took

the forms of beasts; he had married into those stories. He knew where to begin his search. At home.

"Roman. Go with him; keep him on task," Adol instructed as Roman ushered in a new girl to sit at his feet.

William had no need for someone to keep him on task. He was now aching with the desire for power, however it came. He didn't really care for the awkward man who had led him here, but his talents might come in handy along the way, especially if it came down to killing another immortal.

William bowed graciously towards the morbid god before him and then turned and followed Roman back through the corridor and into the main hall. He lingered there for a few moments, once again studying all the expertly crafted artwork around him.

"Who did all this?" William was awed by the intricacies of the designs and carvings.

"Adol, who do you think? He is mighty and powerful, but even the gods want things they can never have."

"What do you mean?" Roman's odd comment had sparked William's curiosity.

"Adol has the power to destroy anything, perhaps even his brothers. He is unimaginably strong, but death is his curse. In his heart he is an artist, a creator, not a destroyer. That is why he envies his brother so. His brother can create worlds and creatures with just the spark of his imagination, while Adol is forced to use his brother's creations to craft his art." Roman was smiling as if he thought the situation was hilarious.

"Still it's amazing, Adol's work. I have never seen anything like it." William rubbed his hand over the smooth surface of a carving that almost seemed to pull itself out of the wall.

"Yes, you fool, but don't you understand it's nothing in his eyes? It's man's work. Adol fashions rocks into beautiful-looking rocks, while his brother paints and fashions the heavens. Adol sees *that* as a god's work, the making of life. So, in his jealousy, he destroys everything his brother creates. Eventually he'll even get around to destroying you and me."

Roman's tone was more serious now and William was impressed with his knowledge and understanding of the situation. Perhaps he had misjudged the man. "I still don't understand; if Odam is so busy creating worlds and universes and all that, why did I see him chiseling rocks?" William was confused.

"It's not Odam, you simple man, it's his other brother, Mikal. He has a place on this island as well, but it's very doubtful you would find him there. He stays very busy with his work." Roman was speaking sarcastically.

"So what power does Odam have?"

"What do you mean? He is a god." Roman's words were frustrating William and making him feel stupid.

"You know what I mean. If Mikal creates and Adol destroys, what does Odam do?" Having last spoken to the strange god only a day ago, William was very curious.

"Odam abides. He is pretentious and self-righteous. Power doesn't mean to him what it means to the rest of the world. I don't know what powers he has, but I don't believe he really uses any. He looks down on both of his brothers, sneering at the suffering they have inflicted on the world. Some say he helps mankind through its toils and troubles, but the truth is that he hates his brother for how they create and take away life. They say he hates the suffering Mikal's flawed creation brings to the created, but I think he is just as jealous as Adol."

After speaking, Roman looked at William for a moment, as if he were waiting for another question, but William remained silent.

"So, what's your plan?" Roman's eyes were gleaming with excitement. "Well, do you know any of these immortals Adol spoke of?" William highly doubted it, but he asked anyway.

"No, but from what I hear, they are nearly impossible to find. They keep to themselves, and there are not many of them."

Clearly Roman wasn't going to be much help with tracking. "What about the one you killed to get your power?"

"I didn't have to kill any immortals to get my power; Adol chooses different paths for us all." Roman walked on as if he didn't want to speak of it.

*All?* "How many immortals has Adol created?" William couldn't help asking.

"Very many, hundreds, or perhaps even thousands over the years. He has been doing this for a long time."

*Thousands!* William was shocked.

## CHAPTER 39

WALKING OUT OF the square opening in the side of the cliff, Roman grasped an inconspicuous knot-like protrusion on the recessed rock and pulled it toward him. The opening sealed, perfectly concealed. William looked out at the waves foaming against the jagged rocks and remembered the story about Roman falling over the cliff and dying right in that spot.

"So what happened to you? I mean, how did you become immortal?" he asked, really wanting to know how he survived the fall.

"Adol found me in a bad position and we made a deal. That was it." He spoke nonchalantly.

"You mean he found you dying on those rocks." William pointed forward as he spoke.

"How could you possibly know that?" Roman retorted quickly. He looked shocked.

"I have spent my entire life working and caring for Jeffrey of Rothber." As he spoke, William could see understanding dawn on Roman's face.

"So he sent you here. I see; they finally figured it out. It took them long enough. That is a very queer family, as I'm sure you have noticed." Roman seemed to be hiding a deeper bitterness.

"Yes, he sent me. He also told me you died falling over this cliff." William's statement was more of a question.

"Well, he is right about one thing; I did fall over the cliff, and I would have died if Adol had not found me lying there with only an ounce of life left in my entire body. You see, Jeffrey's grandfather Caius left me to die on those rocks. I saw him look over the edge of the cliff and then he was gone. He never even came down to check on me." Roman seemed more hurt than angry.

"His face over that cliff was the last I saw of him until thirty years later. I heard he was very ill and only had weeks left to live. Nothing has satisfied me more than the look on his dying face as he saw me, still young and strong. It was a beautiful moment."

William could see the satisfaction still burning in his eyes as he spoke of it.

"So, where to from here?" Roman inquired once again.

"I have heard stories of these beasts for years, and of a family which carries the bloodline."

Roman stopped dead in his tracks.

William smiled to himself at Roman's obvious shock. "Of course, I always thought they were just stories, a family trying to live out its dreams through fairy tales. Apparently, I was wrong." William winced from the pain in his ankle as he spoke.

"Where is this family you speak of? How do you know them? Why would they have told you their secrets?"

"They told me their secrets because I know them well... intimately, actually. The family is my own, at least the one I married into."

"Impossible." A look of excitement and surprise came across Roman's face.

"It's true. The problem is, by the time I met Esmeralda, she was the only child left in the family. We never stayed in contact with the rest of her family. I have no idea where they could be, or even if any of them are still alive, but Esmeralda will know. We will find our answers at Rothber Castle. We just need a boat." William took a deep breath and scratched his head.

"Don't worry about that. I have just what we need; follow me." Roman took off around the cliff and William followed as best he could with his injured ankle. It was only a moment before they rounded the cliff and William saw a boat in the distance, actually more of a small ship. He was exhausted and breathing heavily by the time they reached the vessel.

"Just have a seat, boy; I'll take it from here." Roman shouted enthusiastically.

William was happy to oblige. Finding a small bench near the rear of the boat, William lay on his back and was asleep almost immediately.

# CHAPTER 40

IT SEEMED LIKE an eternity had passed by the time they landed on a narrow beach just a few hours' walk from the castle.

William was confident Esmeralda would tell him everything he needed to know, and he would soon have the power and immortality he now craved so desperately.

It was nearly dark. Good. The children should be in bed by the time he arrived.

Perhaps he could find a way for them all to live as immortals together. If he could just get Solomon to understand, he knew the rest of his family would soon come around.

But first he must talk to Esmeralda. She had the answers; she had the blood.

Time seemed to fly by, and, before he knew it, William and Roman stood only minutes from the castle door.

"What are you going to do, William?" Roman seemed somewhat concerned. "You know that if she has the blood, then we need look no further than right here." His smile was wry.

"Let's hope it doesn't come to that." William looked down shamefaced. "Stay here," he commanded and then hurried up the hill to the castle entrance. He was excited and nervous; the power he so desperately wanted was now within his grasp.

As the door creaked open, William caught sight of his beautiful wife. She was still cleaning the kitchen. The smell of stew lingered in the air, and William could smell onions, tomatoes and all different spices. He had missed those smells, and now he was happier than ever to be home.

"William!" Esmeralda shouted as she turned and met his gaze. She ran to him and embraced him warmly.

"Hello, my love. How have you been?" William spoke gently as he pulled back and gazed into her eyes.

"We have been fine; but we have missed you so much. Let me go wake the boys; they will be so glad to see you." She turned and started up the stairs.

"No, let's let them sleep for now." At the landing atop the stairwell, William took her arm and spun her back around. "I'm just so glad to see you."

"I guess the boys can wait until morning; it will give us a chance to catch up. Tell me all about your journey." She smiled into his eyes most tenderly.

"I will; I will tell you everything, but first I need to ask you about something." He pulled her close as he spoke. He was feeling more and more nervous, and now her face looked worried.

"Is everything all right?" she asked, backing away until her heels nearly met the edge of the landing.

"Yes, everything is fine. Don't worry. Where is Solomon? Is he in bed, too?" William asked, barely able to hold back his excitement.

"No, after dinner he went over to Sara's house. He will be back before long." Her tone was reassuring. "Now tell me, what is it?"

He could feel her curiosity and concern. The two were now face to face on the landing, only inches separating them.

"Do you remember those stories your family used to tell about family members having special abilities?" William was still trying to hide his eagerness.

"Yes, of course I remember those silly stories. Why?" Esmeralda looked confused.

"Esmeralda, I believe those stories are true." William was staring into her eyes.

"True? What on earth do you mean? Those are just stories." She laughed uncomfortably and shifted her eyes to the floor.

"I know the truth, Esmeralda, and I need you to help me find one." William's voice was serious and stern.

"What has gotten into you, William? They truly are just stories." She turned and started back down the stairs, but William grabbed her arm hard and yanked her back around.

"William, you are hurting me," she raised her voice.

"Esmeralda, I tell you, I know. It's no use lying. Now I need you to help me. I have found a way to save our family… and to gain great power." His voice was getting louder as his impatience grew.

"Where have you been, William? What has happened to you?"

He could see her fear as she continued trying to deflect his intent.

"Tell me what I need to know!" He was now bellowing angrily.

"I can't tell you anything. None of it is true, William." She was crying.

"You are lying!" he shouted as he slid a knife from his belt.

"William, no! What are you doing?" Esmeralda begged, just as Roman came through the castle door.

"Just get it over with, William," Roman urged.

"I don't want to kill you, Esmeralda, but I will." Rage seemed to take control of his body. He burned with lust for power, the way he had when he thrust the small blade into the young girl's chest so many times.

"Go ahead and kill me. I have nothing to tell you." Her voice was no longer full of fear, but disgust.

"Well, perhaps you'll tell me to save your children, then. Roman, go find the smaller boy in one of the bedrooms. Bring him down here." William's expression was stone cold as he spewed hate with every breath. The man he once had been was lost. He had transformed into pure, focused lust.

"No, no, no! I'll tell you whatever you want to know, just leave the boys alone."

He could hear the fear flooding back into her voice, and smell it. "I need to find an immortal bloodline. I have to kill someone with their blood to gain my power." His eyes were glaring, and he had a feral smile, even though he didn't realize it.

"I can't send you to slaughter someone, William. I just won't do it." Her demeanor changed suddenly. Her voice was stern, her body straight and strong and determined.

"Not even to save your children?" William was twirling a knife in one hand and pushing Esmeralda until she nearly fell down the stairs with the other.

"I won't send you anywhere else. If you believe this to be true, then take what you need from me. I have the same blood as my family." Her tone was now somber. "Just promise me you won't hurt the children."

William nodded quickly. He was as eager to feel power the way he had earlier. Without one more word, he thrust the knife into her chest and held her for a moment, watching her blood pump out vigorously, before letting her drop and watching as she toppled to the bottom of the steps. Just like before, he leapt from the landing and threw himself on top of her while he continued stabbing, but this time with more purpose.

This time he jabbed under her bellybutton and tore upwards,

ripping through flesh and bone. He kept at it until her chest was split wide open and her heart was visible. Then he cut around her heart, slicing it free of all the tissue that held it in place.

His chest flooded with the thrill of power as he held the heart up in the air like a trophy. Not wasting any more time, he sat down on the floor next to his wife's mutilated corpse and began to eat the raw, bloody organ. He devoured the entire thing in minutes and then waited patiently to receive his gift.

Within seconds, he could feel his entire body start to tingle. He was light-headed for a second, then a burning sensation filled his body, and then a deep calm suffused him, a calm such as he had never known. The pain in his leg was gone. Looking up at Roman, he couldn't hold back a smile.

"Let's go find my son." William was exhilarated. Stepping out of the house, he was eager to try out his new power. He lifted a large stone slab tabletop and hurled it through the air. The massive stone flew at least thirty yards. William could hardly believe it.

"Let's run," Roman suggested.

"Follow me, then," William said.

The pair took off down the valley and headed east along the river. William moved so fast he seemed to fly. He reveled in it...

...and it wasn't long at all before they arrived at Sara's cottage.

# CHAPTER 41

A S SARA AND Solomon approached Sara's cottage they noticed William and another man standing outside as if waiting for someone.

"Why is he here?" Sara whispered.

Looking into her eyes, Solomon could tell she was as surprised to see William as he was. Solomon was confused, but thrilled as well; he hadn't seen his father in years.

"Well, hello, dear Sara. I've just returned, and I'm afraid I'm a bit out of the loop." William's voice and demeanor were dark and taunting—devil-may-care. Solomon thought he might be drunk.

"Sara, come here, please." Solomon wasn't sure what was going on, but wanted to be certain Sara was safe. His father could be a mean drunk at times, and he was covered in blood.

"What a beautiful young thing." William laughed and tugged at his scruffy beard. "Come here, Sara, and let me have a look at you," he muttered as he grabbed her hand and pulled her close.

"Let me go!" she shrieked.

Solomon stepped closer when he saw his father's tight grip

was hurting her arm, and was brought up short by William's unbearable odor.

"Solomon," she looked to him beseechingly as she struggled in his father's grip. From inside the hut he could hear her parents yelling and pounding on the door, but William had blocked the only exit with a large bolder.

"Are you drunk, Father? What is going on? Let her go and let's get you to bed." He was still trying to gently defuse the situation.

"No, Son. I'm not drunk. I'm just especially happy to see young Sara, here." She was now groaning in pain from William's vise-like grip.

"Let her go Father, now! You are hurting her."

"What is that look, Son? Are you upset? Would you like to do something about it?"

William was taunting him. Solomon *was* upset, and confused. This man's threatening and erratic behavior made it harder and harder for Solomon to believe he could be the kind and loving father who'd raised him.

"Let her go, now," Solomon repeated as he stepped towards his father, intent on wresting Sara from his grasp.

"That's a brave lad." William grabbed Solomon by the throat and effortlessly lifted him and held him in the air as he bit down on Sara's neck and began draining her of blood. William tossed Solomon a few yards away as he continued to drink from Sara's veins. He then dropped her nearly lifeless body to the ground.

Awestruck by his father's power, Solomon had trouble believing how effortlessly he'd lifted and thrown Solomon, who was far bigger... but Sara needed him urgently. Leaping to his feet, he charged William.

At the last second, William stepped to the side and, grabbing Solomon by the back of his neck, flipped him into the air. Solomon landed hard on his stomach. Driven now by blind fury, he heaved to his feet again and prepared to launch another attack.

"Uh, uh, uh." William shook his finger and then pointed to Sara lying still on the ground. "She has a little blood left, but not much. If you want her to live, you will do exactly as I say. Is that understood?"

Solomon felt sure she'd never survive, but, unwilling to risk Sara's life further, Solomon agreed.

"First, a test, to see just how dedicated you are, how far you will go to save the ones you most care about."

Solomon thought about Elijah, Malaki, and his mother. He was flooded with icy fear, having seen already that anything his father might ask of him would be abhorrent.

"Build a fire." William's glare was a taunt. "I said, build a fire. Now."

Solomon didn't know what to do. He had a terrible inkling of what William was going to demand of him next.

"No, Solomon, don't. Please!" Sara's weak voice cried out in desperation.

"Shut up." William snarled, spraying her with spittle, then turning back to Solomon. "Do it, or Sara dies."

Solomon had no choice. He gathered some dried leaves, twigs, sticks and a stone. He hunkered down and began building a fire, horrified at what would happen next. The agony he was about to inflict on people he'd known his whole life.

"What's going on out there? Let us out." Solomon could hear Sara's parents pounding at the door and pleading for help. It only took a few moments for Solomon to start a small fire. Then he added a few larger sticks. After only a few minutes, the fire was burning extremely hot, and William called him over.

"Now, take one of those branches and set the roof on fire." He was trying to hold back his gleeful smile of anticipation.

"Please, Father. They will die in agony," Solomon begged

as he searched William's eyes for an ounce of pity, but found nothing.

"It's either them or Sara, and then your family, your choice."

Solomon could hear Sara struggling to get up.

"Solomon, please!" She was barely able to speak; her voice was scarcely a whisper. Solomon hesitated, still trying to figure out a way to avoid this horrifying choice.

"Go ahead and finish her off, Roman. He's not going to do it. He doesn't have the grit," William shouted.

"No! No. I'll do it." Even if Sara was already dead, he couldn't let his family die; they meant too much to him. He only hoped Sara could understand what he had to do. That William had given him no choice. Taking up a burning stick, he walked over and touched it to the dry, thatched roof. The whole place was ablaze in seconds.

The screams coming from inside were horrible, but they didn't last long. After they finally died down, William took a moment to survey the area. "Let's go, Son. The stink of burned flesh is turning my stomach... Oh, and I'll let her live, until she bleeds out on her own. I'm a man of my word."

Sara lay on the ground sobbing and bleeding, her face in the dirt.

"Sara!" Solomon ran to her. Kneeling beside her, he hesitantly touched her shoulders. "Can you hear me? Sara, please say something!" he begged, desperately hoping to hear some sign she would be okay.

She didn't say a word; she didn't move.

"Sara! Please, look at me!"

As she slowly lifted her head, Solomon could find no understanding, no forgiveness in her grim expression, only hate and pain. She did muster the strength for one word, though.

"Go!"

Solomon fell backwards as though her word had been a body blow, as Sara lay her head back on the earth and closed her eyes.

Solomon rose and followed his father. He looked back once, but couldn't see her moving.

She was dead, Solomon thought, as tears welled in his eyes. His life was over, and Solomon knew it. He would never be able to forgive himself for what he had just done. Looking up at his father, Solomon hoped his eyes showed the hate and rage bleeding forth for this stinking, venomous creature who had once been his father.

"That's good boy! You're going to need a lot of that where we're going. Now, come along. If you behave, your brothers might not meet the same fate as these poor souls," William chortled.

"I'm, sorry Sara," he whispered again. His body ached with sorrow and shame as he lowered his head and followed his father without another word. He couldn't allow this terrible fate to befall his own family.

## CHAPTER 42

"WHAT HAS HAPPENED to you, Father?" Solomon asked after a long silence. The man who had been with his father had disappeared a while back, and Solomon and William were now nearly halfway back to the castle.

"It's a long story, my son, a long story. I have been reborn into unimaginable power, and I can give you the same gift." William had stopped walking and was gesturing wildly in his excitement.

"I have no desire to be anything like you, Father. I would rather die." Solomon fired back, and then spat at his feet.

"That can be arranged, but it would be a shame. Then I would have to kill the entire family," William spoke without any signs of emotion.

"What would you have me do that you might spare my family?" Solomon was suddenly frightened again.

"Just follow me and do whatever I say. I am going to make you powerful and immortal. I have been blessed with the power over death; I can take away your brothers' lives and give them better ones, but if I die, they will also die." William turned and continued toward the castle.

After what seemed like only a few moments, Solomon could see his home in the distance.

"Listen to me, Son. Whatever happens in here, just remember I have the power to give your brothers life, even if I have to kill them first, as long as nothing happens to me." William spoke softly, almost as if he was trying to comfort Solomon.

"You are going to kill them?" Solomon shouted hysterically. "No, Father... please, I'll do anything."

"Not necessarily, Son. Anyway, I have the power to give them much more than I could ever take away," William grinned and laughed.

"Help! No! Elijah!" Solomon could hear Malaki crying out as his father opened the castle door and they walked in.

Solomon froze in the doorway, only halfway in, overcome with a feeling of panic. What could he do?

Roman was almost at the bottom of the stairs with Malaki slung over his shoulder when Solomon heard a loud thud followed by a few more. Seconds later Roman handed a kicking and screaming Malaki over to his father, and Solomon, still standing in the doorway, saw Elijah tumble down the stairs and lie still at the bottom.

At first Solomon thought he was unconscious, but he soon dragged himself to his feet.

"Father?" Elijah cried. His eyes narrowed and his brows knitted.

Solomon noticed Malaki had stopped screaming, and then, after a moment, he heard one loud scream and then a cracking sound. He looked over to see his father had just bitten his brother on the shoulder and then snapped his neck before throwing him to the ground. Blood was everywhere.

Solomon stood silent, in shock and horror. His frustration grew and he picked up a log that lay near the door. William looked over at him threateningly, and Solomon recalled his father's words and hoped what he'd said about giving new life was true.

A moment later he saw Elijah lunging for his father. Elijah didn't know! If he killed their father, then Malaki would be gone forever. Reacting to protect his youngest brother, Solomon stepped forward and swung the log like a bat, smacking Elijah directly on the temple.

His brother fell to the ground unconscious. Now in the room, Solomon had a better view over the table and could see a horribly mutilated body. His *mother!* As he struggled not to vomit, shame overcame him and he understood that he, too, was now vile and disgusting. His heart broke. What had he done? What terrible things had he helped his father do?

He ran to his mother's body and knelt down beside her. He wiped the tears falling from his eyes off of her cold, dead face. Behind him, he heard the most awful sound. As he turned to look, he saw his father plant his boot on Elijah's shoulder and pull ferociously on Elijah's head, ripping it from his body.

"You said you would give them new life!" Solomon screamed accusingly.

"If you do what I say, I will bring Malaki back, but you know Elijah. He is too weak; he could never understand what we need to do."

William wasn't convincing, and Solomon's heart was now broken beyond repair. He was burning with rage, but what could he do? He had just lost one brother and didn't want to risk losing another.

He turned around and knelt once again beside his mother's body. As he kissed her forehead, he noticed the pendant she wore lying on her shoulder; he wanted to keep it to remind him of her, but was too ashamed. Rising hopelessly to his feet, he walked towards the door.

Before he could step out the door, William jerked him close

and sank his teeth into Solomon's neck. Solomon almost welcomed his certain death.

"Now, you have also been reborn," William said, smiling.

Solomon was confused, but was soon overcome with a tingling sensation, a great pain in his chest, and then an overwhelming calm. He felt good. He felt strong.

# Ayda
# 1256 AD

*"It's not your strength or your skill that are lacking. It is your discipline. You are a volcano of emotion; that emotion gets in your way. It makes you careless and vulnerable, especially when you are fighting an adversary who cares for nothing." She laid her sword on the ground and walked towards him. "I can teach you the control you need; I can teach you to find your center."*

# CHAPTER 43

THE LETTER FROM the imam instructing the Assassins to surrender the fortress had reached Alamut in advance of the army, so the surrender was swift. Elijah watched as the Mongols raged through his long-time home, destroying all the towers and battlements. He remained in the hills outside the fortress, perhaps because of guilt or shame, but, whatever the reason, he did not want to enter.

Looking up at the nearly impenetrable fortress perched on the edge of a steep cliff, Elijah thought how it was in a much better position to defend than Maymundiz. It could have withstood a long siege, perhaps long enough to dissuade the Mongols, but not his father. If his father really was calling the shots, and there was something he wanted in that library, then he would not stop.

*Perhaps it is better this way.* Elijah exhaled and loosed another arrow that ricocheted off of the edge of his targeted tree. Looking to his left, Elijah saw the Khan walking up the hill to meet him.

"It is done, then?" Elijah asked as he laid the bow on the ground and turned towards the tall man.

"No. Whatever William is looking for was not in the library." The Khan lowered his head and raised his eyes to look at Elijah. "I am going to have to ask more of you." He spoke in a low, tired tone.

"We had an agreement: I give you Alamut and you take me to my father. That's it." Elijah could feel shards of anger shooting from his spine in all directions. This was the second time the great Hulagu Khan had reneged on his word.

"You have to understand, Elijah; I had no idea. They only tell me what they think I need to know. My brother has informed me that what they were looking for wasn't here, and now he is sending me to Baghdad. He now believes it must be there, in the House of Wisdom."

Elijah was breathing heavily as he paced back and forth.

"I haven't any choice, Elijah. Help me take Baghdad, and I will take you to William, I promise," the Khan pleaded.

Elijah stopped pacing and looked at the ground for a moment before looking up at the Khan. "How can I trust you now?" Elijah drummed his fingers against the hilt of his sword.

The Khan narrowed his eyes, acknowledging Elijah's threatening gesture. He was a strong man, not easily frightened. He cocked his chin to the right and smiled.

"You can trust me." He looked back to Elijah. "Because I would see every last one of these monsters struck from the earth, and you know that. I promise you; I will take you to William." The Khan spat on the ground and turned to walk away.

"Hulagu!" Elijah shouted. The Khan turned to meet his exacting gaze. "Bring me your most trusted man, one of your generals. Bring me your second in command." Elijah was still drumming the hilt of his sword.

"What do you want with him?" The Khan's brows tightened together.

"Just bring him to me." Elijah kept his face cold and expressionless.

The Khan sent one of his men to find the general; they were both back at his side in a matter of minutes.

"This is him? This is the man, your second in command?" Elijah stepped closer and firmly clasped the hilt of his blade.

"Yes, I am General... ." Elijah drew his blade and swung it with such speed it was nearly back in its sheath before anyone noticed. The man who had been speaking stood silently for a moment with his eyes wide. Seconds later his head fell from atop his body.

"Your promises mean nothing to me anymore. Now I am second in command. Do not lie to me again." Elijah reached down to pick up his bow and laced an arrow into its string. Turning towards the tree, he loosed the arrow and watched it as it glanced to the side.

"This is outrageous!" Another man standing beside the Khan shouted. The Khan quickly quieted him and stepped to within inches of Elijah's ear.

"You do something like that again, and you better hope you can withstand the force of my entire army," he whispered. "You are not ready to face William right now; he would surely defeat you. You have no control, no faith. I am trying to help you, to teach you, and you disgrace me in front of my men. This will not be forgotten." The Khan lowered his eyes and drew a deep breath to calm his nerves before looking back up at Elijah.

"For now, I cannot accept a commander in my army who has not mastered the bow. Listen and take instruction well so when that day comes, when we finally make it home, you might have a chance." He grabbed the bow from Elijah's hand and quickly fitted an arrow against the string.

"Shooting a bow is all about faith; it starts with faith in yourself and extends to a faith in, and unity with, everything. That faith brings peace; it brings perfection. Perfection is spontaneous right action, with no thought. Don't think about your

target; think about yourself and learn faith in what you can control. Your grip around the bow, only as firm as is necessary; your
pull of the string, even and steady." The Khan seemed to be in a
trance as he talked.

"Aim your bow with the same assurance with which you
point your finger. You don't have to eye your target, just point
with your bow like it is an extension of yourself and trust that
your arrow will fly true." The Khan raised the bow and turned
from Elijah towards the tree, loosing the arrow before the tree
was even in full view. The arrow vibrated proudly from the dead
center of the tree's large trunk.

"Now keep practicing," the Khan snarled as he threw the
bow at Elijah's feet and strode away.

# CHAPTER 44

AS NIGHT FELL upon Alamut once again; the removal and destruction of all battlements was complete. Elijah had practiced with his bow for hours before finally taking a break. He was happy to be back at Alamut. He was anxious to see this through, and to see Hassan.

"Ayda!" Elijah shouted as he saw her exiting the Khan's tent, but she paid no attention. Elijah appeared seemingly out of nowhere and she stumbled into him.

"What do you want, Elijah?" Ayda grumbled under her breath.

"What were you doing with the Khan?" Elijah looked down at her eyes, inspecting each one, as well as her guarded expression. He could never tell what she was thinking.

"Elijah, forget what I said. You were right; you are not a good person. You are no better than the Khan." Ayda pushed passed Elijah and continued walking. "Actually, you are worse. At least he is just following orders." She turned around; her walls had fallen and a look of disgust filled her face.

"What are you talking about, Ayda?" Elijah stepped forward

and grabbed her by both arms. He could see her eyes were now wet with tears; she was obviously distraught.

"You truly are willing to do anything to get what you want. Betraying your own people by negotiating their surrender was one thing, but to stand by for this... ."

Elijah had heard enough; he needed to find out exactly what was going on. He turned and walked into the Khan's tent.

"What is going on?" He shouted before he realized the tent was empty. He demanded the Khan's whereabouts from one of the guards. The guard pointed down the hill, towards the valley at the bottom of the castle. Elijah could see a ferocious blaze and heard loud cheering.

Elijah quickly raced to the bottom of the hill, where he was shocked to see Hassan and the imam in chains. The Khan stood in the front of the crowd directing the entertainment.

The imam was on his knees with his head on a barrel; the executioner's blade dropped swiftly before Elijah could reach the Khan. His head rolled to the Khan's feet; he lifted it up and roared. The rest of the men cheered and roared back, even louder. Two men then lifted Hassan's limp body and another tied his head to the same barrel. Elijah had been betrayed again. If the Khan was trying to make a point, it would be made at great cost.

Elijah redirected himself and rushed to Hassan's side just as the blade was about to fall. Elijah came from behind and clasped the executioner's blade as he held it above his head. Then he yanked it down and rammed it straight through the executioner's back. A number of vampire soldiers pulled their swords and came at Elijah as he shoved the dying man to the ground with his blade still inside him.

Elijah was unarmed. He had left his weapons on the hill where he had been practicing. The first soldier thrust his sword towards Elijah's chest; Elijah quickly turned to the side, avoiding his blow. He held the man's outstretched arm and grasped his sword by the blade. Jerking it from the vampire's grip, he spun around and thrust it into his stomach.

Another vampire swung his blade; Elijah leaned back and the sword swept over, barely missing his face and decapitating the first vampire while Elijah removed the blade impaling him. Elijah then loosened his grip on the blade until it fell just enough for him to grasp the handle firmly. He quickly swung the sword with his right hand until the blade fell across the neck of the second vampire, who was overextended and at the end of his swing.

With two bodies at his feet and warm blood upon his cheeks Elijah was once again caught up in a whirlwind of rage as he reached down and grabbed the other dead man's sword. Elijah was nearly encircled by the Khan's men; he twirled both swords, reveling at the prospect of spilling their blood. As the men pressed forward the Khan's voice rang out.

"Stop!" The Khan shoved through the ranks of his men and appeared in front of Elijah. "You took my best man today. This was in recompense, to show you that you are not in command here."

Elijah's pulse was racing, his breathing fast, his mind teeming with thirst for bloodshed. He quickly raised both swords and tightened them around the Khan's neck like scissors. The masked man's hands moved instantly to his sword before the Khan raised his hand to stop him.

"I have an eternity to find William, so I do not need you as much as you might think. Betray me again, and your entire army won't be able to protect you from my wrath; I promise you that." He closed his eyes and took a deep breath before throwing the swords to the ground and kneeling to care for Hassan. He broke the chains binding his hands and lifted him to his feet. "What have you done?" Elijah shouted as he noticed the bite marks covering Hassan's body.

"I must apologize; my vampires grew hungry in the absence

of battle." The Khan frowned condescendingly as his eyes moved from one bite mark to the next. He turned towards the lot of vampires, who roared with laughter. The masked man stood silently at the Khan's side, gazing at Elijah through the narrow slits in his mask.

"He will live, and the blood of your own men will see it so." With blinding speed, Elijah jerked a man from the gathering crowd and ripped out his throat. He laid Hassan on the ground and held the man's wound over his face, allowing the blood to flow into his mouth. In only moments, Hassan's wounds began to heal, and he regained strength. He grasped the lifeless body as he sat up and pressed it to his mouth, continuing to feed.

A minute later, just as it started to rain, Hassan dropped the body to the ground and rose to his feet, a new vigor and strength corrupting his mortal flesh.

As the Khan's men stood frozen. Elijah rose to stand beside Hassan. He turned his attention to the man wearing the mask.

"Your men seek blood!" Elijah growled. "Well, so do I." He pushed Hassan to the side and picked up a sword lying at his feet. "I would see blood flow, enough to fill the heavens." Elijah watched as blue flames burned through the slits in Roman's mask. "A coward who hides behind a mask, let yours be the first." Elijah spoke as he stared into the blue eyes behind the mask. Roman immediately pulled his sword and came at Elijah.

The masked man thrust his sword towards Elijah's chest. He was faster than Elijah had anticipated, much faster than the other vampires. Elijah tried to maneuver away, but the sword lodged just beneath his shoulder. Elijah spun behind him and leapt into the air as the vampire withdrew his blade. Elijah fell, plunging the blade toward the big man's neck, but he ducked and rolled backwards, avoiding Elijah's blow. Elijah quickly turned and deflected another thrust from Roman.

Elijah's rage was now fiercely focused; he didn't notice the two vampires approaching behind him. Stepping towards Roman, he heard the footsteps behind him just in time to duck beneath their swinging swords. As he turned to quickly dispatch the two men behind him, a fierce pain swelled in his back. Elijah looked down to see Roman's sword jettison through his chest. This time, Elijah spun quickly enough to jerk the blade from Roman's hand. As he spun, he slammed the hilt of his sword against the back of the masked man's head. As the man stumbled forward, Elijah lifted his knee and thrust his leg forward, kicking the big man to the ground.

Roman grabbed a dead vampire's sword, quickly pushed himself up, and turned towards Elijah. He watched as Elijah reached around and pulled the sword from his back. Now holding sword in each hand, Elijah twirled them both as he lifted his head and roared like thunder from the heavens.

The two warriors stood facing each other, both eager and willing for more. The Khan jumped between them before either one moved. "Stop! Please, just stop." The Khan turned towards Elijah. "I am sorry about your friend; I overreacted. Please, just allow me to get you to William." Elijah looked into his eyes and remained silent for a moment before throwing down his swords once more and turning from the Khan.

"Come with me." Elijah pulled at Hassan's shoulder, and the two pushed through the crowd, back towards Elijah's tent. There they sat on the dirt next to the burning embers of an unattended fire. "I can't believe the nerve of that fucking Mongol." Elijah fiercely stroked the bridge of his nose.

"He is a Khan, and a Mongol. What did you imagine would happen when you loosed them upon us? Besides, I would be more worried about the man in the mask." Hassan rested his elbows on his knees.

"Him? He is nothing. Although, I keep wondering who he is, why they keep trying to hide him from me. I have only seen eyes like his once before, but he is not my father, he couldn't be. I think he may be the one who was with my father that night; do not worry yourself my friend, I will kill him soon enough." Elijah looked at Hassan and smiled.

"Don't worry about him?" Hassan nearly shouted. "The man nearly bested you today, Elijah. He is something fierce." Hassan raised his head from his knees and looked at Elijah. "Do you still think all of this was worth it?

"I know you are angry with me Hassan, but I only did what I had to do in order to find my father." Elijah rose to his feet and paced near the dying embers.

"And you think this crazy bastard is really going to take you to your father, or even knows who he is?" Hassan looked back at the fire.

"They know his name, Hassan. There is no other explanation. After we take Baghdad, Hulagu will take me to my father." Elijah pulled a half-burned stick from the fire and twirled it in his hand before sitting back down. "Or he will pay the price."

"Your father?" Elijah heard a condemning voice behind him and turned to see Ayda holding a small pile of firewood. "William is your father!" Elijah could see shock and confusion in her voice as she stumbled and nearly dropped the fire wood. Elijah quickly grabbed her and held her on her feet until she was steady again. "So what you told me about Solomon not being your brother, that was a lie?" She narrowed her eyes and frowned. Elijah wasn't sure if she was mad or empathetic.

"Ayda, what are you doing here?" He took the firewood from her.

"I came to apologize for earlier. I didn't realize that you didn't know. Anyway, I'm sorry." She turned to leave.

"Wait!" Elijah shouted. "Hassan, this is Ayda, the one who saved your life. She informed me, accused me rather, of your impending execution." Elijah opened his hand towards Ayda, as if presenting her to Hassan. Hassan stood up and knocked dirt from his knees and elbows.

"Thank you for your kindness." He bowed graciously and then sat back down.

"You're welcome. I am glad to see you are still of this world," Ayda said, smiling politely. She lingered for a moment more and then began to walk away.

"Wait, please." Elijah rushed over to her as she stopped and turned back to him. "I'm sorry for lying to you. It is hard to..." Elijah paused as he looked up into the sky and closed his eyes.

"It's okay," Ayda's voice was a gentle whisper. Elijah opened his eyes, disappointed to see her walking away once again. He watched as she faded into the blackness surrounding them before he walked back to the fire and sat next to Hassan.

"Elijah, I'm sorry, but I refuse to drink anyone's blood. You have saved my life, only to let me become something I despise. I will not kill the innocent to see a monster live, even if that monster is me." Hassan lay on his back and looked up at the stars. Elijah joined him and pondered his words.

"Those men are not innocent, Hassan." Elijah spoke as he placed his hands behind his head.

"They are human; that is enough," Hassan said flatly.

Elijah raised his head to look at Hassan. *Could he be serious?* Hassan's eyes were closed. He seemed to be at peace. Elijah knew then Hassan meant what he had said.

Elijah lay back down and closed his eyes. He thought about Sara, how he had given her life, and how he had sworn no one else would ever drink his blood. He lay quietly for a few moments, contemplating the fate he had laid upon Hassan.

"You won't have to." Elijah sat up and turned to Hassan. "You will drink my blood. I will cut my flesh every day, and you will live." He laid back down and looked up at the stars once more. No more words passed between them that night.

# CHAPTER 45

AS DAWN BROKE they were only a few hours into their march on Baghdad. Elijah and Hassan were on horseback near the rear of the army when the Khan called for a halt. Elijah wondered why they had stopped.

Elijah and Hassan rested near the Khan's tent. After the previous day's betrayal, Elijah wanted to keep Hulagu Khan close enough to guarantee his *kopis* easy access to the Khan's neck.

Elijah called for one of the guards to bring him an empty cup. Upon receiving the cup, Elijah retrieved his dagger and sliced open his arm from wrist to elbow. Holding the wound open so it wouldn't heal, he filled the cup and handed it to Hassan.

"I can't drink that." Hassan pushed it away.

"You must." Elijah insisted.

"My God would not allow it." Hassan looked up, as if toward his God. This was an aspect of Hassan Elijah hadn't missed.

"Would your God not have you live?" Elijah pressed the cup to Hassan's chest and Hassan grasped it. "You can always die tomorrow if you choose," Elijah added. Hassan looked at him and shook his head before taking a sip and then gulping the rest down.

"Gratitude." Hassan laid the cup on the ground and examined Elijah's new bow. "You are an archer now?"

"I am just trying to find the peace, perfection, unity, and potential the Khan echoes from your fucking lips." Elijah smiled as he watched Hassan study his bow and then place it back on the ground.

"Elijah." One of the Khan's guards walked over. "The Khan would speak with you."

"About what?" Elijah asked as he rose to his feet.

"The Khan, in his wisdom, does not tell me these things." The man insisted, before ushering Elijah and Hassan to the Khan's tent.

"I see you have brought your friend," the Khan commented as they entered.

"He is my right hand, as I am now yours, my Khan. I go nowhere without him." Elijah smiled as he opened his hands and bowed. "What is it you would have of me?"

"First of all, one of my guards saw you mutilating yourself to feed your right hand. The vampires drain and store the blood of the dead, so there is no need for that. Second, I have found a place for you among my men." The Khan rubbed his tired eyes.

"I already have a place, my Khan; I am your second in command." Elijah bowed once again.

"Desist with this game. You have made your point; the men already fear you as much as they do me, if not more. I would prefer to have you in a position where you would be of real use." The Khan stood, placed his hands on the table in front of him, and leaned against it, calling Elijah's attention to the full set of Mongolian armor lying on the table, the kind worn only by their leaders. It was a lamellar cuirass made of hundreds of lacquered rectangular leather pieces, all pierced and laced together.

The lamellae were nearly black, the lacing white; it was of fine craftsmanship.

"Where would you have me?" Elijah finally asked after a long pause.

"I need someone strong, someone the vampires would fear and respect, to lead their company. They only fear me because of the hand that guides me, the one pulling the strings. If it weren't for their fear of William, they would have probably eaten me by now." He sighed as he wiped his forehead with a rag and then sat back down, looking up at Elijah.

"Are you sure you wish this? I might kill them all myself." Elijah smiled; the Khan just stared at him, the spark of life somehow dim in his eyes. "Hassan must be my second in command," he demanded.

The Khan dropped his head for a moment and then looked back up at Elijah. "Fine," he spat.

"Why not have him lead them ?" Elijah gestured to the silent and burly vampire standing at the Khan's side. Elijah had spent his nights wondering what was behind that wooden mask, what features surrounded those bright blue eyes.

"He is my personal bodyguard; I require his attendance. Now go; take your place behind your men. They have already been informed of my decision, and we have set up another tent for you there. Just bring your personal items." Hulagu Khan poured a cup of wine as he gestured for them to leave.

"This is why you stopped the march?" Elijah asked.

"Yes, it is," the Khan replied. "Now go." He commanded with a flick of his wrist.

"Wait." He spoke once more, just as the two were about to exit his tent. Elijah turned back to face him. "You are a commander in my army now. You must look the part." He opened his hands towards the armor lying on the table. Elijah collected the greaves, cuirass and a pair of leather schynbalds, armor to protect the shins, from the table.

"I don't need the rest of that, but I will be delighted to have one of those attractive masks," he said.

"Sorry, the supply was extremely limited." The Khan reached forward and pushed the other pieces of armor towards Elijah, who quickly grabbed his hand. The Khan tried to jerk back, but Elijah held his hand firmly in place. The masked man stepped forward and Hassan pulled his sword. The Khan quickly motioned for his masked guardian to step back.

"What do you want, Elijah?" The Khan groaned uncomfortably as Elijah squeezed his hand tighter.

"Why does he wear that mask?" Elijah turned his head and shouted at the masked man. "Why do you wear that damn mask? What is my father trying to hide from me?"

"Your father?" The Khan's eyes grew wide. "Now, that is an interesting development." He said.

"Were you with my father when he slaughtered my family?" Elijah shouted as he squeezed even harder, threatening to crush the Khan's hand.

"I do not know Elijah and I cannot speak for him; but I do know he would let you kill me before he would remove it. Even I have never seen his face." Elijah stared back and forth between the two men.

"Perhaps we should test that theory." With his free hand Elijah pulled the ancient *kopis* from it's leather holster—that Elijah had fashioned to wear on his back—and pressed it to the Khan's neck. Roman lurched forward threateningly, but paused when the *kopis* drew blood from the Khan's neck. "Take it off!" Elijah shouted. Roman's eyes burned bright beneath the mask as he stared at Elijah.

"I told you he will not!" the Khan groaned with pain. Elijah stared fiercely at the vampire's glowing eyes for a moment more before letting go of the Khan's hand and throwing his armor to Hassan.

"Let's go," he snapped. "I will see that mask ripped from your face one day soon, and then I will know." Before exiting the Khan's tent, he stepped to within inches of the big man and stared up at the now-darkened slits in his mask. "And your fate will be sealed."

## CHAPTER 46

"I DON'T TRUST HIM." Hassan burst out as they entered Elijah's tent.

"And you think I do? After all he has done?" Elijah threw up his hands in frustration. "But there is nothing we can do about it right now." The two gathered up their weapons and other belongings and headed to the front of the encampment to take their place among the immortals.

There was a new, large tent set up at the rear of the vampire camp; guards were in position blocking the front entrance, but quickly parted so Elijah and Hassan could enter. Elijah gave little thought to the hundreds of menacing glances they had received on their way in. Everything in the new tent was identical to his old one, down to the bowl of fruit and wine on the table.

"What do you think?" Elijah tossed the cuirass to Hassan for inspection.

"Well, it's fancy, but you are becoming a fancy man." Hassan smiled and tossed it back.

"A means to an end, my friend, a means to an end." Elijah slid into the cuirass and laced it. He twisted his body to test the armor's flexibility, then quickly drew a sword and sheathed it once again. "It's really not that bad. It's not silk, but it's not that bad."

"I like it." Ayda appeared at the entrance of the tent.

"How did you get in here?" Elijah narrowed his eyes as he continued to twist in an effort to break in his new armor.

"Well, you do own me," Ayda said as she walked further into the tent.

"What?" Hassan's head snapped towards Elijah.

"Relax, Hassan. It's a long story, and it isn't nearly as bad as it sounds." Elijah smiled and walked outside. He surveyed the landscape, the men, if one could call them that, and approached a group of twelve vampires sitting together and filling their cups from a medium sized barrel of blood.

"Where is the blood stored?" Elijah addressed the group as a whole.

*"Foder unha cabra!"* A vampire sitting with his back towards Elijah piped up, and the rest of the group roared with laughter. Elijah pretended he didn't understand the comment, but since he grew up on the Iberian Peninsula, Elijah could understand Galician very well.

"He tells you to go fuck a goat." Another vampire sitting across looked up towards Elijah as he explained. Elijah took a couple steps closer to the man who first spoke and quickly snapped his neck. A few of the other men stood up, but the other vampire who had spoken quickly pressed for them to sit.

"Your friend here will heal from this injury, as you know." Elijah knelt beside the unconscious vampire lying at his feet and pried his mouth open. "But when he does, he won't have a tongue to speak with." Elijah forced his hand into the man's mouth and, grabbing his tongue, pulled back and ripped it from his throat just as the man's eyes were opening. Blood spewed from his mouth like a fountain. He was conscious now as he screamed and thrashed with pain, but he still couldn't move because his neck hadn't yet healed.

"I am your leader!" Elijah shouted, as he held the vampire's tongue high above his head. "You will show me respect and do as I command. When you address me, you will speak in either the Mongolian or the Persian tongue. If you disobey me, I will take you apart one piece at a time." Elijah slung the man's tongue down on top of his chest and lifted an unopened barrel of blood from the ground before returning to his tent.

"Here." Elijah dropped the barrel at Hassan's feet before sitting beside him at the table.

"Elijah, what are you doing?" Hassan lifted the barrel and sat it next to him. His face was stark.

"What do you mean?" Elijah jerked off the cuirass and wiped his hands on a rag lying next to his things.

"I have known for a long time you aren't the same man I met on the road all those years ago, Elijah, but you are slipping into a dark abyss, one from which I fear you will never return."

Elijah looked down at the blood still staining his body and then at Hassan, who was sitting with his head clasped in his hands. Through a split in his fingers Elijah could see the veins, swollen and throbbing, around his eyes.

"I didn't fall; I was pushed," he retorted.

Hassan raised his head and turned to him, revealing the hellish face of the dark nature Elijah had forced upon him.

"And what about me, Elijah; did I fall or was I pushed?" he asked. Elijah shifted his eyes and looked away. "Look at me!" Hassan shouted. "You sold my soul for just a whisper of the possibility of satisfying your passion."

"What are men, if not ruled by the passions that drive us?" Elijah spoke quietly as he turned to look again at Hassan. Sharp pangs of guilt ran throughout his body and softened his eyes as he dropped his head, staring at the rug.

"Men do not have to be ruled by their passions. They may not win every battle, but they can choose to fight. That is a lesson I have tried for too long to instill in you." Hassan reached for the barrel of blood lying next to him and pulled it to his chest. After staring at it for several minutes he ripped opened the top and consumed all it held. Wiping the blood from his lips, he looked up at Elijah, who looked back. Hassan's eyes were wet and shone like glass.

"Only the damned are ruled by their passions. Men always have a choice," he whispered. He stood up and dropped the barrel on his way to exit the tent.

"And what of a man who rules his passions?" Elijah asked. He looked at the ground and spoke with his back towards Hassan.

"Well, those aren't men at all, are they? They are gods," Hassan replied. He paused for a moment before looking back at Elijah.

"Do we... you and I... not now stand as gods among men?" Elijah asked, still unwilling to face him.

"No, we are something much different; we are both slaves. We may have different masters, but we are both slaves, Elijah. The main difference between us now is that you don't have to be. You choose your shackles." Hassan paused for another moment and then left the tent.

Elijah reflected for a few moments on Hassan's words. He thought of the life he had now forced upon him, how he had betrayed the only real friend he had made since becoming the thing he now was. He was a slave to his lust for vengeance; Hassan was correct, and that made him hate his father even more.

Still standing motionless since Hassan had left the tent, he let the fury build within him. He looked down and saw the barrel Hassan had dropped to the ground, saw a drop of blood still glistening along its rim. The sight overwhelmed him, and he screamed out, his guilt and frustration bursting forth. He kicked the barrel, and it scattered in splinters all around the tent.

Looking up, he saw Ayda still standing in the corner. He didn't know why he did what he did next—perhaps he needed a distraction from his fury and guilt, or perhaps he just gave in to the passion that had sparked the moment he first saw her.

He walked towards her with purpose. When he reached her, he grabbed her by the waist and lifted her onto a table sitting in the corner of his tent. Leaning forward, he began to kiss her, first her lips and then her neck and chest.

"Elijah, stop, I can't do this." Ayda whispered as her fingernails sank into his back like claws. Elijah continued; he picked her up again and threw her onto the bed. "Elijah," she whispered.

"Shhhh," he interrupted, on top of her before she hit the bed. He lifted her dress and pushed her farther up on the bed. Her body was soft and smooth; he kissed her stomach and then moved lower as he removed his clothes.

"Please Elijah, stop." As she spoke, Elijah maneuvered between her legs; he moved up, kissing her gently as he went. He kissed around her collarbone and her neck. Ayda's breathing grew harder until he finally kissed her lips and entered into her. She moaned softly for a moment and then arched her back as she wailed out.

Elijah looked into her eyes and saw them begin to glow a bright red. Seconds later, razor sharp claws raked against his back. As she pulled him closer, her hands slid to his side, shredding the flesh around his ribs. He healed instantly. Ayda held his side for a moment before falling back and sinking into the soft bed beneath her.

Warmth built suddenly behind Elijah's eyes. It sizzled and burned as it trickled into the sockets and filled them to nearly bursting.

"What is happening?" Elijah asked, dumbfounded. He pushed to his feet and covered his eyes with his hands. The heat spread to his fingers and palms. "Ohhh!" he sighed, as he fell to his knees.

Then a deep, aching pain seared his bones and teeth for a moment, as if they were compacting, or solidifying. The muscles throughout his body began to burn like his eyes. He noticed a slight change in his hands; they looked larger, as if the muscle and bone had expanded. As he rose to his feet, he examined his body. Everything had changed; he was more ridged and defined. He looked at Ayda, to find her eyes had stopped glowing, but were wide with shock.

"I told you to stop!" Ayda screamed before she raced out of the tent.

"Wait!" Elijah shouted, but she was gone. He stumbled forward to go after her, but the ache in his bones grew so fierce he staggered to his knees before he could even reach the exit. His bones were about to explode. His eyes and muscles smoldered like they were on fire. The pain continued to grow until he could no longer see, and kept intensifying until, blessedly, he tumbled into unconsciousness.

Elijah awoke naked on the floor of the tent the next morning. Remembering what had happened, he jumped to his feet and examined his body. Everything was back to normal; there was no more pain. He immediately went out and tried to find Ayda, instructing the guards standing outside to find her tent, but they returned to report it was empty.

He continued looking for her over the next couple of weeks, but she was nowhere to be found. No one, not even the Khan, had seen her.

# CHAPTER 47

"WHY DO YOU use those swords?" Hassan asked as he thrust his towards Elijah's chest. Elijah twisted his torso to the right and stepped forward barely in time to escape a serious blow. Elijah grabbed Hassan's outstretched forearm as Hassan swung the sword in his other hand at Elijah's calf.

Elijah lifted his knee to avoid the blow. He leapt into the air and forced his fist, clenched tightly around the hilt of his sword, downwards as he fell, to strike Hassan in the face. Hassan evaded his punch, and Elijah's arm shot over Hassan's shoulder. Elijah dropped the sword in that hand and grabbed Hassan's shirt. Pulling him upward and over his shoulder, Elijah flipped him over his back. Hassan landed on his feet and smiled as he kicked Elijah in the back. Elijah grabbed the sword he had dropped and rolled over his shoulder onto his feet, quickly turning to face Hassan.

"Why do you now use two swords? Where is your dagger?" Elijah asked as Hassan stepped forward and sliced at Elijah's left knee with the sword in his right hand. Elijah lifted his leg over the sword and stepped backwards. Hassan sliced with his other hand at Elijah's right leg and Elijah escaped in the same way, once again stepping backwards.

Hassan's momentum was building as he moved forward, and he once again thrust his blade at Elijah's chest. This time Elijah rolled around his extended arm and elbowed Hassan in the back of the head, causing him to stumble forward and fall to the ground.

As Hassan rolled forward, he pulled his dagger from the small of his back and flung it at Elijah. Elijah dodged to the left, but hissed in pain when the blade grazed the side of his face and cut through his ear before planting itself in the tree just behind his head. Elijah grinned and laughed as Hassan grabbed his sword and pushed himself from the ground.

"I see you didn't give the dagger up altogether." Elijah wiped the blood that had spilled from his already-healed wound.

"Never," Hassan growled. Noticing the change in his voice, Elijah quickly looked at his face, which was now transformed. Hassan's eyes looked bloodshot and his cheekbones seemed to swell, and Elijah could see pulsing veins begin to rise around the corners of his eyes. Hassan leapt forward, swinging the sword in his left hand at Elijah's neck. Elijah leaned back in barely enough time to keep his head. Hassan was suddenly much faster; his speed was incredible. He pulled back his sword and then thrust it at Elijah's gut. Elijah knocked the sword to his right and Hassan twisted his arm, slicing at Elijah's leg as he pulled his sword back.

When he noticed the cuts on the outer side of the calf muscle in his right leg, Elijah momentarily questioned his decision to carry single-edged blades. Hassan sliced again, this time with the sword in his left hand. Elijah managed to get his leg above the sword, but was now off balance. When Hassan stepped forward and sliced again with the sword in his right hand, Elijah couldn't step back fast enough. Hassan's sword sliced at his heel; then, pulling his sword back and up, he jerked Elijah's foot out from under him and Elijah fell to his back.

"Ha!" Hassan shouted, as he pressed the point of the sword in his right hand against Elijah's chest.

Elijah knocked the sword away and he sprang to his feet. He quickly looked down as his eye sockets filled with heat. The heat burned through his eyes and then moved throughout his muscles. His hair hung over his face, blocking it from Hassan's view. He opened his mouth wide and then slammed his teeth together to ease the aching in his bones. Then Elijah raised his head, his hair fell back from his face, and he immediately saw confusion in Hassan's expression.

Hassan lifted his swords and walked towards him. The two men stood face to face for a moment, and then Hassan stepped forward, slicing at Elijah's chest with the sword in his right hand. Hassan now seemed to be moving in slow motion as Elijah dropped his swords and rushed forward. He caught Hassan's swinging wrist with one hand and, lifting him off the ground with the other, he slammed the big man onto his back. Hassan shook his head to regain his bearings and then stared up at Elijah.

"Your eyes are glowing," he observed matter-of-factly.

"I know." Elijah smiled as he sheathed his swords and offered his hand to Hassan. He pulled the big man up, and the pair sat down on the hill, looking at the huge army below them.

"What happened?"

"I think Ayda did it," Elijah answered as he rubbed his beard.

"What did she do to you?" Hassan asked as he pulled his swords to his side.

"I don't think she actually did anything; I think she unlocked something that was already there, lying dormant. I have been so focused on finding my father I haven't allowed myself to feel anything but hate and anger." His voice began to trail off. "And guilt." He looked apologetically at Hassan, who nodded.

"I think she helped me to access an area of my soul, or my mind, that has been locked away since I was young," he mused. "I think there is more to this…" Elijah pointed at himself, "… than I knew." Elijah wanted to tell Hassan about Ayda and her eyes, but it seemed wrong to give away secrets that weren't his.

"That is quite remarkable," Hassan said as he studied Elijah's face more closely. "I am glad you have found someone else to take care of you," he smiled, "because I will not fight by your side at Baghdad." Hassan leaned back and sheathed his swords.

"What do you mean? Why not?" Elijah frowned at his big friend.

"I know what they will do to the people inside. I will not be a part of that. God would not allow it." Hassan stood up and walked to the tree behind them to retrieve the dagger he'd thrown.

"You still believe in such things after all you have seen?" Elijah's eyes widened as they followed Hassan to the tree.

"I have been marching with you for a short time now; my only hope is to assure you are not completely overwhelmed by the darkness that surrounds you and fills your heart. I thought my presence here might somehow help you to find your way back, but you are only moving deeper into that void. You isolate yourself almost completely now." Hassan pulled his dagger from the tree and turned toward Elijah.

"Find a way to overcome this Elijah, before it kills you." He held Elijah's stare for a few moments before he turned towards the forest, just east of camp. Mountains in the distance loomed above the forest, which lay on the valley floor. "Are there no good thoughts left on which to dwell, memories of a better time, better company—a woman, Ayda perhaps? Maybe she will do better than I have done to free you from your past. Women have a way of managing such things." He hung his head momentarily and then continued on past the tree line.

"Stay until we get closer; I still need your instruction!" Elijah shouted, his eyes bright.

Hassan paused and turned to face him. "You haven't needed my instruction for years; we both know that. You could take my head in an instant if you wished." He moved a few steps closer.

"It's not just that. You are all I have here, especially since Ayda won't speak to me anymore. In fact, she has completely disappeared." Elijah stood and walked closer to Hassan.

"You know, you have a special talent for keeping people at a distance." Hassan smiled. "It seems I am the only one who can put up with you." Hassan looked at Elijah, at the ground, and then back at Elijah. After almost a minute of silence, he spoke again. "I will stay just a while longer. I will see you to the end of this march, but there is something I require of you in return." Hassan placed his hand on Elijah's shoulder and looked him in the eye; his gaze was intense.

"Whatever I can do." Elijah's brow furrowed as he stared back at Hassan.

"I need you to do something for me, Elijah. It's not going to be easy, but you must promise me that, if I stay, you will do whatever I ask of you." Hassan's eyes narrowed as he tapped Elijah's chest with his finger.

"What is it?" Elijah asked.

"You'll know soon enough. Now, do you promise?" Hassan reached out his hand towards Elijah. Elijah looked at his face for a moment longer and then at his hand; he tried to imagine what Hassan could need, what could be so terrible he couldn't speak of it now.

"I promise." Elijah said, as he reached out and shook his big friend's hand. "But I must know what it is now, please." Elijah begged.

Hassan dropped his chin and stared at the ground before looking back up at Elijah. "Very well, but remember, you have given me your solemn promise." Hassan took a deep breath. "I need you to kill me once we reach Baghdad." The words burst from Hassan's lips, a blasphemy to Elijah's sensibilities. His heart sank. He wished Hassan had asked for anything else; how could he possibly kill his only friend?

"What? No, of course not. I don't even know if I could." Elijah quickly pulled his hand away and turned around.

"Elijah, please. I cannot kill myself; God does not permit it, and I cannot continue living as this *thing*, not any longer than I must. Please, I don't want to slowly starve; I don't even know if that would kill me. You owe me this much."

Elijah rubbed his chin vigorously as he marched back and forth in front of Hassan. *I should have realized*, he thought. *Of course he wants to die, what else could it have been?* Elijah knew Hassan didn't want to live forever, not even if he could be human; they were too much alike in that. So be it. He would grant Hassan the best death possible.

"I promise." He stopped and reached out his hand again. Hassan pulled him into a tight embrace.

"Thank you, Brother."

"Elijah." A guard called from the hillside.

"What is it?" Elijah shouted, as he wiped his eyes.

"The Khan has requested your presence." The guard spoke as he walked closer.

"I'll be there in just a moment." Elijah replied. He watched the guard retreat down the hillside and then turned to Hassan. "Come with me," he said. Hassan nodded and the pair descended from the hill and entered the camp. At the Khan's tent the same guard ushered them in.

When they entered, Elijah noticed a bowl of fresh fruit on a side table next to the entrance. He chose a mango and split it in half before taking a bite.

"What would you have of me, my Khan?" Still chewing the mango, Elijah bowed with a smirk on his face.

"Don't patronize me, you condescending cunt. Sit down." He motioned to a chair across from him at the table.

Elijah complied. He cocked his head to the side and handed the mango to Hassan as he took a seat at the table. "What would you have of me?"

"We have been marching for a couple weeks now, and the blood supply is low." The Khan pulled out his chair and sat, facing Elijah.

"How do you know that? I haven't heard anything." Elijah reached back and took the mango from Hassan's hand.

"That is because you never leave your fucking tent. I told you to lead these animals, and if you can't do it, our arrangement is over." The Khan looked up from the table and stared at Elijah.

"What are you talking about?" Elijah broke the Khan's stare and took another bite of the mango.

"I am talking about two of your vampires killing six of my fucking men, that's what I am talking about." Spittle flew from his mouth as he yelled and slammed his fist down on the table. "Five of my guards were killed trying to detain them after finding them eating one of the soldiers. If they hadn't caused such a disturbance, they might have killed more."

"Where are they now?" Elijah continued to eat the mango.

"They are outside, at the base of the camp. My own bodyguard had to stop them. He has them now. Will you stop chewing on that fucking mango?" the Khan exploded.

Elijah threw the mango on the ground and rose to his feet. "I will take care of it." He turned to leave.

"Wait," the Khan commanded. Elijah paused. "That is not our greatest problem. We need more blood," he repeated.

Elijah turned to face him and threw up his hands. "How do

you expect me to accomplish that? There are no armies out there for us to fight."

"No, but my scouts say there is a small town not far from here. Your men could get there and back in a day's time. I'll have ten of my men follow on horseback with the barrels." The Khan looked up at Elijah.

Elijah's eyes were wide; he glanced over at Hassan, who was shaking his head.

"You can't do this, Elijah." Hassan grabbed Elijah's arm as he was turning back to face the Khan.

"He can, and he will." The Khan rose from his chair as he spoke.

"You want me to slaughter an entire town of innocent people just to feed this rabble." Elijah stepped closer and leaned his hands on the table.

"I need you to lead a company of one hundred of your men, if you can call them that, and do what you must," the Khan pressed.

Elijah looked again to Hassan, who narrowed his eyes and gently shook his head.

"Unless, of course, you can think of another way to feed an army of vampires," the Khan chortled, sure of winning this battle of wills. "You do want to confront your father, do you not?"

Elijah turned back to the Khan and stared at him for a moment. "Then fall to fucking command." The Khan shouted.

Elijah didn't say another word; simply whirled and left the tent.

"And don't leave one drop of blood in that town, Elijah," the Khan bellowed from inside the tent.

"Elijah." Hassan followed him through the camp, but Elijah kept walking. "Elijah!" Hassan shouted and Elijah finally stopped. He turned and walked towards Hassan until the two were face to face, only inches separating them. "Don't do this, Elijah." Hassan's voice was low but insistent.

"What would you have me do? This is the only way to find my father," he yelled.

"Is it worth it, to kill hundreds of innocent people… to lose your soul?" Hassan asked.

Elijah's jaws clenched; he looked at the ground and then turned and began to walk away.

"What could he have done to you, or taken from you, that could be worse than what you are about to do?" Hassan asked.

Elijah kept walking.

"You won't come back from this, Elijah; you will be lost to the darkness forever," he shouted.

Still, Elijah kept walking.

"In doing this, you become your father, perhaps even worse." Hassan was now shouting at the top of his lungs, and Elijah finally paused, but for only a moment. Seconds later he was gone from Hassan's sight.

Elijah walked to the base of the camp, where he could see the Khan's bodyguard and the two vampires he was holding prisoner. Elijah stopped in front of the big man wearing the mask. His blue eyes were so bright they seemed to almost leap from the mask. Perhaps Roman wasn't the man who had helped butcher Elijah's family. Perhaps he was just another vampire lord, one unknown to Elijah, but he knew he didn't like big bastard.

Elijah stared into those flaming blue eyes for a full minute. Those eyes stared back, but he didn't say a word. Seeing those glowing blue eyes triggered memories of the last night he had seen Ayda, and the myriad of unanswered questions forever lingering in the back of his mind, questions about that terrible night so long ago, and about what it had made him become. His eyes could now glow, but he knew he was no vampire lord. He ached to find Ayda and question her; if he was like her, then perhaps she knew something that would help him understand.

Elijah turned from the masked vampire lord to the two vampires standing beside him. Anger consumed him. They were to blame for what he would have to do. His wrath fell upon them with blinding speed as he plunged his hands through their chests. In seconds they fell to their knees, absent their hearts. Elijah glanced back at the mask and the eyes. He roared with fury as he crushed the two hearts he was holding and threw them, blood and veins trailing and spattering at the big man's feet. He stood there for only a moment more before making his way back to his tent.

Elijah entered his tent expecting to find Hassan, expecting, hoping his friend would try once more to talk him out of what he was about to do. But he wasn't there.

Elijah sat for a moment and pondered Hassan's words. For the first time in a great while he thought about Sara. He remembered how many times he had been the great and heroic prince, fighting against all of the wicked and evil forces their childish imaginations could conjure.

He thought about how many times he had saved her from fantasy nightmares, and how he had failed to save her when it really mattered. She had called him her prince, her protector; she saw goodness in him, he had seen it in her eyes. She was wrong; his goodness was nothing more than the reflection he saw in the eyes of those who loved him.

He realized Hassan was wrong. Doing this would not condemn him to the darkness. He was the darkness. There were no eyes left to which he could go; no eyes that could show him any remnant of goodness that might be hidden deep inside. Those remnants had all been ripped from this world long ago. He saw his reflection now, even in Hassan's eyes, and he was worse than any horror he had pretended to fight in his youth.

# CHAPTER 48

ELIJAH AND HIS men could now see the town in the distance. Elijah gathered the vampire crew and instructed them to encircle the town, to insure no one escaped. He reached the town first; there was no wall and only a small number of sentries.

He and his men fell upon them like the horde of monsters they were. They cut down everyone guarding the town in seconds. Moments later he heard a scream from the other side of the town, and soon the place was in chaos. Screams of terror and despair filled the town like a demon wind.

Elijah entered one of the homes and was met by a sword shoved clumsily into his chest. The man left it there and walked backwards to stand protectively in front of his wife. Elijah looked down and stared at the sword still sticking out of his chest. Wrapping his hand around the blade, Elijah pulled the sword out. He looked up at the couple, who stared at him, their eyes wide with horror. He threw the blade to the ground and started towards them.

"What are you?" The man shrieked up at him from the floor where he had retreated in fear, holding his woman. Elijah didn't say anything. "Please, take whatever you want, just leave us unharmed." The man pleaded, as Elijah grabbed the woman by the arm and hauled her up off the floor. Taking the dagger from beneath his arm, he pressed it to her throat.

"Is there anyone else here?" Elijah asked.

"No it is just us, I swear. Please don't hurt her." The man begged. Elijah looked around and saw a table set for four.

"Are you sure?" Elijah slid the blade of his dagger against her throat, making a small cut.

"Please." The man's voice shook with fear. Elijah looked into his eyes and saw his own reflection; he saw his father holding Malaki and threatening death. He understood now. Hassan had been right, after all; this would now be what defined him.

"Stop, stop, I'll tell you, just don't hurt her !" The man continued to beg.

"No, John, no!" the woman screamed in spite of the knife at her throat.

"We have two small children in the cellar." He moved a rug with his hand, revealing a hatch. "Now, please, just take what you came for and go." Elijah continued to stare at him as he put the dagger back under his arm. "Thank you, thank you so much." The man sighed with relief. Elijah stared at him for another moment and then snapped the woman's neck.

"No! What are you doing? I don't understand. What do you want?" the man cried out. Tears were streaming down his face.

"I came here for you." Elijah drew his sword and plunged it through the man's heart. Sheathing it, he pulled up the hatch and saw two young girls staring up at him. Elijah reached down and pulled one girl up, snapped her neck, and dropped her on the floor.

Then he reached for the other one. As he grabbed the second girl child, she looked into his eyes. She placed her hand on his and gently pushed it away. Elijah loosened his grip and the girl walked steadily up the stairs. He saw no fear in her eyes as she came to stand directly in front of him.

She was strong; she made no sound nor any attempt to flee while Elijah reached out and placed his hands on each side of her tiny little head. For a moment she reminded him of Sara and his hands dropped to her shoulders. He fell to his knees and cradled her small face. She was now looking slightly down at him.

As a tear trickled from his eye, she reached out and gently wiped it away.

"Here." She reached out a hand clutched with a piece of braided leather. "I was making this for my father." Elijah accepted the token and stared at it for a moment before stuffing it in his pocket. "Thank you." He stared at her for a few moments more and then dropped his chin to stare at the floor.

When he looked back up at her, he once again saw his father's reflection in her eyes. He was overcome, perhaps in shock over what he had done. No, he had to find his father, and this was the only way. Still, he had never truly considered himself a monster until this moment.

"I'm sorry," he said, as he looked around the room at the bodies. He took a deep breath and quickly snapped the girl's neck, then gently laid her body on the floor next to her sister.

As he left her home, he looked back at the girl's body one last time. He clutched pity and caressed his guilt one last time and then let them go.

He was left with nothing but an unholy rage that engulfed and consumed him. His bones ached momentarily as fire seemed to erupt throughout his body. Out of the corner of his eye, he saw a vampire who was just beginning to string up a body. Rushing over, he grabbed the vampire from the back and spun him around. The vampire swung his extended claws at his face but Elijah caught his arm and held it.

"Oh, it's you. My apologies, my lord." The vampire's voice

rattled. His eyes were wide with fear as he gazed upon Elijah's face.

"I need you to do something for me. Go back to camp and inform the Khan we are going to need twice as many barrels." Elijah tempered the anger in his voice, but still the vampire stood for a moment and stared back at Elijah in confusion.

"Go!" he shouted, and the vampire snapped into action and ran back towards camp. Elijah watched until the vampire was out of sight and then slowly turned back towards the town. The screams had died down. The streets before him had only moments ago been filled with screaming men, women, and children. Now there were only monsters and bodies piled one upon the other.

Elijah saw a vampire draining blood from the hanging body of the little girl he had just killed. He could no longer hold in the madness erupting from within him. He could feel the fire in his eyes as he reached down and washed his hands in the dry dirt and rock beneath his feet. Unsheathing both of his swords, he stalked towards the group of four vampires who were hanging headless bodies by their boots, or feet, or however they could, on tacks and hooks they had driven into the brick wall of a small mosque. Blood raced through his veins as fiercely as the darkness walling his soul as he approached from behind the short and muscular vampire who had taken the girl's head. The vampire turned around as Elijah approached. Without a word, Elijah used his swords like scissors to slice through his neck.

As the vampire's thick frame fell, absent a head, the other three paused for a moment, stunned. In the pairs of eyes staring back at him in fear and bewilderment he saw what he had become, his true form, a monster among monsters. He had completely given into his anger and guilt, and it swallowed him whole.

The vampire to his left was the first to make a move. He

swung his sword, and Elijah spun beneath his arm and swung the blade in his left hand outwards. A rush of relief eased his frustrations when blood sprayed all around him and the vampire's head rolled off of his back.

The other two immediately came at Elijah, one from the right and one from the front. The vampire to his right looked burly and strong, his muscles knotted as he swung his blade at Elijah's neck. At the same time, the one in front of him scythed her blade straight down. Leaning back, Elijah maneuvered just under the swinging blade, allowing it to pass him and block the blade slicing down at his head.

Elijah kicked the vampire in front of him, slamming her nearly through the brick wall directly behind her. The burly one stepped forward and swung his sword once more. Elijah took to the wall. Pushing himself up and out, he quickly spun in the air and fell on the vampire now at the end of his swing, plunging swords through both sides of his neck. Elijah then yanked his swords from the vampire's neck and forced him to stumble backwards. He swung his sword once more and took the vampire's head before he turned back to the one against the wall and sank a sword deep into her forehead before taking her head.

He looked further down the street and noticed a large group of vampires swarming toward him. They flooded the street and the tops of the buildings around it. Elijah charged them. Two vampires were out in front of the rest, and he slid feet-first beneath their blades and removed a leg from each of them. Keeping up his momentum, he threw himself to his feet and quickly leapt forward, tackling a vampire and plunging one sword through his chest and another through his head.

He rolled over his shoulder, onto his feet, and continued forward, toward the thickening horde of vampires. With each swing of his sword he was free, all the madness inside him spilling out through his blade into his victims, emptying him and freeing him from its terrible weight. But only for a moment; it left him hollow and void, an empty vessel into which the darkness would pour itself again and again.

Screams rose from the city once more while Elijah continued to rain down his terror onto the vampires who hadn't yet fled. Then the cries rang out all over, all at once, as if the city itself was screaming, but as Elijah pulled his swords from the vampire beneath him he could see no one else left alive, no one left who could bellow forth such an awesome and terrible cry. As drops of blood fell into his open mouth and he was forced to swallow, he realized he alone was left screaming in the wake of his own madness.

Elijah fell from his knees atop the vampire and flopped to his back on the dirt. Releasing both of his swords, he bathed in the void, the freedom which came upon him only through slaughter and death. Closing his eyes, he could once again see Sara, Malaki, and his mother, alive and beautiful. In the emptiness, his mind was his to control. He didn't see his mother's dead eyes or have to watch his father break Malaki's neck. Through death he could remember the good.

*

"Elijah, I thought you would be here." Sara stepped out from the thicket of trees into a small opening where the waning moon shone through the treetops and lit the forest floor.

Elijah was sitting on the ground, leaning against the large tree that had toppled the year before.

"I waited for you; why didn't you come ?" She spoke softly as she sat beside him.

Elijah was quiet for a moment. "I don't know what to do, Sara." He shuddered as he looked up at her with tears in his eyes. Sara tugged at his tunic, pulling him to her, and he fell over easily, his head onto her knee.

"Shhhh." She gently wiped the tears from his eyes. "Everything will be all right, Elijah," she said as she stroked the hair above his ear.

"Rest easy my love," she whispered, "while I sing you a song. Let it carry your worries away." As she began to sing, Elijah rolled to his back and gazed up at her face. In her he saw beauty and love; he knew grace, as if Venus herself had touched him. In her eyes was a strength and calm that somehow quieted the storm in his mind and stilled the raging tide of hopelessness that had nearly shattered his soul.

Until now, this memory had been completely lost to him. He had not remembered seeing Sara as a human after Solomon had so prophetically pulled her away from him and led her away from their special place in the forest, the one near the toppled tree.

Elijah closed his eyes as peace and warmth filled his soul.

# Sara
# 1186—1190

*"Do you want to kiss me?"*

# CHAPTER 49

ELIJAH AND SARA *had been the best of friends for as long as he could remember. Their mothers had both been servants of Lord Jeffrey and would often bring the children along to Rothber Castle so they could keep an eye on them while they cooked and cleaned. He and Sara had always been overjoyed to play out their fantasies of knights and wizards, dragons and princesses in a real castle.*

*Many times Elijah had to fight his way through hordes of evil knights, powerful wizards, and all sorts of magical creatures to save Sara, the beautiful princess who was trapped in the castle's tower. The kitchen, where they were often confined, had served as an excellent tower. Once Elijah broke into the tower and reached the princess, the danger would grow by leaps and bounds; alarms would sound all over the dark kingdom as every wretched soul therein learned of the hero's plight.*

*The beautiful Sara was a princess first, a real lady through and through, but when surrounded by danger, throngs of evil creatures too vast for Elijah alone to destroy, she would rise to the occasion and fight bravely beside her prince. He always enjoyed playing the game, but as he grew older, it was the deserving kiss the brave prince was bestowed by the rescued princess he most looked forward to. To Elijah, Sara truly was a beautiful princess. He imagined one day she would really kiss him, Elijah the peasant, rather than Elijah the prince.*

*Solomon was only a few years older than they were, but was always very mature for his age. He saw them as children and treated them as such. He never joined in their games. When he wasn't helping his father in the field, he spent his time reading, and occasionally taking walks deep into the forest, where he found solace at a small shrine and in the nature that surrounded it.*

*By Sara's sixteenth birthday, she and Elijah had grown out of playing games in the castle. Still, when they weren't doing chores and helping their families with the rigors of a peasant's daily life, they spent nearly every moment together. They would walk through the forest and by the river. They talked about everything; they held no secrets from each other. Sara spent a lot of time complaining, but Elijah didn't mind, he just enjoyed listening to her voice. That day she had been telling him about how her father had recently begun pressuring her to be more of a lady.*

*"What does that even mean?" she had demanded, extending both arms to keep her balance as she walked across a fallen tree. Elijah took her by the hand to help her down when she reached the end of the rotting log. As she jumped, her foot caught on a limb, and she stumbled into Elijah, causing him to also lose his balance.*

*As he fell backwards, he had no idea what perils might be beneath them, but he could see Sara's genuine fear as she shrieked in alarm. Jerking her hard by the hand, he pulled her to his chest and wrapped both arms tightly around her, holding her in place as best he could as he fell backwards. Luckily they landed on a small bush that softened the fall. Lying on the ground, wrapped intimately around each other, neither of them rushed to get up.*

*"Thank you Elijah!" She kissed him on the cheek and then, placing her hands on his chest, pushed herself up. "I guess you will*

*always be my prince." She was still on top of him, pressing on his chest and looking down into his eyes as she spoke. Elijah could feel himself blushing and turned his head to hide it as he sat up. Lifting her by the waist, he gently slid her onto her knees beside him.*

*He could feel her staring at him intently, but he kept his eyes on the ground in embarrassment.*

*"Elijah, look at me." Hearing her plea, he quickly glanced up and then back down at the ground.*

*"Elijah, look at me, please." She laughed as she spoke. "Don't be embarrassed." Her tone was as comforting as her soft hands against his face when she gently forced him to look up at her.*

*When he met her gaze, the entire world melted away, along with his embarrassment. In this moment there was only Sara.*

*"Do you want to kiss me?" Her soft voice echoed in his mind. Yes, he wanted to shout, but for a second his lips wouldn't move. In that moment of silence he could see her begin to blush. She was nervous.*

*It seemed as if he had been awaiting this moment for his entire life; he had never been more excited, or more nervous. He cleared his throat and shifted his body into a more comfortable position as he gathered his wits to speak.*

*"Of cour —"*

*"Elijah, Sara, there you are; I heard a scream. Are you okay?" Solomon grabbed Sara by the hand and lifted her to her feet as he spoke. "Come on, let's get you home." He continued to hold her hand as he led her away. Elijah watched from his place on the ground while she gazed back at him over her shoulder.*

*In that moment, he was once again a child playing a game, but he was no longer the hero. This time he had been bested, and he watched in defeat while his princess was spirited away. He didn't know until later that evening how eerily, accurately symbolic that moment had been.*

*Knowing the pain it would cause Elijah, his entire family*

*gathered to inform him of his father's plan, how he had negotiated for Solomon to court and eventually to marry Sara.*

*More than three years had passed since that day and though she was never far from his thoughts, he had only seen her once. He had promised to meet her again the next day, but he couldn't bear it.*

# CHAPTER 50

AFTER DINNER, ELIJAH took Malaki upstairs to get ready for bed. After a few minutes spent convincing Malaki to get into his bed clothes, Elijah helped his little brother settle in.

When he finally walked out into the corridor to wait at the top of the stairs for his older brother, he heard anxious whispers going back and forth between his mother and Solomon. Creeping forward to learn why they were so upset, Elijah heard his mother bring the conversation to a close.

"You have put this off for long enough. You know it's going to happen, and so does he, so you might as well get it over with. Elijah will understand." He couldn't see her, but his mother's voice was adamant.

"I just don't want to do this to him, Mother. I can't face him with this; it's going to tear him apart." His brother moved in and out of view, pacing the floor as he spoke.

"Of course it will hurt him, but he will get over it. You have tried your best for your brother, but your father already made arrangements with Sara's. There is nothing you can do now but tell him. Besides, he hasn't seen the girl in years; he's probably over it by now." Her tone had shifted as she tried to comfort Solomon.

*"He hasn't, Mother; I promise you that. I see it in his face every time he looks at me. He still loves her as much as he ever did, and I'm about to crush him all over again. I can't shake the feeling that this is wrong, that I'm betraying my own brother. This isn't the way it's supposed to be, Mother. I can see it in her eyes as well. She has grown to care for me in a way, I think, but she still longs for Elijah."* Solomon's voice sharpened with his anxiety.

Elijah turned to walk back to his room, wishing now he hadn't been so suspicious, or so anxious to know what his brother seemed nervous about at the dinner table. He knew this day would come, but had tried not to think about it. Solomon was right, Elijah hadn't seen Sara in years, but loved her just as intensely as he ever had.

His pull towards her was stronger than gravity; it had been a struggle for him every day... not to cause a fuss, not to leave in the middle of the night and escape with her, to just grit his teeth, lower his head, and bear the weight of it all.

*"Elijah,"* his brother had seen him and was calling from below. *"Elijah, come down here; I need to talk to you, Brother."* His voice was shaky; Elijah just stood there silently for a moment with his back turned and his eyes shut. For a moment he thought he might lose control, but finally took a deep breath, gathered himself, and then turned around.

Elijah looked into his brother's eyes and saw a desperate longing for acceptance. He took pity on him for a moment; he hated what was happening, but loved his brother with all his heart. Elijah closed his eyes and clenched his teeth as he gently rubbed his fingers across his eyelids. He knew what his brother wanted, but didn't know if he could give it.

*"Elijah, you know I don't want to do this to you, but I also can't do this without you; I can't do this without your blessing, Brother. I need you to tell me it's okay."* Elijah could see tears welling in Solomon's eyes as he, too, struggled to fight them back. Elijah once

*again closed his eyes, trying to calm himself enough to speak. After a long moment of silence, he took a breath and finally began.*

*"Brother, I love you more than life. I would gladly take up any hardship to keep it from your shoulders. Neither time nor space, nor any happening, could dull the love that I have for you; it will always be there, no matter what you do. But I am afraid that is the most I can give you, because Sara is my heart, and it is against all the laws of heaven and nature for a man tear out his own heart and end his life. I cannot do it, Brother, but I will let you do it for me. I will lie on this table and hand you the knife to cut the heart from my chest, and I will hold you blameless. That is the best I can do." A single tear rolled down his face as he spoke.*

*Solomon looked at him teary-eyed for a few moments and then nodded in acceptance.*

*"I do love her also, Brother; I want you to know that," he said softly, then turned and went out the door. In all of Elijah's life, there was never a more hollow or more deadening sound than the door slamming behind Solomon as he walked out of the castle that night.*

*Upstairs, Malaki had been waiting for his brothers, and when he heard the door slam below, he decided to investigate.*

*"Where is Sol going?" Malaki asked his mother as he peered down from the top of the stairs. "Don't worry little one, he'll be back. He's gone to see Sara." Esmeralda tried to comfort her youngest son. She knew how jealous Malaki could be when he had to share his brothers' attention, especially Solomon's. It didn't help; he was upset.*

*"Why didn't he tell me?" Malaki pouted; Solomon should have at least told him he was going to leave. He had been waiting patiently for his elder brother to come to bed, certain he could convince Solomon to tell him at least one grand tale of dragons and danger before Malaki had to go to sleep.*

*His hopes shattered, young Malaki ran across the bedroom and plopped down on the bed next to where Elijah was now lying, the boy's arms crossed over his chest and tucked in defiance. A fierce frown pursed his lips and flared his nostrils.*

*"What's wrong, little brother?" Elijah asked dully. The look on Malaki's face would have at any other time made Elijah smile, but at this moment it was hard to even pretend interest.*

*"I'm never going to fall in love, Elijah, and you shouldn't either!" Malaki grumbled jealously. The look on the child's face was now serious, and his tone was grave as he warned Elijah of the perils of love.*

*"You are right little brother; I promise to try my best." Elijah forced a smile and then kissed Malaki on the forehead. "Don't worry, I will never love anyone more than you little brother, and neither will Solomon. Don't be so hard on him." Elijah said, trying to comfort the boy. Malaki looked at Elijah for a minute, as if considering his suggestion, but as he scrunched his nose once again Elijah knew his advice would be ignored.*

*Waiting for Solomon's return, Elijah listened to his younger brother's chatter a long while. He could sense Malaki's voice losing its fervor as he drifted off to sleep lying next to him on the small bed. Tired from his own labors, the soft bed beneath him and the fresh smell of soap rising up from the sheets around him made Elijah's eyes grow heavy and, though he tried to fight it, he, too, fell asleep.*

# CHAPTER 51

I T WAS A long walk to Sara's house, especially at night, but Solomon had a lot on his mind and was glad for the extra time. Elijah had been in love with the girl for as long as he could remember, and tonight Solomon's actions would change everything. He had already received permission from her father, and the marriage had been arranged; the proposal was just a formality.

Still, his trepidation grew as the distance to her cottage shrank. Soon he could see her face.

There she was, smiling as she sat on a small wooden stump on the hillside and watched fireflies dance. She truly was a beautiful creature and would make a wonderful wife.

In the years since their betrothal, Solomon truly had fallen in love with the young woman he'd once seen as just a silly little girl. If it only concerned him, this would be the easiest decision of his life. When she noticed him approaching, she gestured gracefully towards the fireflies and smiled politely.

"What's wrong?" she asked.

"Could we take a walk? I need to talk to you; it's important." He took her hand to help her up, and Sara glanced at him again, looking perplexed, but came along willingly. After walking a few minutes in silence in the near dark, Sara grew impatient.

"Solomon, please, we've been walking forever. Tell me what's wrong." She stopped walking and leaned against a large tree.

"Do you ever think about your future?" Solomon stood beside her and braced himself on a low branch.

"Of course I do, every day. Why do you ask?" She reached around the tree and picked at the bark.

"Just walk with me a bit more; we are almost there." He began to move faster and Sara did her best to keep up. "Here we are." Solomon smiled and opened his arms to encompass the landscape. Beneath the moonlight Sara could see a small cottage, an expanse of grass, an old garden patch, and a steep hill capped with a huge stone.

Taking her hand, he led her up the hill to the stone. "Do you remember this stone?" Solomon asked as they climbed.

"Of course I do; this is one of the places Elijah and I used to play when we were small." As she spoke, she walked around the stone and carefully caressed its side. "It brings back so many memories." A smile lit her face as she turned back to Solomon.

"How many of those memories are of me?" Solomon already knew the answer.

"Come on! I want to show you something else ..." Solomon jumped off of the rock and ran towards the forest.

"Where are we going now?"

Solomon didn't answer, just watched to make sure she kept pace as he led her into the woods and a few minutes further.

"Do you remember this place?" he asked, his voice cracking. The toppled tree was mostly rotted and sprouted with seedlings, but she remembered it well. How could she ever forget?

"What are you doing, Solomon?" Her voice was also shaky as she tried to hide her emotions.

"*Tell me your memory of this place, please.*" Solomon knelt down and grasped her hand.

"*This is also where Elijah and I used to play.*" She gasped for air, and tears sprang to her eyes.

"*Is this where I found you two after your father sent me looking for you? Is this where I found you with Elijah the night we all learned you and I were to be wed?*" After he finished speaking there was a long moment of silence.

"*Please Sara, tell me, is this the place?*" Solomon's eyes were red as he held back tears.

"*Yes Solomon! This is the place! You know this is the place!*" She sat on the ground and began to cry.

"*Does this place still mean anything to you? Does it hold value?*" Solomon stood. He could see in her expression as she gazed at every tree, every leaf, every stone, it was still precious to her.

"*I only have one more question left.*" Solomon spoke quietly as he grasped her hand. "*Sara, do you love me?*" In the quiet moment, Solomon stared into her eyes, as if trying to see into her mind. Sara looked away nervously.

"*Not the way you want me to.*" She lifted her eyes to meet his.

"*Do you still love Elijah?*"

Sara's head jerked upright, her eyes narrowed, filled with anger and sorrow. "*Why would you ask me that? I haven't even spoken to him in years.*" She turned to hide her face, but her feelings were transparent.

"*Sara.*" Solomon grabbed her by the arm and twirled her around. "*Elijah is still in love with you. He loves you as much today as he did yesterday and three years ago. I do love you Sara, but I also love my brother, and I will not stand in the way of your happiness together.*"

He pulled her close and forced a smile. "*I am calling off our engagement; I don't care what our fathers say.*" Solomon twirled her away, but held on to her hand. "*Please, Sara, let's get back. Let me* take you to Elijah." He was eager to get back to the castle and tell his brother the news.

"Yes, please!" She was all smiles and giggles; her heart leapt with joy. "But we need to tell my mother first." The pair raced back to Sara's cottage, even though she was nervous about what her mother might say. As they approached the cottage, they saw two figures standing outside.

# CHAPTER 52

SUDDENLY A TERRIBLE pain tore through Elijah's beautiful vision, and then another, but he refused to open his eyes for fear of waking far from the sweet peace that had vanished at the onslaught of pain that ripped at his back and seared through his mind.

"Pick him up." A deep voice vibrated next to his ear. Elijah could feel bodies on all sides of him, propping him up, and then another vicious sting, this time in his back. Finally Elijah opened his eyes to see a vampire holding the grips of the two long swords protruding from Elijah's abdomen. He tried to move back, but was met by an iron-like grip around his neck. He didn't fight; he wanted to die, hoping it would take him back to his vision of Sara.

"Move backwards to the wagon." It was the same voice. The vampire in front of him took a couple steps back. "Now get out of the way!" The voice grew louder. He pulled the two swords from Elijah's body and quickly moved to his right. Elijah saw a large wooden wagon with huge iron wheels carrying an iron box. There was a sudden stinging sensation as another sword was pulled from his back. A hand around his neck pushed his head down while someone kicked him from behind, forcing him into the open box.

*Why won't they just kill me?* He struggled to turn, to see enough to figure out their intent, and just before the door was shut behind him he saw the familiar mask and glowing blue eyes. Then he saw it; a scar in the shape of a cross just below the masked man's ear. Immediately, he was transported to the past. There was someone on top of him, holding him down, and he saw a man holding Sara. The man's eyes were glowing an icy blue; as he turned his head Elijah saw a cross-shaped scar below his ear.

"It *is* you!" he shouted as the heavy iron door clanged shut.

He heard iron scraping against iron as someone locked the door. He heard chains rattling and another lock clicking into place, but he could see nothing, only darkness. Elijah pounded on the walls of his prison; he pushed as hard as he could, but couldn't get any leverage from his cramped position inside the tiny space. He couldn't believe the man who had helped his father kill Sara had been so close to him for so long. He was angry; how could he have been so stupid? Why hadn't he remembered that scar sooner? He had suspected the man's identity for a while, so why hadn't he simply ripped the mask off instead of endlessly wondering?

The wagon carried Elijah back to the camp; he heard cheers and laughter as they passed through. Finally the wagon came to a stop. He heard footsteps, people moving around him.

"You were able to capture him?" Elijah knew that voice; it was the Khan. "Good, but now what to do?" Elijah could hear him pacing around the wagon.

"Kill him." Elijah heard the voice that had caged him.

"He is strong; we don't even know how strong, but at least strong enough to kill more than twenty vampires single-handedly." Elijah smiled to hear the Khan's concern.

"When I got there he was weak, just lying on the ground; but no matter, I assure you that I can deal with him."

"Nonetheless, I recommend you put that box on a fire and let him smell the stink of his own burning flesh as it continues to heal and burn at the same time. If that doesn't kill him we will try something else in a few days," the Khan instructed. "Did the men find his friend?"

"No; it seems he fled the camp when the men left to raid the town," the man in the mask replied.

Elijah was relieved to learn he hadn't condemned Hassan yet again to a terrible fate.

"Make sure to station a few vampires here to watch the wagon at all times," the Khan commanded. Elijah heard someone pounding on the outside of the box. "Elijah! I would have taken you to your father and let him kill you, but now you will die here, all because you couldn't follow simple fucking orders." He tapped on the outside of Elijah's box a couple of times, as if punctuating his comments, before Elijah heard him walking away.

# CHAPTER 53

F ROM THE EDGE of the forest, Hassan peered down at the Mongol force in the depths of the valley. Earlier that day Hassan had watched the giant in the mask force Elijah into a metal box.

He had been keeping an eye on the Khan earlier when he saw a vampire hurrying through the camp to inform the Khan Elijah needed twice as many barrels. Soon more and more vampires raced into camp, hysterically telling tales of Elijah's rampage, of his madness.

Hassan had sprinted to the town, hoping to save him, but was too late. After watching them force Elijah into the box, he hurried back to camp, where he sneaked into a guard's tent and quickly disguised himself as a human soldier. He had been only a few yards away, watching through a slit in the guard's tent, while the Khan ranted at Elijah in his iron prison.

Hassan himself thought Elijah probably did deserve death for what he had done, but not at the hands of the Khan. Three large vampires were guarding the wagon, which was opportunely stationed at the edge of the camp. Still, Hassan needed a distraction.

As night fell, Hassan descended from his concealment in the trees, down the mountain to the valley floor. He circled the camp and crept through the main force at the rear of the army encampment. The mortals would be asleep, so this should be the easiest way in. His steps were quick and light; he stayed in the shadows, away from the torches.

His plan was simple, but he wasn't sure it would be as effective as he hoped. Grabbing two oil-filled vases, Hassan slipped between the tents and campfires until he came to the front edge of the vampire camp. From there he could see the two wagons stacked with barrels of blood at the opposite edge of the camp.

The vampires were celebrating Elijah's downfall and the renewal of their food supply with barrels of wine the Khan had provided, so it was easier than he had expected to get past them. Hassan walked to the edge of the camp and merged with the darkness.

Cloaked in the night, Hassan made his way to the outermost wagon at the front of the camp. He walked quietly around the wagon as he emptied the vases of oil over the barrels, saving only a small amount. The nearest torch was at the edge of camp and there was a vampire walking directly beside it. Hassan immediately saw his opportunity to act as he watched the tall, bald vampire slink past the torch, clearly on his way to get more blood. When he was almost at the first wagon, Hassan raced over. Grabbing the torch, he ran back to the wagon, doused the vampire with the remaining fluid, and set him ablaze.

As his screams pierced the darkness, Hassan torched the wagons and vanished back into the night. He circled the camp towards Elijah and waited for the commotion to draw a crowd. His plan worked; within seconds the fire had drawn all but one vampire away from the wagon. Hassan rushed down the mountainside and plunged his dagger through the side of the remaining vampire's head.

"Elijah, are you in there?" Hassan whispered.

"Hassan. What are you doing? You need to get out of here!"

"I'm going to free you first." Hassan quickly unrolled a small cloth parcel and retrieved two small metal tools. Kneeling down, he went to work on the lock. He was finished in a matter of moments and began unraveling the chains around the box. As he dropped the chains to the side of the wagon, the door swung open and Elijah pulled himself out.

"Let's go." Hassan grabbed Elijah by the arm and helped him down from the wagon.

"Not yet. I need to find that mask-wearing ghoul." Elijah turned around and looked towards the Khan's tent.

"This isn't the time Elijah, but I'm sure you'll be glad to see this." Hassan pulled the Great Khan's sword from his back and tossed it to Elijah.

"How did you get this?" Elijah asked, his smile warming Hassan's soul. He loved Elijah the way he imagined a man cared for his son. They were nearly the same age, but Hassan's experience, wisdom, and maturity, combined with Elijah's youthful appearance, had left Hassan as the voice of reason, the anchor that held them in place as much as possible.

"How do you think? I am an Assassin." Hassan was pleased to remind him of where they both had gained their mastery. He longed for those days; he now knew he hadn't appreciated his life the way he should have. He reached to embrace Elijah and the world disappeared before him.

# CHAPTER 54

"NO!" ELIJAH SHOUTED as the tip of a sword tore through the front of Hassan's neck. As the sword was retracted, Hassan fell to the ground gurgling, his neck nearly severed.

As Hassan fell, Elijah looked up to see the mask and the glowing blue eyes that had haunted him for weeks now. A deep surging pain struck Elijah's heart; pressure twisted against the inside of his chest, like something trying to break free. He grabbed his chest and fell to his knees at Hassan's side.

"Here, drink this." Elijah bit through the veins in his wrist and pressed it to Hassan's mouth. He realized now how much he needed Hassan, and he was truly afraid. Hassan was all he had left, and he didn't know if he could survive losing everything again.

"No; please, let me go." Hassan turned his head to avoid the blood.

"This is my fault; let me fix it," Elijah begged.

"Please, I have compromised as much as I am able. My God would not allow this." Hassan struggled once more to avoid the blood. Elijah closed his eyes for a moment and then looked up at the mask. The blue stare seemed tangible; Elijah's eyes were now dry. A hard thud crashed against his chest and he quickly looked down to see Hassan's hand.

"No, Elijah, what I couldn't accomplish in life, allow me to accomplish in death. I have tried to make you feel; please, feel this. This pain is your humanity, your salvation. You will never get what you want without it... what you really want... peace."

Elijah watched as Hassan's palm slid from his chest. "God," he scoffed, "how can the damned believe in such things?" He felt tears burn his eyes, but allowed a hint of a smile as he looked back into Hassan's eyes.

"Elijah, there is good in you. Your damn stubbornness and your vengeful spirit cause you to do wicked things, but as long as you can feel there is still hope. Don't ignore all the evil things you have done, all the harm you have caused.

"Feel it. No matter how much it hurts, feel it, but don't let it control you. If you numb yourself to the pain, you will lose yourself completely. It's not how you feel, Elijah, but what you do that matters. I will vouch for you on the Day of Judgment, my friend, my brother, and one day a cool breeze will blow though the depths of hell." Hassan's grip loosened from around Elijah's cuirass and his eyes glazed over. He was gone.

"I hope you are right, my friend, but either way, you will live forever in the thoughts and memories of every life I touch and every life I take." Elijah closed Hassan's eyes and kissed him on the forehead before rising to his feet. He closed his eyes for a moment and tried to choke back his emotion. Hassan's words echoed in his mind, but he couldn't do as his friend had wished. All of his pain and anger stormed out from his heart to his fingers.

"Now we finally will have our moment alone," the deep voice resonated from behind the mask, the giant wearing it now standing directly in front of Elijah. Elijah looked up and watched as the big man removed his mask. His face and his glowing blue eyes brought back memories of Sara's death.

"You have made a fatal mistake," Elijah growled. The rage within him could not be described as he gazed into the glowing eyes of a man who had robbed him of so much. "You are nothing more than my father's dog."

"My name is Roman, and I am no one's dog. I am here because I choose to be. I like getting my hands dirty." Roman smiled and laughed; without warning, he punched Elijah hard on the chin and knocked him backwards. Sheathing his sword, the giant stepped forward and cracked his neck to each side. His eyes burned brighter as sharp bone claws burst through the tips of his fingers.

Elijah had never received such a blow; devastating pain mingled with sorrow to confound him as he stumbled backwards and fell against the wagon. A fist full of claws raked across his face and then ripped at his chest again and again. Hassan's words were fresh in his mind as he struggled to gather his wits.

"Or don't you remember?" Roman jeered as he unsheathed his sword.

Elijah had all but given up until images of Sara's bloodied body flashed in his mind. He remembered the funeral pyre he had built for her, the bracelet which still hung from his wrist, and then the two coins he had placed in her mouth so she could make it back into his arms.

Elijah opened his eyes and drew in a deep breath; he was slumped over, only the wagon behind him keeping him on his feet.

*I'm sorry Hassan*, he thought, as Roman thrust forward his sword. *I do not have the power to control my pain. All I can do is what's most natural to me; unleash it.*

"I remember," he whispered as he stopped the sword at his chest with both hands.

"What?" Roman asked as he placed both hands on the sword and pushed even harder. Elijah held the blade firmly in place.

"I remember!" He growled as he looked up at Roman. Elijah could feel the burning sensation which meant his eyes were beginning to glow. He gritted his teeth as the heat moved through his muscles and made his bones ache. His eyes burned hotter and hotter as he slowly pushed the sword away from his chest.

Roman pulled his right hand from the sword and swung his claws at Elijah's face. Elijah jerked the sword away from Roman with his right hand and caught his swinging wrist with the other

"This is not possible. I am a vampire lord; you cannot do this." His glowing blue eyes began to dim after Elijah dropped the sword and lifted him up by his neck. "What are you?" he asked, the words barely able to find their way to his lips after Elijah threw him back nearly ten feet.

"Here." Elijah unsheathed his ancient sword and threw it to Roman. "That is a Spartan sword. It once belonged to the greatest Khan of them all, Genghis Khan. Before that, it belonged to the great Spartan king Leonidas the Brave." Elijah stepped around the big man, who quickly took the sword and pushed himself up.

"It is said that thousands of men have lost their lives on the edge of that sword. I think that is probably a great exaggeration. Still, many believe there is much power in that sword," Elijah spoke calmly while Roman examined it. Elijah drew his other sword; he held it up for a moment and then dropped it at his feet.

"I am a vampire lord. You dare face me without a weapon?" The big man hid his fear behind a broad smile. Elijah remained silent. "Your father was right about you. You are an arrogant little shit," Roman bellowed.

"You have no name," Elijah said. "You are no one. You have

no recourse; you will die here today and time will erase you. You will be one of the countless devils who died trying to reach beyond their grasp, trying to kill what can't be killed, trying to fight against the abiding strength of my immortal will." Elijah spoke in a calm, even tone, and then quickly leaned to the right to dodge the sharp edge of Roman's sword.

"Tell me what you are. How can you still live after we killed you? Why are your eyes that color?" Roman demanded, his expression grim as he lunged forward. Elijah quickly maneuvered to escape the blow and grabbed the outside of Roman's sword hand. Spinning around Roman's outstretched arm towards his back, Elijah yanked the small *kopis* from beneath his arm and plunged it upwards into the base of Roman's skull.

"We all have many faces; we each are different things to different people. In this moment we are the same, you and I," Elijah whispered as he removed the dagger. Roman fell to the ground, moaning. "We are the two faces of Janus, the god I worshiped as a child, the god of transitions, beginnings and endings. Today I offer you an ending to your miserable existence and you offer me a new beginning, where I walk beyond the reach of pain and anger."

Elijah reached down and retrieved the Spartan sword. He stood above Roman, who was crawling and calling out for help. He kicked him to his back and stood with one foot on his chest.

"I give you death as you give me life." Elijah smiled as he brought the blade down and separated Roman's head from his body. He watched Roman's eyes as they glowed bright again for only a second and then dimmed as his head rolled away from his body.

Elijah walked slowly back to Hassan's body He closed his eyes and heard Hassan's words one last time. Taking a deep breath, he let it all in. He tasted guilt, anger, and pain one last time before he swallowed it down. Then he turned it all off, and was once again left with the bittersweet taste of emptiness.

By this time a huge crowd had gathered. Elijah picked up his other sword and sheathed it as he calmly observed the horde of vampires and humans alike gathered between Elijah and the Khan.

Elijah began walking toward the Khan, Spartan sword in one hand and Roman's head in the other. As he reached the edge of the horde they began to part, leaving no obstacles between him and the Khan.

"I don't know what you are planning to do, but without me you will never get to William." The Khan stammered and took a couple steps back.

"I will lead your army. I will collect your blood from wherever I can find it. I will take Baghdad for you, and then you will take me to my father," Elijah commanded. The Khan's eyes were wide; he couldn't speak. "If you betray me, you will end up like *this!*" Elijah threw Roman's head at the Khan. He sheathed the Spartan sword in the leather scabbard on the back of his cuirass and walked back to his tent.

"That's a nice sword. It looks familiar," the Khan yelled after him.

Elijah paused for a moment before turning back with a smile. "Yes, it's funny how such things find their way to deserving hands." Elijah smiled again and continued towards his tent.

# CHAPTER 55

"ARE YOU OKAY?" Elijah heard a familiar voice and lifted his head to see Ayda walking into his tent.

"Why are you here?"

"I heard about Hassan." Ayda came closer and stroked her fingers through Elijah's thick, curly hair.

"I'm fine." Elijah whispered as he looked back down at the floor.

"Look at me, Elijah." Ayda cradled Elijah's chin and forced his head up. "I know you're not fine."

"You don't even know me." Elijah slapped her hand away and stood up. "Just get out!" He pointed to the exit.

"I will leave for now." Ayda looked towards the exit and then back at Elijah. "I just wanted you to know that you can call on me if you need a friendly ear."

"Call on you?" Elijah laughed. "I haven't even seen you in months. I thought you were my friend, or something near to it. I had questions, and you just disappeared," he yelled.

"I do care for you, Elijah." Ayda stepped forward and again reached for Elijah's face. "I just didn't know what to do. I was confused; I still am."

"If you care about me, then tell me what I am." Elijah grabbed her arms and forced them down to her sides.

"You think I know what you are?" Ayda responded, shaking her head.

"You know." Elijah clutched at his head, making a frustrated noise, and turned away, then whirled back and pointed at her. "Your eyes were glowing bright red, and then my eyes started to glow as well."

Ayda wouldn't look at him. She stared into space while her fingers played nervously with a seam on her gown.

"Elijah, you are not like me." Ayda looked back up at him when she finally spoke.

"How do you know? What *are* you?" Elijah asked, his eyes wide.

"It doesn't matter, Elijah, but you are not like me. I know that much." She stood up and walked towards the exit.

"Wait!" Elijah shouted and she stopped. He stood up and walked towards her. "How do you know that?" Taking her by the arm, he gently spun her around and looked into her eyes. "How do you know?" he asked again.

Ayda remained silent for a moment. She broke Elijah's stare and looked at the floor. "Because your eyes glow yellow, like the light of dawn; they remind me of the yellow amber gemstones formed by fossilized tree resin. I have never seen eyes like that before," she looked back up at him as she spoke.

Elijah was stunned. He had been almost certain they were the same. He stumbled backwards and caught himself on the table before sitting. Ayda rushed forward and sat in the chair next to him.

"Elijah, what is wrong?"

"I'm fine," he said. Actually, he was somewhat disappointed. While he had believed he was like Ayda, he thought he had finally found a hint of belonging. That now vanished.

"Elijah…" Ayda began to speak, but was quickly cut off.

"I'm fine, I said. At least my eyes aren't blue. Just go." Elijah raised his head and looked at her. She reached to touch his face, but he caught her hand. "Go," he growled.

Ayda stood up. "I'm sorry." She bent down and kissed his cheek before leaving.

Elijah sat alone, staring at the table. He was more confused than ever, as he recalled the lonely emptiness of being truly alone. Without Hassan he was truly lost; there was no hope of finding his way out from beneath the weight of the void, nor did he want to. With the darkness as his home he would be able to make the decisions and bear the horrors he would have to unleash if he was to find his father. He needed his hateful emptiness now more than ever; he needed to revel in it, lest all he had done be for nothing.

# CHAPTER 56

"DON'T HOLD. HOW many times have I told you not to hold?" Hulagu Khan shouted at Elijah as he was about to loose an arrow.

"How do you expect me to aim if I don't hold?" Elijah shouted back.

"You don't aim, Elijah. I have tried to teach you this for months now. Remember, your..."

Elijah cut him off. "I know, I know. Trust my body; my eyes and my body know where the arrow needs to go. It's all non-sense. It just doesn't work!" Elijah loosed an arrow and missed an ear hanging from the city gate. Behind the gate Elijah could see countless men, women, and children hanging headless, drained of their blood.

"You always have too much going on in here." The Khan stepped closer and thumped Elijah on his forehead with his right index finger. "It is good you have rid yourself of your guilt and anger, at least for now; the true test will be when you see your father."

Elijah nodded.

"Emotion is weakness, and it clouds your mind. Now you

just think too much, you try too hard." The Khan took a horse by the reins and pulled it over to Elijah. "You have a problem with control. You always try to control things, but you can't, not always. Sometimes you have to let go. Now get on the horse." The Khan handed the reins to Elijah, stepped to the rear of the horse, and smacked its back.

"What? Why?" Elijah asked as he pulled the reins to his right, forcing the horse to turn so he could see the Khan.

"Do you really want to kill your father?" the Khan asked as he took a step forward and stroked the horse's neck.

"Of course I do, but what does this have to do with my father?" Elijah demanded. After a moment of silence he clapped his hands to get the Khan's attention.

"William is not one of these cursed creatures roaming around my camp; he's not even what Roman was. He is much stronger, and, unless you learn to control your mind, you haven't a chance."

"I have learned. I don't care anymore." Elijah responded sharply.

"You might have learned to kill mercilessly, without guilt or shame, or even anger. You may be able to chop the heads off of these women and children and string up their bodies without a second thought, but there is one thing you still care about: your father. Let go of it Elijah, or bury it deep; you will only be able to beat him when you no longer care to.

"It's a paradox, I know; it's not fair, but it's true. You will never get what you want until you learn to let it go." The Khan leaned forward and took the horse's reins. "Do you understand?" he asked, watching Elijah intently.

Elijah nodded. The Khan did seem to speak in circles, but Elijah thought he was beginning to understand him. Elijah was beginning to learn that his anger—what he had long considered his greatest ally—could hold him back, and cloud his judgment.

"Have you ever heard of the great Hindu warrior Arjuna?" the Khan asked as he took the bow from Elijah's hand. "He had a bow called Gandiva; it was the mightiest of bows, forged by the gods themselves." Hulagu Khan examined the bow in his hands. Pulling back the string and flexing it, he admired it as if it were Gandiva.

"Why are you telling me this?" Elijah cocked his head slightly to the side and opened his eyes wide. He was getting more and more frustrated with the Khan's incessant lectures.

"Because extinguishing your rage is just the first step." The Khan leaned forward and slapped Elijah's chest. "Right action separated from thought and detached from consequence," he said, spacing the words out like he was chipping them in stone.

"What does that mean?" Elijah's frustration was obvious.

"Arjuna went into battle and killed hundreds of men, even his own family members, but it wasn't because of Gandiva. Arjuna learned how to separate his actions from his mind and heart." The Khan tapped his head with his index finger, and then his chest. "It's like walking, you don't think about it, you just do it. But more than that, Arjuna separated himself from the consequences of his actions. He took the right steps and left the outcome in the hands of the gods, or whoever." Hulagu stroked the horse's nose as he spoke.

"If the man shot an arrow at someone, then he obviously wanted to kill or at least wound them," Elijah argued, glaring at the Khan.

"You are incorrect" Hulagu's voice grew louder. "Arjuna did his job. He nocked the arrow to the bow, pulled back the string, and let go. He even knew where the arrow would go, but after it left his bow it was no longer his concern. He didn't care where the arrow landed; he removed himself from desire, from satisfaction, from disappointment, from all attachment.

"He fought for Krishna. You fight for me. Now do what

needs to be done! Whether with your bow or your sword, move swiftly, set death on its course and get out of the way. Remove yourself from the consequences. Now get on the horse!" the Khan shouted as he slapped the horse on the back once more.

Elijah stepped to the side of the large black creature and pulled himself up.

"Here." Hulagu threw Elijah the bow. "You have one arrow. Ride along the wall and loose the arrow just as you reach the gate. Remember; don't worry about hitting the ear. Don't aim, don't hold, just loose the arrow because that is the plan which has already been set into motion. Once the arrow has left your bow, it's no longer of concern, and neither is the ear. Now go." The Khan slapped the horse hard and it took off, carrying Elijah toward the edge of the city wall.

Elijah rode to the edge of the wall and turned the horse around. He looked at the ear, then at the Khan, and again at the ear.

"Remember; your arrow is already through the ear. It's been set into motion; you just have to play your part. Set your mind free!" the Khan bellowed.

Elijah closed his eyes for a moment as he took a long slow breath. *This is it*, he thought as he kicked the horse hard, urging it forward. The horse reared slightly and leapt forward, thundering in a straight path, paralleling the city wall. As the horse moved closer, the bloodied red ear shone against the black gate like a beam of light escaping the darkness.

Elijah dropped the reins and raised the bow which had been clutched tightly in his left hand. His eyes remained on the ear. The rhythmic pounding of hooves striking the ground as the beast barreled forward and the sound of his own shallow breaths echoed through his mind, freeing him from thought, just as a lantern clears out the darkness from every small corner of a room by filling it with light.

The two sounds grew louder, merging into one, and then there was silence. Time and space distorted and then disappeared altogether as Elijah pulled back the bowstring. Everything seemed as one; there was no longer any distance between his arrow and the ear. No longer was there any desire or concern about where the arrow would land. He knew what was going to happen, but was, truly, detached from the consequences; he didn't care.

Elijah gazed upon the oneness of the universe as he let go of the string and loosed the arrow. As the arrow left his bow, everything snapped back into its own space; the world he had just seen as one was now a great jumble of distinction. Again he heard the pounding of hooves as his chest expanded with breath. He lowered the bow to his side and picked up the reins with his right hand while he watched the arrow slice through the center of the dangling ear, then brought his mount to a stop just in front of the Khan.

"See, it's as easy as letting go." The Khan smiled at Elijah and then turned and walked towards the gate, laughing at his own words.

## CHAPTER 57

# 1258: SIEGE OF BAGHDAD

"NOW THAT WE have arrived, what is your plan?" Sitting at the end of a large mahogany table covered with lavish helpings of wine, fruits, and fresh meats, Elijah pulled loose a grape and tossed it into his mouth.

"I offered him terms, but that was just for show; my brother wants this city." The Khan was sitting at the other end of the table with his commanders and advisors surrounding him. "We have the best engineers from all of Asia. I have positioned men on both sides of the Tigris, forming a pincer around the city. Once this siege starts, it won't last long." Hulagu Khan smiled and turned to Kitbuka, his confidant and greatest general, for his opinion.

"Now that we have surrounded the city, sir, I believe we should begin." Kitbuka was a tall, well-spoken man.

"What of their forces?" the Khan asked.

"I have positioned engineers at certain points in the river;

if they come out in force we will break the dikes and flood the area behind them; they will be trapped, sir," Kitbuka assured the Khan.

"Excellent. Begin digging a ditch around the city, then. Move all siege engines and catapults into position," the Khan commanded as he rose from the table. He dismissed the others and approached Elijah, who was still seated, eating grapes.

"Have you told them why we are really here?" Elijah asked as he looked up from the plate of fruit in front of him.

"I have told them everything they need to know. They are soldiers—my soldiers." The Khan stepped forward and placed his left hand on Elijah's shoulder.

"You don't believe they have the right to know that their lives will be lost in pursuit of some book which may or may not be in that library?" Elijah's eyes followed the Khan as he circled behind him.

"Rights, ha," the Khan chuckled. "What would a murderous creature like you care about rights? That you would even ask me that, after all the young, innocent blood I have seen you spill, shows there is no hole deep enough to compare to the depths of your arrogance and hypocrisy."

The Khan's words pierced the walls in Elijah's mind; as he closed his eyes he could see a beautiful girl child reach out her hand to wipe a single tear from his cheek. He rubbed the braided leather token he had woven into his cuirass as a constant reminder of the monster he had become.

"It's okay." The tiny voice echoed in his mind for a moment before being violently interrupted by the sharp sound of cracking bone. Elijah could feel the vibrations in his hands as the girl's neck snapped. He saw his hands around her small jaw; her body went limp as he caught her in his arms and gently lowered her to the floor beside her sister. Elijah took a deep breath and his thoughts descended into a peaceful silence.

Suddenly, a horn blasted in the distance and Elijah opened his eyes.

"What is that?" Elijah asked as he turned to face the Khan.

"Get to the front; they are coming out," the Khan barked. Elijah dashed to the edge of camp and stared towards the city just as the gates began to open. He moved into position at the rear of the vampire army as twenty thousand soldiers on horseback poured from the city gates. It was a sizable force, a formidable wall of rested and well-fed beasts and men.

"Archers!" Elijah heard Kitbuka shout from behind him as the horsemen fell into formation and began to charge. The drumming of hooves grew louder and louder as the enemy soldiers were drawn farther from the comfort of their strong walls.

"Fire!" The moment the commander shouted the order, an army of arrows rose into the sky and came crashing down on the incoming force like a blanket of iron.

Hundreds of horses and men alike fell to the ground; the moaning of dying men and the grunting and screams of dying horses filled the air.

"Ready, fire!" Another barrage of arrows rose and fell. Men continued to fall from their horses, the casualties mounting. It seemed they had vastly underestimated the size and effectiveness of the Mongol archer forces.

Still, the soldiers continued to charge. As they pulled farther and farther away from the city, water began to gush in behind them from the Tigris. The dikes had been broken and the rising waters trapped the horsemen outside of the city. With no other option, they continued forward.

"Break position!" Kitbuka yelled. The archers, already on horseback, disbanded, encircling the enemy and picking them off with stunning accuracy. It seemed Elijah's men would see little action today.

Suddenly, a great horn sounded from within the city walls.

All of the fallen horsemen rose to their feet and leapt to topple the archers, tearing them from their horses and cutting them down like they were sheep. The men still on their horses continued forward.

"They are vampires, attack!" Elijah shouted, shocked at this development. The uninjured horsemen, who had reached Elijah's forward line by now, leapt from their horses with swords drawn and fell on Elijah's men, who were caught off-guard. Slicing and biting, the soldiers from Baghdad were slowly and inexorably hacking their way through Elijah's vampire troops.

Elijah and his vampires were outnumbered and the archers were all but decimated; they needed a new plan. He raced to the back of the camp to speak with the Khan. The Khan was on his horse staring down at the new developments when Elijah approached; his eyes were wide with shock.

"Did nobody think of this?" Elijah shouted as he appeared next to the Khan.

"No, of course not, and they shouldn't have. How is it possible they have been able to feed twenty thousand vampires within the confines of a city?" The Khan removed his helmet and slammed it to the ground.

"What are we going to do now?" Elijah asked as he reached down to pick up the Khan's helmet.

"What do you mean, what are we going to do?" the Khan raged as he dismounted his horse. "This is why you are here. You killed hundreds of my men on your own," he shrieked as he grabbed Elijah's cuirass and hauled him forward before pushing to the edge of the hillside. Elijah looked down the hill at the collision of evil upon evil.

"Not thousands," Elijah stated as he threw the Khan's helmet back on the ground.

"Win me this war, Elijah." The Khan stepped forward and put his hands on Elijah's shoulders. "You are not the man I met so long ago. With a clear mind you can cut them down, all of them. Even if we survive, Elijah, I will not be able to take you to your father, unless we win this battle. That is the truth." As he finished speaking, the Khan tugged at Elijah's right arm and Elijah turned to face him.

"Goddamn!" Elijah shouted and turned his back to the Khan as he drummed his palms against his temples. "You are right !" His eyes began to heat. "There is no way they could have kept twenty thousand vampires fed within the city walls. The Caliph must have sacrificed half of his army just before we attacked. These vampires are newborns!" Elijah turned back around, his eyes wide and glowing fiercely with conviction.

"What does that matter? They are destroying your vampires as we speak!" The Khan cocked his chin up and squinted his eyes.

"That's because they outnumber us three or four to one. Listen, they get stronger as they get older. If you have good fighters, men like Hassan, they can kill these things." Elijah was speaking quickly.

"I have the best soldiers in the world," Hulagu boasted.

"Then prove it; send in everyone, right now! We can snuff them out in one concentrated attack" Elijah grabbed the Khan by the back of the neck. "Trust me, sound the attack."

The Khan turned to Kitbuka and nodded. The general immediately blew three blasts on his horn; the Mongol infantry and cavalry charged as one.

Elijah rushed back to the front lines. He reached down and took a handful of dry dirt, scrubbing it between his hands before drawing his swords. He closed his eyes and took a deep breath. His heart rate began to slow as his mind cleared. The warmth in his eyes grew and flooded his body; his bones ached momentarily and then the pain subsided.

Just before he opened his eyes Elijah heard the whooshing

sound of a sword swinging towards him. Bending forward, he ducked just beneath a vampire's swing before leaning back and slicing through the vampire's neck with both his swords. Elijah opened his eyes and watched the vampire's head roll off of his shoulders before raising his foot and kicking the headless body to the ground.

As the body fell, another vampire leapt forward. Elijah quickly turned to his side to avoid a thrusting sword. Elijah held the vampire soldier's wrist beneath his left arm as he forced his sword-clenched fist forward, breaking the soldier's elbow. He then jerked his hand to the right, slicing off the soldier's head.

As another head fell to the ground, Elijah moved the sword in his left hand over his shoulder and against his back, just in time to block a slicing blow from another newborn vampire soldier. Turning around, he swung his sword straight through the vampire's neck.

Elijah quickly diverted thrusting blows from his left and right. He knocked the soldier on his left to the ground with his elbow as he turned and pushed the soldier on his right past him, sending his thrusting sword into the neck of a third vampire. Elijah swiftly chopped the head from the falling vampire he had pushed past him and then turned to his left as the other one jumped back onto his feet.

Joined by two more soldiers, the vampire swung at Elijah's head. Elijah ducked beneath the blow as he blocked swinging swords from both sides. He lunged forward, plunging his sword through the head of the vampire in front of him. Dropping the sword in his left hand, Elijah spun to his right and ripped through the vampire's chest with his hand.

At this point, everything seemed to be moving in slow motion. Elijah acted without thought, detached from consequence. He avoided every blow as he moved through the horde of obstacles. Completely untouchable, he easily deflected and destroyed every soldier who came near. He leapt over piles of bodies and brutally battling groups to cut through clusters of vampires who were about to overpower the Khan's soldiers.

Behind Elijah, the entirety of the Khan's force descended upon the newborn vampires and, though the Khan's forces were significantly depleted, the battle was soon over. Elijah stood at the front of the Mongol horde, staring at the high walls around the city. He was eager to have this finished.

# CHAPTER 58

"IT'S NOT OVER yet. With our forces so depleted, how do you plan to take the city?" Kitbuka demanded as he leaned forward against the table.

"As long as there are no more vampires, everything should go as planned. We still have a sizable force, siege engines, catapults. We can still do this." Elijah looked around the table and then at the Khan.

"No, we have to do this." The Khan was painfully aware of what his brother, the Khagan, dead to heart beneath William's evil whispers, would do to him and to his army if they didn't succeed here. "Pull the catapults and other siege engines into place in front of the gate and to the east wall. Send the vampires in over the other walls and have them destroy everyone they find," the Khan commanded as he stood and dismissed the generals.

"Not you." Elijah heard the Khan's voice behind him as his grip landed firmly upon Elijah's shoulder.

"What do you mean?" Elijah snapped as he turned to face the Khan. His heart was racing with anticipation of death at his fingertips.

"I don't want you to go in. You are still not ready, Elijah;

you are not detached." The Khan lifted his hand from Elijah's shoulder and placed it on the side of Elijah's neck as he leaned forward. "Look at you. You are oozing with lust for bloodshed." He whispered accusingly and then straightened. Elijah frowned and began to grind his teeth. "Today I need you to be Arjuna; get on your horse and pick their archers off of the wall. I will have someone else lead the vampires," he commanded.

Elijah took a deep breath as he stood. He stared hard at the Khan before eventually moving to obey. He rushed back to his tent to retrieve his bow and quiver, fitted the leather straps of his quiver over his shoulders, and took up his bow before mounting the speckled grey stallion given to him by the Khan.

The horse was small compared to the ones he had known as a child, but it was fast and agile. Collecting the reins, Elijah pressed his heels gently to his mount's side, urging him forward, and the pair raced through the camp and toward the city. In the distance Elijah could see the Mongol vampires climbing the city walls. Catapults and ballistae volleyed a steady barrage of boulders and missiles over and against the walls.

Elijah dropped the reins to his mount's neck and grabbed an arrow from over his shoulder. Using his legs and weight, Elijah maneuvered the horse around the city. One after another, Elijah picked off enemy soldiers who were pouring oil and shooting fiery arrows at the Mongol vampires as they climbed the wall.

It wasn't long before horns began to sound from back at the camp, ordering a retreat. *The enemy was well prepared. This won't be as simple or straightforward as Hulagu had hoped.* Elijah thought as he rode back to camp.

# CHAPTER 59

"WHAT IS THE plan?" Elijah spoke as he entered the Khan's tent.

"I need your blood-eating bastards to man the catapults." Hulagu Khan spoke quickly as he looked up from his desk where he was writing something. "It will take a bit longer, but as soon as we break through these walls, we will flood the city with your monsters and end this." He looked back down and continued to write. "Here, send this to the Khagan." Hulagu handed the letter to a man standing beside him and turned back to Elijah. "As soon as those walls fall, I want you to lead your men inside," he said.

Elijah nodded and left the Khan's tent, heading back to his own at the rear of the camp to retrieve his weapons. As he entered his tent, Elijah heard a noise behind him, just beyond the campfires. He saw a pair of eyes watching the camp from the safety of a darkened tree line. The eyes were glowing red; immediately he thought of Ayda and decided to investigate. He couldn't allow anyone to sabotage this victory, not even her.

Elijah picked up his swords and slipped out the back of his tent. He exited the camp from a different side and crept closer to the place he had seen the possible saboteur. Using the skills he had learned as an Assassin, Elijah silently maneuvered through the forest.

He was shocked by what he found. He couldn't see it well, but he knew it wasn't Ayda. It was a great beast, a kind he didn't recognize. From his vantage point, Elijah could only see the beast's thick tail, the muscles bulging from its right hind leg, and its huge paw; he had no idea what it was.

Elijah drew his dagger as quietly as possible, but the beast took off before he could make a throw. Elijah watched the beast disappear behind a tent at the edge of camp. Elijah rushed to intercept it, but when he reached the edge of the tent, he found nothing. Elijah opened the tent to investigate and spied a naked girl with smooth, caramel skin and silky dark hair.

"What are you doing?" Elijah asked, now thoroughly confused. The girl gasped as she turned around.

"Elijah! What are you doing here?" she screamed in protest while covering herself with a gown lying next to her feet.

"Ayda, did you just see or hear anything strange outside of your tent?" Elijah demanded as he stepped through the entrance and pulled it closed behind him.

"What are you talking about?" Ayda frowned and furrowed her brow. Elijah remained silent. "Please turn around," she pleaded. Elijah, unsure of what to do next, obeyed her request.

"I'm sorry; I thought I saw something lurking at the edge of the camp," he said. "What *are* you doing?" Elijah looked back over his shoulder at the weapons and maps lying around the tent.

"I am preparing for battle, just as you should be doing. Now turn back around," she scolded. Elijah turned around for a moment and then turned back to face Ayda, who was now clad in leather from head to toe.

"What are you wearing?" Elijah asked.

"My night clothes," she said sarcastically. "I can't very well fight in a gown, can I?"

"You aren't listening to me! I saw a beast run behind your tent and disappear." Elijah's brow furrowed. "Did you hear or see anything? It's strange, but I got the feeling the beast was planning something." His eyes darted around the inside of the tent and were snagged by a unique-looking weapon—a sword, very gently curved, with an angled tip. It was beautiful; but when he reached out to touch it, Ayda quickly intercepted him.

"A beast that can disappear and make plans? Are you sure you are well, Elijah?" Ayda laid the sword on the other side of her, keeping it close.

"Yes, I found it while searching for you. I saw your eyes glowing in the forest; you must have been close to it. Perhaps it followed you into camp," Elijah surmised.

"And then disappeared?" Ayda narrowed her eyes. Elijah eyed her condescending look and then shook his head; he knew it sounded crazy. As he stood there, his eyes scanned the tent once more.

"What is all of this? What kind of sword is that?" Elijah took a step closer. "And why is a servant girl preparing for battle?"

"It's just something I made. You must have realized by now that I'm not simply a servant. I am doing some special tasks for the Khan, and you must leave now." Ayda backed up and placed her hand on the hilt of the sword behind her.

"It all seems just a little suspicious," Elijah said as he stepped forward and placed his hands on the table on either side of her, caging her between his arms. "You can't kill me, you know," he said as he leaned forward, pressing her against the table while he reached for the blade of her sword. The closer he got to her, the less he thought about his suspicions and the more his mind sank into the depths of her beauty. Their lips were nearly touching. "I think you should come with me, just to be sure," he said as he shoved her sword off the table.

"Elijah, please, forget you ever saw me. I have important work to do." She gently pushed him away and straightened her back.

"I'm sorry Ayda, but I will not allow you to interfere with me, with my plans; let's just go talk to the Khan," he said, his voice uncompromising.

"You give me no choice, then," Ayda submitted; her voice trembling and her eyes hollow. "I will follow you," she said.

"Good; let's go." Elijah took her wrist and turned around. As he turned, Ayda quickly yanked her hand loose and placed her hands firmly on Elijah's head, one near his ear and the other across his face to the side of his chin. As she snapped his neck, a familiar pressure followed by a sharp pain left him unconscious.

# CHAPTER 60

"KA-*BOOM!*" ELIJAH AWOKE to the sound of an explosion and the whump of a wall collapsing nearby. Quickly recalling what had occurred with Ayda, Elijah was immediately confused.

*What is she up to?* Rising to his feet, he saw the maps he had noticed earlier and quickly pored over them. The map on top seemed to be of Baghdad, and she had marked an X on it. He also found notes in a language he did not recognize.

"At least I know where she is going," he muttered. Elijah took the map and raced toward the city just behind the horde of Mongol vampires. The familiar smells of blood and death surrounded him once again as screams began echoing throughout the city.

Just inside the walls, Elijah unfolded the map. He quickly found his own position in relation to the X that marked a complex in the center of the city. Unsheathing one of his swords, he rushed towards the complex. Convinced he didn't have time to get caught up in battle, Elijah avoided the main roads; he raced through alleys until he reached his destination and entered through an atrium.

He nearly stumbled over two bodies with severed heads when he opened the door into a room adjacent to the atrium, only two rooms from the X. Severed heads and limbs led the way from room to room. Elijah no longer needed a map. As he entered the room marked X, his eyes widened. *A library?*

"What are you doing here?"

Elijah looked over his shoulder to find Ayda. "You tried to kill me." Elijah accused as he turned to face her.

"I'm not an imbecile; if I had wanted to kill you, you would be dead," she replied while retrieving a piece of parchment from the book she was holding.

"You might be surprised. I'm not so easy to kill," he stalled, as he lifted the blade in his right hand. "What is that?" he asked, pointing the tip of his blade toward the parchment. "Is that what the Khan is looking for?" He stepped closer.

"Listen to me, Elijah; you have no idea what this is. I can't let him get his hands on it." Ayda folded the parchment and stepped backwards.

"Normally I wouldn't care either way, but I need that. I have a deal with the Khan." Elijah sheathed his sword and raised both hands in an attempt to calm her. "Just put it down and I will let you go."

"It is not the Khan who concerns me. Your father, William... he must not find this." Her eyes were wide as she pleaded with him, slowly easing away from the wall.

"Don't worry about my father; I will take care of him. What do you know of my father? Who *are* you?" Elijah's eyes narrowed as he maneuvered closer.

"No, Elijah, you are not ready. He will kill you. Come with me and I will answer your questions. I don't want to kill you," she said with conviction.

"You, kill me?" Elijah laughed.

"Find the library!" the Khan's voice boomed from the atrium.

Ayda opened a pocket below the breastplate of her leather armor and placed the folded parchment inside.

"I am sorry, Elijah; I must go." She drew her sword and backed toward the door where Elijah had just entered. Before she reached the door, it swung open and two men raced through in single file. Ayda plunged her sword through both men's chests with one thrust and leapt through the door before their bodies hit the ground. Elijah quickly followed through the first door, and then through two more, but he couldn't find her. She had vanished.

"Fuck!" Elijah yelled as he turned back toward the library. He had cared for Ayda, and didn't want to believe she would deliberately hurt or thwart him. But his anger grew, and his pain at her betrayal and disappearance hit like a battering ram to his heart. Why hadn't he just killed her?

# CHAPTER 61

"WHAT ARE YOU doing here?" the Khan fired when Elijah entered the library.

"I followed Ayda; she took something from one of the books and disappeared." Elijah rubbed the sweat from his forehead as he picked up a book and threw it to the Khan.

"What is this?" the Khan growled as he flipped through the book.

"It is the book from which she retrieved a parchment."

"Why did you not stop her?" he roared.

"I tried; she was too fast. She even broke my neck." Elijah rubbed the back of his neck as he spoke, his anger building to epic proportions.

"You mean to tell me a little servant girl overpowered you and outran you?" The Khan's eyes narrowed; Elijah could understand his suspicions.

"I have come to believe she is far more than a servant girl." Elijah took a step forward, towards the Khan.

"Or perhaps you took it. It does seem more likely, does it not? Certainly more likely than the great Elijah being overpowered by his own slave girl." The Khan handed the book to a man standing behind him. "See if there is any significance to this book," he instructed before turning back to Elijah. The man beside him took the book, bowed and left.

"It does, indeed, seem more likely, Great Khan, but it is not what occurred." Elijah's voice vibrated as he stared at the Khan. He took a deep breath in an attempt to calm himself.

"Do you want us to detain him?" Kitbuka asked the Khan.

"No, it doesn't matter." The Khan spoke after a long silence. "The Khagan wants him, and so does his puppet master. Elijah will come with us peacefully because we are taking him exactly where he wants to go. Look through the rest of these books and make sure there is nothing else we need; throw everything we don't need into the river." The Khan turned back to Elijah. "Are you ready to meet your father once again?"

## CHAPTER 62

E LIJAH DIDN'T EVEN turn to look when he heard the
heavy wooden doors boom shut behind him. Anger and
anticipation crept into his chest when he saw his father at the
top of the stairs.

He took a deep breath and exhaled hard to rid himself of
emotion. "I hear you have been looking for me," William said as
he calmly descended the stairs and entered the courtyard.

"Yes, for many years now, ever since you butchered my family," Elijah replied as he leaned his head to the side to crack his
neck. He looked around at the guards surrounding the yard; he
was certain they were vampire. Elijah's rage was growing with
every breath, but he tried hard to choke it down; the Khan's
admonitions were ever-present in his mind.

"Well, here I am; what is it you need? Have you come to kill
me?" William gulped down the blood remaining in his wooden
chalice and tossed it to the ground as he circled the enclosure.

"I would like some answers first."

"Very well, ask," William answered after a short pause.

"The night you came back, the night you killed my mother,
were you already vampire?" Elijah asked flatly.

"No, I was not, not yet." William smiled.

"Then I just want to know why." Elijah stepped closer to his father, who was now standing still; they were finally face to face.

"Why?" William laughed. "You want to know why. You are still such a child." William turned and ran his fingers along the marble fountain at Elijah's side. "You know, I used to be like you. I used to play into the fictions of right and wrong, good and evil, but the problem with fictions is, by definition, they are not real. The only thing that matters, the only thing that is real, is power, the ability to do more, unlike your mewling impotence." William turned back towards Elijah as he spoke.

"You know, there is not much difference between us. I have heard of your endeavors, of all the innocent blood you have spilled." William stepped closer. "You enjoyed it, didn't you? Don't deny it; I can see it in your face."

Reaching behind him, William pulled a sword from the scabbard at his back. "Do you recognize this?" It was King Leonidas' *kopis,* the one Hassan had given to Elijah. "Thank you for bringing it home, by the way. It belongs to the Khagan," his father smirked.

Elijah rushed forward to grab the sword, but William quickly knocked him to the floor open-handed. "A bit touchy, aren't you? Elijah, you've always had such problems controlling your emotions." William laughed as he reached down to help Elijah off the ground.

Elijah slapped his hand away and jumped to his feet. "No, I did not have a problem with my emotions. Not until everyone I cared about was brutally slaughtered in front of my eyes. Let's get this over with," Elijah growled as he closed his eyes. The rage growing in his chest thundered throughout his body.

"Elijah, my gentle son, if I had wanted you dead, you would be dead by now." William sheathed the sword behind him.

"I have heard that a lot recently, but I am not easy to kill."

Elijah reached into his cuirass and pulled out Roman's mask; he had retrieved it from the Khan after killing Roman. He threw it on the ground at William's feet.

"Ah, Roman. He was always such a fool," William said as he picked up the mask and examined it idly. "You have done me a service. The man was uncivilized; all he did was get on my nerves." William tossed the mask away. "The truth is, I am proud of you, Son. I have heard how you were instrumental in the taking of Baghdad. Even though you managed to let a servant girl slip through your fingers."

William looked at the ground as he spoke, and then slowly shifted his eyes to watch Elijah. "Don't worry about her, though; we have news she is traveling to Japan, so that will be our next conquest. I will have what I seek." He raised his head and smiled.

"What exactly are you searching for?" Elijah asked.

"Surely you don't expect me to tell you," William scoffed.

"It doesn't even matter. Everything I did was in order to reach you, to watch you die squirming beneath my own hand as the devil blue in your eyes flares one last time and then fades away." Elijah's eyes narrowed slightly as the now-familiar heat permeated them.

"Wow, there they are, those yellow eyes I've been hearing about." William paused as he stared into Elijah's eyes. "Elijah, I will be honest with you. Despite the weaknesses brought on by your pathetic thirst for vengeance and a misguided and unintelligible sense of self-righteousness, you are a true anomaly. But I know what you are; I can tell you. I want you with me; you could be my right hand, my second in command." William said proudly as he lifted his chin.

"Where is Solomon?" Elijah asked as he looked around the courtyard once more.

"Don't worry about him; he is far away," William flicked

his fingers carelessly before turning to look as the doors to the courtyard opened behind him.

"Just give me a weapon and let us end this," Elijah growled through clenched teeth as he glared into William's eyes; his heart thundered with fury.

"As you wish. Hulagu, bring him a sword." The Khan unsheathed the sword Elijah had forged long ago and walked over to him.

"*Remember!* No desire, no attachment; he must simply be another nameless face... or you will not win." Hulagu Khan whispered in Elijah's ear as he leaned in to hand him the sword.

"Yes, well, he's not." Elijah accepted the sword and took a deep breath in an attempt to clear his mind. The Khan was barely out of the way when William lunged.

Elijah was caught off guard, but reflexively knocked the sword to the side as it sliced through the flesh just above his elbow. William smiled as he took a step back. The stinging pain in Elijah's arm helped to slightly dampen his rage, allowing him better focus.

As Elijah's arm quickly healed, he stuck his sword in the ground and untied the side of his cuirass before sliding it over his head.

"I agree. Let us make this a bit more interesting. The result will be the same, either way." William removed his armor and stepped towards Elijah as he sliced his sword downward from his right.

Elijah deflected William's sword and then backhanded him across the face. William stumbled backwards a bit, but quickly gathered himself.

Again William lunged, keeping Elijah on the defensive. The blow was deflected, but William quickly spun and backhanded Elijah hard, knocking him back against the fountain. William chopped down, forcing Elijah to lean back over the fountain while he blocked William's sword. Their swords were locked as the two immortals stood face to face. Elijah's eyes burned hotter. Like engulfing flames, they shone in opposition to William's icy blue.

"I still sometimes dream about snapping your little brother's neck, and how easy it was. I remember his dead eyes; it was beautiful." William grinned, delighted to see the effect of his words on Elijah's face. His targeted taunt had met its mark and fulfilled its purpose.

At that moment, Elijah was undone. He let go, and a tidal wave of emotion surged, crashing through all of his walls and barriers. They went smashing to the ground, leaving him bare, standing at the brink of oblivion. His expanding rage erupted and powered him with an unholy fury, focused towards annihilation.

Elijah kneed William hard in his midsection. As William stumbled, Elijah leaned further back over the fountain and kicked his father hard in the chest, sending him crashing against the stairwell.

Dawn seemed to break in Elijah's eyes as they burned with the fierceness and color of the sun. His aching bones drove him to the ground. As he fell to his knees, he rammed his sword into the dirt, then picked up a handful of parched earth and rubbed it between his hands. The world seemed to be moving in slow motion as he rose to his feet; grains of sand seemed to fall from his hands one at a time as he stood and dropped them to his side, clasping the hilt of his sword. He twirled the sword in his left hand before switching to his right and continuing towards his father, who was already on his feet.

"That's more like it, Son," William smiled.

Elijah stalked forward, swinging his blade furiously. William deflected every blow, and Elijah kicked him once more; he fell hard against the cracking stairwell.

"I like your eyes," William said as he pushed himself upright with his arms and waited for Elijah to attack again.

As he hurried forward, Elijah saw William's eyes begin to glow brighter. Elijah swung the sword to his left, but William quickly stepped forward and grabbed his wrist, stopping his arm mid-swing. With his free hand, William grabbed Elijah's neck and lifted him high off the ground before slamming him down on his back with great force, knocking the sword loose from his hand. As he hit the ground, Elijah elbowed William hard in the side, forcing him flat on his back.

Elijah reached for his sword as William fell, but it was just out of reach. William rolled over, hacking his sword down towards Elijah's chest. Elijah shoved himself out of the way just in time to see William's sword plant into the sand.

Elijah quickly stretched and reached again for his sword, but just as he touched it, a searing pain tore through his back. He looked over his shoulder and was surprised to see William's sword still planted in the sand.

"Stupid boy!" William's voice was echoing behind him.

"Ahhhhhhh!" Elijah cried out as another searing pain erupted in his back. Suddenly there were hands on his shoulders and back; someone was rolling him onto his back. Drops of blood crashed against his chest as his back hit the ground; he saw William's face and bloody dagger looming just above his chest. Again and again William rammed the knife through Elijah's chest and neck.

"Filet him and drain him of blood. Then crucify him on the prow of the fleet flagship heading for Japan. Keep his wounds open; make sure he does not heal." William's voice seemed miles away, but a blurry figure still hovered above Elijah for a moment. Then it was gone.

"I am sorry, Elijah, but I told you that you weren't ready." It was Hulagu's voice, and the last thing he heard.

# CHAPTER 63

"CRRRRRR-ACK!" ELIJAH WAS jerked awake by a bolt of lightning. All he could see were dark, raging waters, whose crashing waves battered against him again and again. He tried to move, but couldn't, as if he was stuck in a vat of thick mud. Mustering all his strength, he looked to his left and then to his right; his hands and arms were nailed into the wood behind him. He had been sliced open from wrist to elbow, and his wounds were tacked open to keep them from healing. He saw others crucified alongside him, but they looked dead. He continued struggling to no avail; he was too weak.

"Okay, it's time." Elijah heard a familiar voice above him. He saw a rope fall from the deck and watched a cloaked figure climb down. "Stupid boy!" the figure scolded as it removed its hood.

"Ayda? How…? What are you doing here?" Elijah mumbled.

"I'm saving your life. Now be quiet. Are you ready?" Ayda asked brusquely.

Elijah nodded the best he could as she grabbed his wrist. "You need to leave, right now. They are looking for you… going to kill you," Elijah croaked as he moved his arm weakly, trying to shake loose from her grip.

"You listen to me. You are right; I am taking a big chance, believing in you. But we can discuss this later. Half the ships have already sunk in this storm; this is our best chance." Ayda whispered as she pulled Elijah's left arm free.

"Our chance for what?" Elijah asked, barely able to speak.

"Our chance to escape." Ayda replied as she reached down and pulled his feet through the nails holding them in place.

"Escape where? Land is too far away; I don't have the strength to swim," Elijah admitted as Ayda pulled his last hand free and caught him by the chest as he fell.

"Just try to hold on." She threw his left arm around her shoulder and jumped into the raging sea.

Elijah continued to phase in and out of consciousness, the relentless cold and pummeling waves reviving him and then smashing him back under countless times.

His body, landing hard and then scraping against the sand, finally waked him fully. "Ayda?" Elijah's voice was still weak and his vision blurry. Out of nowhere, a fist smashed against his face and once again he was lost in darkness.

# CHAPTER 64

E LIJAH SAT UP coughing when icy water once again invaded his mouth and nose.

"Wake up!" Ayda shouted as she soaked him with another bucket of water.

Elijah shook his head, hard, trying to clear his mind while also examining his surroundings. He was in some sort of primitive dwelling, much like the one where his family had lived before moving to the castle.

"I saved your life?" Elijah asked. Ayda's brows lifted haughtily as she dropped the bucket.

"No, I saved your life. You arrogant—" she began.

"Stop; I have heard it before." Elijah held up his hand. "And my father? What happened to him?" he asked as Ayda handed him a cup of water.

"Don't worry; he is thousands of miles away," she said.

Elijah examined his body, which was beginning to heal, and then sighed and closed his eyes as he leaned back. "No! I must find him!" Elijah attempted to leap to his feet. "Ahh!" he shouted and grabbed his chest.

"You can't; you're not even healed yet. You need to rest, and even if you were healthy, you are still not ready," Ayda raised her voice when he tried to interrupt.

Elijah's last clear memory hit him like a hammer between the eyes; even with all of Elijah's strength, his father had still beaten him. He didn't understand why he had been unable defeat his father, but he had to try again.

"Thank you for your help, but you do not understand. This is all I have; nothing else matters." Elijah slowly rose to his feet.

"Listen, I can help you, but you must give me time," Ayda said as she grabbed his arm and helped him to a chair.

"Help me? How could you possibly help me?" Elijah looked at the table in front of him and then up at Ayda.

"I brought you here, didn't I? From more than a mile out to sea. I just might surprise you," she said with a slight smile. "You won't need long to heal. Just give me a few days, and if you still want to leave, I won't stand in your way," she said as she tossed Elijah a piece of fruit. He ate one and then another, and then another.

"What kind of sword is that?" Elijah pointed at the sword he had first seen in her tent back at camp.

"That is not just a sword. It is a katana. It is the weapon of the Samurai, whose way of life I have grown to deeply respect." She picked it up and gently caressed the blade. "Rest now; we will begin in the morning."

# CHAPTER 65

"HOLD THE SWORD with two hands!" Ayda shouted. "This is fucking ridiculous; I am fighting the air. It's a waste of my time. I'm sorry; I have to go." Elijah dropped the blade and began walking toward the path leading through the mountains to the east. "Where are the horses?" Elijah stopped and scanned the landscape.

"What horses?" she shrugged.

"The horses we rode here. I distinctly remember galloping," Elijah answered as he turned to face her, the sound now clear in his mind.

"You were dreaming; now pick up the sword," she demanded.

"No, thank you for all the help, but this is pointless." Elijah continued on the path.

"Stop!" Ayda shouted, and he did. "Fight me, right now," she urged. "If you can beat me, then you may leave." She picked up the katana and threw it to Elijah.

"I appreciate all you have done. And I don't want to kill you; you don't even have another sword." Elijah looked at the sword for a moment and then at Ayda. He had missed her when she left him, and he knew he would miss her again, but he had to leave. Killing his father meant everything.

"I don't need one," she said as she stepped closer.

"You might think you know me, but you don't. I will kill you without a second thought; I have killed hundreds of innocents, women and children included." Elijah raised the sword.

"Show me," she pressed.

"If you insist." Elijah quickly stepped forward and brought the katana chopping down towards her neck. In an instant his hand was frozen in midair. Her back was against his chest and her right arm around the back of his neck. Leaning forward, she slung him over her shoulder and onto the ground.

He leapt to his feet immediately, lunging forward with the blade, but Ayda spun to escape it. She trapped his wrist under her right arm, and with her left palm she struck the back of his elbow hard, snapping it. Letting go of his wrist, she struck him once more in the back and sent him crashing to the ground once again.

"Stop playing with me, Elijah! Really fight! " she yelled.

"You are crazy if you think I'm going to kill you," he said.

Picking up the sword, Ayda stalked towards Elijah's broken body with purpose. When he rolled to his back, the katana was already at his neck.

"Are you ready to learn now, or are you going to continue to act like a stubborn child?"

Elijah snapped his arm back into place and pushed himself upright. Grabbing the sword's blade, Elijah pulled her closer, forcing the blade through his shoulder. Once he had pulled her close enough, he grabbed her throat with his right hand and pushed himself forward until he landed on top of her.

"Do you yield?" he shouted as he squeezed her neck harder and harder. Pushing up with her hips, Ayda flipped Elijah onto his back and rolled on top of him. Quickly pulling the sword from Elijah's shoulder, she pressed the sharp blade hard against his neck.

"I'm not sure what you are or how to kill you, but I bet severing your head will work." She pressed the blade harder against his neck until blood began to pour.

"Maybe, maybe not. Let's try it and find out." Elijah grabbed the blade and pulled hard until it sank more than an inch into his neck.

"You *are* crazy!" she shouted as she jumped to her feet with the sword. Elijah lay on the ground for few moments until the wound healed and then pushed to his feet.

"Do you still not understand?" Elijah asked, wiping the blood from his neck. "I have longed for death for as long as I can remember. The only reason I am still alive is hate. I need to kill my father. Then I'll be happy to kill myself." Elijah turned and walked once more towards the path.

"Wait, Elijah. I can help you. You are not lacking in strength or in skill. It is your discipline. You are a volcano of emotion, and that eruption of emotion is what gets in your way. It makes you careless and vulnerable, especially when you are fighting an adversary who cares for nothing." She laid her sword on the ground and walked towards him. "I can teach you the control you need; I can teach you to find your center." Racing up to him, she stopped and gently placed her hand on his bare chest.

"You mean to be detached, without desire, like Arjuna?" He tried to walk around her, but she stepped to the side and blocked him once more.

"Yes and no. That is a good example, but you have misunderstood Arjuna. He was filled with emotion and conflict; he was torn apart by some of the things Krishna asked him to do, like killing his own family," she said.

"Like my father. I have no respect for anyone who would kill their own family."

"No, not like your father. Arjuna was doing what he thought was right, what his god wanted him to do," Ayda insisted, pressing harder against his chest.

"I have seen too many people do evil in the name of their god. It is still just as evil, even if they truly believe it is the will of their god." Elijah's voice was now just a whisper.

"The point is, Arjuna had no magic way to turn off his emotions; he simply controlled them. Once he made up his mind about what he needed to do, he put everything else aside and focused on the task at hand, one action after another. Actually, the principles in the story of Arjuna, and in Hinduism in general, are foundations of the principles of Buddhism and for the Samurai Code." She placed her hands on Elijah's shoulders. "I can help you if you will let me."

He was silent for a few moments as he stared at Ayda, trying to figure her out.

"Okay, but first tell me about what you took from the library in Baghdad, the piece of parchment my father wants so badly." Elijah couldn't take his eyes off her; even here, far from civilization, and in the midst of his chaos, her beauty confounded him. He leaned forward to kiss her; she closed her eyes as their lips touched, but then turned her head and pushed him away.

"We can't do that; it's not why we are here. And I'm sorry, Elijah, but I cannot tell you about the library, either." She took a deep breath after she spoke; her voice was stern but apologetic. Her eyes shifted to her feet as she dropped her head slightly.

"I don't even know what you are; why would I trust you?" he asked as he tipped his head to look into her eyes. He hoped to see something that would give her away, but she was well guarded.

Ayda stared at the ground for a moment longer and then lifted her face to look at him. "Because I've only ever tried to help you."

# CHAPTER 66

"THE KATANA IS a weapon of control. Once you can control the katana and master the *katas*, you will be able to master your emotions." Ayda slowly unwrapped the silk from around her blade and handed it to Elijah.

She didn't know why, but she was determined to help him. She was convinced he was special, important somehow. She worked with him every day, and every day they grew closer. Elijah spent years with her among the snowy mountain peaks, where they found solace in each other's company and distance from worldly cares.

His time was spent meditating and mastering control and discipline through the precise and intentional movements of the *katas*. Nothing was free or spontaneous; his hard-handed teacher had an ever-watchful eye that directed his every move. Every lunge, every slice, every step was choreographed as if he were the star in some lonely ballet.

"Slow down!" Ayda screamed. Elijah knew what was coming next, the fierce lash of a carefully braided leather training whip.

He had spent his life unleashing the rage he held just slightly beneath his skin; he believed it had kept him alive. "Why am I doing this? I am not going to need to move slowly when I kill my father," he moaned under his breath at the sting of the whip.

"I have told you countless times, Elijah, it is not your speed, or your strength, or your skill that are lacking; it is your discipline. Performing the *katas* will fill that void, giving you the control you need." She snapped the whip once more; Elijah glared at her for a moment, huffed, and then resumed dancing with his sword.

Eventually, he discovered a sort of peace in the hollowness of his mind as he sat motionless on that snowy mountain ridge for months at a time, or as he spent days practicing his *katas*. However, it was not a lasting peace; it faded every time he left that comfortable vacuum. As the years passed and Ayda's guard slowly fell, he began to notice hope fading from her eyes. Every time he looked at this woman he cared for so deeply he saw a growing disappointment and sense of failure.

"I'm not making any progress." Elijah spoke over the table as they ate dinner. "Even now, all I can think about is my father and my family, about revenge." Elijah rubbed his forehead.

"I know, and until you can find a way to forget about revenge, forget about yourself, your brother, and your father, you have no hope. You cannot win this battle with hate in your heart." Ayda rose from her chair. "I'm going to lie down," she said as she turned toward her bedroom. As she was turning, Elijah caught her hand and pulled her back.

"Please do not blame yourself. In more than a lifetime, no one has been so kind to me. To see the possibility of hope when it's not there is a beautiful thing," he said, gazing into her eyes. As he pulled her closer, he brushed her hair behind her shoulder and then placed his hands on each side of her waist. "My scars are just too deep; you've done everything you can do." Elijah held her tight and pressed her tearing eyes against his shoulder.

"I love you, and I always will," he whispered as he gently

pushed her back and cradled her soft face in his hands. He looked into her eyes for a few seconds before leaning forward and kissing her. Then he slowly pulled the tie around her waist to loosen her robe. Ayda held his wrist for a moment and then dropped her hands.

Elijah continued pulling the tie until her robe fell to the ground. She was as exquisite on the outside as she was the inside. Elijah continued to kiss her as he walked her into her bedroom and removed his own robe. As he laid her down, the two became as entwined and inseparable as the Earth and the Sun, as the mind and the body. She was truly a magnificent creature.

Late that night Elijah crept out of her room. He finally had something to live for besides revenge, something worth living for. His mind was at ease as he began to dress himself, and he imagined a possible new future, a long life in the mountains, with Ayda. After dressing, Elijah reached for the lonely necklace lying on the table, the last article of his peasant vesture. As he examined his mother's necklace and remembered his vow, he realized that his hopes for a life beyond war and revenge were no more than fantasies. All of his grief and hate came flooding back as he donned the necklace he had removed from his mother's mutilated corpse all those years ago.

For the next few hours he sat at the table, considering what could be and what should be. As he stroked the braided leather, he had tied around his small *kopis*, the only thing Ayda had been able to retrieve for him, he knew; he could never be good for anyone or anything until he had exacted the vengeance that might mend his crippled soul. He looked at the bracelet hanging from his wrist and thought about Sara. For a moment, pangs of guilt worked at eroding his sanity, guilt for his affection for Ayda, as if it in some way betrayed Sara's memory.

It had been lifetimes since she died, but he still loved her fiercely. He wondered if she would feel the same; if she would even recognize the man he had become. She had made him promise to find his princess. He imagined there would never be another more special than Ayda. Still, all the pain he had endured and inflicted had changed him at his core, and if he had to choose between Ayda and his vengeance, he knew what his choice would be. He stroked the braided leather around his *kopis* one last time to remind himself of who he was. He could never deserve her.

# CHAPTER 67

AYDA WOKE UP and a smile graced her face as memories of the night spent with Elijah came rushing back.

"Elijah!" she sang out, full of life, as she rose from the bed and slipped into her robe. But when she stepped through the bedroom door and into the kitchen a pain tugged at her throat, as if someone were squeezing and yanking it down, into her stomach. The sight of Sara's old leather bracelet lying on the table was Elijah's bitter farewell. She knew he was gone, for good.

She sat down at the table and her tears soaked the bracelet she clutched to her chest: the only reminder of the fool's errand she should have given up on years ago.

Still, in spite of everything, she hoped beyond hope he would find his way. She believed in him; she loved him.

# KHALID & EMIRA
# 2014 AD

*"...An immortal's entire demeanor is different from a human's; there are subtle differences in the way they carry themselves, how they stand and move. All that power is hard to hide from someone who knows what to look for, and, for me, knowing what to look for can be a matter of life and death."*

# CHAPTER 68

SOLOMON HAD BECOME accustomed to adulation at an early age. Even in his youth everyone had seemed to look up to him—to admire him. He had been a beautiful young boy, and as he grew he only became more handsome. Now his angled and muscular jaw was a foreboding reminder of his strength and the power he could unleash. For Solomon, the downward glances of professors and students passing through the corridor were expected, even in a place as distinguished and proud as Princeton University's Nassau Hall.

*Prof. Tariq Amon* read the plaque on the door. Solomon was glad to finally be standing here, ready to enter the professor's office. He knocked twice, and after he heard the shuffling of papers and the squeaking of an office chair wheeling around, the door swung open.

"Come in." The professor's voice was pleasant but rushed. Solomon's imposing presence and disposition immediately informed the professor who his visitor was. "I just got off the phone with your associate, and as I told him, I'm no expert on the ME, or the Tablets of Destiny, as we call them today. I do know the ME are merely part of a legend from ancient Assyrian mythology. They are certainly not real," he spoke with conviction and an amount of empathy, as if he were concerned for Solomon's disappointment.

"I know the legends professor." Solomon's voice was deep and gravelly. His expression was uncompromising. "Is there anything else you can tell me; anything at all?" The professor had been scribbling something on his notepad. He tore the page loose and handed it to Solomon: it read, *Khalid Gondal, 245 Caleb Ln., Rallo, VA.*

"This is the name and address of a former colleague of mine, now retired. I've heard he has become something of a recluse, but he is brilliant, and he knows more about mythology than anyone alive," the professor assured Solomon while he adjusted his glasses.

Solomon stared at him for a moment, watching for any tells which would reveal that he was lying, but, seeing none, he snatched the paper and left the professor's office.

# CHAPTER 69

ELIJAH AROSE WEARILY. Like Atlas, the weight of the world, his world, his immortal curse, weighed heavy on his shoulders. He should have been too strong to be sluggish and uneasy on his legs, but so often his incorruptible form was no match for the unrelenting and unseen albatross that forever clung to his mind. Hate alone propelled him.

He looked in disgust at the three women lying naked on the king-sized bed behind him. As the night waned, so had his passion, and the all-too-familiar stench of used women, infused with the strong odor of clashing perfumes and rose-scented oils, now sickened him. He was tired of this life, this charade of indifference… but most of all, he was tired of himself.

He laughed sarcastically. The irony of the situation was not lost on him. After nearly a thousand years, he still couldn't be honest with himself.

It was easier this way; seeing himself as apathetic allowed him to hide from his true feelings, from the fact it still mattered. The sting of his childhood betrayal was just as sharp today as it had ever been, and the lifetimes of failure, of allowing himself to be eluded, had taken their toll. So he chose to take whatever small pleasure he could from the distractions he sought when his frustrations grew nearly unbearable.

"Where are you going?" A soft, muzzy voice from behind him nipped at his nerves. One of the girls sat up in the bed and playfully pawed at his right thigh. Without a word, Elijah shoved her back down.

His heart seemed to have died when he lost Sara, and once more when he came down from the mountain where he had spent so many years with Ayda. No one could take Sara's place, but it was Ayda he dreamed of now. He had spent many lonely nights thinking of her, longing to feel her warmth, wishing he had been able to remain with her on that mountain and forget about this world forever.

But he knew that was just a fantasy; he loved Ayda, but he couldn't shut out his past. He was a warrior; the need for battle and blood had become a part of him long ago. The blood of his family had been his oath. He had fought many battles since then, but the important ones were yet to come.

Elijah had left Sara's bracelet with Ayda. Now, his mother's pendant resting against his chest and the tattered and worn miniature horse tether bracelet—that was now known as an infinity sign—clinging to his wrist, were nearly the only tangible pieces of evidence left to remind him his story was still true, he had loved more than once, he had been betrayed, and there was still blood to be spilled.

Over many lifetimes, Elijah's memories had slowly faded away, especially the good ones. Trying to find one to cling to was a bit like grasping at air. Only the most important ones remained, the ones that left a truly lasting impression, and unfortunately for Elijah, only a precious few of those memories were happy ones.

He had a random memory of his mother kissing him once on the cheek and then on his forehead, but he couldn't see her face.

He remembered lying next to Malaki and listening to Solomon tell tales of adventure and derring-do, and he remembered Sara every time he noticed the bracelet hanging on his wrist.

He remembered the fear that had consumed him when he thought he had lost her, the cool of her wet dress as she tied the bracelet around his wrist, the wet lock of hair he pushed away from her face when he first kissed her, and the inexplicable pain and burning rage that became him as he watched her body burn. But most of his pleasant memories, at least of late, revolved around Ayda. He feared forgetting, that one day he would wake up and remember nothing. Even now, voices sometimes eluded him, and sometimes faces were hard to recall. He feared being lost in this world that had become so foreign to him.

Elijah slid into his Armani jeans and his black canvas shoes. Picking up his shirt and jacket, he opened the hotel room door, needing to get out of there before he was forced to speak again. The comparatively fresh air from the corridor drifted into the open doorway and refreshed Elijah's senses. The welcome change sharpened him. Donning his shirt and swinging his jacket over his muscular shoulders, he shut the door quietly and walked down the corridor.

As he went through the hotel lobby, Elijah could feel his pulse racing. This had been a long time coming. He stepped out into the night, shuddering as a cold wind rushed across his cheeks and down through the open collar of his burgundy leather jacket, but it didn't matter, not tonight.

Nothing could bother him tonight. After so many years of searching, he was finally closing in. By the time Elijah had left Japan, the Mongol Empire had splintered and dissolved. Elijah had no idea then where to find William and Solomon. Or how.

He had been forced to return to an expanded version of his original method, which had relied mostly on luck and been confined to a much smaller area. In just the past hundred years he had visited thousands of churches, temples, synagogues and mosques, hunting his father and brother through Europe, Asia, and the Middle East. He was constantly on the move; he hadn't had a real friend since Ayda.

One thing he did remember was Solomon's habit of seeking refuge and solace at holy places: shrines, altars, places of worship. Solomon had often said it was important to reflect, to allow the beauty outside of your body to resonate within. Elijah hoped this habit, this ritual, would eventually lead to his discovery, that it would eventually bring him face-to-face with Solomon and his father.

He had picked up hints of his brother's presence a few times, but always too late. Once, in Greece, he had met a woman who remembered seeing his brother at the great Temple of Poseidon at Sounion just three weeks before. Since the day Ayda had pulled him off the prow of the Khagan's ship, that was the closest he had come to facing his betrayers.

Fortunately for him, his brother's presence was extremely imposing, nearly unforgettable. It seemed everyone remembered him, even if the encounter lasted only a moment. Because of this, Elijah was finally close. After centuries of missing his father and brother by years and months, he was now only days behind them.

Through sources of his own and recent personal accounts, Elijah had traced them to this specific region of the United States. He didn't know exactly why they were here, in the eastern part of the Commonwealth of Virginia, of all places. He only knew they were looking for something. Still, he didn't know what they could find in a place such as this; he couldn't imagine Ayda had brought the parchment all this way.

Elijah didn't care why they were here; all that mattered was finding them. He would search every temple in Eastern Virginia if he had to; someone would remember seeing his brother. He was anxious to get started. The town was filled with churches and temples, but most of them could be ruled out.

Elijah knew his brother; he knew his admiration for art, especially in architecture, would lead him to the most elaborately and artfully designed temple in the city. There were only three possibilities he had noticed the night before, two large Christian churches and one small but beautifully designed mosque.

He would begin with the mosque; it would be less crowded and quieter. If his brother was in the area, that is where he was most likely to be. The mosque wasn't far from his hotel; he was there in minutes.

Stepping into the foyer, he took off his shoes as was required. The musty heat of a freshly vacuumed carpet penetrated his nostrils, making it a little harder to breathe. He had come to hate religion, and thought it ironic he had spent so many lifetimes traveling from temple to temple.

He was not really expecting to find anything here in this little mosque in Carlisle, Virginia. Experience had taught him the uselessness of hope. It seemed only to lead to disappointment, but fate had brought him here for a reason.

He had spent more time at mosques than anywhere else over the years, so he knew all the customs and traditions and it was easy for him to fit in. Not wanting to wash up and go into the prayer room, he was relieved to see a middle-aged man walking past him towards the door. The man was Elijah's height, but thinner; he carried himself with confidence.

As he approached, the sweet smell of jasper soap washed across Elijah's face. The man looked Elijah directly in the eye and nodded. His demeanor was uninviting, but Elijah didn't have time to wait for the perfect candidate. He took the opportunity to quickly ask about his brother; he described him the same way he had so many times before. Elijah noticed a flicker of recognition in the man's eyes as he began to speak.

"I remember him distinctly. I saw him three days ago." The man's eyes were wide and his voice was filled with certainty. "He had the most tired-looking eyes. He couldn't have been more than thirty, but he seemed to carry lifetimes of pain."

By the man's broken accent, Elijah could tell he was far from home, and by the deep scars on his hands and face he knew the man was no stranger to pain himself.

"He was at the *masjid* in Rallo, a small town ninety miles south," the man concluded, helpful, but by no means pandering. As soon as he finished speaking, he quickly slipped into his shoes and exited the building.

Elijah had been caught off guard. It had been a while since Elijah had ran into someone who had seen Solomon. He had forgotten how Solomon seemed to be carrying sorrow that he didn't deserve. Still, for a brief moment empathy played its hand, and for the first time in centuries he remembered why he had admired his brother so long ago. But his nostalgia was quickly trumped by visions of his brother's betrayal. He had spent centuries trying to excuse Solomon, trying to imagine what could have happened to warrant his brother's actions. There was nothing. *My brother was the great deceiver*, he thought. *His pain-filled eyes are nothing but lies.*

Elijah slid his feet into his shoes and scrambled for the door as visions of killing his brother filled his mind and warmed his soul. Dreams and visions of revenge were the only true pleasures he had known for centuries. Losing his loved ones had been difficult, but being betrayed by the person he loved and trusted most, his big brother Solomon, had stripped him of his soul. Over the years his anger had seemed to change focus, moving from his father to his brother. He sometimes thought it was because he had been able to face his father and see him for the monster he was; he had yet to face his brother.

The things Elijah had done still haunted him; if it hadn't

been for Ayda and Hassan he would have been lost in darkness forever. At least now he was able to live without being dogged by constant bloodlust, to move about in the gray areas without making ripples. People still feared him everywhere he went. They no longer greeted him with the warmth he remembered as a child, but he was no longer a child, nor was he the murderous monster he had been, despite the guilt that was an ever-present reminder of a past he couldn't leave behind.

The years of meditation he had spent on that mountain had taught him to control that part of himself to some degree. He was able to live amid the masses, and, for the most part, to go unnoticed.

He still killed when he had to, but only vampires.

# CHAPTER 70

KHALID HOOKED THE nozzle back onto the gas pump and then screwed in the gas cap before closing the lid. He climbed back into his truck and pulled the door closed, watching idly as a red sports car turned off of the interstate at the first Rallo exit. It pulled into the gas station and parked a couple pumps ahead.

Khalid watched as a man stepped out of the car. The flat white bottoms of his black canvas shoes dipped slightly into a puddle of water and fuel. The liquid splashed up around his shoe and broke across the top as it rippled outward, storming to the edges of the puddle like tiny title waves.

"Who is that?" Khalid mused.

"I have no idea." Emira looked up from the book she had been reading and followed Khalid's eyes to the man who had just emerged from the red car. "Why?" She looked at Khalid, but he didn't answer. Khalid wasn't paying attention; he sat still, his eyes fixed intensely on the man in front of him.

He watched as the man took off his sunglasses and tossed them into the passenger seat. He took a step backwards and extended his arm; his index finger pressed against the door and didn't give way at all as he slowly forced it shut.

Khalid's eyes narrowed as he continued watching the man's every move. He walked around the back of the small red car to the station entrance; every step was controlled and purposeful. Khalid's vision honed in on the man's fingers as he folded two of them behind the door handle and pulled the stubborn door open steadily. Khalid's focus shifted to the man's feet. They remained flat on the ground; his body weight remained centered above them until the door was opened wide enough for him to carefully step through.

"Did you see that?" Khalid turned to Emira who was still watching the door as it shut behind him.

"See what?" she asked, turning to face Khalid when he opened the cab door.

"Stay here; I'll be right back." Khalid stepped from the truck and slammed the door before she could respond. As he walked into the station market, the sweet smell of gasoline was abruptly replaced by the stench of stale cigarette smoke and chemical cleaners. The small store was a complete mess. The supplies were lacking and filth crept out of every corner.

"Sixty dollars on pump three." The stranger stepped forward and smacked a hundred dollar bill down on the dusty counter. The cashier seemed more concerned with texting on his cell phone than attending to the customers on the other side of the counter.

"No problem." The fat little man continued to toy with his cell phone for another moment and then began punching away on a cash register with both hands.

"And I need directions to the local *masjid*," the man added. Khalid knew he would have no problem finding it; the newly found fear of Islam in the west had put Islamic centers on everyone's radar. Khalid had lived through the Crusades and, despite the atrocities he had seen committed on both sides, he had also seen how the strict discipline at the heart of Islam brought order from chaos. He found it shocking and unfortunate that the desperate acts of a few tortured souls had caused entire civilizations to fear one of the greatest and longest-lasting systems of social order the world had ever known.

"The what?" The voice coming from behind the counter had a sharp twang. The cashier squinted his eyes and crinkled his forehead as he spoke.

"The Islamic center, the mosque." The man's tone rose slightly as he explained. This was Khalid's chance; he needed to find out why this immortal was here. It hadn't been more than a few days since the last vampire had come into town; he feared they knew too much, but wanted to be sure before informing the council. Perhaps this was his chance to find out. He decided to take advantage of the man's olive complexion and dark features.

"I thought you might be one of them." Khalid stepped forward, towards the counter; his stentorian voice echoed behind the man's shoulder and he spun around. Khalid forced a broad smile as he stared down into the stranger's eyes.

Khalid stood a beast of a man, towering over the smaller immortal; everything about him was huge, as if he had been carved out of a monolithic stone. Still, the man staring up at him showed no signs of fear or surprise. His eyes seemed empty, void of any emotion, impossible to read. He seemed to be in his early twenties at the most, but that was just his appearance. His young trendy look was just a façade.

"I apologize." Khalid stretched out his huge paw, attempting to maintain *his* façade of friendliness. His skin was a bit darker than the olive color of the smaller man and his black hair flowed neatly back behind his ears, stopping near the bottom of his neck. Khalid had been told he seemed superficially like a contradiction, like a polished grizzly bear blanketed by a quiet, yet ferocious, intellect. So he tempered his intimidating form with a wide grin hiding beneath his dark beard, only exposing the brightness of his teeth.

"My sense of humor doesn't always go over so well." Khalid kept his deep voice monotone and revealed nothing. He watched as the man finally lifted his hand to shake. As their hands met, Khalid's seemed to swallow the smaller man's hand whole. He sensed the stranger was trying to read him, but knew he would get nowhere. Khalid's strength was obvious, but nothing else was. He hid his constitution well, behind an impenetrable stone glare and practiced smile. Still, he took the man's hesitance as suspicion and decided to be more careful in any further interactions.

"My name is Khalid," he said, retrieving his hand.

"Elijah," the man replied, putting on an empty smile.

"I'm headed to the *masjid* now, you can follow me if you'd like." Khalid forced a friendlier tone.

"Yes, I would like that very much," Elijah said, while rubbing his hand on his jeans, as if he had just pulled it from the belly of some beast. Khalid could see he was attempting to hide his suspicion behind a practiced mask of warmth and charm.

"Great, I'll meet you outside. I'm in that white truck, just follow me out." Khalid pointed out the window; he watched as Elijah's eyes followed his finger to the large four-door truck parked at the gas pumps.

"Thank you," Elijah replied, nodding before turning back towards the cashier.

Khalid exited the market and walked to his truck. He walked around the back and opened the door, climbing in just in time to see the passenger door close. He watched Emira walk towards Elijah's car, and he began to climb back out of the truck, but stopped when he saw Elijah out of the corner of his eye.

"What are you doing?" Khalid growled to himself, as he pulled the door closed. He wanted to jump out and grab Emira, but couldn't risk seeming even more suspicious. His eyes followed Elijah while he walked towards his car. As he approached, Emira turned towards him and their eyes met.

Elijah stopped dead in his tracks for a moment and stared at her. His lips parted slightly as he glanced around with wide eyes. Gathering his composure, he nodded towards Emira and then pressed forward. Seeing her had clearly shaken him; Khalid could see the man was taken aback, but couldn't understand why. She was a beautiful girl, to say the least, but that wouldn't be enough to cause such a reaction from a careful and practiced immortal.

"Impossible." Khalid whispered. Looking through the windshield, he could see Emira's supernatural glow. She shone as if there were something luminescent woven throughout her body, just below the skin. There was no way Elijah could have seen it. Only the Council could see the light; vampires were dead to such light. As Khalid continued to watch Elijah, he was struck with concern. As the other man pumped his gas, his eyes were repeatedly drawn back to the girl standing across his car. Something about Emira had shaken him, it was obvious, and, if not the light, what else could it be?

Emira's long auburn hair hung nearly to the middle of her back. Her eyes were a medium brown with a hint of green; together with the girl's dark hair, they contrasted beautifully against her fair skin. Her small frame was thin, but she had curves where she needed them. The girl's features were soft, but gently defined. They flowed seamlessly together, to complete a vision of beauty.

"Don't just stand there, Emira; say something!" Khalid muttered to himself.

"Can I help you?" Elijah growled. Khalid could see him trying to keep his focus elsewhere, but he couldn't. Emira didn't say a word; she just stared at him.

"What are you doing, Emira?" Khalid huffed beneath his

breath. This was the most awkward situation Khalid had seen, possibly ever; now he *had* to make sure Elijah followed them. Khalid hadn't killed in years, but he couldn't let this immortal go, not since he might have somehow seen Emira's light.

"Can I help you?" Elijah asked again, as he tried to hang up the nozzle, but missed, his attention being pulled in two different directions.

"I love your car." Emira finally spoke, widening her eyes and smiling suddenly, as if she had just been awakened from a trance. Her eyes hadn't landed on the car since Elijah walked out of the station, leaving little doubt of what she was really interested in. She lingered a few moments more, as if she wanted to say something or was perhaps waiting for Elijah to say something. She shifted her weight uncomfortably when Elijah finally attached the nozzle. Khalid watched Elijah close his eyes for a moment and take a deep breath before slowly turning to face her.

"Do you wash windows?" Elijah's voice was sarcastic and condescending, but his eyes, the same eyes that had seemed hollow and void in the station, were now bursting with emotion. Still, he continued with his obvious charade of indifference.

"Sorry." She spoke politely, holding her composure with a peaceable firmness and turning towards the truck.

"Wait." Elijah's voice quaked. "I'm sorry, please," he begged. "Where did you get those?" Khalid watched as Elijah moved towards Emira with focused intensity. Khalid quickly opened the door to jump out, but stopped when he noticed Elijah's attention was now focused more specifically.

"Get what?" Emira asked as she turned to face Elijah, who stopped suddenly. Following his gaze, Emira clutched her necklace.

"Where did you get the silver deneros on your necklace?" he asked, pointing a trembling finger towards her clutched hand.

Emira seemed confused for a moment as she watched the man's jaw quiver.

Khalid was dumbfounded to see the man transform before his eyes; this was not at all the same man who had stared Khalid down with cold and empty eyes. Still, Khalid wouldn't be fooled; there was no way Elijah could have been so completely unraveled by her necklace. Khalid was certain now; this immortal had somehow seen her light and must die.

"Do you collect old coins too?" she asked. A smile lit her face as she unfastened her necklace, holding it out for Elijah to see. "I have two of them. Go ahead, have a look." She stepped closer to Elijah, who seemed awestruck. He slowly reached out his hand, as if he wasn't sure what was real; as his hand drew closer, he seemed increasingly lost in his mind. His eyes welled with tears as he took the coins from her hand.

"Are you okay?" she asked, peering into his face. Elijah didn't answer. He stood quietly staring at the coins cupped in his hands. A tear trickled down his cheek and he suddenly shifted his gaze to meet Emira's.

"Sara?" His voice flooded with emotion as tears began to stream down his face in earnest.

"I'm Emira." Emira reached out her hand and watched as Elijah slowly responded in kind. "Are you okay?" she asked again.

Khalid was more confused than ever; if this was an act, it was a good one.

"What are you?" Elijah asked, his wide eyes shifting between Emira and the coins. Emira looked stunned.

"I'm sorry. I don't know what you mean," she said. Elijah stared at the coins for another moment before clenching them in his fist. His attention suddenly turned to Emira; his eyes focusing on hers like laser beams as he held out his clenched fist. Emira immediately retreated; she was obviously intimidated by the abrupt change in his demeanor.

"Ready, Sis?" Khalid shouted as he opened his door and leaned out. Elijah's eyes turned to Khalid; confusion fell upon his face once more as he opened his hand. Emira slowly took the necklace; she glanced back numerous times as she walked to the truck. Elijah's eyes slowly moved between the pair until Emira disappeared into the passenger seat.

Leaning from the open door, Khalid pointed his finger towards the road in the direction they would be heading. Elijah looked and then nodded before climbing back into his small red car.

"What were you doing?" Khalid scolded Emira as he slammed the door. She sat quietly, looking at the coins on her necklace. "Emira, what were you trying to do?" Khalid asked again.

"Do you think he could see me?" Emira asked as she turned toward the big man. Her face contorted with emotion. "From the first moment, I sensed he could see me."

"I don't know." Khalid admitted, placing a hand on her shoulder to comfort her.

"Is he a vampire?" she asked. "I thought they couldn't see me, I mean, my light. That is what you said." Her voice was accusing.

"I'm not certain he was able to see you; maybe those coins reminded him of something," Khalid said as he pulled out of the gas station, watching carefully through his rearview mirror to make sure Elijah followed.

"Where did Ayda get these coins, anyway?" Emira asked as she fastened the necklace again.

"I'm not sure," Khalid admitted. "But don't worry, everything will be fine. I promise."

"How could everything be fine? He asked me *what* I was!" Emira screeched. Khalid just looked at her for a moment and kept driving.

## CHAPTER 71

A RRIVING AT THE *masjid*, Elijah pulled his car into an empty space two cars over from where Khalid had parked. The noise and vibration beneath him ceased when he twisted the key. The slight jerk from the braking car sent the air freshener dancing in circles around the rearview mirror. A subtle waft of freesia drifted gently against his face and filled his nostrils. As he opened the car door, he saw Khalid standing between him and the truck.

"Why is it you are here?" Khalid demanded. The tone of his voice had hardened. Elijah remained silent as he stared up at the man from the driver's seat of his car. His mind was still focused on the coins he had just seen and the girl who wore them. After several moments, Elijah stepped out of his car and shut the door behind him.

"What do you want with the girl?" Khalid asked; he seemed certain in his accusation. Elijah's perpetual glances towards Khalid's truck must have betrayed his burning compulsion.

"I need to talk to her." Elijah tried to step past the beast of a man, but Khalid quickly maneuvered to cut him off. Elijah lowered his head for a moment and closed his eyes; he took a deep breath, attempting to calm himself. "I just want to talk to her." Elijah forced the words between clenched teeth.

"First, you are going to talk to me." The big man pressed his fingertips against Elijah's chest and gently pushed him backwards. Elijah gave.

As his back pressed against the car behind him, Elijah retreated once more into his mind. Since leaving the station, he had been over and over what had just happened, trying to make some sense out of it.

"Now, tell me what you want," Khalid growled as he stepped forward. Elijah remained silent. "What do you want with Emira, and why are you here in our small town? Are you visiting someone?"

Khalid's questions jarred Elijah from his temporary trance. "Yes. I mean, no; I am just here to speak with the imam," he said, taking a deep breath to gather himself once more.

"I'm sorry, Elijah, but there is no one like that here. We work together to keep this place alive." The big man's voice held subtle hints of frustration; he seemed almost jaded. He furrowed his brow and rubbed his chin. "A few of us take turns making speeches and teaching lessons from the *Quran*; we rotate weekly," the big man continued.

Elijah wasn't surprised by their system of rotation; he had seen this many times. Many Islamic communities in the West, especially in the United States, were very small, and the members were often busy professionals. Still, they managed to maintain their Friday prayer services.

"You said a few of *us*, does that mean you are a part of the rotation?" he asked as he straightened up and reached to stroke the pendant hanging from his neck; this old habit still broke through sometimes when he was nervous.

"Of course," Khalid answered. His tone heightened with curiosity. "What exactly are you looking for, Elijah?"

Elijah appreciated the big man's candor. He tried his best to focus; he took a deep breath, but his mind remained fuzzy. He didn't feel like himself.

"I'm looking for someone. I heard he was here, three days ago," Elijah explained. "If you saw him you would remember; he stands out. He is a very large man, nearly your size." Elijah paused as he rubbed the bridge of his nose. Despite the vast amount of time Elijah had spent hunting his father and brother, this was not the conversation he wanted to be having right now; his mind was still focused on the girl.

"Are you unwell?" Khalid asked. "It looked as if you had some kind of breakdown back there."

"People are drawn to this man I seek for a reason I can't explain. He is extremely compelling," Elijah continued, disregarding Khalid's question. He had described Solomon so many times the words seemed to speak themselves.

"I remember him; yes, his presence demanded attention. He came to last Friday's prayer; his name is Solomon." Khalid hadn't been impressed. His voice was filled with disgust, his stone-like countenance permeated with contempt.

"What do you know of him? Do you know where I can find him?" Elijah asked. The revelation had drawn him back to his purpose; excitement burned through his palms. Elijah would finally come face to face with his betrayers, and this time he would bring an ending, for them all. In the wake of his vengeance, their world would come crashing down around them. His chest tightened with anticipation.

"I know nothing except he is not here today; he drives an older model black sedan." Khalid closed his eyes, as if he were searching his mind for more information.

"It's a Mercedes." A small but familiar voice piped up from inside the truck.

"Yes, a Mercedes," Khalid agreed. "What is your association with him?"

"I have none," Elijah said. His demeanor had noticeably changed. Thoughts of revenge had cleared his mind and focused it on the task at hand. "I am going to kill him," he said flatly, "and I am only seconds away from killing you if you don't get out of my way." Elijah clenched his teeth as he stepped forward and focused all of his attention on the big immortal standing between him and the answers he sought.

"Is that so?" Khalid cocked his head to the side to stretch the muscles in his neck. Since his days at war, Elijah had seen hundreds of vampires fall beneath him due to their ignorance of who and what he was.

"Yes, and if it wasn't for the girl I would have killed you already. I have killed your kind by the hundreds," Elijah admitted, tired of the back and forth. He closed his eyes and stretched his fingers as he straightened his jacket.

"What do you want with the girl?" Khalid demanded again.

Elijah watched the muscles in his neck tense and flare. Elijah considered just ripping through the big man, but decided against it; he would try once more to reason with him. He was close to finding his betrayers and needed to be sure his mind would stay clear of the angelic little creature hidden behind the dark tinted windows of Khalid's big truck. However, he knew the big man would need an explanation before that was possible.

Elijah was struck by a sudden trepidation when as he noticed Khalid's truck rolling backwards into the road. He could hear a vehicle racing towards them from the same direction they had just come. Forgetting discretion, Elijah quickly slipped past Khalid; as the big man spun around, Elijah leapt into the air and pushed against his chest with his left leg. Khalid flew backwards and slammed against the small car Elijah had acquired from long-term parking at the airport while Elijah rolled over the hood of the truck. He grabbed the door handle and jerked it open, halting the vehicle. The opening door pulled a gentle breeze, carrying the young girl's scent into his nose. The smell was a poison attempting to steal his soul.

"What are you doing?" Emira sounded startled and confused. Elijah was surprised to see the girl peering up at him from the driver's seat. Hidden by the tinted glass, she had crossed over the console and was now backing the truck out of the parking lot herself.

And the glow he'd seen had all but disappeared. Elijah suddenly noticed the subtle vibration in the door handle and listened to the quiet turning of the truck's engine. He was embarrassed his distractions had caused him to make such an obvious mistake, but even more, he was glad to see the girl was unharmed.

Emotions were twisting inside him into a tangled web as he watched the vehicle he had heard moments ago zoom by. The situation was very awkward. He found himself trying to act normal. It was like trying to walk for the first time; he had never tried to do it deliberately before and was failing miserably. Khalid was back on his feet and moving towards him. Elijah could see he wanted an explanation. They both did.

Elijah's thoughts suddenly turned back to the tiny young woman who had disrupted his single-minded purpose. He was furious. After his mother was murdered, he had tried hard to snuff out his sensitivity in an attempt to end the pain that plagued him. It hadn't worked. He was still blanketed with it. He could only purchase relief from the sensitivity by being ferocious.

Elijah's demeanor hardened; the hints of emotion in his face disappeared. He looked sharply at Khalid as his left hand clenched the open door; the metal bent beneath his fingers. Khalid stopped.

"Please," Khalid said. "Leave her alone; I will tell you whatever you want to know. Just let her go."

Suddenly, Elijah felt a soft warmth on the inside of his right hand as it rested against his leg. He turned back to the girl; as their eyes met, he could feel the tension lifting. The light that permeated her being had brightened once again. The expression on her face was no longer an accusation. There was now interest and empathy in her eyes as she slipped her hand deeper into his grasp.

"Thank you." Her tranquil voice comforted him, and the coins hanging around her neck transported Elijah back in time. A deep sentiment welled in his chest and the awkwardness of the situation completely melted away.

Elijah could feel his muscles loosen. The rage in his stomach was snuffed out like a flame and that strange euphoria from earlier overcame him once again. His body softened as his mind flooded with precious memories from his youth; the memories he was most often not able to explore.

\*

His mother's life had been an arduous one, but she had always managed to make time for Elijah and his brothers. She watched over them with great care. He remembered every delicate curve of her face as she sat on that old familiar stone and told the stories he grew to know by heart.

The skin on her hands was thick and coarse from doing far more than her share. He could see her fingers running across the twine and turning the needle as Malaki begged for just one more story.

\*

Elijah was brought back to the present by an implacable grip tightening around his arm. Khalid spun him around and pinned his back against the truck with one arm beneath his chin and the other across his chest.

The air about him suddenly turned cold once again as Elijah envisioned his mother's body wrapped tightly in that tattered old cloth. He thought about the huge stone now resting beside her grave, its only marker. The warm memories of his mother's soft voice and gentle touch were replaced by nightmarish visions of his mother's defiled and mutilated corpse lying bare on a cold stone floor. He could hear Malaki's shrill cries.

Fever was once again burning inside his chest. What would have been disconcerting to most people brought Elijah back home and filled him with composure; he was much more comfortable with hate than empathy. He was tired of the emotional rollercoaster ride he had been on since leaving the gas station. He opened his eyes to reveal two burning amber rings encircling his pupils.

"It's you." Khalid's eyes widened. Elijah took advantage of his surprise and pulled loose his right arm. Forcing Khalid's right elbow down from his chest, Elijah spun from beneath the big man's hold and backhanded him hard across the face.

"Yes." Elijah leaned back and slammed his right foot into Khalid's chest. "It is me!" His voice thundered across the empty lot as Khalid slammed against the truck.

"You're not a vampire." Khalid said, looking up at him.

"No. I'm something much worse." Elijah exclaimed. His jaw fell open as his tongue ran across his front teeth. Elijah could feel a faint smile break across his face; he seemed to thrive in the madness of war. Undone by the emotion from his encounter with the girl, Elijah became the monster he had cast off on Ayda's mountain.

Rushing forward, Elijah's left hand smashed against Khalid's throat, forcing his back to slide further down the side of the vehicle. Elijah's fist pounded against the side of his face again and again, despite Emira's desperate cries. Khalid's head snapped up suddenly and he caught Elijah's fist in his giant paw.

"I am, too," Khalid growled.

Elijah watched as the big man's eyes began to blaze beneath his dark brows like two fiery embers. He reached for the open door with his other hand, slamming it and forcing himself up in one motion. As he gained his footing, Khalid's fist rammed against Elijah's chest like a hammer and catapulted him backwards. Khalid continued forward with lightning speed; Elijah's feet were off of the ground by the time his back slammed into the brick wall of the *masjid*. Elijah didn't fight; the fiery red that was still blazing in the man's eyes mesmerized him, and brought back a flood of memories.

"Ayda." Elijah spoke slowly, as if in a trance. He didn't mean to say it; it just came out. Understanding eclipsed the big man's face once more and his eyes slowly dimmed to black. He stepped back and dropped Elijah to his feet.

"I know who you are, now," Khalid huffed. He seemed disturbed by the revelation as he bent over and rubbed his knees. "I understand it all now, why you are here, your brother, why you can see her light." The big man straightened up and looked back at the small girl sitting in the truck. "Ayda told me all about you, and how you left her on that mountain." His tone suddenly turned cold as he looked at Elijah; his stare nearly pierced him like a sword.

"So you are like her." Elijah rolled his shoulders forward and then tugged his jacket back into place. He closed his eyes; he could feel the heat dissipate from behind them. "You are not a vampire either."

"I should be... like her, I mean." Khalid forced a laugh.

"What do you mean?" Elijah asked.

"Nothing." Khalid waved his hand as if to dismiss his last

statement. "Yes, I am like her, and from what I hear, you are some kind of anomaly." Khalid narrowed his eyes.

"I am something." Elijah sighed, then glanced toward Emira. "What do you mean by 'her light?' What is it? What is she?" Elijah spoke fast. He was fascinated; he needed to know.

Khalid quickly hushed him, and then something entered Elijah's mind that changed everything.

His eyes suddenly widened. "You are like Ayda," he repeated, as if in a trance; he closed his eyes as thoughts tumbled through his mind. "That is why they are here, because of the parchment she stole from them at Baghdad."

Elijah's voice trailed off as he was stricken with fear for Ayda. Had his father come here after killing her?

Khalid narrowed his eyes; his stony geste was disturbed for just a moment and Elijah could almost feel his anger.

"She stole nothing." Khalid snapped, turning once more to the girl, as if he were guarding her from something, perhaps from Elijah.

"Did they kill her?" Elijah asked as he ran his fingers through his hair and began to pace. "Did they kill her? Are they here now because they got to her and she led them to you?" he shouted.

Khalid remained silent; he had regained his composure and now stared at Elijah through two black eyes that gave away nothing.

Elijah turned back toward Khalid; maddened by his silence, Elijah could feel heat creeping in behind his eyes and knew they were beginning to glow faintly. He stepped toward Khalid and looked up into the big man's dark eyes. He could see the certainty in them had faded. Elijah waited for him to answer. His impatience grew with every silent moment until heat surged through his body and the light of day filled his eyes. "Is she dead?" Elijah roared as he lifted the big man off the ground and pounded him against the brick wall.

"I don't know. I haven't been able to get in touch with her since they showed up," Khalid finally admitted as composure poured back into him. He had been left speechless by those uniquely yellowish eyes.

Elijah dropped him to his feet and swore with frustration. He knew if his father had killed Ayda, he would be irretrievably lost to the darkness continually nipping at his heels, the darkness that had once been his home.

"Here is my phone number. I will be at the motel we passed on the way in. Call if you see Solomon or any of his companions." After speaking, Elijah handed him a small scrap of paper with a phone number scribbled on one side.

"I will, if you leave now and forget about the girl." Although he was calmer, Khalid's walls had temporarily been shaken and he was much easier to read. His voice was full of hope, desperation even, that Elijah would comply.

"Ayda trusted me; now you need to trust me." Elijah paused for a moment and cleared his throat. "If she is alive, she is the only friend I have in this world; I need to know. Call me if you hear from her. Please." Elijah's concern for Ayda now exceeded his need to talk to the girl in the truck, but he didn't know what to do. He didn't even know if Ayda was alive, and if she was, he had no idea how to find her.

Confusion and uncertainty swamped him. Driven to learn *now* how to help Ayda, or whether she was even alive, he was finding it hard to force himself to leave. Also, the coins seemed like a clear link between Emira and Sara; he was reluctant to leave her alone before he could find out what she was and how she and Sara were connected. Also, Khalid and the girl were his only link to Ayda and to his brother.

Still, Elijah knew he would have to fight to stay, and Khalid seemed quite capable of protecting the girl for now. He believed

Khalid would call him, if only to keep him away, and he needed to blow off some steam anyway, so he decided to leave.

"What do you intend to do once you find them, your family?" Khalid asked. "Ayda told me what happened last time," he prodded, finally breaking Elijah's stare and looking down at the concrete.

"I'm going to kill them," Elijah growled. "I'm not the same person I was all those years ago." Gathering himself, he looked once more at the faint light shining through the window of Khalid's truck and then strode to his car.

# CHAPTER 72

ELIJAH HAD BEEN sitting in his hotel room for a few
hours, lowering the level of a bottle of Kentucky straight
bourbon whiskey; his thoughts were on Ayda as he paced. He
had to make sure she was alive and well. She had saved his life;
he owed her. He loved her.

Throughout the centuries, ever since he had descended
back into the world from that mountain in Japan, whenever he
drowned his thoughts and feelings with spirits, which was nearly
every day, he had brooded about his life. He thought of Sara,
and mourned her daily… but she was gone, and there was nothing he could do about it, so most of his thoughts and regrets
were about Ayda.

He wished he could start over, he could take back everything and rewind time to the last night he had seen her, when
he had left her magical form lying in that bed. In his fantasy, he
would make very different choices. He would give up his foolish
quest and stay with the woman he had grown to love so deeply.
He hated himself for leaving her.

Still, in the back of his mind he knew his dream of making different choices was just a fantasy. In the end, this is who

he was: his miserable purpose, and nothing more. His life was a woeful symphony, composed by only a few, but the ending would be his to write. There was no room for happiness here, and no time for a new composition.

The darkness was his and he would own it, but allowing fantasies of Ayda during his quiet moments kept him sane; they were the raft that kept him afloat when he no longer had the strength to swim in the dark waters of his soul. The thoughts and memories of what could have been were his only warmth when the dark nights got too cold for even a soul as black as his.

Elijah's spiraling misery was interrupted when he became aware a light tapping at the door had escalated to the most awful noise as someone now pounded incessantly from the other side. The noise grew with Elijah's impatience until he was forced to deal with it. Perhaps it was news of Solomon.

"What the hell do you wan—" he pulled up short as he was flooded with an awesome light. It was Emira, the girl from the gas station, standing awkwardly in the doorway. Definitely not Solomon, but he was pleased all the same.

"Come in," he said, as graciously as he could to make up for his rude greeting.

"Here." She shoved a Styrofoam container into his chest and marched past him.

"You came here to bring me a sandwich?" Elijah asked when he opened the container. "Is there news of Solomon?" His hopes were high; why else would she be here?

"Yes." The girl spoke quickly as she paced the floor. "No. I mean, yes to the sandwich, and no to Solomon. I thought you might be hungry." She said.

"Th…" Elijah opened his mouth to speak but was quickly cut off.

"Are you going to shut the door, or are you encouraging me to leave?"

Elijah had been so startled by this entire encounter and hadn't realized he was still leaning against the open door holding the Styrofoam container.

"Of course not," he said as he carefully closed the door.

"My name is Emira, by the way. We weren't introduced earlier." She walked to the bed and sat down.

"Yes, your big friend made sure of that." Elijah's words came out with a croak; he was still entranced by the girl's aura. "But you told me at the gas station."

"I suppose I did." The girl paused for a moment. "Why are you so interested in my coins?" she asked, as she clutched her necklace.

Elijah had no idea what to say. He considered unloading the truth in its entirety, but thought it might scare her away. So many idiotically romantic notions had crossed his mind. He even considered perhaps this girl was Sara's reincarnation, but had quickly dismissed the idea. Although he found it silly and amusing—he wasn't the type to believe in signs and fanciful notions—he couldn't completely suppress the idea the universe, in its infinite wisdom, had given Sara a glimpse of his future, and now the universe was trying to speak to him. But he didn't know exactly what it was trying to say.

"I have seen coins like those before," he said finally. "I actually used to have some." Elijah set the open Styrofoam container on the table. The sweet smell of mayonnaise filled his senses as he unwrapped the chicken salad sandwich and took a bite.

"That's the only reason you can come up with?" Emira asked, as she narrowed her eyes and lowered her chin.

"Yes, well, they also remind me of someone I knew a long time ago." He didn't want to lie, but thought it best not to be too forthcoming.

"Khalid's sister?" she suggested. "She is the one who gave them to me."

"That man has a sister, a real one? I would hate to meet her," Elijah chuckled. "No, her name was Sara." Elijah smiled as he thought of her, of her contagious joy and delight in life. Elijah closed his eyes for just a moment. He realized his eyelashes must have been a bit wet because he could feel them clinging together briefly as he opened his eyes again. "It was a long time ago." He ducked his head slightly and wiped his eyes before pouring another glass of bourbon, tossing it down, and then pouring another.

Suddenly, Elijah felt something soft brush against his hand; he looked down to see Emira attempting to take the glass away from him. He held on to it for a moment, but gave in after seeing the empathy pooling into her eyes. After placing his glass on the desk, the girl took his hand and gently pulled him over to the bed. His nostalgia, along with the whiskey, was making his compulsive attraction to her much harder to resist.

She placed her other hand on top of his as he sat beside her. Her touch seemed to cleanse his soul and free him from the pit of despair into which he had fallen so long ago.

"What are you?" he asked. His eyes began to close; he couldn't stop it, he didn't want to stop it. "What is that light?" Elijah's eyes were completely closed and his head was gently resting against Emira's shoulder. "What do you want from me?" he asked after a moment of silent relaxation. His voice trailed off as feelings of beauty and wonder permeated his entire being.

"Hey! Wake up." Elijah heard Emira's voice and then a loud clapping sound that snapped him back into reality. He quickly stood up and looked down at her in confusion.

"I wasn't asleep; I don't sleep." He spoke sharply.

"Well, I think you've had a bit too much to drink then, because you were asking me some really weird questions." she accused. She looked confused.

"No, alcohol doesn't do that to me," he protested.

"Well." She paused.

Elijah could tell she was disappointed; she had clearly been hoping for something more, he didn't know what.

"Tell me what happened today, outside of the *masjid*. You nearly yanked the door off my uncle's truck." Her tone was accusing.

"I'm sorry, I just thought you needed me," Elijah confessed unwillingly. It was almost as if he *was* drunk, or delirious; he hadn't been able to stop the words that emerged. In one sentence he had given away more about himself than he ever meant to. "I mean, I thought you were in trouble." Elijah was trying, but couldn't find a way out of this lapse in guise. "I thought the truck was rolling into the road, and I could hear an oncoming car. I didn't realize you were driving."

"I see. You do that a lot, that kind of crazy, overprotective kind of thing?" Emira asked. She seemed nervous and uncomfortable as she rose to her feet and began pacing.

Elijah understood then she wasn't concerned with how he had stopped the truck, but why. He had tried to save her from an imagined danger and she wanted to know why. That was surprising, and a relief.

"I'm always eager to help," he lied, in an attempt to discourage her from digging any further.

"Okay," Emira spoke slowly. "You *are* a bit odd, aren't you?"

Elijah was somewhat offended; he had never been seen as odd before. At least no one had ever told him he was, but now he was definitely feeling a bit odd.

"I suppose so," he replied. He didn't understand why he felt awkward. He had been with thousands of women over the years, with never a hint of awkwardness.

But then he had never wanted to actually talk to those women, nor had he cared for an instant about their feelings or what they thought of him... at least not until he knew them well enough to actually have feelings for them. He had grown up with Sara, and he had bartered with an entire fortress for Ayda; he wished it were still that simple. "It's fine for you to talk, but I'm not the one who glows," he teased.

"What? You are definitely an odd one," she said, seeming to withdraw a bit.

"Why are you toying with me?" he asked as he walked back to the desk and lifted the glass of bourbon he had poured earlier. "Why won't you two just tell me the truth?" he said before downing the whiskey and turning to face her. "What *are* you?" he shouted.

The girl's mouth fell open and she stood up. Elijah could see she was dismayed and offended.

"I'm so sorry; I didn't mean to shout. This has been a very upsetting day; please stay." Elijah didn't know what to do, if she did know, she was hiding it well. What reason would Khalid have for keeping this from her?

"I'm not like him, if that's what you mean. And I don't mean to be secretive, but vampires aren't supposed to be able to see my light." She relented a bit and sat back down on the bed.

"I'm not vampire!" Elijah's tone was accusing.

"I know, I mean, I figured that, but what does that make you?" Suddenly, Elijah could hear something vibrating in Emira's pocket, but she ignored it.

"Are you going to answer that?" Elijah asked; he was glad for the distraction.

"No, it's just my uncle Kal. I'm supposed to be at home; if he knew I was here he would kill me, and then he would kill you," she said sheepishly.

"I don't know about you, but I'm not at all easy to kill. Believe me; people have been trying for a long time." Elijah poured some more bourbon. Frustration and curiosity consumed him; he was drawn to this girl and she had an effect on him he could not deny. No matter what caused this distraction, that made her dangerous, and he needed Khalid's cooperation; he couldn't risk making an enemy out of him now.

"I have lived with Khalid for ten years," Emira continued. "He is a great man, but he is stubborn and overprotective." The girl looked over at him as if she wanted Elijah to empathize.

"Your uncle, or brother, or whatever he is, has been around for a long time, as have I. You seem to have lived a happy, sheltered life; this safe little world he has created for you is a blessing, even if it is a lie. There are things out there you have only seen in your nightmares and on your television screen. You would do well to heed his advice and go home." Elijah deliberately spoke harshly, disguising any hints of concern for the girl with blatant rudeness. It was for the best, at least for now, until he could figure out what Khalid was concealing from him about her light, and why.

"You don't know me; I have seen more than you know." Emira's eyes strayed from his face; she seemed to be lost in her own memories. "Khalid's sister gave me these coins almost ten years ago; that is when she found me." Emira rubbed one of the coins dangling from the chain around her neck. "She is the reason I started collecting these old things to begin with." She gazed at Elijah for a few seconds, searching his expressionless face for answers.

Elijah imagined she was looking for the man whose heart and body had leapt into action when he believed she was in danger. He was in there, but Elijah had shoved him back down out of sight, so deep she could never find him.

"So you and Khalid are not actually related?" Elijah asked as he poured more bourbon and quickly threw it back.

"No, he just calls me Sis." She lingered awkwardly for a moment, as if she were waiting for him to become someone else, as if she refused to believe she was wrong about him.

"I think you should get home." Elijah spoke without even turning back to face her.

He could feel her eyes on his back as she paused for a moment before turning and walking to the door without another word.

Elijah was anxious and uncomfortable. He didn't want her to leave disappointed. He didn't want her to leave at all. He wanted to tell her everything; he wanted to know about her and the big man who called her *Sis*, but he couldn't bring himself to stop her. Regret sank in deep as he heard the door slam behind her.

# CHAPTER 73

EMIRA WALKED BRISKLY along the catwalk outside of the motel room. Her cheeks burned with embarrassment. Why had she come? Why did she think a man like Elijah would be interested in her? What was wrong with him? He made her feel elated, warm and safe one minute, and the next he seemed explicably cold.

Walking down the steps on the outside of the motel, she noticed two dark figures standing at the bottom, on the opposite side of the handrail to her right. It seemed strange, but she was too frazzled to be cautious and decided to walk past. Unfortunately, the hairs on her neck were tingling by the time she reached the last step.

The men who had been standing to the side of the rail suddenly spun round and blocked her passage. The man on her left was tall and thin. The other one was thicker, more muscular-looking. Both men smelled like garlic and stale cigarette smoke, and they were standing entirely too close. Emira's pulse raced; these men meant her harm!

"I'm sorry, me dear, but we didn't catch yer name." The thin man spoke with a thick accent. Both were cloaked in the shadow of the overhanging catwalk, but she could see the curves of the thin man's face as the shadows danced around it.

The flickering light of a hanging lamppost lit the ridge of his long, thin nose as it came to a sharp point. His cheekbones were high and obtrusive, but gave way to large sinkholes just beneath them on both sides. He looked almost malnourished, but his manner showed he wasn't.

The man to his left said nothing. Next to his shoe, a dull red ember took its last breath, turning bright red before vanishing into the darkness like a collapsing star. She took a step backwards, up the bottom step. She considered running back to Elijah's room, but another man was at her back before she had the chance.

"Don't worry, we just want to talk." The voice coming over her shoulder from the next step up wasn't a bit convincing. All of her frustration turned to terror as it became clear she was trapped. She wanted nothing more than to see Elijah's face appear at the balcony. She tried to scream for him, but her throat was frozen with fear. Realizing she had stopped breathing, she forced her lungs to expand and a sharp sting pinged in her chest.

"My name is Emira. I just want to go to my car." She was barely able to force the words out. Her voice was vibrating with fear, and the trio started to close in like a pack of dogs.

Relief rushed over her when a figure appeared behind the two men in front of her. His demeanor was menacing. The hunters had become the hunted. As the two men in front of Emira turned to meet Elijah's exacting gaze, Emira darted between them. She squeezed Elijah's left bicep hard and tucked herself safely behind him—this stranger who was once again coming to her rescue. Satisfaction filled her. These assholes were about to get what they deserved.

Elijah glared balefully at the three men. Men who would dare attempt to extinguish a light they couldn't even see. They meant nothing; he would be doing the world a favor to rid it of these vermin. He stepped forward with malicious purpose. The three men recoiled, as if they could sense the death awaiting them at Elijah's hands, their own dire fates reflecting back at them in his eyes.

Emira watched the veins pulsing in Elijah's neck; she could feel his muscles tighten as his body moved with deadly purpose. Unexpectedly, her tender nature burst through her heightened emotions. She tugged at his arm with all her might, but it was like holding onto a huge stone hurled across the expanse of space.

She could see terror and bewilderment in the men's faces as he lunged forward. Her feet skidded across the concrete and then came off the ground. The three men turned to run, but didn't have a chance. Their deaths approached with blinding speed.

"Nooo!" Elijah heard a loud scream. It was close. It was impossibly close! The sound startled him from his lethal focus. He suddenly noticed a pressure release from around his arm. It was Emira's hands, slipping away as he jerked forward. She was falling hard toward the concrete steps.

Elijah's focus shifted immediately. The three men disappeared from his mind along with everything else. All the hate that burned inside him evaporated as compassion and deep concern took its place. In this moment, Emira was all that mattered.

Mustering enough composure to find a solution, he relaxed and turned his rigid, lunging body to dead weight. Hurtling through the air, he rotated and pulled her towards him, holding her close. His left hand cupped the back of her head, pushing her forehead firmly to his chest. His right arm, wrapped tightly around her waist, held her tiny frame steadily in place and out of harm's way.

A deep sense of relief overtook him as his back and head smashed against the edges of the concrete steps; he couldn't help but think of holding Sara in that same position when he fell from the overturned tree long ago. The pain of the impact was searing. A large chunk of the step fell behind him as he lifted his head to check on Emira. She looked shocked and frightened, but she was fine. A sense of composure slowly crept into her face.

"Oh, my God, are you all right?" Tears welled and soon came rolling down her pale cheeks. Her aura of light had all but disappeared.

"I'm fine; everything is fine." He wiped the tears from her face. "I promise," he said. The tears stopped and color flooded back into her face; her light slowly began to expand once again. Bringing her to her feet, Elijah knew he had a lot to explain. He expected a barrage of questions, but got only one.

"Are they gone?"

Elijah was silent for a moment, unsure of what she meant.

"I think so," he said after a moment of consideration, only then recalling the men whose lives Emira had just saved. "I'm sorry," he said, wandering aimlessly.

"Why? You just saved my life." She meant it, too. Elijah could see it in her face.

"I also almost killed you; I should have better control of my emotions." He spoke quietly as he raised his eyes and met her gaze. "I have spent hundreds of years living in the void, the space between caring and conviction. Your coins and light have shaken me to my core. I'm sorry. I was so angry. If I hadn't heard you, you might have died." The hate, which had so quickly evaporated, was finding its way back into Elijah's soul as he thought of how easily he had just lost control.

*Ayda would be disappointed,* he thought. His body hardened noticeably as frustration flooded him.

"But you did, and you saved me." Unbelievably, considering what he'd almost done, she was actually trying to comfort him… even though she was still afraid. Elijah could feel it. She seemed to fear losing him, as he feared losing himself, to the sea of grief and hate that seemed to overtake him so easily.

Emira pressed the side of her face against his chest and grabbed him hard around the waist. His body warmed with emotion; she somehow melted away the ice that grew so quickly around his heart.

"Will you tell me about her, the coins, the girl who obviously meant so much to you?" she asked in a whisper.

"AHHHHH!"

"What was that?" Emira was startled by a loud scream, but what came next was even more alarming. The sound was horribly biblical. They heard the crushing of bones, the ripping of flesh and the gnashing of teeth. The wet noises of raw flesh being gobbled. Elijah grabbed Emira by the arm and yanked her behind him.

"The noise came from the other side of the motel." Elijah's voice was steady; his composure seemed to comfort the girl, but she maintained her tenacious grip on his arm. He could feel every tiny fingernail nearly piercing his skin. He didn't mind it. Elijah liked having her close. If she couldn't be a million miles away from whatever caused that bloodcurdling sound—then she needed to be as close to him as possible.

"I'll tell you about her, but we need to get back to the room first." He hurried her up the stairs and was on her heels all the way to the room, then closed the door behind him as they entered the room and latched the security chain.

"Now, what would you like to know?" Elijah sat down on one of the beds and leaned forward with his elbows on his knees.

"Well, how did you meet her?" Emira asked brightly, like a child awaiting a bedtime story. Elijah thought about it for a while, about how much bullshit he should mix in with the truth. He wondered how much she knew about all this, about the man she called her uncle. She obviously knew about vampires, and he was certain she couldn't have missed the display put on by him and Khalid at the *masjid*.

"How long have you known Khalid?" Elijah finally asked, after a long silence.

"If you're asking me if I know he is special, that he has been around for a very, very long time, then the answer is yes. He took me in when I was young; he has kind of been like a father to me since I lost mine."

Elijah watched the vibrant eagerness drain from her face as she plopped down on the bed across from him and crossed her legs.

Elijah found himself speechless yet again. Humans' awareness of immortals had dropped dramatically since the Middle Ages, so he wasn't used to speaking openly with them. Still, this girl clearly wasn't a mere human.

"He told me about you as well. He wants me to stay away from you, obviously." She propped her hands on the bed behind her and leaned back.

"I'm not a vampire," Elijah repeated.

"I didn't say you were, but you're not like Kal either, are you?"

The girl looked up at him; her dark eyes were once again filled with excitement. She was taken with him, even fascinated. He could see it all over her face and, despite any meaning that might be in those coins, he had to snuff it out. He couldn't deny she intrigued him; she plagued his mind with a desire he hadn't known since lifetimes past, but he knew he could only bring her pain.

"So, your true curiosities surface once again?" Elijah rose from the bed. This time there was no distraction, no way to change the subject. "I may not have sharp claws or fangs, but I am far worse than you could imagine, far more dangerous than any vampire." He walked to the table and poured another bourbon. "I have slain vampires by the thousands. I have slaugh-tered entire towns, towns filled with innocents, filled with humans. I have peered into the eyes of a prophet, a child, and snapped her neck without flinching." Elijah drank the bourbon and took a step towards his tormentor.

"You want to know how I met Sara? First let me tell you how I met the only other woman who ever cared for me." He didn't give the girl in front of him time to respond. "I bought her from the Mongolian Empire. I traded my best friend and my people." Elijah took another step forward.

"You traded all that just for a girl?" Emira asked. Her eyes were wide with awe, as if he had made some sweeping romantic gesture with his bartering.

"No, she was just something the Khan threw in for good measure," he answered. He took another step forward and was now standing directly in front of her. The sweet fragrances of her skin lotion and shampooed hair washed over him as he leaned over her and placed his hand on the bed behind her. "I am the worst kind of devil you could imagine, worse than you can pos-sibly imagine, in fact, and Khalid is right. You need to stay away from me."

Emira's eyes were like two black holes compelling him for-ward; his face was just inches from hers now. He hated what he was doing, but he had to. No matter how much he wanted her, no matter how she possessed his mind, and no matter why she had those coins, he couldn't allow her into his life, not if he cared even a little. His life was too dangerous. He was too dan-gerous; he chased after death, and the passenger seat on that ride was no place for a young, vulnerable woman. He would tuck her away as another fantasy, another notion of what might have been.

She slid backwards on the bed, allowing herself room to breathe, but Elijah crawled forward until he was once again uncomfortably close. She tried to move further back, but her back hit the wall. Elijah heard her swallow hard as he moved closer.

"What did you see when you peered into the little girl's eyes?" she asked. She was trying to hide her fear, but her voice was shaky and her lip was trembling.

"I saw the devil... my own reflection," he said. His mind went back to that moment as it had so many times before. In that child's eyes, he had seen his future; he had seen who he would become. He had seen his father. Hassan had been right; he had lost his soul that night.

"What do you see when you look into mine?" Emira's voice brought him back. He stared into her eyes for another few moments.

"I see nothing." He lied; her eyes betrayed her secret. They were enamored with him; he hadn't yet filled them with dis-appointment as he had Ayda's. This girl saw goodness in him. But then she hadn't known him long enough to know better, and although it scared him, it also moved him in other ways. It pushed him out of his comfort zone. Her youth and innocence gave her the eyes to see what others could not, or perhaps what wasn't even there.

Either way, she was somehow hard-wired to Elijah's emo-tions. They surged like rolling hills every time she was near. She forced him to feel. She broke through the guise of apathy, which was the only dam holding back an ocean of feelings he couldn't handle. Elijah climbed off the bed and walked to the table where he threw back another shot of bourbon.

"I don't believe you," she exclaimed as she scooted back to the edge of the bed. "You obviously cared deeply for someone once," she said as she tucked her hair behind her ear.

"That was a long time ago." Elijah closed his eyes. "You can come to care for anything, even a slave, if it's around long enough." Elijah's thoughts turned to Ayda. "Khalid was right; you shouldn't be here," he repeated as he turned around and walked back towards his bed.

"If you don't want me to stay, then just tell me why you are here. Tell me what happened between you and Khalid earlier; tell me the truth, and I'll leave."

Elijah turned around to see her expression dull; he had disappointed her again. He was also disappointed, but it wouldn't be good for either of them if she stayed.

BOOM! They both jumped and looked towards the door. BOOM! Another blow to the door, even louder this time.

Elijah looked at Emira; she was trembling. He was suddenly stricken with anger, even rage. Had this girl not been through enough? This was the second time tonight she had been filled with fear, and with good reason.

"Emira, look at me." Elijah walked over to her bed and knelt down and leaned in close. "You are going to be all right. I promise; there is a reason I have been alive for so long." Elijah tried to comfort her; he wanted to protect her. He rubbed his thumb across her face and then rose and walked towards the window.

"Can you say the same about your friends?" she asked with shaky bravado. Elijah looked back at her. The question had caught him off guard. He thought about Sara and Hassan, and how he had been unable to save either of them.

"No, but I never had many friends, either," he answered as he opened the shades a bit to look out the window. He couldn't see anything from there. "Looks like they gave up and left," he said in a low voice.

"Do you think it was the men from before?" She had crawled to the back of the bed.

"Sure, probably," he said. He didn't want her to be afraid, but he knew those men wouldn't have come back. This was someone, or some*thing*, else. "Stay in the room; I'll be right back," he instructed as he walked to the door.

"No! Please, stay with me." She pleaded, beckoning for him to come to her.

"Emira, I will not let anything bad happen to you." He walked back to the bed. "I promise you, whatever is out there, no matter how bad, how dangerous, vicious, or dark, I am much worse." Heat flooded his eye sockets and rushed through his body; he could tell the spark of amber that lit them gave her comfort.

"You promise?" she asked as she curled up against the wall.

"I do." Elijah watched as she nodded and most of the fear seemed to leave her eyes. Her trust in him was comforting, even though it was misplaced. "Here." He looked from her face to his wrist and then back to her face.

"I'm going to let you borrow this." He flipped the leather loop on his bracelet over the knot and it fell into his hand. "I don't have much. This is one of the single most important things I own; it means more to me than you could possibly imagine. Give me your hand." Emira surrendered her arm to his gentle touch.

"BOOM!" This time the knock rattled the door hard; it almost broke from its hinges. Elijah saw Emira shaking and heard her heart begin to pound beneath her chest, so he didn't even look back.

"Look at me," he said calmly. She looked up as Elijah looped the bracelet around her wrist and then clasped her hand inside his. "If I lose you, then I lose this, and I am not losing this, not tonight." He let go of her hand; the bracelet was so big she had to hold it to keep it from falling off.

"Stay right here. I'll be back," he assured her. She nodded and Elijah turned back to the door. "Lock the door behind me," he whispered.

## CHAPTER 74

ELIJAH STEPPED OUT onto the catwalk and heard the chain rattle from inside as Emira locked the door behind him.

"What a heroic display, Brother!" A deep voice heralded from beneath the catwalk. Elijah's entire body shivered and his pulse quickened. A second later, his entire body was burning from the inside out.

*Solomon!* It had been nearly a millennium since Elijah had heard his voice, but he recognized his brother immediately.

"I nearly swooned when you whisked her up in your arms. You've made quite a mess of the steps, though," Solomon paused his falsely jocular commentary. Elijah remained silent; he could hear a slight chuckle from below. "But don't worry, Brother; I took care of the nasty lot of them. Scum like that shouldn't be allowed to roam the Earth, not with such precious and helpless creatures about."

This was the moment Elijah had been waiting for! His body went rigid, nearly every muscle contracted at once.

"Are you going to look at me Brother? Please don't be rude." Solomon's voice sounded the same, but he spoke differently.

Elijah had never before heard him sound cold and condescending. He wanted so much to rip out his brother's throat, but even more, Elijah needed an explanation. Deep down, he still held out hope his brother had a reason for what he had done all those years ago.

Nine-hundred-year-old memories flooded him and rocked Elijah from his momentary petrification. His body's temperature continued to rise with anticipation, and he could feel his bones solidify and expand. He had dreamed of this moment a million times.

"I'm going to hurt much more than your feelings," Elijah growled as he vaulted over the balcony and landed directly in front of Solomon. His right hand clenched tightly around his big brother's muscular neck, and he felt amber fire burn bright in his eyes.

Fresh blood was smeared at the corner of Solomon's mouth and he smelled of death, but he didn't struggle; he wasn't afraid. Elijah wasn't surprised by his brother's lack of fear, but by the warmth eclipsing his tired face.

"That is not very courteous, Brother. Now, embrace me," Solomon demanded.

The thought sickened Elijah. He was appalled at Solomon's audacity, that he would speak to him as if they were anything but enemies, as if they were still brothers.

"Brother." Solomon spoke softly as he reached his hand slowly towards Elijah's face. There was nothing menacing about his gesture, but Elijah quickly knocked his hand away—this creature was no longer his brother.

"I thought you were dead. All this time Elijah, I thought you were dead!" Solomon's expression was now jubilant.

Elijah was confused, but didn't waver. "You thought Father killed me when he nailed me to that ship? Everyone seems to forget how difficult it is to kill me." Elijah could feel his fingers tightening around Solomon's throat.

"No, Brother. I know nothing of that; I would never harm you." Solomon whispered; he seemed offended and confused.

Elijah could hear the abhorrence in his voice, but he didn't believe him, not after what he had witnessed.

"But I did see Father rip your head from your shoulders," Solomon continued.

His apparent sincerity piqued Elijah's curiosity for a moment, but he quickly brushed it aside. Solomon couldn't be trusted; he would probably say anything at this point, with his life being held firmly in Elijah's lethal grip.

Elijah's confusion disappeared and his purpose became clear; he was finally going to finish what he had set out to do all those years ago. His strong hand clenched even tighter. Solomon remained still; he seemed to welcome death at the hands of his brother.

Then Solomon stirred briefly. "Mal..a..ki," he gagged out in spite of Elijah's viselike grip.

Hearing Solomon say his little brother's name infuriated Elijah; it inflamed his already turbulent spirit and he started to pull back his arm as his fingers sank deeper into Solomon's neck.

"Malaki is still alive!" Solomon managed to croak the words out just moments before he would have lost his throat.

Startled, Elijah loosened his grip. "What do you mean? How? I saw Father break his neck. I know he wasn't part of yours and father's twisted betrayal." Elijah stepped back as confusion clouded his mind and his eyes cooled, dimming to their normal dark brown.

"Mine and Father's?" Solomon sounded shocked and offended. "What exactly do you remember of that night?" Solomon asked; his tone was accusing.

"I remember enough!" Elijah exclaimed. "I remember

Malaki screaming. I remember Mother's body, broken and bloody on the floor. And I remember you, Solomon, big brother. I remember you helping Father. I remember you striking my head with that log." Elijah was once again smoldering with the anticipation of revenge. "I saw Malaki die with my own eyes. I saw Father snap his neck just before you blindsided me." Elijah's face was burning; he was bitter and enraged.

"And I saw you die that night also, but here you are. Father was already a vampire when he snapped Malaki's neck; do you not remember him biting Mali first?" Solomon asked. "Malaki is alive."

Solomon sounded sincere, but he always had. Elijah found himself wanting to believe his big brother, but, after all he had seen, there was only one way he could be sure.

"Bring him to me," Elijah demanded, staring fiercely at Solomon.

"I can't," Solomon asserted as he shrugged his shoulders and raised his hands in the air.

"Liar! If he were still alive, you would have some proof!" Elijah shouted.

"I can't bring him to you because I don't know where he is. Father hid him from me all those years ago, but he has promised me if I help him, he will return Malaki alive. That is the reason for everything I have done, every wrong step I have taken, and every time I have stood by and allowed the most terrible things to transpire. It is also the reason I stopped you from attacking Father. I believed Father was the only one who could have brought Malaki back to life. I didn't know the bite itself would have restored him." Solomon stepped closer to his brother as he begged for acceptance.

Elijah backed away instinctively, but he was torn. If his brother was telling the truth, then Elijah had the explanation he had sought. He could finally make sense of Solomon's actions and forgive him. He wanted to believe his brother, but it wasn't easy to give up on a millennium-old desire for vengeance. It wasn't easy to trust him again, especially after Elijah had seen Malaki die with his own eyes.

"You are a much greater fool than I remember if you believe that nonsense, or if you think I am willing to. Malaki is dead. Some people may be harder to kill, but the dead stay dead, there is no coming back from that," Elijah bellowed.

"Are you serious, Brother? In nearly nine hundred years of killing our kind, you have never watched someone turn?" Solomon asked; confusion suffused his face. "They usually die first."

Elijah's thoughts immediately turned to Sara. She died before coming back as a vampire. And Hassan, the same thing had nearly happened to him. Perhaps his brother was telling the truth. Perhaps Malaki *was* alive. If being a vampire could be called living, because if what Solomon described was true, then Malaki must be one of the creatures Elijah had hunted all his life.

Elijah did recall now that William bit him first, but he thought William had killed him before giving the boy a chance to turn. Hope suddenly bloomed in his chest. He looked up to see Emira hanging over the rail of the catwalk listening to every word. She looked disgusted.

"I have never fed on the living. I am not vampire," Elijah said.

"I know, Brother; our father has told me. But if you are not animated by blood, then what?" Solomon asked.

"I do not know how or why I am, but I do know you and I are very different. Perhaps hate is what fuels me and keeps me young. Perhaps when retribution and punishment have dealt their hands, I will fade away with the light of that day." Elijah spoke boldly; the words resonated from the depths of whatever bit of soul he had left, and he could see Solomon understood, however well he could.

"I am deeply sorry for the mistakes I have made that hurt you, but Father will kill Malaki if I don't obey him. I have never known what else to do. I can't just let Malaki die; watching Father kill you was more than enough to break me," Solomon admitted.

For the first time, Elijah began to sympathize with his brother. What Solomon described made more sense than anything else Elijah had considered.

Elijah looked up and saw Emira leaning over the rail. "Go back inside," he mouthed, but she just shook her head.

"Since that day," Solomon continued, "I have been biding my time. I have killed thousands of men over the years, draining them of their blood to stay young and strong. I have done far too much evil for no good to ever come of it. So I will continue doing whatever I must do to get Malaki back." His tone was changing. He no longer sounded apologetic; he was speaking as if this revelation should somehow vindicate him.

"And we're close, Elijah. Since he turned me, and led me to the creature who made me into this," Solomon lit up his eyes to emphasize his point; he too was a vampire lord, "Father has been looking for something, and he has charged me with helping him. He has promised me, when this object is in his hands, Malaki will be freed."

Solomon smiled as though he had made a conclusive point. "This has been a long, hard road, but we can finally have our family back, Elijah. Father has traced whatever he is looking for right to this area. There is a man here with connections to it. He claims to be simply a scholar of sorts, but father believes him to be much more. He is part of an order charged with protecting this secret, these tablets, or whatever they are, for hundreds of years, if not more. The man's name is Khalid Gondal. He hasn't given us anything yet, but he will." Solomon's voice resounded with enthusiasm. Excitement radiated from his smile, fueled by an obvious belief he was on the verge of finding Malaki, but his words filled Elijah with foreboding.

"Please, help us. Help me to save our brother. We will take what we need from this man, and then we can have our family back," Solomon implored.

"And what about Mother? Will you raise her from the grave where I placed her, repair her body, and fill her with life?" Amber lightning bolts seared through his eyes.

Solomon lowered his head as he closed his eyes. "I'm sorry Elijah, but I swear to you, I had nothing to do with that."

Elijah didn't know what to do. He wanted what was left of his family back. He wanted to trust Solomon and to save Malaki, but not at such a cost.

Ayda had warned him of the dangers of letting his father find whatever this thing was. Regardless of Solomon's reasons for helping their father, William was evil. Elijah knew his father could not be trusted. They needed to discover a different way to rescue Malaki.

# CHAPTER 75

ELIJAH GLANCED UP once more to see Emira still standing on the catwalk. She had heard his brother's plans for Khalid and his appeal for Elijah's help. She looked desperate; her light was gone and her dark eyes were pleading with him, as if he was her only hope.

Elijah stood silent for a long time, taking it all in, doing his best to carefully weigh his brother's words.

"I hear you, Brother. You were weak and you made bad choices, but those choices were your own. I can't allow your choices to hurt another person whom I care about." He looked up at Emira and she seemed consoled.

Elijah didn't understand how this girl who barely knew him could put so much faith in his decency and his abilities. Elijah couldn't understand the confidence she placed in him, but it strengthened him all the same.

"Who you care about!" Solomon exclaimed. "You don't even know him." He stated.

"You are right, but I do know people who care about him." Elijah's eyes shifted towards Emira and then back to his brother. "Besides, we can't trust Father's word. It is too dangerous to let him get his hands on this parchment. There has to be another way," Elijah insisted.

"No, there is not. Father is too strong already." Solomon's enthusiasm dimmed. "You would put these people before your own family?" His question was an accusation.

"That is not what I'm doing. Listen to me Solomon. I believe you, but this will not bring Malaki back. Father will not give up his hold over you, but, if we work together, we can defeat him and save Malaki." Elijah's pulse was racing once again with anticipation. He hoped his brother would recognize his fool's errand and join with him.

"Please reconsider, Brother," Solomon growled. "Father doesn't give second chances," he said ominously. Elijah could see him growing angry as his eyes began to flicker with sparks of icy blue. He wasn't going to come around, at least not yet.

"Elijah!" It was Emira's voice and it sounded like she was in pain. He lost all thoughts of Solomon as he wheeled around to see the horror before him. His father was holding Emira over the rail of the catwalk by the back of the neck. She was clawing at his hand as she screamed.

Elijah's chest tightened and he was stricken with terror. He tried to run to her but was stopped cold by his brother's tight grip around the neck and abdomen.

"I'm sorry, but I warned you, Brother. I will do whatever I must, no matter how unspeakable, to save Malaki," Solomon whispered.

"Make a move and she's dead." His father's voice echoed down from above, monotone and completely devoid of emotion.

"I still don't know how I'm alive Father, but I now know why. I know my purpose, and it will end with you." Elijah's voice rumbled from behind clenched teeth.

"Perhaps it will end with me, but not in the way you would like." His tone was patronizing. "We have seen how this ends more than once, Elijah. You are only alive because I have allowed it. So listen carefully. I will not allow your petty lust for vengeance to get in the way of what I mean to achieve. For your brother's sake, I will leave you be. But you must leave this place immediately. If I find you anywhere near here after tonight I will kill you and the girl." William looked at the frail creature he was holding suspended over a deep drop. "Come, Solomon. Leave him," William commanded.

The rigid grip around Elijah's neck released and was gone as the two escaped into the darkness. He wanted to go after them, but his intent was shattered by Emira's screams. As he raced to stop her fall, all thoughts of his father and the revenge that could be his withered and died.

He dashed across the parking lot and made it just in time to feel her small frame land against his outstretched arms. She was safe, and although he didn't have his revenge, she still had her life. He could feel it beating strong and fast within her chest. Looking down upon her beautiful face and feeling her soft skin pressed against his, he was happy with the choice he had made.

He stared into her eyes for so long, he thought he might never let her go, and her soft eyes made him think she might be glad of it. Finally, he gently placed her on her feet and looked off into the darkness where his brother and father seemed to have vanished.

Emira looked at his eager gaze and her heart clenched with sorrow. She had heard most of Elijah's conversation with Solomon and understood him much better now—his rage, his passion—but more than anything, she understood his pain and his need for vengeance.

"I'm sorry," she whispered.

"For what?" Elijah continued to stare off into the vastness of the night.

"For coming between you and your revenge. If you hadn't

been worried about me, you could have gone after them," she said, her voice almost a whimper. Elijah turned to face her. He was completely surprised by her demeanor and tone of voice. She really was sorry... not afraid, and not judgmental, but sorry.

*What has happened to this girl, that she understands the value of vengeance?* The thought made his heart ache, and he hoped, for once, his instinct was wrong.

"Don't feel bad." Elijah stepped close and took her hand. "I didn't stay for you; I had to get my bracelet back." By the time he finished speaking it was back on his wrist. "How much did you hear?" he asked, feeling uneasy.

"Everything." Her voice carried hints of guilt.

"And you believe all that?" He spoke mockingly, but secretly hoped she did. He wanted to let someone in.

"Yes," she said. "I saw it with my own eyes." Her voice was resolute.

"Come on, we need to get your things. You need to get out of town tonight." Elijah grabbed her by the wrist and started for the stairs.

"Wait." As Elijah turned around she slipped her arm around his neck and then fell into his arms. Her touch was gentle and comforting; it brought to mind every good memory Elijah hadn't realized still lurked somewhere within him. Elijah was strong-willed, and his passion was fervent, but it was becoming harder and harder not to need anyone, especially now, with all the new hopes and emotions jumbled together with uncertainty, and Emira's nearly magical attraction, to cloud his mind.

In her arms he was hopeless. No matter how hard he tried, he couldn't muster an ounce of enthusiasm for the hateful purpose which had driven him for so long. He cupped his big hand along the side of her face and pressed it against his chest as he stroked his fingers through her silky dark hair. He was once again intoxicated by her scent.

"I was just kidding before; I wouldn't have let them hurt you," he said quietly. His chin rested sideways against the top of her head; his words were just a whisper.

"I know. I've known you my entire life. I've been waiting for you," she replied. Elijah didn't understand, but he didn't question her. He also didn't understand why she trusted him, or why he wanted so desperately to let her into his world, but in that moment he didn't care. It felt good; she felt good.

"You know I'm not going anywhere. I'm not going to leave Khalid, or you," she said firmly as she pulled away and looked into Elijah's eyes.

"I will take care of him. I just want to know you are someplace safe first."

Elijah's knew she could tell he was sincere; he could tell she trusted him, but he could also see her mind was made up.

"Let's just get to the room; we will talk there." Without hesitation, Elijah turned and started up the stairs, Emira right behind him.

"I'm sorry, but I have nowhere to go. Besides, I am safest here, with you and Khalid." Elijah could see it was pointless, but he had to try.

"Emira, they *will* kill you," he warned.

"They would have to kill you first," she replied immediately, with complete confidence.

Elijah didn't know what to say. He had just met this girl, but the connection, which had begun with a couple of coins, was winding its way around his heart. Still, killing his father had to be his first priority, especially since there was a chance Malaki might be alive somewhere.

"I am not the great man you seem to believe I am. I might not drink human blood like my brother, but if you knew some of the things I have done, you wouldn't be so quick to trust me, especially with your life." The conflicts now eating away at him, the new information about his brothers, left him open to human connection as never before, but he still wanted to be careful not to mislead her, or to fall helplessly into her web.

"Are you the spider?" Elijah asked.

"Are you?" she responded.

Elijah took a deep breath and tried to clear his mind. This light-hearted conversation was a nice change.

"I am the spider and the fly. I weave the very web that entraps me." Elijah smiled. "My father was right," Elijah said, circling back on point. "I have never been strong enough to defeat him, and if he believes I care for you, or that you are something unique, that places you in a great deal of danger." He wanted to know more about the girl and her light, but decided this wasn't the time.

"I do know the things you have done. You told me, remember? I'm not afraid of you." Emira turned the conversation back where she wanted it.

Elijah took a deep breath and poured another shot of bourbon.

"And it doesn't matter how strong your father is. You are not like him, Elijah, as much as you seem to think you are. Your power comes from somewhere else. It's nothing supernatural. A hero's strength always comes from the wells of passion and reserves of strength in his mortal mind. It's your will and dedication, your grit and determination. Your tenacity will get us through this." She spoke with fervor. Elijah couldn't help but smile. The girl was spirited, but had obviously watched a few too many movies.

"This isn't a storybook," he laughed.

"My father, he was a tenacious man, too. He believed a person's loyalty and his determination revealed more about his character than all other things combined." She smiled and then sighed as she poured her own glass of bourbon.

"What are you doing?" Elijah quickly grabbed the bottle before she set it down.

"I'm not a child." She huffed before choking on the bourbon; it quickly made her eyes water and her lips purse as she coughed and asked for something to wash it down.

Elijah didn't have anything else, so he ran a glass of tap water.

"Are you serious?" she croaked. She looked like she was about to throw up.

"It's all I've got."

Emira snatched the water and chugged the entire glass. Clearing her throat, she tried a wobbly smile. "Wow! Remind me not to do that again."

"If you're not going to leave, then we need to warn Khalid." Elijah reached for his phone.

"I already called him, when I heard your brother talking, but I promise you, he will not leave town either."

Elijah had figured as much.

## CHAPTER 76

E MIRA RAN TO the door, completely unintimidated by the
ominous thudding from outside, and swung it open. It was
Khalid. He bouldered through and grabbed Elijah by the neck.

"I told you to stay away from her; now look what you've
done." His eyes were blazing.

"Stop!" Emira shouted. "He saved me," she proclaimed.

Khalid seemed not to hear her, as his grip around Elijah's
neck only tightened. Elijah remained still, not wishing to further
inflame the man's rage. He needed him.

Emira stepped closer and placed her hand on the beastly
man's shoulder. Immediately, Elijah felt Khalid's grip loosen
and saw his eyes dim to normal. Elijah stepped back and Emira
darted past Khalid to tuck herself beneath Elijah's arm, grasping
him tightly around the waist.

"What were you thinking, Emira? That could have been anyone," Elijah scolded as he stood awkwardly before Khalid with
the man's tiny progeny clinging to him like an adorable little
leech, sucking out all of Elijah's hate, all of his pain and his guilt.

"Sorry." Emira shrank deeper into his grasp. Khalid's head
cocked to the right, his face looking confused; he had obviously

missed a lot. Elijah could see his anger. Clearly he didn't like that his "little sister" was so taken with Elijah.

"Let's go, now." Khalid demanded. "Solomon and William are at my house, but it won't take them long to realize they are looking in the wrong place. Emira, you ride with me, Elijah will follow us. I know a safe place."

Emira looked up at Elijah as if for guidance, or even permission.

Elijah knew Khalid was strong, but no match for his father. So, if she was going to stay in the area, Elijah preferred to watch over her himself. He didn't hide his disapproval.

"Why don't we just ride together and leave Elijah's car here? I think it's safer if we stay together," Emira suggested.

"The only way you will be safe is if they think I left town. My car needs to disappear," Elijah replied. Khalid nodded his agreement. "And we need to find Ayda," Elijah added.

"You know Ayda?" Emira pulled away in protest. "Why did you not tell me?" She was obviously upset.

"It doesn't matter." Khalid cut in. "She is fine. I talked to her just moments ago," Khalid assured him.

Elijah closed his eyes as a rush of relief cascaded upon him like a waterfall of peace and hope. "Where is she?"

"Somewhere safe," Khalid replied and then turned his attention to Emira. "If what you told me on the phone is correct, then they want this man you're clinging to gone, and they'll use you to make sure it happens. I've dealt with these types of creatures before and, believe me, they'll do absolutely anything to get what they want." Khalid's face was expressionless as he spoke.

"I'm sure you have seen a lot, but not like this. My father is the most powerful individual I have ever encountered. Just ask Ayda; do not underestimate him," Elijah warned before turning to Emira.

"Right now they are after Khalid and whatever they think he

knows. The more distance I can put between you and him, the better I will feel." Elijah didn't want to force anything, but he knew he was right, at least as far as Emira was concerned. Emira looked at Khalid, hoping to find some kind of consensus and he reluctantly nodded. He obviously knew Elijah was right.

"Okay, you ride with him, but follow closely; I'll be moving fast. It's not far away, but nobody can connect me to it." As Khalid finished speaking, Elijah grabbed his duffle bag and followed them out the door.

## CHAPTER 77

THEY MADE A left out of the motel parking lot, but after that there were too many rights and lefts in the dark for Elijah to remember exactly how to get back. Then the white truck in front of him veered unexpectedly off the road to the left.

Elijah couldn't see a road, or a trail. He wasn't sure his little rear-wheel drive car would make the climb up the slick, grassy hill, but it did, and finally the truck came to a stop in front of a huge pond. Khalid got out of the truck and motioned Elijah to pull beside him.

"This is it?" he asked, parking his car where Khalid indicated.

"This is as far as your car goes, I'm afraid." Khalid pointed to the pond in front of them that stretched far out into the darkness. Elijah realized Khalid was right. Emira and Elijah climbed out the car and the three of them took a moment to look around.

"Will you do the honors, or shall I?" Khalid smiled broadly. It reminded Elijah of the first time they met.

"You know, you were right," Elijah said.

"Yeah, about what?"

"Your sense of humor is shit." Elijah said. He retrieved his duffle, put his car in neutral and sent it swimming to the depths of the pond. "All right, now it's your turn." Elijah smiled with satisfaction. Khalid quickly turned to Emira in protest, but she nodded her agreement.

"Shit. You're right." Khalid shook his head ruefully as he opened the trunk and retrieved two large suitcases.

"You travel light," Elijah teased.

"These are Emira's." Khalid laughed and dropped them at Elijah's feet before walking around to the driver's side of his truck and pulling out one small duffle bag. "I travel very light." He grinned.

Emira leaned over and kissed Elijah on the cheek, as if to say thank you, and skipped ahead to walk with Khalid.

Kicking Khalid's huge truck into the deep abyss of the pond, Elijah knew the big man had gotten the last laugh, but he didn't care. Ayda was safe, and, for the moment, Emira was as well. The tide might not yet been turning, but it was at bay, and it was just good to be laughing at all. And after lifetimes of solitude, he was happy to part of something again.

Elijah picked up the bags and the trio walked in silence around the side of the pond and over a large hill. They were half-way down the other side of the hill before the small cabin came into view. Elijah couldn't wait to have a few moments alone with Khalid; he wanted answers.

"And I thought we'd be roughing it." A crooked smile broke across Elijah's face.

"Well, I've been around for a long time, and I've learned it is always handy to have a few good hiding places." Khalid's laugh was just a façade. Elijah was learning quickly not to underestimate the beast of a man. He wondered just how long Khalid had been around, how long he had been protecting these ancient secrets, if there were any.

Walking into the dank and musty cabin, Elijah could hardly

breathe. Emira sneezed as a breeze came in from the open door and blew dust everywhere. It was as if the door hadn't been opened for months, or maybe years. Elijah thought for a moment it might be better to sleep outside on the grass.

Khalid chuckled as he pushed past the pair and walked over to what looked like a huge granite fireplace. He pressed against the giant stone and moved it about three feet to the right with ease, revealing a large opening and a stone staircase that descended a full story beneath the earth.

# CHAPTER 78

KHALID USHERED THEM down the stairs and pushed the huge stone back into place. The underground section of the cabin, which was actually more like a compound, was intricately decorated and fully furnished. The air was fresh and clean, as though there was a circulation system filtering the air and pumping it in.

The place seemed to have every amenity. There was a large square stone in the center of the room that functioned as a coffee table. It was bracketed on two sides by antique-looking leather couches, both of them large enough to easily support Khalid's massive frame.

On both sides of the stairs were large, fully furnished bedrooms, with desks, end tables, and even bathrooms. Across from the stairs, the living room opened into an impressive library. It was complete with books, a ladder, and five huge bookcases. Elijah was impressed; he greatly enjoyed the smells of aged leather and parchment.

"I'll take the couch. The two of you can have the bedrooms... separate bedrooms." Khalid glared threateningly at Elijah, who threw his duffle bag into one of the bedrooms and then very conspicuously placed Emira's bags in the other. He threw up his hands to show his submission.

The big man before him was fiercely guarded. Elijah could rarely tell what he was thinking, and he gave no hints about when he was joking or being serious. This man was careful. The only chink Elijah had seen in his armored guise was in the way he dealt with Emira. He was attached to her; he was her ferocious guardian.

"Okay, Papa," Emira smiled and laughed. Turning from Elijah, she looked at Khalid and pointed her finger at him as she narrowed her dark eyes at him playfully. He could be harsh at times, but it was easy to see how much he cared for the girl.

Earlier she said she had lived with him for the last ten years, since Khalid's sister had found her. Elijah wondered how exactly that had come about, and what they wanted with the girl.

Elijah had heard her speak of her father; she remembered him as a man of principles. After losing him, Elijah imagined it had been easy for Emira to grow close to this beastly man, who also seemed to be principled. She had told Elijah he had been like a father to her since she had been under his care. Elijah imagined she would never have made it this far without him. It was obvious she loved him deeply.

"All right, I'm going out to build a fire." Khalid said sheepishly. Emira obviously held sway over the man, but Elijah couldn't blame him. Her playful innocence had softened Elijah's skin, allowing her to get underneath it much faster than anyone ever had before.

The girl was something of a siren, it seemed, but it didn't matter. It was too late, at this point, to be concerned with her intentions. Elijah knew resistance was futile. He had tried to fight it, but she had somehow stolen his heart; it was hers, as if it had been waiting for her all these years. His only hope was not to be eaten alive, at least not yet.

"Are you sure that's the best idea? What if someone sees?" Elijah asked.

"We are in the middle of nowhere; surrounded on all sides by hills. Trust me, no one will see anything," Khalid replied. He seemed certain, but Elijah still wasn't convinced.

"I just think we should be a little more cautious," Elijah suggested. He didn't like the idea of having Emira out in the open while they were being hunted, especially with a large fire pointing out their exact location like a neon sign.

Khalid just stared at him. Clearly he didn't appreciate being questioned about his ability to care for Emira. He was a dangerously stubborn man.

Khalid huffed threateningly before turning and stomping up the steps. The noise from his breath echoed down the stairwell in a deep growl.

Elijah got the message. He realized there was no way to change the man's mind, especially not with words. Still, he wasn't going to sit by and watch while anyone, including Khalid, put Emira's life in danger.

It might have been hard for anyone else to understand how a couple of old coins could mean so much, but he was certain they were a sign. They had pointed Emira out to him; they had brought the two of them together. And he wasn't about to let anything tear them apart, at least not until someone could give him a better explanation for his feelings and the staggering number of seemingly random events that had needed to unfold in order to bring him here, to this very moment... as if they were pawns, no more able to change their fates than all the men who had fallen beneath Elijah's blade.

Watching Khalid storm up the steps, Elijah could feel his own anger and stubbornness rising to match Khalid's. He started for the stairwell with every intention of stopping the man, who seemed now to think just like the beast he appeared to be.

Suddenly, a soft hand resting against Elijah's forearm forced him to stop.

He turned to face the small woman holding his arm. It was as if she were a lioness, able to sway his purpose with just a swipe of her beautiful paw. The only difference was her touch; it carried infinitely more power than any beast. Elijah looked into her eyes; her stare was condemning and sympathetic at the same time.

He knew what she wanted, but he also knew his first thought in this moment must be for her safety. Elijah knew his face and body were visibly tense, and most people would back away at the threat. Emira tugged on his arm and drew him in close, as if she knew he wasn't going to let go easily.

Every nerve in his body was warmed and softened, as if he had been drugged. He knew it was the wrong decision, but there was nothing he could do. Her hold over him was growing with every touch; it now seemed impenetrable and inexhaustible.

He understood her silent plea and relinquished his obstinacy.

# CHAPTER 79

"I'LL JUST GO out and have a look around, then. Will you come?" Elijah was hopeful.

"You two go ahead; I'll have a bath." Emira twirled her hair as she spoke.

"It's fine. I'll just stay in and read for a while." Elijah said. After the night's occurrences, Elijah didn't want to let her out of his sight.

"No, go ahead. I would like for you and Khalid to have a chance to get to know each other better. I'll be fine. You'll be just outside." She seemed comfortable enough, and besides, Elijah was anxious to talk to the big man alone. He knew anyone coming in would be drawn to the fire first, and Elijah trusted deeply in his acute senses; nothing would sneak past him, not tonight.

Reaching the patio, Elijah could see Khalid in the distance. He was hunkered down in front of a pile of twigs and leaves. Soon, he piled on larger sticks. He stuffed a crumpled piece of paper under the wood and lit it with a silver Zippo lighter. Walking into the flickering firelight, Elijah dropped an enormous log right next to the fire.

The smell of burning wood lit his nose and his imagination.

He was immediately transported hundreds of years back in time, to the night his mother had died. It was a memory that had never before surfaced. His subconscious must have noticed and remembered more than he realized in the terrible fury of that night.

\*

*He was back in his childhood bed. He was asleep, or mostly asleep.*

*"Tell me Esmeralda, or, I swear to God, I will cut your throat right now. I know your family. I know the stories, and I know now they are not just stories. It's all real, isn't it?" His father's voice had been furious.*

*"I can't tell you anything, because it is not real; they are just stories, legends. You have gone mad," his mother had protested.*

*"You can't lie to me Esmeralda. I have heard it from a source who is unimpeachable, and I know you are a part of it." His father's tone had transformed. He no longer sounded angry, but devoid of emotion altogether.*

*"If what you say is true, then what does it matter? If I were really part of some secret society bound to protect hidden truths, would I reveal them to you, even at the expense of my life?" Her voice lacked fear. It was ferocious and stubborn. Elijah had never heard her speak in that manner his entire life.*

*"Maybe not yours, but your children's, perhaps? Roman, go get the small boy, now!" William shouted.*

*"No, please! Those are your children too." Elijah could hear the fear pierce his mother's voice.*

*"Then tell me. I know you know something," William's voice was dark and lacked any empathy whatsoever.*

\*

"Elijah, Elijah, are you okay?" Elijah was yanked back into the present; he could see a hulking figure standing before him, snapping his fingers.

"I'm fine, I was just thinking about some things from my past." Elijah said. His face felt parched and cold, as if it were lifeless and drained of color, and, from the way Khalid was looking at him, Elijah could see it was.

"You know, I'm starting to like having you around to do all the grunt work," Khalid joked as he sat on the bench-sized log Elijah had just dropped next to the fire. "What exactly is your story? How did you come to meet Ayda?" Khalid looked up from the fire and stared at Elijah with suspicion.

"I was an Assassin at Alamut in Northern Iran. Ayda was with Hulagu Khan's army when they forced us to surrender. I made a deal with the Khan and stayed around; eventually Ayda and I became close." Elijah stepped over the log and sat down beside Khalid.

"And just how long of a story do you have?"

"What do you mean?" Elijah stalled, but knew exactly what the big man wanted to know.

"I mean, just how long ago did your past actually begin? How long have you been consorting with blood-letters?" His tone was patronizing.

"I'm not what you think I am. I do want to kill my brother and my father. I have never fed on human blood, or any other kind. I know Ayda would have told you that; and if Emira told you what she overheard at the motel, I'm sure she would have mentioned that part, too." Elijah's voice got louder as his impatience with Khalid's ignorant assumptions grew.

"Then what exactly are you?" Khalid asked.

"I believe it's your turn to answer a few questions," Elijah replied. The conversation had gotten a bit heated. "Tell me what the girl is, and why you try to hide it." Elijah's question was a not-so-subtle accusation.

"That is none of your concern. In fact, she is none of your concern," Khalid stated with finality.

Elijah closed his eyes and rubbed the palms of his hands against his temples. He was becoming more and more agitated.

"It is my business. It's no coincidence she is here in the midst of all this madness, right where my father is looking for some object Ayda told me long ago will make him even more powerful. I need to know what's going on. I need to know what you are and what your plans are for the girl." He could see Khalid was growing anxious, because he began to shift positions nervously.

"I love that girl. You need to know that, but it is not the only reason I watch over her. She is very special. All I can tell you is, if the vampires found out what she is and got their hands on her, it would be disastrous, even catastrophic. Beyond that, I can tell you nothing," Khalid admitted.

Elijah could see concern in his eyes, and he could also see he wasn't getting any more from the man, at least not now. "I wonder why, then, my father did not notice anything different about her when he was holding her in his arms?" The question had been troubling Elijah since his father had disappeared.

"Luckily, vampires can't see her light. If they could, we wouldn't have a chance." Khalid leaned forward and rested his elbows on his knees, dropping his forehead into his hands.

"Yes, I forgot; she told me that much. Does she know anything more?" Elijah asked. "About her importance I mean."

"She knows enough, what she needs to know." Khalid replied. "What would be the point in telling her more? So she can spend her life in paranoia, always looking over her shoulder, even more afraid than she already is? Would that be better?" Khalid's voice got louder as he became more defensive. Elijah didn't like it, but he understood the man's feelings. "Now, let's get back to you," Khalid shoved his face close to Elijah's.

"I don't know what I am. I woke up this way," Elijah shrugged. "There was no instruction manual or teacher to tell me who I was or to help me adapt. One minute I was lying helpless on the ground watching my family be brutally murdered by men I cherished most dearly. And the next thing I remember was waking with a strength and speed that defied everything I knew; everything about me had intensified, including my desire and my determination. You don't have to worry about me; I'm not your enemy."

"I hope you are right, but you understand it just doesn't make any sense. I have been around a long time and have never heard of anything like that, anything like you. You and your father carry the same power and were birthed on the same day; you must carry the same curse. I don't know what has come between you and your family, but when a family becomes immortal, it's usually as a family. I'm willing to guess you had a hand in it." Khalid's words were a terrible accusation. His tone was condemning.

Elijah nearly flew through the air, and he was at Khalid's throat in a split second. As they landed hard on the ground, Elijah's grip tightened around Khalid's neck. With tremendous force, Khalid thrust his body upwards and slung Elijah over his head.

By the time they hit the ground Khalid was already on top of him. Elijah could feel razor-like claws at his throat. With all his might, he pressed in on Khalid's right elbow, just releasing the tension enough to get his hands beneath the big man's torso. Pushing forward, Elijah slammed his palms hard against Khalid's chest, lifting him a few feet into the air above him. Lifting his powerful thigh, Elijah thrust the heel of his shoe underneath Khalid's chin and flung him backwards.

Khalid flipped over in midair and landed on his feet. Letting out a deep, bone-chilling growl, he turned around and ripped off his shirt. The two seemed equally matched and neither knew fear; their dark pasts had robbed them of it.

# CHAPTER 80

"NO, PLEASE, STOP." Elijah heard a shrill, small voice cry out behind him. He could tell Khalid had also heard it, as his fierce stare had shifted and was now focused behind Elijah.

*Emira.* The thought frightened him; she might be in trouble. He quickly turned to see her nearly at his back. Her body collapsed into his like two puzzle pieces falling into perfect conjunction. He imagined it was like a double shot of heroin would feel to an addict after a long jones. He didn't know if he was in love or addicted, or if there was a difference.

"You stupid boys! What are you doing?" She was nearly crying as she pounded her fist against Elijah's shoulder, still wrapped in his arms. Elijah's heart sank as he realized he had let his emotions get the better of him once again. He had upset Emira and possibly put her life at risk. The man before him might not be the one he would choose to accompany him on this journey, but he was the one who was here. He had proven himself strong, and willing to protect Emira, and for that, Elijah was thankful.

"I'm sorry. I promise it won't happen again. I just got carried away." Elijah whispered, his mouth pressed against her ear.

"No, it was my fault. I was poking my nose where it didn't belong. I do apologize Elijah. Emira, I'll be on the couch." After apologizing Khalid gave Emira a hug before walking inside.

# CHAPTER 81

"LET'S TAKE A walk." Emira turned back and took Elijah's hand, pulling him forward, away from the fire.

"Where are we going?" He didn't want to take her very far from the cabin.

"Don't worry. We won't go far," she assured him. It was night, but a nearly full moon lit the fields and valley around them. Winding their way through a thicket of spruce trees, he found the strong smell of pine a welcome change from the nauseating effect of smoke from the fire.

"Can I ask you something?" she asked shyly.

"Sure," Elijah sighed. He could imagine the questions reeling in her mind and braced himself for the worst.

"Well, are you... are you a v-vampire?" she stammered nervously. Elijah wasn't sure whether she was afraid of offending him or of having her blood drained. "I mean, I know I asked you before, and I heard what you said to your brother, but—"

"No, I'm not a vampire. I mean, I don't think so. The desire to consume blood has never burned in my mind or body. I have spilled enough blood to fill the heavens, but it has never found its way to my lips. It might sound silly, but as I told my brother, perhaps when he and my father lie dead beneath me, when my purpose is finished, my vow complete, perhaps then the ghost that keeps me alive will depart as well." Elijah spoke in a low and solemn voice. This had been his hope for as long as he could remember.

"You want to die!" she gasped.

He was silent for a moment as he stopped and gazed, nearly unaware, at a pinecone lying at his feet.

"What I want is an ending; I want all this to be over. I want to close my eyes and fade away. There was an artist from your time, well, a little before your time, his name was Tupac Shakur, and his words reflect how I feel in a lot of ways. He embraced death; he said his only fear of death was coming back reincarnated. I think when a man, or a woman," he gestured politely towards Emira, "has struggled for so long, it is only natural to desire an ending." Elijah lifted his head and looked into her eyes.

"What about heaven? Don't you want to go to a better place, a place filled with happiness?"

"No, I want an ending, endless unconsciousness. I truly hope, when I do die, that it can all be over, no heaven, no hell. Let it be finally the end of an ugly story and a wretched man." Elijah was overcome with emotion as his eyes traced the soft curves of her face and bathed in her brilliant aura. "Life is pain. The Buddha taught that pain comes from our attachments, our desires, and he was right. Any form of consciousness that exists will have to come with those desires and attachments, love and hate, and it all leads to pain."

He reached forward and caressed the side of her face as he brushed a wisp of hair behind her ear. "Believe me, when you have been around as long as I have, you understand just how much life is overrated. There is no version of an eternity, besides one where I do not exist, that would appeal to me. I just want this to be over, finally and truly."

"Well, I hope that's not the case. I will take the good with the bad before I give up on attachment altogether," she asserted.

"Tell me that again in a thousand years." Elijah grinned.

She squeezed his arm tightly, resting her head against his shoulder as the pair walked a little further and came upon a small creek. They stood in silence for a long while, just listening to the music of water flowing from rock to rock.

"I'm sorry," she said quietly, as she wrung her hands and then turned to Elijah. She seemed to see right through him.

"Sorry for what?" He turned and started back towards the cabin. Quickening her pace, Emira caught him by the hand once again and coaxed him to face her.

"I'm sorry for what happened to you and your family," she said softly.

Elijah was quickly becoming uncomfortable. Once again his emotions were rising and falling like an elevator. He was not used to empathy, and he didn't react well to it.

"Yeah, well, you weren't supposed to hear about all of that," he snapped, his tone growing colder and harsher by the moment.

"I didn't really hear everything, but I heard enough," she said, pulling him to her by the tips of his fingers.

Elijah pulled his hand away and continued walking. He was growing more and more uncomfortable about his feelings for her, about how she affected him. He couldn't understand how, after so long, he could suddenly feel this way about someone again. How could he trust it?

He was afraid he was fooling himself, seeing what he wanted to see rather than what was truly there. Perhaps he was confusing his feelings for Sara with feelings for Emira, believing in a fantasy because of the coins hanging from her neck, quite possible the very coins he left to burn in the pyre.

She darted in front of him and blocked his path.

"Why would you be sorry? You weren't there; you didn't

sit idly by, looking into my little brother's eyes while my father snapped his neck." He closed his eyes, and that entire night seemed to flash through his mind, sudden and complete as a bolt of lightning. The conversation was beginning to stir up old, dangerous feelings, feelings Elijah had attempted to bury over and over again.

"I just meant I'm sad you had to… to endure such pain and loss," she explained.

Elijah didn't want to hurt her, but anger and frustration were reaching the outer edges of his composure.

"And what exactly would you know about either one? You're just a silly girl looking to be entertained," he growled, his emotions beginning to boil over.

"I'm sorry; I didn't mean to upset you." Emira's eyes were wide with shock. The sudden shifts in his demeanor were making her nervous.

"Do you have any idea what you've gotten yourself into? How you've complicated things for me?" he demanded. Her questions had brought to the surface all of Elijah's old memories and griefs. He didn't know what to do with them, how to force them back into the dark corners of his psyche.

"I know I've caused you grief. You had one goal in life, a single-minded purpose, allowing nothing to get in the way. I know you hurt, and I know I may have complicated your plan, but I didn't mean to." She paused for a moment and took a deep breath. "But don't walk around pretending you are the only one who has ever been hurt. I have also experienced pain… and loss."

Elijah could see tears welling in her eyes.

"I was only eight years old," she said, "when the Army of the Republika Srpska marched into our village. Mother hid me in the cupboard just before five soldiers broke through our door. I could see through a crack in the cupboard door. Two men held my mother down and another one raped her. My father tried to stop them, but there was nothing he could do. The other two men tied him to a chair and forced him to watch as they took turns with her." Tears began to leak from the corners of her eyes as she spoke.

"When the soldiers were finished, they spat on her and called her a whore. They were laughing and joking as they hacked at my father with a machete for fun, or maybe they just didn't want to waste a bullet. I did nothing. I sat quietly and looked into my father's eyes. He held my gaze as long as he could, until life vanished from his eyes."

"Now it's my turn to apologize, Emira. You don't have to tell me this." Elijah's folly now filled him with guilt and sympathy. He stepped closer and reached out for her, but she backed away.

"Just listen," she demanded, taking another step back as she wiped her eyes. "When the soldiers left, my mother took a small knife out of a drawer in the kitchen and jammed it into her neck twice. She was dead in seconds, but I know it wasn't the knife or the blood loss that killed her. It was those five faceless men who I wouldn't recognize if they were sitting across the dining room table. It was the world, watching as I was, through a crack in the cupboard door, as General Mladic led his ethnic cleansing campaign, which had been underway for more than three years by the time my village was raided."

Elijah could hear the anger and frustration in her voice. He remained silent.

"They were just a ragtag group of thugs; any real army in the world could have stopped them. It's never what you can do, but what you are willing to do that matters. That is what you have Elijah, an absolutely unstoppable will. That is what's so beautiful about you, and about the hero character in general." As she spoke the last sentence, she stepped forward and pressed her index finger against Elijah's chest.

"Why do you keep saying that?" Elijah forced a laugh.

"What is it in your wild imagination that paints me a hero?" He asked.

"You remind me of my father; there is good in you, even if you refuse to acknowledge it. You have reserves of strength I can recognize because I've seen it all before—in my father. I have rested easy in the depths of his passionate commitment. It's nothing supernatural or overtly noticeable. It's much more than that; it goes much deeper... it's... maybe it's primal.

"It's a look of resolve a dying father gives to his daughter to comfort her in his last moments of life. It's a determination and desire for justice that carries a man through thousands of miles and hundreds of years without losing an ounce of fervor. There are very few men with that kind of grit. I have to admit, when I heard your story I almost couldn't believe it. I was blown away." She laughed playfully and batted her eyelashes.

Elijah was moved in spite of his determination to remain aloof; to realize someone had so much faith in him was inspiring. It made him want to be the man she imagined him to be. But, for her own good, for her safety, he could not encourage her interest in him, or allow her to continue believing in her fantasy that he was a good man.

"There are a few things wrong with your story. First, I'm not good; I'm about as far from good as someone can be. Second, I haven't traveled thousands of miles over hundreds of years for justice. I couldn't care less about justice. I've come for blood, and vengeance." Elijah closed his eyes and took a deep breath. Her words had touched him, but he was stubborn. Still, his regrets were mounting like ash from the hope and joy he had experienced from being with her. He realized now that, in his astounding selfishness and impulsivity, he had once again leapt to a conclusion based on his own cynical beliefs.

"Well, sometimes, they are one in the same thing. And sometimes people on the outside of a situation have a much clearer perspective. If you were really so bad, we wouldn't be in this situation right now." She smiled wryly.

"How do you know I'm not right where I want to be? How do you know you and Khalid are not my bait?" He knew he'd made his expression intimidating, piercing and vicious, but could also tell she wasn't buying it.

"I'll take my chances," she said. Her laugh sang the song of a siren once again as it compelled him forward, closer to her. "Read me the inscription on your pendant." She pointed to the necklace that had worked its way from beneath his shirt.

"This was my mother's," he said, lifting it up to admire it. He didn't need to read it; he knew the words by heart. "'Everything begins and ends with a will, and a purpose is only as strong as the will that propels it'." He looked up to see her eyes tracing the circling words.

"See, do you not think that pendant found you for a reason?" She smiled wide as she hesitantly touched the pendant. As she dropped her arm back to her side, the moonlight struck the coins on her necklace and Elijah was reminded of why he had taken such an interest in her in the first place. He decided he needed to tell her the entire truth about Sara.

"Emira, I need to tell you about those coins." He tucked the pendant back under his shirt and reached forward, rubbing his fingers against one of the coins on her necklace; it was lying at an angle against her prominent collarbone. A rush of memories filled his mind and he was overwhelmed; tears sprang into his eyes as he began to speak. His voice shook as he explained about Sara and the coins, about how much she had meant to him and why he was concerned that what he was feeling in his moments with her, Emira, might just be his feelings for Sara projected onto her.

"I understand," she said as she reached out and cupped the side of his face. Her empathy and demeanor took him aback.

She might have been young and impulsive, but she risked a lot and seemed sure of her decisions despite the risk. She was brave, and Elijah admired her for it.

He didn't know if it was because of the coins, or the way her soft touch brought peace and ease to his mind, or if it was because he was so tired of being isolated and alone in his grief. But, for the first time since Sara had died, he completely dropped his guard, and he didn't feel guilty about letting her come closer.

"I'm truly sorry about before. I had no idea what you had been through. I just lose control sometimes." Elijah rubbed his hand across hers, which was still nestled against his face, and then cupped it between his and held it at his waist.

Her reply was poignant. "It's okay, I'm just glad you are here with me now. I don't want to lose you to that darkness that always seems to be lurking just below the surface."

"Yes, it's definitely there." He knew she was right. It was so easy to give into that vacuum. "That darkness is who I am, or who I've become. For nearly a millennium I have carried it and it has carried me. It has been my comfort and my strength." Elijah gently tugged at her hand and started walking back towards the cabin.

"You are wrong. Your true strength comes from somewhere much deeper, much more powerful." Her conviction and her insights continued to confound and delight him. She had a passion to rival his own.

"It's all I've known—the pain, the struggle, the passion, the defeat, and the eventual victory that will end only in death... a tragic romance, indeed," he spoke bitterly.

The fire ahead of them seemed to grow larger and larger as they approached. Elijah could once again smell the smoke; it wasn't so bad in small doses.

"It just seems like it would be so tiresome to carry around that much hate," she said. She was right. It was a terrible burden, but it was Elijah's to bear, and he couldn't let it go, not until he was finished. It fueled him.

"How do you keep from hating? The men who murdered your family and the world that let it happen?" Elijah echoed her words back to her as he turned and looked into her eyes.

"I couldn't for a long time. I burned with hate and thoughts of vengeance, just like you do now. It was Khalid who taught me how to find peace, to let go of what I couldn't change. He is truly a great man.

"But don't get me wrong," she added, "I completely understand you. I gave up my hate partly because there was nothing I could do about it. I don't even know what those men look like. In your case things are much different." She spoke with a wisdom elusive among mortals and immortals alike. Beyond right and wrong, it spoke to the core elements of who he was and conferred a strange sense of peace and rightness.

Elijah stomped out the fire and they walked back into the cabin. He felt good; he felt understood.

# CHAPTER 82

E LIJAH SLID OPEN the fireplace. Before starting down the stairs, he wrapped his arm around Emira's waist and turned, leaning his back against the wall beside the stairwell.

"There is something else I can't get off of my mind," he admitted. His trouble connecting hadn't completely vanished and he was feeling somewhat awkward now, as he spoke. She seemed to sense his uneasiness and placed calming hands flat against his chest. He could feel his heartbeat thundering against them, but her touch was soothing. And his heart rate began to slow as he was once again swept away in the calming tide of her aura.

"Please tell me; I want to help you, Elijah." She stepped closer and leaned her right ear against his chest.

"It's what my brother said. I am confused about what I should do for the first time in my immortal life," he confessed as he rubbed her shoulders and gently pushed her back.

She stood quietly; her eyes encouraged him to continue.

"My stubbornness tells me to ignore it and continue down this path; after all, I have spent so much time and energy to get here. But if I am honest with myself, and look at the situation through the new eyes my brother's revelation has given me, I am no longer certain." Releasing his grasp on her shoulders, Elijah pressed his hands against his face and then cupped them around hers.

"You see, my brother was a great man," he mused. "He was everything my family needed after my father left. He loved us. I know he did, and we loved him, fiercely." As he spoke, Elijah could feel emotion stirring, rising to a boil within him and leaking into his voice.

"We all looked up to him, even Mother. That is why this has been so confusing. My little brother was so young when William, our father, left, Solomon was the only father figure he ever really knew. I listened for hours sometimes as Solomon told our little brother... his name is Malaki... told him bedtime stories that went on and on as Malaki begged for more and more and more." He paused for a moment and looked at her, noticing a faint smile steal across her face, and then realized her smile only mirrored his own; she was smiling back at him!

"I entertained Malaki a lot of the time, since Solomon was always working, always taking care of things for the family. I loved Malaki and he loved me, but it was Solomon who made his face glow, and I know Solomon loved him just as much. I don't know how bad he has become, but I finally know why, which has changed everything." Elijah could feel a strange rush of excitement building.

"What do you mean?" she asked. Her smile was now gone; confusion and fear seemed to have taken its place.

"I don't know if it was because of shock, or anger, or just my damned determined focus, but I didn't take enough time to think about it earlier. The more I consider it, the more it makes sense. Solomon was never a monster; he was a loving man, so how could he change overnight? That is what has always haunted me." The words seemed to tumble over each other, riding on waves of enthusiasm.

"Elijah, he is a vampire; that changes a person," she said warily. Concern and disapproval clouded her face as she spoke.

Elijah could see she understood and didn't like where he was going with this conversation, but it didn't matter. He knew what he had to do.

"Sara was a vampire, but it didn't change who she was on the inside," Elijah explained.

"I don't know, Elijah; I'm not sure what you are getting at. You told me she killed people, even children." She was now stroking his neck and jaw, but retreated when the muscles in his face tightened and the soft curves she had been stroking transformed into rigid edges. He didn't look at her; he clenched his jaw and closed his eyes. The space between them grew tense; it was obvious her comment had crossed a line.

Elijah shook it off as he opened his eyes and looked at her. Her aura had shrunk; he could see she was apologetic.

"He was telling the truth back there; my little brother is alive somewhere!" Elijah nearly shouted. A rush of joy overcame him as he finally said aloud what he had been almost afraid to believe. "But what do I do about it? I can't follow in my brother's footsteps and become another of my father's pawns, just waiting and hoping William will release him eventually. I also can't just charge off and kill them all, as has been my only plan and purpose for so long."

He looked at Emira to see her reaction. Her eyes were filled with empathy as she leaned against him once more.

"You are the only person who can decide what you should do. Khalid and I will support whatever decision you make." She rested her head against his chest again as she spoke. Elijah knew she was right. He wrapped his arms around her waist until she was tightly fitted against him. The gentle ebb and flow of her confidence was soothing, no matter how he pushed against her, she always found her way back. It compelled in him a desire to confide in someone again.

Elijah thought about all the time he had spent being confused and angry. Perhaps he had been wrong about Solomon all along. He was still angry and still confused, but the situation seemed very different now. He had hope, hope nourished by this tiny gem of a girl, resting snug against his chest. Hope his little brother might still be alive, and hope the man he had looked up to in his youth might still deserve his trust and respect.

"I need to speak with my brother. I have to try harder to get through to him."

"Are you sure?" she asked. She seemed shocked, and a bit clumsy, as Elijah led her down the steps and slid the huge stone back into its place.

When they entered the basement of the cabin, they found Khalid leaning back on one of the huge couches, reading a book. He didn't even look up as they entered the room.

"Khalid, I need to talk to you." Elijah's tone was pleasant but austere.

"Okay." Khalid promptly set his book down on the couch, clasped his hands between his knees and looked up at Elijah.

"I need to find my brother." Elijah spoke emphatically, certain Khalid would object.

"So I heard," Khalid said. "You think your little brother might still be alive and you are willing to risk Emira's life to find out." His tone was viciously condemning.

"No! Never! I wouldn't risk harming her for any reason whatsoever, but if my little brother is still alive, it changes everything!"

"Not for us. They still think I have something they want and they'll kill us all for even a chance to get their hands on it." Khalid leaned back and put his feet up on the table as he spoke.

JoSHUA A. CHAUDRY

"What I am trying to tell you is, if my youngest brother is still alive and Solomon has only been following my father's orders in the hopes of saving him, then Solomon may not be a monster at all. There is a chance I could convince him to work with me and find another way to save my little brother." Elijah's words, when he heard them spoken aloud, shook his confidence. Hope his plan would succeed seemed dim, even to him, but he wasn't going to back down.

# CHAPTER 83

"DO ME THIS kindness first." Khalid spoke in a calm voice and gestured his open hand towards the couch beside him. "Sit for a while and let me tell you some things you might not know about your family, and then, if you still want to go, I won't object." Khalid sounded sincere, and his willingness to compromise was a welcome surprise.

"Sounds fair," Elijah agreed. He knew he was asking for a lot of trust, and, between him and Khalid, there wasn't much trust to spare. "But let me ask you something first," he continued. "How did you know what I was when we first met?" he asked as he took a seat on the couch next to Khalid.

"Well, according to you, I still don't," Khalid noted. Putting his feet on the ground, he sat up and rubbed his knees. His tone was sarcastic, but friendly enough.

"I mean, how did you know I was different, immortal?" Elijah pressed as he leaned forward, mirroring Khalid's own position. He was curious. The beastly man intrigued him; there was an air of mystery and wisdom about him.

"As you well know Elijah, the longer you live, the more you learn to pick up on subtle things. I have been around for a long,

long time. Your father and brother are not the first immortals who've come to me looking for the ancient wisdom known simply as the ME. When you've seen enough of them, you learn to recognize certain things. An immortal's entire demeanor is different from a human's; there are subtle differences in the way they carry themselves, how they stand and move. All that power is hard to hide from someone who knows what to look for, and for me, knowing what to look for can be a matter of life and death." Khalid pulled a glass fitting from the top of an expensive-looking whiskey bottle and poured two glasses as he explained. He took a sip from one glass and handed the other to Elijah.

Elijah was impressed with Khalid's knowledge and once again wondered if perhaps Khalid and Ayda were cut from the same immortal twine as was he, or if the color of his eyes truly eliminated that possibility, as Ayda had suggested.

He threw back the whiskey. "What is this ME? Why does my father want it so much?" he asked. His voice rose with his curiosity.

"It's smooth, isn't it?" Khalid noted with pride. "It's thirty-year-old single malt."

"I prefer bourbon, but it is good," Elijah nodded. He could see Khalid swell with contempt and was immediately sorry. He had no idea the lion of a man would be so sensitive about his scotch.

"Like I said," Khalid continued. "Over the years, many immortals have come looking for this knowledge, but no one has ever found it, because it doesn't exist." Khalid rubbed his eyes and took a deep breath as if he was about to give a long, rehearsed speech.

"The legend of the ME comes from Assyrian mythology. There is no real description of exactly what it is, no consensus, only various beliefs and opinions. Some so-called experts believe it is a collection of actual stone tablets, similar to the Ten Commandments in Judeo-Christian and Islamic mythology. Others believe it is a collection of glyphs, scrolls, or books; some even believe it is a single piece of parchment. There are also various beliefs surrounding the number and makeup of the rite or rites. Some people believe there are many different tablets scattered across the earth, each conferring a different supernatural gift, while others believe there is just one sacred writing, providing one sacred gift." Khalid paused to take a deep breath as he poured another helping of whiskey.

"The mythology is quite simple. It states that in the beginning there were three gods, existing beyond time, in a state of perfect unity. The gods acted as one; having a unified will and purpose caused a perfect synchronicity and harmony to exist throughout the universe. The three *brothers,* if you will, ruled in this manner until the creation of mankind. Mankind was the jewel in their crown, the pinnacle of all of their achievements; never before had a life form been created with such a capacity and thirst for knowledge. Although greatly lacking in power, humans had an intelligence and will to rival even the gods. They were the first creations to question the world around them; they even questioned their creators." Khalid took another drink from his glass and then topped it off. Elijah could see he was conflicted regarding the audacity of man. The story seemed to mean a great deal to him, as if the telling of it exacted a toll.

"Man's questions and opinions brought light to the fact the brothers were uniquely specialized in their powers, and this provoked pride and envy between two of them, who both desired to prove the superiority of their power," Khalid continued, before finishing the last drop of whiskey in his glass and then leaning forward to stare intently at Elijah.

Elijah straightened and returned Khalid's stare. "I don't believe in fairytales," he said, "or gods, but Ayda did take

something from the House of Wisdom. She said it was impera-
tive my father not get his hands on it. So, tell me the truth;
what did she take? And why is it so important? Why would so
many immortals believe the ME does exist?" Elijah was tired of
secrets; he was determined to get what he could from Khalid,
and although the big man was beginning to open up, it wasn't
hard to tell he was being purposely vague and trying to throw
Elijah off track with his sarcastic tone.

"Is that true?" Emira asked. Her tone and expression were
sharp and condemning. Khalid became noticeably uncomfortable; the incorrigibly proud man was suddenly softened by
Emira's accusing stare.

"Just listen. Let me finish telling you the myth, and then I'll
tell you what I know." Khalid's voice was nearly a whisper; Elijah
was vividly aware of his deep reluctance.

"The god Mikal, known as the god of light and creation,"
Khalid continued, "was proud of his power to bring life into
the world. It is said he has spent ages making all different kinds
of creatures and beasts, including man. His brother, Adol,
is known as the god of darkness and death. He despises his
brother's power; he is envious of him, and spends his time taking away all his brother creates, turning light into darkness and
life into death." Khalid paused for a moment and once again
poured more whiskey. Emira shot him a disapproving look, but
he tossed it down anyway and then continued.

"This is where your father comes in," he said. "Adol is the
god who creates those like him, these immortal blood-letters,
vampires as they have come to be known. He empowers them
with death; the more life they consume, the stronger they
become." Khalid's voice was now a monotone. His guise of
imperturbability surrounded him once again.

"Wait, I thought you said it was all just a myth," Elijah
interrupted, sure Khalid was still hiding something.

"I said the ME was a myth, not the entire story." Elijah caught him backtracking and wasn't going to let him off the hook. "Anyway, will you let me finish?" Khalid's imperturbability hadn't lasted long, and he was becoming noticeably frustrated by Elijah's questions. "The third brother god is named Odam; he is also known as the breath of man and the spirit of the earth. It is said he took notice of man's plight and was compelled towards compassion.

"He didn't like the way his brothers played with life and death, and he wanted to help man in his struggle. It is said, in his anger and compassion, an immense power was birthed in the form of knowledge. He wrote this knowledge down, and it is believed by many that these tablets, glyphs, or tombs contain knowledge that can give humans or immortals god-like power. They are said to be able to empower even the gods." Khalid's voice began to rise. His passion for the subject was now bursting forth, flooding his voice with hints of excitement.

"The most popular theory is, whether there is only one or many tablets, there is only one rite, or ritual, either inscribed on one tablet, or perhaps scattered throughout multiple tablets. The rite is known as the Apotheosis. Adol apparently charges his immortals with the task of finding it. He believes he must keep it out of his brother's hands. He believes the rite will give him the power to create life and make him the most powerful of the gods.

"However, if one of his immortals, like your father," Khalid frowned in Elijah's direction, "were to find the rite, be able to decipher it, and dared to defy Adol, he could perform it himself and become extremely powerful. At least, that is what some believe." The excitement in Khalid's voice had quickly transformed to sarcasm. He obviously wanted Elijah to believe he wasn't convinced.

"But that still doesn't explain what Ayda took or why they

would come here, to you." Elijah's curiosity caused him to continue pressing the big man.

"Well, it is said, when Odam created these tablets, he also created an order of immortals to see to their protection, to be their guardians. The rite is only to be used by a member of that order, and only in the direst of circumstances, like if Odam himself were somehow killed, and mankind had no other option. I spent much time as a professor trying to help people understand these myths and, unfortunately, I got a name for myself. Because blood-letters can tell I am not human, the ones who know of the ME and the order automatically assume I am involved, that I am one of Odam's immortals," Khalid explained while he tugged his ear.

"As far as Ayda is concerned, she can be naïve; she might believe in such things. For all I know, she might have thought she had found it." Khalid chuckled, probably trying to sound condescending, but, as far as Elijah was concerned, he had already given himself away. Still, Elijah knew there was more to be revealed.

Khalid's secretive nature was beginning to remind Elijah of his own past. Over the years of their friendship, Ayda had been persistently vague and secretive about anything to do with her past. It sounded crazy, but maybe this was why; maybe this was all true.

"Are you one of Odam's immortals, a guardian of the ME?" Elijah didn't know exactly what to think and was becoming more and more intrigued. He had experienced many things in his life which most people would think impossible, so he saw no reason to rule this out.

"I told you, the ME is just a myth," Khalid declared. He seemed guarded once again.

"What are you, then?" Elijah asked him straight out, hoping to rattle him enough to get something.

"Why would I go to mosque if I truly believed in all of this? That wouldn't make any sense," Khalid finally said, and then stared blankly down at the coffee table.

"It would be a good cover," Elijah prodded. "Besides, you already admitted to believing in these three gods." Khalid didn't reply; he just continued staring. After a long silence, Elijah realized Khalid wasn't going to discuss the subject with him any further, so he decided to give up, at least for now.

He wanted to ask Khalid about his own eyes and if he thought they might be of a similar kind, something he thought Ayda had dismissed too easily. But after noticing Emira had wandered into another room, Elijah took the opportunity to pry into another subject in which he was deeply interested. "How long have you known Emira?" he asked.

"How did I know that's what you would want to discuss? Death and danger all around us, and you can't get your mind off of her, can you?" Khalid raised his voice; he seemed threatened.

"Death and danger I'm used to; death and danger are my life. Emira is a welcome change," Elijah responded unapologetically.

"You know you are not good for her." Khalid was like stone.

"Well, I'm sure you're right." Elijah was leaning calmly back on the huge couch. "Besides, I've got more urgent things to worry about right now. You just keep her here and keep her safe; I'll take care of my brother and my father," Elijah assured him.

"Are you boys talking about me?" Hearing Emira's voice, Elijah looked up to see two beautiful bare legs stretching down from a familiar T-shirt. "I stole this shirt from your bag; I hope you don't mind." Her voice was melodic.

Talking to Khalid had made Elijah tense, and he was glad to feel the warm tenderness of Emira's presence. He looked over at Khalid and could see he was also grateful for the beautiful interruption.

"I don't mind. It looks better on you anyway," Elijah

laughed. He loved to see her smile; it seemed to make everything else disappear. Elijah stood up and took her hands in his. Looking into her eyes, he was sad to see her smile had disappeared and she looked worried, as if she already knew exactly what he was about to say.

"Emira, I have to go," he explained. Her expression didn't change. "I need to know for sure if my little brother is alive. Khalid will be here to protect you." He glanced back at the big man on the couch, who was now writing in a notebook.

"Don't worry, I will be back, and I will make sure no one can hurt you." Elijah stood there gazing into her eyes for a moment, almost waiting for permission. He wanted her to understand.

"I know. Please, just don't die." She fell into him as she spoke and hugged him with all the warmth in the world. Being immersed in her light gave him a strange, overpowering feeling, as if it were suddenly fueling him, strengthening him. With her blessing, he was ready.

"Where will you go? How will you find them?" Khalid's deep voice rose behind Elijah.

"I guess I will start with the *masjid*. Hopefully they'll find me." As soon as the words were out of his mouth, he realized he actually didn't have much of a plan.

"Here." Khalid stood up and handed him the piece of paper he had just been scribbling on. "That is directions back to the *masjid* and to my home from there."

Elijah accepted the scrap of paper and thanked him, then said his goodbyes and took off up the stairs. He could still hear Emira's muffled sobs as he slid the fireplace shut behind him.

## CHAPTER 84

USING THE DIRECTIONS Khalid had provided, Elijah was easily able to follow the path that had brought them in. As he passed the pond, he gave fleeting thought to the red sports car resting forever at the bottom. Within seconds he was at the road, and then the *masjid*.

The night air was cool as he walked around the building; he could almost see his breath. The lights were off inside and the parking lot was deserted. This wasn't where he needed to be.

The other address and directions Khalid had given him were easy to follow, and it didn't take him long to find his way to Khalid's front lawn. When he checked around the house he could tell someone had been there not long ago, but there was no sign of anyone now.

Inside, the house was a wreck. They had turned the place upside down looking for their prize. The drawers were all turned over; everything was scattered on the floor. Walls were busted in, couches torn apart. It looked as if wild animals had been locked in there for weeks.

Maybe that's all his brother was anymore, an animal. He had spent hundreds of years believing just that, but now he had reason to hope he might have been wrong. But where was Solomon? Elijah had one more idea.

He left the house and ran along the road, back to the first thing he had seen when he entered this small town. Walking into the gas station, the saw the same fat man sitting behind the counter, still punching away on his cash register with both hands. Elijah got in line behind a young man who seemed to be dressed up for a special occasion of some sort. He reeked of far too much cologne, but it was better than the stench of stale cigarette smoke that filled the small building.

"You're back." The fat little cash register puncher stated as Elijah stepped up to the counter.

"Yes. As a matter of fact, I need to ask for more directions." Elijah spoke politely.

"Well, I can't just give out directions if you don't buy anything; didn't you read the sign?" The man motioned to the front of the counter. "Hah!" he chortled as Elijah followed his finger. "I'm just joshin' ya. What is it you need, buddy?" The man asked between belly laughs.

Elijah was still smiling, trying his best to be patient and friendly.

"You are funny," he said, still managing to maintain a grin. "I was just wondering if there are any nearby churches."

"Yeah, well, there's lots of churches. What kind are you lookin' for? I thought you were a Muslim, anyway." The man looked confused and bored. He was eager for lengthy conversation, but Elijah didn't have time.

"Is there a big church, one with stained glass windows or any elaborate religious décor?" he asked.

"Yes there is, but it's a catholic church; I don't think you want to go there. They don't like Muslims much; they don't even like me, and I ain't nothin'." The man's slow speech and tendency to blather on and on was really nipping at Elijah's nerves.

"Thanks for the warning. Now, just tell me where it is." Elijah snapped, trying hard to hold in his frustration.

"Well, it ain't far. It's on the main highway, just a couple miles east."

"Thanks." Elijah could hear the man mumbling on, but he was out the door before he could hear enough to make any sense of it, if there was any sense to be made. It wasn't long before he could see the steeple and the stained glass in the distance. His chest was welling with hope. It all seemed to make sense now, at least the part about Solomon.

Solomon was still his brother; a brother he loved dearly. He had simply been forced to do some horrible things for the sake of Malaki. If Elijah could just talk to him alone, they could figure something out together. Solomon had always been a reasonable person; he just needed to know there was another way to save Mali. Elijah didn't know what that other way was, but was confidant there must be one, and he believed they could figure it out together.

He stopped just a few blocks from the church and stared up at the glass. This was the moment of truth. If Solomon was inside, Elijah would finally know for sure if he was still the brother he remembered or the monster he had been in Elijah's mind for so long.

He walked the last two blocks slowly, remembering some of the best times he'd had with his big brother. He hoped that man was inside, and he hoped they wouldn't have to kill each other.

Elijah walked up the steps to the big double doors at the front of the church. He took a deep breath and pulled on the enormous, elaborately carved handles.

# CHAPTER 85

A S THE DOORS swung open, a gust of wind raced across Elijah's face, carrying the scent of burning wicks and melting wax. The smell immediately drew Elijah's attention, and he looked to his right. There were a number of candles still burning; pools of hot wax surrounded some, as if they had been burning for some time now. The main altar was opposite the entrance, directly in front of him. As he turned his head towards the front, he saw what he was looking for.

"Come and sit with me, Brother." Solomon spoke before Elijah had taken even a step.

"You knew I would come?" Elijah asked. He was surprised. He had been one step behind his brother for so many years, it was a bit unsettling to find him waiting this time. Elijah walked forward, towards the answers he so desperately sought.

"I knew, after what I told you, your hope and curiosity would outweigh your hate." Solomon was sitting on a pew in the front row on the right side of the main altar. He had been staring up at a vivid and gruesome portrayal of a crucified Christ since Elijah walked in; he hadn't once looked back.

"Is it true? Is Malaki still alive?" Elijah asked.

"Yes, Brother, it's true." Solomon's tone was somber and melancholy.

Elijah didn't understand. "Then we will find a way to save him; we'll kill Father if we have to." Elijah's voice was full of enthusiasm as he tried to convince and inspire his older brother.

"You don't understand, Brother." Solomon's voice turned harsh. Elijah could see his frustration. "Father is the only way; he is the only one who knows where Malaki is. To kill Father would be to kill Malaki." Solomon's voice was filled with certainty; he seemed convinced and defeated as he hung his head.

"Just come with me, Solomon; we will find a way. I am no longer angry with you. I see now you have only been trying to protect our little brother. There is honor in what you have done." Elijah knelt beside his brother; his eyes were alight with hope.

"You still don't understand, little Brother. Until tonight, I had been able to lie to myself, make myself believe I was doing the right thing. After all, I was trying to save my brother, just like you said. That is how I have excused all of the horrors I have committed." Solomon's voice was cracking as he turned to face Elijah.

"When I saw the fury in your eyes and the disgust in your face this night, as you looked at me for the first time in almost a millennium, I realized the monster I had become. I couldn't hide from it anymore.

"You have always been strong Elijah," Solomon sighed, "and your judgment has always been true. That is the real reason Father killed you and hid Malaki away; he knew I was weak. He knew he could use Malaki to control me, that I could easily deceive myself into believing I was doing what was right." Solomon once again hung his head in shame and defeat as he stared at the faded purple velvet carpet beneath them.

"I have killed thousands of innocent people, Elijah, and I now know, after seeing the way you looked at me tonight, that even if I manage to save Malaki, the look on his face will be the same as yours, once he sees what I've become. Malaki would despise me for saving him, saving him only to live free in this cage of vampirism, to be a monster like me. That is what he is; it must be, if he is truly alive. He will have to kill to survive, just as I have." Solomon stood up and looked around, as if he were searching for something—anything—to bring him a sense of peace.

"I don't even know why I come here anymore. There is no solace, no peace left for me... not anywhere." Solomon looked at his brother.

Elijah looked on, now feeling only pity for the man he once loved and hated.

"I'm sorry, Elijah; I have been on this path for too long. You showed me the monster I have become, but it doesn't matter; I will be whatever I need to be to save Malaki. I pray you will help me, that I won't have to kill one brother to save the other. Please, put aside your hate for our father, choke it down, and let us get this done, for Malaki." Solomon knelt beside Elijah and took his hand. "We are family, Elijah. What is more important than that? Would you really put these people you hardly know before family?" Solomon's gaze was an accusation.

"The family I have left has betrayed me and left me for dead more than once. Solomon, I know Father, and I know he can't be trusted, not to release Malaki, and definitely not with something that could make him even more powerful than he already is. We have to stop him." Elijah spoke with conviction.

"I can't allow you to kill Father, not yet," Solomon swallowed as he paused. "He has assured me many times that if anything should happen to him, Malaki would also find his way to the underworld. I know you don't want that to happen to our little brother. If you help me to free Malaki, then I will help you kill Father." Solomon rubbed his brother's hand between his own and looked him in the eye.

"Join me." Solomon dropped Elijah's hand and stood up. "Join me." He held out an open hand, as though hoping Elijah would take it. "Join me, Brother." Solomon begged.

Elijah looked up at the man who had once been his beloved big brother; he could see his desperation.

"Let us do this together, for the sake of our little brother." He reached his hand further toward Elijah.

"Please, just come with me and we will take Father together; we will force him to tell us where he is keeping Malaki," Elijah pleaded.

Solomon dropped his hand as he hung his chin once more and stared at the ground. "You are not listening, Brother!" he shouted. When he looked up, Elijah could see whispers of blue shoot through Solomon's eyes. "I'm sorry, Brother; sometimes it's hard for me to hide my frustration." Solomon smiled. "There is no other way." His tone grew dire; the expression on his face was grim, but Elijah could see the weariness behind his emotion and determination. "I have waited hundreds of years for this opportunity; I'm not going to risk it on some ill-conceived scheme. Please come with me, and let's save our brother." Solomon once again extended his hand.

Elijah didn't know what to do. He would risk the world to save his brother, but not on his father's word. Elijah knew his father needed Malaki to control Solomon, and there was no way he would give that up willingly.

"Father is not going to give you Malaki," Elijah said, standing up. "Can't you see that?"

"After he gets what he wants, he will have no more need of me. If Malaki is alive, he will give him to me." Solomon held out his hand towards Elijah once again.

"I can't help you, Brother. We can't let Father get what he

wants, who knows what he might do with it?" Elijah watched as Solomon dropped his hand to his side.

"I am not the man I once was," Solomon replied, "but I love you, Brother, and I wish you luck. However, I warn you, I will do whatever it takes to get our little brother back, and I'm terribly disappointed you are not willing to do the same. If you place yourself between me and the chance to find Malaki, I will do what I have to do."

"I know you, Brother, and I know you are only doing what you think is right," Solomon continued. "I will not hold it against you if you have it in you to kill me and Father. You will only be doing what I cannot, releasing both of your brothers from the purgatories in which we live. If you see an end to this, Brother, please remember me as I was, and if I have to cut you down, know I will mourn you for as long as I live."

Solomon reached over and pulled Elijah into a warm embrace. The oddly familiar feeling of his brother's strong arms around his chest brought to the surface of Elijah's mind memories that he had buried deep. He was overwhelmed, like a child who was once again in his big brother's loving arms. A tear fell onto his cheek from Solomon's eye; it moved Elijah to tears. He had never seen his big brother cry, not even as a child; he had been their fierce guardian, their protector. Elijah wondered if, over the course of centuries, this was the first time his brother had been brought to tears.

"You would have me kill you, Brother? And Malaki?" Elijah asked as tears streamed down his face.

"If you do, don't weigh yourself down with guilt, for you will have freed us. Death is a peace we should have known long ago, if I had only been strong enough to accept it."

Elijah heard the weariness in Solomon's voice. When he finished speaking, Solomon kissed his brother on the forehead and was gone.

Elijah raced to the door, but saw nothing, no hint of where his brother had gone. He was overcome with grief. Things hadn't turned out at all as he had hoped. It had been much easier to imagine killing his brother when he hated him.

Now all of Elijah's hate was focused, burning in one direction—towards his father. It burned with a renewed passion, stronger and hotter than ever as he raced back towards the cabin. He was eager to see Emira and have this passion dulled, at least for now. For the time being there was nothing he could do about his father, but he would find him soon enough.

## CHAPTER 86

SLIDING THE LARGE granite fireplace shut, Elijah was pleased to hear the chattering voices below. Emira was in his arms before he could reach the bottom of the steps. Her touch and smell refreshed his spirit and dulled the anger and pain that pervaded him.

"I'm so glad you are okay!" She squeezed even tighter. "Did you find your brother?" She looked briefly at his face and then squeezed him again as if she could sense things hadn't gone well. "Were you not able to find him?" she asked.

"I found him," Elijah said dully; he didn't want to talk about it.

"Well, was he not willing to speak with you?"

Elijah could see she wanted him to elaborate; she wanted some kind of explanation. "We spoke," he said softly, his face tense with pain. "He's lost; he is hopeless."

"What did he say?" she pressed.

"It appears my recent hopes were unfounded. My brother Solomon believes my father has been holding our little brother prisoner since the night he butchered my mother. He believes by helping William he will be able to save our brother. He believes once Father gets what he wants he will release Malaki."

Elijah gently pushed Emira back and closed his eyes as he rubbed the side of his neck. "If I believed that for a second, I might reconsider what side I'm on, but I know he won't, even if he is still alive." Elijah sighed. Suddenly, he noticed uncomfortable glances back and forth between Emira and Khalid.

"We need to know we can count on you; that your family ties won't get in the way of what we are trying to do here. Your family is evil, wrong, bad; you know this!" Khalid exclaimed.

Elijah glared at him, but Emira must have seen his tension and sorrow, because she touched him softly on the face and pulled him to face her. Elijah closed his eyes and took a deep breath to calm himself.

"My brother is not a bad man; he is just a lost soul doing what he can to save his brother, grasping at straws, hoping all he has done is not in vain. I love my brothers, but I will do what I think is right. I need vengeance, and I believe and trust what Ayda told me long ago: we can't let my father get his hands on whatever he's looking for.

"Solomon embraced me as a brother and wished me luck. He said killing him would only free him from his eternal nightmare." Elijah spoke as if he were in a trance.

"Did you kill him?" Emira's voice was soft but penetrating.

"No!" Elijah snapped back. Her question evoked painful emotions. She retreated a step, and Elijah could see he had hurt her feelings. "I'm sorry, Emira. I'm just all messed up right now. I have wanted to kill my brother for nearly a millennium, but couldn't find him. Now I have to kill him; I need to kill him, but I'm not sure I want to." Elijah looked up at Emira and then at Khalid, who immediately looked suspicious.

"So he is just going to let you kill him?" She sounded confused.

"Emira, leave the man alone; at least give him a minute to catch his breath," Khalid begged, but it wasn't going to help. She obviously wanted answers.

"No, it's okay. Besides Ayda, you guys are the closest things I have to friends, and you deserve to know." His voice was now calm, his manner collected. "The answer to your question, Emira, is no," he stated calmly, but then, he was suddenly numb, inside and out, as if he hadn't completely processed the truth.

"But that doesn't make any sense. You said he asked you to kill him," her voice grew higher with her confusion.

"Not exactly; he just acknowledged we were on colliding paths and wished me luck in the ensuing collision. I think he has been traveling down a certain road for so long, he doesn't know how to change course. If there is another way to save Malaki, it would mean all the atrocities Solomon has committed would have been for nothing. I don't think he can handle that." As he spoke, Elijah pictured the gentle Solomon he knew in his youth and his tears began to well again.

"A lot of things have happened to my brother. He was always strong, but he had a gentle soul. He has been forced to do things, in his righteous but misguided attempt to save my little brother, things the man I knew could never have countenanced or withstood." Elijah was speaking fast and pacing the floor as if he was on to something.

"I think those evil deeds have twisted his gentle soul; in order to cope and keep pressing forward for the sake of Malaki, his soul was forced to twist and bend until it broke into two pieces. The brother I loved is still in there; I spoke to him tonight. There is also a darkness in him; the same darkness that is in my father." Elijah paused. "He is to blame, for all of this." Elijah said viciously

"What about your little brother? How will you save him?" Emira's sweet voice was filled with concern for a boy she'd never met. Elijah reached out and pulled her close to his chest, wrapping his arms around her waist.

"If he truly is still alive, Malaki has spent hundreds of years in a prison of some sort, either corporeal or locked in his mind in some kind of coma. Solomon spoke as if they had both been living in some kind of purgatory, Solomon's created by his own hand." He was speaking quickly again, but he was still holding onto Emira, looking into her eyes.

"So, what are you going to do?" Khalid's deep voice came rumbling from behind her.

"I'm going to do what I came here to do. I'm going to kill them all." His vision was concrete, despite his somber feelings of regret.

"Solomon is right. Even if I could save Malaki, he could never find peace or happiness living as a vampire, feeding off of innocent people. The only true way to save him is to bring him the peace in death he is owed. So that is what I must do. Solomon assured me Father's men have orders to kill Malaki if anything happens to him. Besides, I have learned from experience that good men can't live as vampires; they either fall into darkness, or they find a way to kill themselves." Elijah looked down at the floor. Tonight had been a crushing disappointment.

Emira leaned forward and leaned the side of her face against his chest. The pressure made him realize his heart was beating hard and fast, like a war drum.

"I'll be in the bedroom." Elijah gently pushed her back and cupped her face in his hands for a moment. He squeezed her once more, softly, and disappeared into his designated room.

## CHAPTER 87

FRESH AIR FILLED the room. The linens on the bed smelled clean. A gust of lilac floated up from the bed as Elijah turned down the sheets. After taking off his clothes, he climbed into the bed and pushed his feet underneath the wool blanket at the foot of the bed for warmth.

In the living room he could hear Emira and Khalid talking. At first they were speaking in quiet, serious tones; Elijah could hear Khalid express concerns about his allegiance and Emira defend him. Soon they began joking, arguing and carrying on. He heard his name more than once. Elijah closed his eyes and listened to the melodic rhythm of Emira's light, sweet voice. Although he could hear every word of their conversation, he was no longer paying attention.

It seemed only moments later a soft touch gently rubbed against his arm. He opened his eyes immediately, as if only aroused from a brief reverie, and quickly rotated his head and shoulders to the right. He was surprised and comforted to see just what he had imagined.

Emira was lying in the bed beside him with her hand lying gently on his arm. Her fingers were tucked just beneath the short sleeve of his shirt. She recoiled slightly as he turned, but he quickly caught her wrist.

"No," he said, clasping her left hand in his own as he tucked his arm tightly against her abdomen, just beneath her breasts.

"I thought you were asleep," she whispered.

*I don't sleep,* he thought. He pulled her tighter, until her back was pressed firmly against his chest.

His tight grip was unexpected and a little uncomfortable at first, but the discomfort quickly eroded as Emira realized, even in the midst of all the night's danger and chaos, she was not afraid. She had never felt safer than she did in this moment, beneath Elijah's heavy and capable arm, in the clutches of the same hands that, only hours earlier, had nearly squeezed the life out of one of the strongest-looking men she had ever seen. She lay with a lion, and she knew it.

She knew this man was dangerous, but not to her. His touch had proven to be as ferociously gentle with her as it had been savage around Solomon's neck. The strong, steady beat of his heart thumping against her back was soothing. She thought about the warmth of his breath on her neck while she drifted off to sleep.

The delicate bit of vibrant life beneath his arm had gone limp, all except for the surprisingly tight grip she had on his wrist. It was as if she was afraid he might disappear. The smell of her hair and neck were enchanting, and he was most definitely under her spell; she was the best thing he had known in centuries. She was a goddess.

He thought about his discussion with Khalid about all the different gods. Elijah wasn't concerned with them. Here, now, tangled in Emira's arms, she was the only god that mattered. From this moment on, he would kneel only to her, worship only her. She alone deserved such adulation. She gave him hope, but could she revive his heart? Could she undo the scars left from losing Sara? From leaving Ayda? That, he didn't know, but at least he had hope.

Elijah suddenly thought about the thousands of girls he had been with over the years… and how he had treated them like animated tools, only there to ease his mind and body. For the first time he was sorry for, and disgusted by, his actions, but Emira's tight squeeze quickly relieved all the bad feelings. She made him feel wonderful and alive for the first time since he was young.

Everything about this girl surprised him. For more than eight hundred years, all he had known was pain, anger, and a gripping need for vengeance, but in the powerful presence of this tiny package all of those feelings melted away. He was left with an unimaginable peace. At least for the moment, nothing else mattered; he was right where he belonged, where he wanted to be. Entangled with this tiny goddess, he could finally rest.

## Elijah: The Reckoning
# 2014 AD

*"I'm going to kill them all."*

# CHAPTER 88

ELIJAH OPENED HIS eyes to the sting of a cold wind blowing through his room and across his bare chest. Then he remembered where he was and the events of the night before. He was momentarily comforted by thoughts of Emira's warm body lying next to him... but only now, as he reached across the bed, did he realize she wasn't there.

She was gone. His heart surged with fear as he leapt out of bed and searched every room. Thoughts of his father ripping open her chest crashed against the inside of his head like tidal waves.

*What has happened? How did I let this happen?* he thought frantically. Then a stunning realization sank in.

For the first time in almost a millennium, he had fallen asleep. He was furious, at her for making him so weak, but, most of all at himself for not protecting her, for losing his wits when he needed them most.

If she were hurt, there would be a reckoning that would stir the earth and everyone on it; it would shake the very foundation of the universe; the heavens would tumble down, and he would see these *gods* punished and parted from their heads. For ages to come, the children of men would feel his pain, but no one would suffer more than he. He would be punished by an eternity of despair from which he would never relieve himself.

As he ran up the stairs, he could see the stone slab had been pushed open and feel a cold breeze rushing down to the basement floor. Bursting into the outside air, he was relieved to see Khalid standing just feet from the pile of wood and ash which had been a roaring fire the night before.

"Khalid!" he shouted. As Khalid turned around, Elijah could see the somber look on his face—something was most definitely wrong. He immediately scanned his surroundings to find Emira.

He followed Khalid's eyes, and he saw it, on a hillside in the distance, the very thing he hoped never to see again. Camouflaged directly beneath an old hickory tree, he could see his father, and in his vicious grip was Emira. It seemed like just moments ago she had been nestled safely against his chest. *How could his father have stolen her from beneath his very arm? Maybe she walked out on her own.* Elijah's thoughts were racing.

The sleep had disoriented him; he had only a vague sense of time. The sun was nearly halfway up the eastern sky, so he knew it was some time in the morning. Seeing Emira in his father's hands again enraged him. His eyes burned with fury as his solidifying bones ached and slightly expanded. There was only one thing he knew to do. He raced towards his father. One way or another, this was all going to end right now.

Khalid intercepted him just yards before he reached his father and Emira. Khalid's grasp around his chest was like a prison.

"Elijah, stop." Khalid whispered in his ear. "He will kill her, and I know you don't want that."

"Listen to your big friend, my son. Put away those yellow eyes, boy, or do you need another lesson in manners?" William lifted Emira in the air by her throat and twisted her chin slightly as she struggled to breathe. "You don't want another innocent girl's blood on your hands, do you?" he chortled. The snide reference to Sara only heightened his fury and his eyes burned hotter.

"Elijah, look!" Khalid shouted as he released him. Elijah looked. Emira was struggling less and less; she was about to die. Elijah took a deep breath and closed his eyes, when he opened them again they had dulled to their natural brown.

"Good." William sat the girl down on her feet, holding her loosely by the back of the neck. "My foolish boy, did you really think you could turn your brother against me? I own him," William boasted. Elijah looked at Solomon, who was standing beside his father and staring at the ground. He wouldn't look Elijah in the eyes.

"I told you I was a monster, Brother. Did you not believe me?" Solomon's voice was steady, but Elijah could hear his shame.

"You led them here, Solomon? You brought them to my door after I reached out to you last night?" Anger and the pain of betrayal were once again building in his chest. "You are both monsters, and I will have your heads," Elijah roared.

"Settle down, Son. It wasn't your brother who gave you away; my people are everywhere. They followed you from the church last night, after Solomon had already left. Did you not know we would be watching you? I told you to leave; I gave you a chance." He laughed condescendingly.

"Let her go, Father. This is between you and me," Elijah tried to sound fierce and firm, but he could hear the pleading in his voice.

"No, Son. I have no interest in you. This is between Khalid and me. He has what I want." Elijah turned to Khalid, who looked defeated and apologetic.

"Give him what he wants," Elijah demanded.

"I told you last night, I can't."

Elijah suddenly remembered their earlier conversation.

"He doesn't have it!" Elijah shouted. "He told me last night; it does not exist." Elijah's voice was cracking with emotion.

"Come on, Elijah, we have been here before. We all know how this ends. Hand it over, or I will do everything to her I had to do to poor Sara." William handed Emira to Solomon and motioned for him to take her away.

"Kill her in one hour, unless I say different." He shouted over his shoulder, almost indifferently. Solomon nodded and was gone.

"Khalid is lying to you, Son, and you better find the truth or your girl will find only pain and... .eventually... death." William's tone was arrogant and threatening as he walked closer to Elijah and Khalid.

"I will break you in half, old man!" Elijah lunged at his father. Grasping him by the neck, he hurled him towards the pile of ash. When William stood, Elijah gripped him firmly by the chin and bent the man almost double over the huge tree trunk he had ripped from the ground the night before. His father seemed surprised by Elijah's strength. "You will pay for what you did to Sara!"

"Old man!" William laughed. "You are as old as I am." The disgusting stench of death was all over the man. Fresh blood stains were on his collar and neck.

"I have no time for games, Father! Where is he taking her?" Elijah was burning with fury and impatience.

"I told you, I can't have you meddling in my affairs," William said as he pushed himself nearly upright.

"I should kill you right now," Elijah growled, pushing him a little harder against the tree until it started cracking under the stress.

"Go ahead, but it would be the girl's death sentence, and your little brother's as well." William smirked.

Elijah's heart sank for a moment as he thought of Emira and Malaki, and the real possibility he would never see either of them again. His grip dropped to rest on his father's neck.

"Tell me, Father, where is Malaki?" He tried to sound accusing, but knew his voice was filled with hints of desperation.

"Malaki is in a very safe place, far away from all of this." William's continued smirking raised a murderous fury in Elijah; he wanted nothing more than to end his father, in gory battle, right now.

"Is he even still alive?" Elijah demanded.

"Oh, yes, he is very much alive," William drawled.

Elijah was barely managing to resist his urge to tear his father limb from limb.

"Know this, Father. I *will* kill you, and in doing so, I will give Malaki the peace in death he deserved so long ago. I may not be able to do it today, but, believe this—your fate is certain." He twisted his father's head to the point of snapping it and then suddenly let go.

"Fair enough, Son." Rubbing his fingers beneath his jaw, William straightened. "But not yet. Today, you will put your tail between your legs and leave this place. We will take your friend here and… well, we'll do whatever we have to do to discover all of his dirty little secrets."

Elijah looked up at the mountain of a friend beside him. In Khalid's eyes he could see many things: remorse, frustration, but not fear. He wasn't afraid of William, or the two other immortals standing near them.

Elijah thought of the gruesome and horrifying things his father would do to him, to force him to talk. The most dreadful thought, which Elijah knew to a near certainty, was the big man would not break, even if he did know more than he was letting on, if not for Emira's life, then surely not for his own.

Elijah's choices were impossible. But he couldn't do anything to risk hurting Emira, which included allowing Khalid to face the wrath of these three immortals on his own. He turned to Khalid.

"Run!" He shouted as he jumped on the man to his father's immediate right and twisted his head in a complete circle. He lifted the man off the ground and, swinging him by the head like a baseball bat, he hit another of his father's immortal goons in the back and knocked him off of his feet.

Khalid was not one to run. His instincts told him to fight. He was not afraid, and he could not leave Elijah there to die, especially after the sacrifice he had just made to protect him, but fighting these men could lead to Emira's death.

"Stop!" Khalid's voice thundered through the hills. "I will give you what you want." Everyone else was silent; no one moved. Elijah was shocked. "Leave us now, and bring Emira to my home tonight at dusk, unharmed, and, on my honor, you will hold in your hand that which you seek." His expression was cold and his voice solemn.

"Give it to me now." There was excitement and determination in William's eyes.

"I can't. It is not here." He seemed to be telling the truth, at least as far as Elijah could tell.

"Agreed, then." William was shaking his head and walking towards the big man. "But know this. If you are lying, you are all dead, starting with the girl." William picked up his nearly-decapitated man and he and his other goon disappeared into the forest. Elijah was shocked by Khalid's revelation, and appalled at how he had risked Emira's life by waiting so long to speak up.

# CHAPTER 89

E LIJAH TURNED TO Khalid and, without warning, slammed his fist into the big man's chin, sending him stumbling to the ground.

"What were you th—" Before Elijah could finish speaking, the ground around them began to rumble and the world seemed to vanish behind a blinding light.

"Hear me now." A voice thundered all around them. Elijah thought his head would explode. He looked over at Khalid who was also covering his ears. "I am Mikal." The expression on Khalid's face grew grim. Elijah looked up to see the glowing form of a huge man; he seemed to be made of pure energy. The brightness of his glow was so blinding Elijah had to shield his eyes and look away.

"I have empowered you to one end and one end alone, to take your revenge and end my brother's most unrighteous quest for power. I chose you because I knew your hunger for vengeance would lead me to the truth about these rumors. If this rite does exist, if my brother has truly found a way to elevate a creation to a godlike level or beyond, then you cannot let it fall into the hands of Adol, or your father. I will not allow you to turn away from our righteous path, not for any reason, especially not for a mere creation, a girl.

"Your goal is now within reach," the booming voice continued.

"If you don't seize it, if you let anything distract you, if you give your father what he wants, I will relieve you of your power. I will rob you of your vengeance forever, and you will wither and die. A thousand years of decomposition will catch up with your empowered corpse in just minutes, and you will be no more. There are no other options. You must press on towards your destiny; be not compromised." The voice thundered so loudly Elijah could barely understand it. And then it was gone.

Everything was suddenly back to normal; the light was gone. Elijah's thoughts raced, as if his mind couldn't accept what had just happened and was searching for some alternate explanation.

Khalid studied his confused countenance for a moment, and then climbed to his feet to face Elijah.

"I knew you were different," Khalid was in awe, and his tone was gentle. "But I never imagined. One family commissioned by two different gods; now it all makes sense." Khalid reached out and grabbed Elijah by the shoulder as if to comfort him.

"What do you mean? Did you see that? What *was* that?" Elijah was staggering with one hand still over his ear.

"You were right. You are nothing like your father, or your brother. You are much, much different." Khalid's eyes were wide.

"What are you talking about? Who was that?" Elijah was still in shock.

"Listen to me, Elijah. As you well know, there are immortal beings on this earth—you being one of them. These immortals are the way they are because they have been empowered by the gods." Khalid grabbed him by both arms as he spoke.

"Yes, yes, you told me all of this last night." Elijah spoke frantically.

"Remember I told you of Adol? He is called the Lord of Death and Decay. The ancients described him as having no vestige of kindness or mercy. He was considered evil because he took what people held most dear—their lives.

"In some ways Mikal is the yang to Adol's yin, if you will. He was worshipped as the God of Light, the bringer of life. He wears the visage of goodness and all kinds of creation spring from him."

Khalid spoke so fast Elijah frowned, trying to keep up.

*"I am Mikal."* Elijah was taken back to only moments ago, when he heard that thundering voice. He had seemed more like a tyrant than the bringer of life.

"The vessels of Adol, like your father, their numbers are vast. Adol creates them and charges them with one purpose, to make chaos and to snuff out the life in his brother's creations and increase his own power on this plane. Lately, his main concern has been finding this rite." Khalid paused and took a deep breath and then continued.

"Adol can't create life, but he can alter it. That is why vampires have to feed off of the living to stay alive, because Adol himself does not have the power of life. Instead, they have to steal their life from Mikal's creations. You, on the other hand, are empowered by the god of life himself, that is why you are fully sustained and your body and power want for nothing.

"You told me the ME didn't exist." Elijah was brooding.

"I'm sorry, my friend. I lied to you. I had to. How was I to know the son of Adol's vessel would be the hand of Mikal? It's insane. The ME is dangerous and powerful. Mikal is right; we can't let your father get his hands on it."

"Hand of Mikal?" Elijah was still shocked and hadn't put it all together. *"I am Mikal... I empowered you,"* the words echoed around his mind. "So you think I have been made immortal by Mikal?" Elijah still didn't know if he believed any of this. He hadn't believed in gods since he was a boy.

"Yes. It is the only thing that makes any sense. You are one of the most powerful immortals I have ever met, and you don't feed on blood. That is exactly what you are." Khalid seemed certain.

"It never occurred to me. I have never heard of such beings. It makes sense he would pick you, though, with the hate you already had for your family." Khalid's logic seemed solid.

"So, why isn't Mikal concerned with getting this rite for himself?" Elijah inquired.

"Well, the legends say he never believed they existed, but I guess he does now." Khalid looked around at the havoc created by Mikal's outburst. "Like I told you before, the ME are said to have been made by Odam, the god of will and the spirit of the earth, to protect men from the gods." Khalid turned away, running his fingers through his thick, black hair.

"To protect from the gods—plural—but you said Mikal was good." Elijah frowned in confusion.

"Are you not listening to me? I said he was light, I said he was creation, but I only said he puts on the visage—the face, the pretense—of goodness. In the end he is just as arrogant and power-hungry as Adol; just as careless towards the sufferings of man. Tell me, Elijah, what do you imagine causes more pain, to live or to die? What causes more suffering—life or death? Neither cares about us; their only concern is for power. That is why they have been locked in battle for millennia."

Khalid's words resonated deep in Elijah's mind. Life *had* caused him much pain. He hadn't known death, but he had longed for it many times. He couldn't imagine death being any worse than life, at least the life he had known.

"Then what about the other brother?" Elijah was desperate. He hoped there was goodness somewhere in the heavens.

"Odam, the god of will. Like I said, he is called the spirit of the earth or the breath of man, that's what the ancients called him. He left us long ago. He was the only vestige of righteousness in the heavens. He tried to protect man, but he loved his brothers too much to harm them, and finally their tireless quarrelling drove him away, far away." The tone in Khalid's voice had changed drastically. Before, it had been as if he was reading out of a book on mythology, but now he was angry, even personally invested. Elijah didn't understand.

"But before he left, as I told you before, he made his own race of immortals. Their only charge was to hold the planet together, and to fight the very gods above them, it seems." Now Khalid seemed bitter and sarcastic as he threw up his hands in defeat.

"The truth is, I think he is weak and afraid," Khalid admitted. Bitterness colored every word he spoke, and Elijah was beginning to believe Khalid was either crazy, or hurt.

"So there's not much difference between him and the others?" Elijah said with disappointment.

"No, there is. I'm sorry. I was just being emotional and dramatic. Odam has a deep respect for mankind. He sees us as sacred and beautiful. Gods know little if any suffering, which is why he so admires us and carries us through our most difficult times. He sees much beauty and strength in our perseverance in the face of pain and suffering, tragedy and loss, and eventually death." Khalid's tone had once again changed; his voice was now filled with love and admiration.

"Gods do not know death, and Odam believes the way we live and love, with the knowledge of our mortality, and in the face of our damnation, is very romantic. We have an ending, an eventual finality that will come as surely as the sun will rise and set; that is what makes everything count, every moment meaningful, every breath a gift, every kiss a precious flower that withers and fades, only remaining in the vastness of what was and will never again be. Odam's eternity of experience and wisdom has led him to the conclusion that nothing lasting can be beautiful, because beauty comes in the passion of moments and lives that fade." Khalid's voice shook with emotion.

"Death is what allows us to live. Death is what makes us alive. He envies us and he respects us." Khalid's tone grew strong, but gentle, like a heavy load had been lifted from his shoulders. "He does not see himself as above us, or better than us, as his brothers do. That is the difference."

"That is all well and good, but how can you say Mikal is right? If we don't give my father what he wants, Emira will die." Elijah spoke with absolute conviction.

"Elijah, Odam has empowered me for longer than you could imagine. My only charge has been to protect the ME." Khalid rubbed his chin and looked at the ground. "I love Emira with all my heart, but I can't risk the balance of the universe to save her."

Elijah could see he was sincere, but…"That's not good enough, Khalid. You can't just let her die!" Elijah shouted.

"What exactly would you have me do?" Khalid asked.

"I say fuck the gods! Fuck the balance of the fucking universe—fuck the universe altogether! You are worried about a universe out there that doesn't care shit for you. What about Emira's universe? It's going to disappear. I'm willing to sacrifice my universe to save her, since, when I hand over that rite, I'm a dead man."

Elijah threw up his hands. "I'm tired of seeing the people I care about die. What is the fucking universe without the people we love?" Elijah could see his words weighing on Khalid's mind as he stared blankly at the ground, rubbing his forehead.

"Elijah, there is something else you should know about Emira." Khalid looked up at him, his eyes burdened with pain. "She is *The Key* to the rite. Your father has her. If we also give him the rite, then he will have everything he needs," he sighed.

"So the rite itself is useless without Emira?" Elijah asked as he stepped forward and placed his hands on Khalid's shoulders. A faint smile quirked his mouth.

"Yes. She doesn't even know yet, but she is the only one who can read it." Khalid admitted.

"Then the decision is easy. We can save Emira and maintain the balance; we just have to make sure we save her. My father doesn't know anything about her. He has no idea she is special." Elijah smacked his palms victoriously against Khalid's chest, his voice filled with enthusiasm.

"That's right! Vampires can't see her light. That *is* the only way we are able to protect her. They know nothing of *The Key*," Khalid mused.

"Well, let's do it, then. Let's get her back." As he spoke, Elijah searched Khalid's face for consensus.

"You heard what Mikal said. Are you truly willing to give up your life for a girl you scarcely know?" Khalid asked.

Elijah nodded firmly; he could see Khalid was inspired by his willingness. "I am a wretched being; her life is worth infinitely more than mine. As long as I take my father with me, I will die smiling. I'll have to do it immediately after we make the trade, since I don't know if I will have minutes or seconds... but either way, I will have to be very quick. My life is of little consequence to me; it's definitely not worth hers. I live only for vengeance; she sees so much more." Elijah gazed at Khalid, his eyes pleading and bleeding hope at the same time.

"Okay. Let the gods fight their own war. Let's save Emira," Khalid agreed. "If we see an opportunity to save her without giving up the rite, we'll take it. Otherwise, we just have to make sure we save Emira."

Hope was now ready to burst from Elijah's chest. This was the best death he could imagine... to save Emira and have his vengeance before Mikal took his power and his life.

"I'll take care of my father, but it will be on you to get Emira out of harm's way." If the course of tonight's events unfolded as he envisioned, he would be dead and his loved ones avenged by morning.

## CHAPTER 90

"WHAT ARE YOU doing?" Elijah yelled when he saw Khalid walking back into the cabin.

"I'll be right back." Khalid shouted over his shoulder. Standing out in the middle of nowhere, Elijah surveyed the landscape around him.

*How serene and lovely.* It was a shame he had been on such a beautiful planet for so long and never cared to notice its majesty, all the beautiful life and color. *Textures*, he thought of Emira and her smooth skin; the way her soft lips had felt against his cheek, her warm breath on his chest, and how her heartbeat had echoed through his mind and into eternity. She set him free.

He also couldn't help thinking of Ayda. He still loved her, and the thought he might never see her again saddened him; but knowing she was out there in the world, somewhere safe, gave him comfort. He wished he could have seen her one last time, to embrace her, and to apologize for the life they never had.

It confounded him that his love for Emira began with a couple of old coins. He wondered what would have happened if Ayda had found those coins, if he had seen that necklace lying on her collarbone instead. He imagined it would have changed everything.

Elijah slowly turned his head as he heard Khalid's thundering footsteps emerge from the cabin. In his hand was a tiny piece of parchment. As he reached Elijah, he extended his hand with the piece of parchment clenched tightly in his fist.

"I have never known nor trusted one of your kind. You may not be one of Adol's immortals, but you are still the vessel of an unholy god. I am not trusting what you are, but who you have proven yourself to be." The gravity of his voice was daunting, and Elijah still didn't understand. Khalid opened his hand and thrust the parchment closer to Elijah's chest.

"Take it, now. I must go." Khalid spoke quickly as Elijah accepted the parchment and read the small inscription on the top,

*Apotheosis*, it read. Elijah was still confused for a moment, and then clarity washed over him like rain as he remembered their conversation last night.

"This is it? This little piece of paper is what immortals and even gods have been searching for, for ages?" Elijah asked. It seemed incredible. It seemed so insignificant.

"Yes, that is it; it's not the paper that's important, it's what's on it." Khalid's tone was condescending. Elijah knew the paper itself wasn't important, but he had expected the thing to be a little more impressive-looking.

"That's great! We can negotiate with my father now." Elijah was bubbling with enthusiasm.

"It's not that simple," Khalid said slowly. Elijah could hear his concern. "This is only part of it; there is a council of my kind. I must go and meet with them; I must convince them to give me the other piece." Khalid's worried face told Elijah the task was unlikely to be easy.

"I'm ready. Where are we going?" Elijah asked.

"*We* are not going anywhere; the council doesn't like outsiders," Khalid shifted away after speaking as if to close the subject.

"I'm coming with you. What if they won't give it to you? What if you have to take it? You will need me," Elijah demanded urgently.

"It won't come to that," Khalid waved his hand sharply and dismissively.

From the look on his face, Elijah guessed he found the thought of fighting his own people very disturbing. "But what if it does?" Elijah stepped close enough to be almost literally in his face.

"Okay," Khalid responded after pacing and muttering for a few moments, "I hate this, but you're right. Saving Emira is the most important thing. But we must not tell them about her light. If they learn William already has *The Key*, there is no way they will help us."

"Why don't they know?" Elijah frowned in confusion.

"Her light just started a few days ago. *The Key* is always reborn into a human family in one of our bloodlines. We watch over the children of our descendants until one of them is revealed to be *The Key*. With all the vampire problems of late and… well, you, I just haven't had time to tell the others yet. Also, once they find out, she will be taken away, moved around, better protected. I guess I just wasn't ready for that. Only Ayda knows, fortunately." Khalid raised his busy brows and looked challengingly at Elijah. "How fast are you on your feet?" he asked, smiling.

Elijah knew he'd just thrown down a friendly, competitive gauntlet. "Fast enough to keep up with you," Elijah grinned back. Khalid shook his head doubtfully. "Where are we going, anyway?" Elijah asked.

"Kentucky." Khalid spoke as if it were just across the street.

"Kentucky? How will we get back in time to meet my father?" Maybe this wasn't the best plan.

"As long as you can keep up, we shouldn't have a problem." Khalid smiled again, tauntingly, and then took off toward the woods. "Are you coming or not?" he yelled over his shoulder as he disappeared into the tree line. Elijah heard thunder, the sound of heavy footfalls and then nothing.

Elijah quickly took off after him. He couldn't see Khalid ahead, but the path left by the huge man would have been hard for anyone to miss. He seemed to tear through everything in the forest. But Elijah was fast; he knew he would soon catch up.

# CHAPTER 91

ELIJAH HAD BEEN running his fastest for at least an hour, and the only sign of Khalid continued to be the brutish path he had ripped through the thick underbrush. He had crossed roads, mountains, and even rivers. *How fast is he, anyway?* Elijah was amazed, and impressed.

As he passed over a thick, trampled briar patch, Elijah noticed a bit of blood and a large tuft of black fur caught on one of the thorns. Had Khalid run into trouble? Had he been attacked by something? Knowing how strong and capable the man was, Elijah didn't bother to worry. He felt sorry for the poor beast that had gotten in his way.

It was a couple hours later that Elijah crossed over a small creak and saw Khalid leaning against a large tree, buttoning his shirt.

"You are faster than I thought," he smiled at Elijah.

"Obviously not fast enough. How long have you been here?" Elijah was curious as to just how fast Khalid was.

"Only a matter of minutes; you were right on my heels the entire time, it seems. Of course, I did clear the path," Khalid beamed proudly.

"Are we close?" Elijah was worried. If they took too much longer they might not make it back in time to save Emira.

"Yes, it's just over that mountain." Khalid pointed as he spoke. "Don't say anything; let me do the talking. Your presence here alone is going to upset him." He seemed even more worried now.

"*HE* will be upset? I thought you said we would be meeting with a council." Elijah was once again annoyed by the big man's secrets and half-truths.

"I am hoping to avoid the council." Khalid paused for a moment and took a deep breath. "The man who lives here is named Arhan. We don't have a leader, but if we did, some might say it is Arhan. He is the guardian who keeps the other half of the ME. Technically we would have to call the council for any decision of this magnitude, but I'm hoping he will cooperate." Though his words were somewhat optimistic, Khalid's voice told an entirely different story. "Follow me," he commanded and raced up the hill with Elijah close behind.

## CHAPTER 92

E LIJAH WAS SURPRISED by the view from the top of the mountain. The valley below was completely cleared of underbrush. In the very center stood a large wooden cabin that seemed the exact opposite of Khalid's small hideout. It was two stories high, and a large crescent window stretched across both stories.

There was a huge wraparound porch extending along three sides of the building, and the back door opened to a set of stairs that climbed down to meet a rocky path leading to a gazebo. The gazebo was intricately designed; it was round, with delicately carved rails stretching from the waist-high walls to the cone-shaped roof.

As they approached the cabin, Elijah could see it wasn't made of treated lumber. Instead, the logs were bare, sanded and cut to fit together perfectly. Their texture was rough and dry. The wood still smelled like wood; the cabin's look and smell reminded Elijah of something beautiful from ages past. He imagined the walls inside looked similar to the outside, with no drywall or insulation.

According to modern standards the house would be

considered raw and unfinished, a work in progress, and perhaps even unlivable. Elijah could remember a time not long ago when it would have been considered magnificent. He had lived long enough to recognize the gem the structure truly was. The man who built this was an artisan, an expert at his craft.

The landscaping, which encircled the house, was also elaborate. The same logs that made up the house framed the flower garden; they were artfully designed and crafted to fit together end to end like puzzle pieces. The garden started in the front of the house with two small rectangular flowerbeds on each side of the walkway stretching from the front steps.

From there, it flowed artistically back around the house and along the rocky path to the gazebo, where it climbed up the gazebo walls and filled the gutter-like flower bed which flowed seamlessly around the inside. The beds themselves were filled with beautiful and exotic plants of all types and colors, some Elijah didn't even recognize. The beds were kept in immaculate condition, clearly watched over meticulously; every plant had its place, and nothing was out of place.

Walking up the front steps, Elijah stopped just behind Khalid on the porch. He waited quietly, taking in the artistry around him, while Khalid knocked on the door. Seconds later, Elijah's attention was pulled away from the parade of color around him by the slight creaking sound of the front door slowly opening.

Looking towards the door, he was surprised to see a short man. No, he was actually Elijah's height and build; he just appeared short next to his enormous friend, but *everyone* looked short next to Khalid. Elijah didn't know why, but he had assumed all of Khalid's kind were men of beastly proportions. Arhan had Khalid's same dark olive skin tone and black hair; they could have been brothers, except for the size difference.

"Khalid, what a wonderful surprise. What are you doing

here?" The man spoke with Khalid's same strange accent while he smiled and pulled Khalid into a strong embrace. Khalid stepped back a pace and shook hands. Arhan noticed Elijah and frowned. "Who is this man you've brought to my door?" The words burst from his throat like an accusation.

Elijah could tell he was a distrustful man, and he certainly had good cause.

"This is my good friend, Elijah; he and I have grown very close," Khalid reassured the man who still blocked the doorway. "We have come because Emira is in danger and I need your help."

A look of uncertainty crossed Arhan's face, and his brow furrowed. Elijah got the feeling this kind of request was out of the ordinary.

"All right, come on, let's talk inside." Arhan certainly wasn't happy about the intrusion, but seemed to be doing his best to be polite. He motioned the two men into the house and shut the door behind them. "Have a seat and I'll make some tea." Arhan walked the pair into the dining room and pulled out two chairs. Elijah looked over at Khalid anxiously as they sat down.

"There is no time for tea and cookies, for god's sake," Elijah hissed.

Khalid seemed to get the message. "Actually, Arhan, we are in quite a hurry." Khalid was speaking politely, but he was obviously nervous, at least to Elijah.

"Okay, old friend, tell me what you need," Arhan said. He seemed more interested now as he pulled a chair up to the other side of the table. Khalid's demeanor was usually like stone, and his obvious distress now might have been what made Arhan uncomfortable.

"Do you trust me?" Khalid asked.

Elijah was losing his patience; he wanted Khalid to get to the point.

"What kind of a question is that? Of course I trust you, Brother. What is this about?" Arhan's volume was growing with his curiosity and irritation.

"What I am about to ask you—" Khalid was interrupted as he spoke.

"We need the other half of the parchment," Elijah blurted. They were running out of time, and his frustration and impatience had gotten the better of him.

Arhan shot to his feet in protest, his face scored with anger and disbelief.

"What have you told him, Khalid?" the man demanded as he slammed his fist on the table. "We keep our secrets for a reason. Our council has but a handful of members left, thus you *know* secrecy is our primary defense against our enemy's vast and growing numbers."

"He knows everything; he is also an immortal, but a friend." Khalid knew this would send Arhan over the edge, but hoped he could reason with him.

"You brought a blood-letter to my home! You told him I am the keeper! What has come over you, Khalid? This is an outrage!" Arhan shouted, his anger boiling over.

"No. He is an immortal, yes, but made by Mikal." Khalid hoped this would console the man a bit.

"Impossible!" Arhan's eyes were wide as he tugged vigorously at the tuft of hair on his chin.

"It's true, Arhan. I saw it myself, heard and saw Mikal while he spoke to this man, and he is a trusted friend." Khalid spoke softly, in earnest. "I'm sorry to ask this of you, but, as I said, Emira is in trouble and I need that parchment to save her life. Will you help me, Brother?" Khalid begged; his voice cracked with emotion.

Arhan's face suddenly flooded with sorrow, as if he knew Emira was like a daughter to Khalid.

"You know I can't just give you my half of the rite, Khalid, the two parts have been kept separate for thousands of years. We can't take the chance of letting them both fall into the wrong hands." His expression was sympathetic, but he spoke resolutely. "Besides, any decisions made about the ME have to involve the entire council; you know that," Arhan finished piously.

It was obvious he wanted to help his old friend, but Elijah sensed that for him it would mean betraying everything he had lived for and fought for, everything good friends had died for over the ages.

"Please Arhan, we have to save her; are you really willing to sit back and let an innocent girl die?" Elijah leapt to his feet, his voice condemning.

"Elijah, quiet!" Khalid glared at him threateningly.

"No, we are running out of time; we need the parchment now." Elijah snapped back; he was yelling.

"I'm sorry, I can't give it to you. One life is not worth risking the ME." Arhan's tone was uncompromising.

Pacing the floor as the man spoke, Elijah decided Arhan was being completely unreasonable, and he became more and more furious. Arhan's words sent chills all through him. It was time for him to act. They were clearly wasting their time with talk; this man could never understand. He stopped pacing and looked directly down at Arhan, who was still seated.

"You are wrong; she is worth everything." His voice was now calm and his eyes were fierce with resolve. He was going to take the rite by force.

"Let's go outside." Khalid jerked Elijah's arm as he spoke, as if he were trying to deflect a disaster before it started. Elijah resisted for a moment and then grudgingly followed the big man. He was fuming as they stepped out onto the porch.

"You've got to calm down, Elijah." Khalid said quietly.

"How can I calm down? How can you be calm? Emira is

going to die if we can't get what we need from this stubborn fool." Elijah suddenly realized he was practically screaming and took a deep breath in an attempt to calm himself.

"Losing your cool is not going to help us, or Emira. I promise you I will do whatever I have to do; you just remain calm and stay out of the way." Khalid was still quiet, but convincing.

As the two walked back in through the open door and into the foyer, Arhan was still sitting at the table with his arms folded in defiance.

"Please, Arhan, just hear me out, and if I can't convince you over a cup of that tea you mentioned, we will go." Khalid asked politely, as if he was sure the man was reasonable and would at least listen to their plea.

Arhan looked curiously at Khalid for a moment and then sat up straight in his chair. "Okay, I'll hear you out; let me put on some tea." His manner took a friendlier turn as he walked out of the room.

"What are you doing?" Elijah whispered. He was looking at Khalid expectantly, trying his best to be patient.

"Just wait a moment." Khalid was staring intently at the passageway through which Arhan had disappeared.

As soon as Elijah heard cabinets opening, Khalid jumped up and headed to the door as if he was leaving. Elijah was frustrated and confused until he saw Khalid take a detour into another room, moving with speed and stealth. Elijah quietly rose from his chair and followed him, but by the time he made it to the passage where Khalid had detoured, the big man was already walking back out.

His eyes looked nervous as he used them to signal Elijah back to his seat.

Elijah sat, but wondered whether Khalid had a plan or was just going to rely on this stubborn immortal to help them save Emira. The two were back in their seats just in time to hear the teapot whistle. Seconds later, Arhan came back through the passageway carrying a tray with a pot and three steaming cups of tea.

Elijah saw only one solution. Driven by urgency he practically ground his teeth; his mind was racing. His fears for Emira's life were increasing with every second they wasted in this place. He decided to give Khalid a bit more time and then he would do things his way.

"Here we are." Arhan spoke pleasantly as he laid the tray in the center of the table. The putrid stench of some unknown herb in the tea was filling the room around them. Elijah was finished; he stood up quickly, intent on ending this madness.

"Actually, Arhan, we need to get back. I realize now we are not going to be able to convince you, and we are just wasting our time here. Our efforts would be better spent elsewhere. We need to come up with a new plan." Khalid spoke politely, disappointment in his voice.

"No Khalid, we have no other plan; there is no other way!" Elijah shouted.

"Let's go." Khalid spoke sternly and pointed to the door. He was making it hard for Elijah to trust his judgment, but once again he forced himself to the door and back out onto the porch. But if Khalid didn't have a plan, he would take matters into his own hands immediately.

Khalid stepped out behind him and shut the door.

"What are you doing? We need that parchment!" Elijah exclaimed in frustration as Khalid quickly stepped closer to him until they were standing chest to chest. The look on Khalid's face was one of shame.

"Don't say another word. Just take this and go." Khalid spoke quickly as he thrust a piece of paper into Elijah's pocket.

"Is that the other piece? How did you—"

"Yes, I stole it," Khalid interrupted, "now, get out of here before he figures it out." Khalid's nervousness was uncomfortably clear.

"What about you?"

"I will be there as soon as I can," Khalid promised. "But I have to deal with this first. I have to face Arhan and tell him the truth about what's going on. Now go. You have everything your father is looking for. If he gets it... well, let's not think about that. I will try to meet you at my house, just before dusk. If your father gets there before I return, try your best to stall him; but if you must choose between Emira and the rite, just give it to him. To hell with everything else. I'm tired of sacrificing time and friends for a god who doesn't seem to care anymore." Khalid threw his hands in the air.

Elijah turned to run; within seconds he was back over the mountain and out of sight.

# CHAPTER 93

KHALID WAS COMPLETELY overwhelmed by guilt; he had just betrayed one of his oldest friends and now he had to face him. It wasn't going to be easy to explain why he had just given an outsider the very thing they had guarded with their lives for the last few millennia, or how there was a fair chance it would end up in Adol's hands.

Khalid took a deep breath and walked back into the house, his heart pounding. Arhan was in the library; he was leaned back in an armchair reading a book. He turned and looked at Khalid as the door slammed behind him.

"Khalid, I already told you there is nothing I can do. You know how sacred and dangerous that rite is. I really wish I could help, but I'm sorry." Arhan's voice was firm but apologetic.

Khalid's face was somber as he hung his head in shame. Tired and sad, he said, "I'm sorry, Arhan. I had to; I couldn't let Emira die. I couldn't lose her."

Arhan jumped to his feet; shock and fear suffused his face as he ran to a bookshelf and opened a copy of *Of Mice and Men*. He flipped through the pages frantically, but didn't find what he was looking for.

"What have you done, Khalid?" Arhan's voice was shaking. He ran to the door, looking for Elijah, but saw nothing.

"He's gone, and you'll never catch him; he's too fast." Khalid's tone was still apologetic but certain.

"I hope you understand, there will be serious repercussions for what you have done here." Arhan turned from the door, running his fingers through his hair as he spoke. "I have to call the council. You sit, and stay right here. I can't help you; after what you've done, you will have to face the council's judgment." His voice vibrated with anger and frustration.

Arhan walked into the living room across from the library and retrieved a telephone. Khalid listened while he made one call after another. He said it was an emergency and called for an immediate council meeting.

Khalid knew where they would meet. It wasn't far, and was actually on the way back to Virginia. With a lot of luck he could convince his brothers to help him before handing down their judgment, if for no other reason than to retrieve the ME. He knew he would probably be executed for what he had done, but he didn't regret it. He wasn't worried for himself; he just hoped he could make it back in time to help Elijah and to rescue Emira.

"Come with me Khalid. We are going to meet with the council, where your fate will be decided." Arhan's voice was filled with sorrow. Khalid was his oldest friend, and he was now escorting him to a grim fate. Killing an immortal like Khalid in the traditional manner was a difficult and gruesome task.

"All is well, my brother; please feel no shame or regret for your actions here. You are only doing what you must." Khalid tried to console the man he had loved as a brother since millennia past. Arhan embraced Khalid once more and then stalked through the door; Khalid followed close behind.

Arhan was strong and fast, but Khalid kept pace with ease. He knew this could be his last hour, and a million thoughts raced through his head. Most of all, he hoped Emira would be safe; his life meant nothing compared to hers. Khalid had lived long enough, but Emira was still just a child in his eyes.

He was comforted when he thought of Elijah; he had been wrong about him. He knew Elijah would do whatever it took to see to Emira's safety. He was strong and fierce. Khalid could think of no one he would trust more with her life. She and Khalid were both lucky to count him as a friend. Still, Khalid knew Elijah's fate. After turning over the rite, he would die, and then there would be no one left to protect Emira, not unless Khalid made it back in time. Desperation consumed him.

For the first time in centuries Khalid thought about his youth and his mortal family. He remembered his mother and his sisters; he could almost see their faces, see them smiling and splashing him as they played in the Indus river. All kinds of memories popped into his mind and stirred his emotions, memories he hadn't realized were still vivid.

Khalid remembered the first time he went hunting with his father. He still had the bone blade his father had fashioned for him as a gift to celebrate his first kill. He had many lifetimes of memories, but only a few that mattered.

His short mortal life had been infinitely more meaningful than all the ages since. The vastness of his immortality dulled everything. His life had become unlivable until the day he met Emira. That was the reason he wanted so badly to hide her aura from the council. She had brought him back to life, and he didn't want to lose her. Watching her play as a child had given him new eyes, her eyes. When he was around her he could see the world as she did, as new and beautiful, like he was experiencing things for the first time, just as she was. His love for her had nothing to do with what she was.

Khalid didn't know how, but he was determined to make it back home tonight. Judgment could wait till morning. The landscape around them was beginning to change and Khalid knew they were getting close. He didn't know how many would be able to make it to this emergency council gathering, but he hoped for a large number. He was already seeing signs of the others, tracks and trampled paths merging as they grew closer.

## CHAPTER 94

E LIJAH WAS STILL worried, but now a bit of hope crept
into his soul. He was grateful to Khalid; he had an inkling
what it must have meant for him to make such a sacrifice. He
hoped Khalid's brothers would understand, because Elijah knew
he needed Khalid at his side when he faced his father. But after
the way Arhan had reacted, he doubted it was likely.

He raced back along the path Khalid had trampled out,
pushing himself as hard as he could. He was fast; he just hoped
he was fast enough. After all these years of searching and longing for vengeance, he had finally found his father. And he was
surprised to realize revenge wasn't the only thing on his mind.

His thoughts were about Emira. He had seen how ruthless
and savage his father could be, and he didn't want Emira to meet
the same fate as Sara. He couldn't let that happen. Buried in the
depths of his subconscious was the idea that, in some small way,
saving Emira might make up for how he had failed Sara. The
thoughts drove him forward, each step becoming a leap more
powerful than the last, rocketing him forward and into the air. It
was almost like he was flying.

Although his anxiety and fear made the trip feel like an

eternity, his passion had driven him with such speed he made it back to Rallo with more than an hour to spare before dusk. He was filled with relief. He was in time to make sure Emira would be okay, even if it meant making the trade.

Now back at the cabin, he discovered it was the last place he wanted to be. He was anxious to see Emira and get this over with. He hoped Khalid would make it in time, but either way, he would do what he had to do to see Emira safe.

He couldn't stop thinking of Solomon, and the conversation they had the night before. It still didn't make sense to him; he still couldn't get his mind around his brother's story.

Was it all true? Had his brother really been infused with some kind of evil he couldn't shed? Emira's question last night was poignant, but Elijah realized something was off about his brother's story.

If Solomon had really wanted Elijah to kill him, if he really wanted to be freed from his misery, then why would he still fight at his father's side against Elijah? If he thought it best for Malaki to be freed by death, why would he not kill their father himself?

Elijah was missing a piece of the puzzle. There had to be something else, something Solomon hadn't told him. He was hiding something, or he was just lying altogether? Could it be even the bit of decency Solomon had shown at the church was just a charade? Had he really been the one to follow Elijah and discover their hideout at the cabin? Had his big brother once again betrayed him?

Elijah was growing more furious and confused as the questions raced through his mind. In many ways, Elijah was a simple man; he didn't like to complicate things. He saw life mostly as black and white, good and bad; although his life was filled with gray, in his mind there wasn't a lot of room for it.

Elijah tried to push the questions and frustrations out of his mind. He was alone now, with only these tiny pieces of parchment. The top line was all he could read; it was in Aramaic. It seemed unimaginable these bits of paper were so precious to so many. What could these tiny inscriptions say that could be so important, that could mean the difference between death and life, man and god?

He didn't care. This rite was a means to an end. It might have the power to destroy the heavens, but he would surely give up heaven to see Emira safe, and to finally see an end to his father.

Elijah rose from the steps on the cabin porch. Although there was still nearly an hour before dusk, he wasn't going to spend it here. His brother had said he could no longer find peace in the temples, but he still kept going, hoping to once again feel the bit of warmth that had once settled his uneasy spirit.

A sudden urge came over Elijah, and he decided to make one last stop before he met his most probable ending at Khalid's house. Moving as fast as his legs could carry him, he passed the large pond on the other side of the hill from Khalid's cabin and had soon made his way back to the highway. In just a matter of moments, he was there.

Looking up at the building before him, Elijah tried to figure out his purpose for being here. As he walked up the stairs to the front door, he hesitated for just a moment before pulling it open and walking inside.

# CHAPTER 95

AS KHALID AND Arhan reached the top of the mountain pass, their destination burst into view. In the distance there was a giant cliff that recessed just a bit as it met the ground, forming a shallow cave. They were close enough for Khalid to see the twelve large stones positioned in a circle at the base of the cliff. Three men and two women sat waiting on the rocks. Their faces showed confusion and condemnation as they watched Khalid approach and take his place in the circle beside Arhan.

"Although the entire council should be present for such decisions, I believe the gravity of this situation requires us to act now; we have no time to wait." Arhan stood and spoke forcefully.

Ubaram, the man sitting directly across from them, stood and glared at Khalid. "Tell us Arhan, what exactly is the situation?"

"Yes, explain exactly what our brother has done, and then let us hear from him," Ku-aya demanded. She was a beautiful woman who had long favored Khalid. Arhan stood once more to speak, but Khalid motioned for him to sit.

"I know I have a lot to explain. We have spent what seems like an eternity guarding this rite and, not only have I handed it over to an outsider, but I also stole it from a brother. I have betrayed you all." Khalid spoke apologetically, but he did not regret his actions, not even if it cost him his life. Shouts of outrage and condemnation swarmed like wasps around him.

"I know the consequences of my actions will be dire; I know my punishment must be severe. But I urge you to postpone this judgment, for there is no time to waste. You all know, or have at least heard of, the girl in my care, Emira."

The group seemed to nod in unison.

"She has been taken by a group of blood-letters, and they are threatening to kill her unless I give them the ME. I gave the rite to a man I trust entirely, and he is meeting them tonight to negotiate for her release. If we leave now, we may still make it in time to save Emira and the ME." Khalid spoke with urgency; they needed to act now.

"We all know what happened to your family, Khalid, and to your daughter," Ubaram stood and spoke. "We sympathize with you, Brother, but it does not give you the right to do what you have done tonight. Your betrayal is unforgivable; the only suitable punishment is death." He spoke with fervor, as if to rile the council.

The reactions to Ubaram's words were mostly in agreement. Ku-aya seemed to be the only one willing to give Khalid a chance. Still, he wasn't worried about the judgment; he was worried about the time. It would take more time to reach a consensus, time they didn't have.

"How dare you? Kill me if you like, but please don't share your false pity with me or the council. This has nothing to do with my family!" Khalid jumped to his feet and was screaming; he was outraged and disgusted. "What would you know of family, anyway, Ubaram?" Khalid sat back down and dropped his head in frustration and disgust. They were running out of time.

"Ubaram is right; he has broken our most sacred law. Not

only has he betrayed, us, he has betrayed our purpose. He has betrayed the reason we exist and he has betrayed Odam. He can't go unpunished; we must kill him now." Ditanu was a man of few words, so when he spoke, the council paid attention.

Khalid respected him very much; they all did. His words stung Khalid sharply, partly because he respected the man so much, and partly because he knew Ditanu was right. Shouts of agreement went up all around the circle; not even Ku-aya could disagree. Khalid himself couldn't disagree, but having a chance to save Emira, even if it was just a small one, made it all worth it.

Ku-aya stood up and walked over to Khalid.

"I'm sorry." She said, as she kissed him gently on the forehead. Her face was filled with grief; it was no easy task to kill one of Odam's immortals in accordance with their traditions, and the scene was about to become gruesome. Knowing his fate was sealed, Khalid stood up and walked to the center of the circle.

"I know your judgment here is righteous and just. I have no arguments, and I absolve all of you of any guilt you might feel when this is over. Just please listen to my final plea. Once this is over, I beg you, rush to my house in Rallo as quickly as you can; you still might have a chance to save the ME and Emira."

With that, he kneeled down and hung his head in submission. As the council crowded around, he looked up once more at Arhan. "You know my friend Elijah; please go and help him. There is not much time left. Emira is *The Key*. You have to save her; you can't let our enemies get their hands on both the rite and *The Key*." Khalid lowered his head in peace. Now they knew Emira was *The Key*, he was fully confident, after killing him, the council would help Elijah.

Khalid could feel his brothers next to him; he remained silent and still as they grabbed his every limb and began to pull ferociously. He didn't fight back; what they were doing was just.

# CHAPTER 96

E LIJAH STEPPED INTO the *masjid* with less than an hour before dusk. He didn't know why he had come. Perhaps somewhere deep inside he was still that little boy following in his big brother's footsteps.

Long ago Solomon had recounted to Elijah how he found such peace in places of worship. He said it made him feel safe. Elijah had respected his brother so much he, too, began to frequent the stone shrine near their home built to honor Janus, the god of transitions.

Unlike his brother, Elijah had never learned how to do things in moderation. Where his brother seemed to be able to unload his burdens and absorb what he needed from his spiritual endeavors, Elijah always left feeling useless and condemned. Prone to obsession, it was hard for him to allow even the most remote insignificances slide by without careful consideration.

He knew this could be a good quality. It could help one through many challenges and in many facets of one's life, but Elijah quickly learned, when it came to religion, this quality could become debilitating. He came to see sin in everything he did. He felt condemned when he laughed at jokes and awkward when he didn't.

He soon realized religion would cost him everything. In his mind, religion left no room for all the imperfections that came with being human. If he followed every directive and steered clear of every sin he had read about or heard mentioned, he would soon be an invalid.

Solomon was quick to tell him not to be so hard on himself. He reminded him to take everything in moderation. But Elijah couldn't live like that; in his mind things were either right or wrong, good or bad, there was no in between, no room for *salt*. He had no special way of deciding which directives to obey and which to ignore.

Eventually he began to hope none of it was true; that there were no gods, or god. He lived in an area where Christianity and Islam had been mixed in with Greek and Roman mythology. The constant condemnation continuously beating against him began to wear on the few beliefs he did have. These moments of weakness allowed his intellect to shine through and question his faith.

*If a god made me exactly who I am*, he thought, *and placed me here in this life to have these experiences, how can he blame me for doing exactly what he knew I would do and made me to do?* With all the questions incessantly colliding in his mind, it hadn't been hard for him to give up his faith altogether, and the sting of his brother's betrayal caused him to lash out against everything that reminded him of Solomon.

Solomon had been the one who guided him into his faith and through the questions about his spirituality. So the faith he had in this brother's beliefs and guidance died along with the faith he had in his brother—which turned out to be a much greater loss. He would have more easily imagined being betrayed by God himself than by his own big brother. The loss of religious faith had been insignificant, but the other nearly killed him.

Then why was he here, in this *masjid*, spending what might be the last hour of his life in the house of a God he didn't believe in? Was he unconsciously hoping to find some sense of solace to prepare him for the chaos that lay ahead of him this night? Despite his qualms about religion, and the bitterness toward it that had grown in his heart, this was the closest thing to a home he knew.

He had spent most of his life running from temple to temple with only hate and vengeance in his heart. He had taken care to follow their rituals and customs, so as not to offend or gain unwanted attention, but he never allowed himself to empathize with the worshippers, to open his eyes and heart and try to experience things from their point of view. He thought them ignorant, and pitied them; he remembered what it was like to be shackled in those same hateful chains.

Or was that just a shield? Perhaps he was simply afraid of being let down or of being found wanting. He remembered the last time he tried to grapple with religion and how it had scarred him—as if the gods and his brother had all just walked away and left him to die.

Elijah slid off his shoes and ritually washed his body. He walked into the prayer room, and there on the floor was one lonely man, on his knees in prayer. For a moment Elijah considered running back out the door, but with his own mortality looming, he had no time to be afraid.

He found a place beside the old man. He took a deep breath and began the prayer he had recited thousands of times, in thousands of places around the world, but never in earnest—until now. His body and tongue seemed to move on their own. He didn't even have to think about it. It was like walking. After praying for a number of minutes, he laid his forehead on the ground and closed his eyes.

As he stood up and walked out the door, he was met by what seemed for a moment to be a ghost from long past.

*Sara?!* Speechless, Elijah couldn't believe his eyes. The two were immediately pulled together by a force much like gravity. There was nothing to be said, no time or room for words. As they came face to face, everything else seemed to disappear. Elijah wrapped his arms around her and kissed her gently on the lips.

After he kissed her, Elijah noticed her eyes were red and welling with tears. He closed his eyes as one tear fell from the corner of his eye and mixed with the rain. Opening them again, Elijah could tell there was something much different about her. She was no longer vampire, and she seemed to glow like Emira. He tucked his hand around the back of her neck and pulled her to his chest.

To touch her after nearly a thousand years of yearning was too much. He was overcome. As his legs buckled beneath him, the pair slid to the ground, once again wrapped in each other's arms beneath the pouring rain.

He couldn't believe, after more than eight hundred years of longing, he had finally found the woman who had consumed his thoughts. Everything about her brought back the most wonderful memories and powerful emotions. They also brought back memories of Ayda and of Emira, his love for them both, and of how much Emira needed him, right now.

"Is it really you?" Elijah spoke between muffled sobs as Sara remained firmly pressed against his chest but didn't say a word. As Elijah gently eased her away, he could see she was smiling. She reached forward and brushed the rain and tears from beneath his eyes. "How is it you are here?" he asked.

Still she didn't speak. A million thoughts raced through his mind; there was so much he wanted to say.

"You have to let me go, Elijah," Sara said softly. Elijah extended his hand as he stood; he helped her up and pulled her back into his arms.

"I don't want to," he whispered.

"You still have that old thing," Sara smiled as she looked at the bracelet on his wrist, then turned around, wiping a tear from her eye.

"I have missed you so much," he said, trying to get her to talk, to explain why, how his Sara was here. "I am so sorry."

"For what? You were the good in my short life, my one true love."

Elijah didn't know how to respond.

"It is okay, Elijah. I know you have lived and loved. Elijah, remember? I once urged you to find your princess; and said you were destined for great things." Sara's voice was calm and soothing. "I love you, and I always will, but you have much work to do. You have to let me go. Emira needs you now. You must protect her; she is more important than you know. Not just for the world, but for you." Sara stepped closer as she spoke and the moonlight fully illuminated the soft curves of her face. Elijah was familiar with every beloved curve and hollow. She looked exactly the same; her beauty was paralyzing.

"Sara, I'm so sorry; I didn't know what to do. Please forgive me." Elijah's face contorted with his inner pain as he rubbed his hands across his face. "I can take you away from this place. I will deal with Solomon and my father; you will never have to see them again. I will protect you; I am stronger now than you could believe." Elijah stepped forward, arms outstretched again.

"Still my prince, I see." Sara gently caressed the side of his face. "Don't be sad, Elijah. I'm free now. I'm happy, and you did nothing wrong. I asked you not to bear the guilt of my death because it's not yours to bear. Please go now. Emira needs you, and you need her," Sara insisted.

"I don't think I can. I don't know how to defeat my father." Elijah lowered his head.

"Yes, you do. You are the strongest and bravest man I have ever known, and, whether you believe it or not, you are a good man." She gently forced his head up and looked deeply into his tired eyes.

"You must forget about your father and what he did to me and the rest of your family. You have to find something you care about more than revenge, Elijah." She placed a hand on each side of his face. "I have to go."

"No, please stay! I can't do this without you." Elijah gently placed his hands on top of hers.

"I can't, Elijah. You have finally found your destiny, but before you can grasp it, you have to let go of the past. You have to let go of your guilt, and you must believe you deserve a new life. Believe in yourself Elijah; everyone else does." After she spoke, she kissed him gently on the cheek; she looked into his eyes for a moment as a single tear graced her face.

"This is a dream, isn't it?" he was almost too afraid to ask.

"Yes, and you need to wake up now."

Leaning into her embrace, Elijah held her tight and, for a brief moment, they were once again dancing in the rain.

Elijah opened his eyes and saw he was still on the floor of the *masjid*. It was nearly dusk now, and Elijah knew it was time to go, but he was grateful and glad to have finally found a small portion of what came so easily to his brother, the true value of spirituality. As he got up to leave, the man beside him grasped Elijah's arm. His grip was firm for such a frail-looking man.

"Peace be with you, my son," he said softly in English.

"And with you," Elijah replied solemnly as he turned and walked to the door. Stepping outside the *masjid*, Elijah could feel the foreboding darkness creep in around him, falling down with the rain.

The time for reflection was over. He needed to be ice cold if he was going to save Emira.

# CHAPTER 97

"WAIT!" ARHAN SHOUTED as he jumped to his feet. Pressure immediately eased in Khalid's core and his limbs as the council members turned to listen to Arhan. "Ubaram might be right, but this matter—the execution of one of our own brothers—cannot be decided without the presence of the entire council." His voice was uncompromising.

Khalid's aching limbs were dropped one by one as everyone backed away. "Besides, Khalid is right. If a blood-letter already has *The Key* and is about to come into possession of the rite, then there are infinitely more pressing matters at hand. This is a matter for tomorrow. Tonight we must fight," Arhan inspired the council members with vigor and enthusiasm.

Khalid looked around and saw almost everyone nodding in agreement.

"It's settled, then. The matter of Khalid can wait. For now we must hurry to save *The Key* and retrieve the ME." Arhan spoke quickly as he turned and took off through the forest at a speed that surprised Khalid. He quickly followed, and one by one, the others fell in line.

Khalid was somewhat relieved, but it was getting very late.

He was afraid they might not make it in time. His concern for Emira, and the hope he might still be able to save her, gave him a newfound strength as he powered past Arhan with tremendous speed.

He was soon so far ahead he could no longer hear the thundering footfalls behind him.

# CHAPTER 98

ARRIVING AT KHALID'S house, Elijah dropped his duffle bag on the ground in front of the concrete porch steps. Opening it, he pulled out his small *kopis*, still encased in its leather holster. He hung the *kopis* beneath his left arm and slipped on his burgundy leather coat to cover it.

As he straightened, a cloud of thoughts drifted through his head. Twilight was the most mesmerizing part of the day. Darkness and light danced together like two old lovers; they kissed like a couple who had been long separated. The lines between right and wrong seemed to disintegrate as the two energies moved in unison to the harmonious duet played by life and death.

He could smell the flowers in the minimal landscaping around Khalid's house. He noticed their colors, how vivid and beautiful. His hate and guilt had caused him to miss out on so much over the years, but seeing Sara, even if it had been a dream, had lifted a huge weight from his shoulders. Beauty seemed to fill and surround him, but none more than his memories of Emira and the certainty he would do anything to save her.

Looking out across the field, he saw a lonely, moss-covered

tree. It was somehow passionate, even romantic, like the Greek tragedies his mother had told him and his brothers in their youth. It was alone in the large expanse, separate from the fold, from the comfort and protection of the forest. All it knew was the company of a small wildflower enjoying comfort and protection beneath its large canopy, but the tiny companion, too, would fade with the season, and once again the tree would be completely alone.

He thought of Emira and how, if he survived the night, her entire life would be only a matter of moments compared to the infinite expanse of his cursed immortality. Just like the tree, he would be left with only the desperate hope that the sun would rise again tomorrow and warm his sturdy frame. The tree's branches began to look like arms and hands as it seemed to ignite with life, a life Elijah had never noticed before, both enduring and unyielding.

*How old are you, tree?* Elijah wondered, feeling empathy, as if he was somehow connected to the hopeless giant. It was by far the largest oak Elijah had ever seen. Its frame was massive, but more than that, this tree had mettle. It had grown strong and tall in a field where no other tree dared to sprout. It wasn't concerned with the world around it, only the small but beautiful flower resting safely at its side. The tree reminded Elijah of himself.

*Are you older than I am, tree?* Elijah wondered. He doubted it. White oaks generally lived no more than four hundred years, less than half as long as Elijah had walked the earth. Still, this tree was different; he was definitely much older than any oak Elijah had seen. The tree's tenacious spirit and stalwart will had kept him going all these years, but for what purpose? Elijah knew his own purpose, and once he had completed it, he would be happy to finally meet his end.

What does this tree have? What secret did he refuse to share that was so special? So special it would cause him to push on with such determination, and against all odds? Elijah was vexed as his attention turned to the small white flower at the base of the tree.

It was the tree's opposite, young and frail. Its existence would be only a blink, a fleeting moment in the long life of the enduring tree. The flower was radiant and bursting with life, completely oblivious to the fact it would soon wither away. Even in the twilight hour, the flower seemed to glow beneath the dark shadow of the tree.

She would be sure to return every year with the ides of March. The tree gave her protection from the elements, the harsh tides of life that erode the spirit without hesitation; the winds, the rains, and the heat. She received much from the giant tree, but what, if anything, did she give back?

Elijah forgot himself in this moment. Even the world around him, the world he had known for almost a millennium, seemed so foreign, and made such little sense. Elijah had simple aspirations. The covetous nature that only seemed to increase throughout mankind confounded him, and his father was the worst of all.

The contradiction between this and the simple nature of revenge, his terrible purpose, which had driven him for hundreds of years, forced him to the edge of oblivion, where he questioned nearly everything he thought he knew.

There were now only two certainties in his life: his father and Emira. Knowing the danger of being distracted at such a time, Elijah turned back to the task at hand.

Carefully walking around the house, he was more than happy to see the place presently deserted. He hoped his father would arrive late, giving Khalid more time. He needed the big man at his side tonight.

Elijah's usual look of calm indifference was gone. He was growing anxious. He hoped the big man was okay.

The grassy expanse behind Khalid's house disappeared into a dense forest. Elijah heard footsteps coming towards him from beneath the forest canopy. He hoped it was Khalid, but feared it was not.

# CHAPTER 99

B Y THE TIME Khalid reached Rallo it was already past dusk and only the waning moon illuminated the night sky. There were no signs of his guardian brothers and sisters behind him, and he had no idea how far behind him they were. Fear tugged at his chest as he thought of Emira; he had no time to waste.

Was he too late? From his cabin, he didn't take the route following the road; he knew a shortcut. Passing the cabin, he didn't even slow down; he plowed straight into the thick bush across the field from where he had broken into the valley surrounding his cabin.

The bush, the underbrush, the trees, nothing could slow him down as he pressed on and tore through the dense forest. He only stopped so he could survey the situation when he reached the edge of the forest just beside his house.

# CHAPTER 100

WHEN SEVERAL FIGURES emerged from the tree line
Elijah saw it wasn't Khalid and his council. It was his
father, with his nasty lot of immortals. And Emira. His concern
for her forced him forward, and he rushed to meet them.

Closing the gap between them, Elijah could see her clearly.
He was relieved she was still alive, but he didn't know for how
long. William's left hand was tightly clamped around the back
of her neck. His hold was so vicious Elijah could barely hear her
shallow breaths, and her light had disappeared.

Solomon was standing to William's right, directly in front of
Elijah. Two more blood-letters were standing to William's left.
Elijah thought himself enormously underestimated if his father
believed this lot of immortal thugs would intimidate him.

Emira's muffled whimpers were growing louder, and the
sounds tore through Elijah's soul. It took every ounce of will
he could muster to remain frozen and calm. Every part of him
clamored to rush forward, to tear William limb from limb, but
he knew that would put Emira at grave risk.

Elijah closed his eyes and took a deep breath. He pictured
Ayda's face, the mountains, the snow. Staring blankly into their

faces, Elijah tried to retreat into the peaceful vacuum in his mind he had once known; he knew it still existed somewhere in there. He was biding his time, still hoping Khalid might make it.

Elijah knew he couldn't stall them for long; time was running out. Without Khalid, he had no choice. It was up to him to make the biggest decision of his life, alone. Handing over the ME could mean a shift in the heavens. The power of his enemies would increase dramatically.

More than that, Mikal's warning was plain. Handing over the ME would mean an end to Elijah's immortality, and his life. The vengeance, which for so long had been his sole purpose for living, would be gone forever, completely beyond his reach.

He had no choice. To defy his father now would mean Emira's certain and immediate death. Avoiding Elijah's eyes, Solomon looked down as he extended his hand.

"Just give it to me, Brother." Solomon spoke softly; he looked like a broken man, pitiful and defeated, only a fraction of the man Elijah had so admired in his youth.

"I will kill her, Son." William pressed his hand hard beneath Emira's delicate chin. Her spine could be crushed in an instant.

"Stop!" Elijah knew he was out of options. He reached in his back pocket and pulled out the two small pieces of parchment. He reluctantly handed them over to his brother, who in turn unfolded the documents and handed them to William.

William looked them over thoroughly. "You have done well, Son. This is it. I have seen partial drawings and etchings, but never the entire thing. Astounding, isn't it?" William smiled, clearly pleased with himself. He looked once again at the rite and then back at Elijah.

"And now I must apologize, Son, but your lust for vengeance has caused me too many problems. I can't allow this to continue. I would rather not kill you, but I can't have you meddling in my affairs, so I hope this time the message will get through to you:

your quest for revenge only ends in the deaths of those you love. I will take this beautiful life you seem to hold so dear. And then you must let it be over, Elijah."

William looked down at the tiny girl in his vicious grasp and jerked up harder on her chin. Emira screamed in pain; her voice was saturated with terror.

"Don't worry, my son; it will be quick." William forced a somber expression, but Elijah knew it was just a façade, and, as he expected, it lasted only a moment. The faint smirk that stole across his father's face burned a hole straight through Elijah's chest.

# CHAPTER 101

EMIRA'S SCREAMS RIPPED at his heart, but he was outmatched. What could he do? Even if he was able to defeat the immortals before him, he couldn't do it in time to save Emira.

Watching her struggle in his father's lethal grasp, he realized he was right back where he had been all those years ago. He could see Sara, viciously torn apart by William and his man, and he could see Malaki's body fall lifeless after his father callously broke his small neck and threw him to the floor.

The fire in Elijah's spirit was extinguished, defeated by vampires, these pathetic, undead animals. They were a species he had come to hate; they were horrible, vicious creatures, and if he somehow made it through this night, he would make it his mission in life to kill every last one.

But the concerns of the present outweighed his hatred, and he was jerked back into reality. He couldn't let this happen again. He couldn't let his father or his father's minions kill another one of his loved ones. This time he would not stand by and do nothing.

He had to act, and he had to act immediately, because he

might have only moments left to live. Handing over the ME had been his death sentence; he was already on borrowed time.

Now that he could see what his father's true plan had been all along, Elijah was glad Khalid hadn't made it back in time. Khalid was a strong man, a brave man, but he wasn't sure if he had a place here, on this field of Titans.

Emira's eyes flooded with tears. She had been trying to be strong, but couldn't hold back any longer. Elijah could see her beautiful face contorting with fear and pain.

"Elijah!" Her scream rang out like a cymbal as William's fingernails dug deep into the skin on her neck. The desperate cry jerked Elijah out of his defeated mindset and hardened his resolve. One thought resonated deep and dominated his entire being.

*Emira needs me, now!* His vision was clear. This was not going to happen, not to Emira.

"Stop!" Elijah shouted. "You need her."

"What are you talking about, boy?" William laughed as he slightly loosened his grip on Emira's neck.

"They call her *The Key*; she is the only one who can read the ancient text. Not even your god can read it." Elijah smiled.

"You lie!" William shouted in protest. As he looked around at his comrades, his grip around Emira's neck loosened even further. Seeing his opportunity, Elijah made his move.

In a whirlwind of fury, Elijah turned his back on his brother and pressed his toes into the earth. With a power nobody could have anticipated, not even Elijah, he rushed forward, his steps thundering.

A glint of fear lit his father's eyes for the first time, and before William could react, Elijah had pried his arm away from Emira's neck and shoved it skyward. With one fluid motion, he leaned back and, raising his powerful right thigh, Elijah hammered his leg forward and buried his foot into William's chest, catapulting his father backward several yards before he finally crashed to the earth.

Solomon remained frozen where he stood. Without hesitation, Elijah raced back to his brother and snapped his neck, dropping him to the ground. William was still lying stunned when Elijah rushed to Emira's side and hauled her into his arms.

He was free and his spirit alive, now that she was safe. Still, he might have only seconds left, and now that Adol's men knew Emira was *The Key*, there was only one thing Elijah could do to guarantee her safety forever. He had to kill them all.

Setting Emira safely behind him, Elijah stalked back towards his father. Before he could make it, two of his father's thugs emerged in his path from behind the oak tree, separating Elijah from his father.

It didn't matter. These demons and their kind had taken from him everyone he had ever cared for, and they were now trying to take that which he held most dear, someone who had come to mean more to him than anything—maybe even revenge. He would make sure their mistake was never repeated.

With lightning speed, Elijah drew the small *kopis* from under his coat and rammed the point of the blade hard into the throat of the man standing to his left. He pushed until the man's feet left the ground and the sword pinned him to the tree at his back. The immortal who had been standing next to him now lunged at Elijah.

With one swift motion, Elijah jerked his sword out of the tree and swung his arm to the right, slicing through muscle, arteries, and bone. His arm extended, sword in hand, he turned his head just in time to watch the lunging immortal swallow his blood-polished blade. The blow nearly severed the demon's head.

Elijah rushed back to Emira and quickly spun her behind him, staying between her and Solomon, who had now reawakened. At least for the moment, he was the only threat remaining.

"I never wanted things to be this way, little Brother." Solomon's apologetic voice was sincere, but not fearful. "I hope you are strong enough," he continued, his face expressionless.

Elijah didn't say a word. William emerged from the darkness opposite Solomon, and Elijah stepped back towards the house, keeping Emira as far from danger as possible.

"Very impressive!" William cheered as he dusted off his jacket. "I won't underestimate you again, Son." His smug grin had disappeared. "You are strong, but you haven't a chance against all of us." William glared at Elijah while he spoke, but then a smile lit his face once more.

*All of us?* He was confused; he looked around, but saw only Solomon and his father. He looked into his brother's eyes, and, as he had expected, there was no vestige of the brother he once knew and loved. He saw disappointment, regret even, but a deep resolve to follow his father's orders—whatever they might be.

But Elijah wasn't afraid; he was on fire.

This was the moment he had waited for since he opened his eyes and raised his head from the cold stone floor of Rothber Castle. Some time during that terrible night he had been baptized in blood and birthed into immortality.

Now he would finally have his vengeance. It would have to be now; this was his last chance. If he didn't take his revenge now, he would never have it. Soon he would be a weak and dying mortal.

"Still not convinced?" William's tone was patronizing, but that didn't matter. Elijah knew tonight would be his. William raised his hand toward the forest in showmanship fashion as four more immortals emerged from the shadowed tree line and walked to William's side.

This changed everything. If Emira hadn't been standing behind him, the extra muscle wouldn't have mattered. He still believed he could see an end to Solomon and William before he was overtaken. He knew his rage would see him through.

He wasn't afraid of death, but there was something much heavier than death weighing in the balance. He couldn't take his revenge without leaving Emira open and defenseless.

He had to make a decision now, before his time ran out.

## CHAPTER 102

H E THOUGHT IT would have been much harder, but it was the easiest decision he had ever made. He would leave his vengeance unclaimed. There would be no reckoning, no retribution for the vicious murder and betrayal of his family. Emira was his choice. Her life for his vengeance was more than a fair trade.

She had already given him more than he had ever imagined possible, more than he ever believed existed, more than revenge ever could have granted him. She had given him hope. She had given him life. For a brief moment, she had allowed him to see himself as he had been so long ago, as a good man.

He suddenly understood the tree. He was the tree, the tree who lives for the flower. He lives for the flower, because no matter how much he gives her, she always gives him more. He gives her protection and allows her to live, but she gives him life and beauty and shows him how. Emira was his flower. She was his redemption. And now he would be her savior.

Painfully aware he could have only seconds remaining, Elijah turned to face her.

"Just take me away from this place," she pleaded between sobs.

"I can't go, but you must."

"Please, just come with me! You will find another time, one better suited for revenge." Her mind was racing. Why would he not just grab her and run? What could she say to make him listen?

"It's not about revenge anymore, Emira. I'm losing my strength. I'm dying, and what I said about you was true. You are *The Key*, and if I don't stop them now, you will be in danger for the rest of your life." He framed her lovely face with his hands and gently stroked her cheeks as he spoke.

"I don't understand," she sobbed.

"Listen to me, Emira. When I handed my brother that piece of paper, my fate was sealed. The god who made me immortal warned me that if I did that, I would lose my power and quickly die. So you see, this is the only chance I have to make sure you are safe." Elijah was pleading and trying to console her at the same time.

"You knew! And you still did it… for me. No, please tell me that's not true." Emira's voice was sharp. "You miserable, selfish man," she shrieked and slapped him across the face as tears continued to roll down her cheeks. She closed her eyes and took a deep breath. When she opened them again, she had stopped crying and hugged Elijah as tightly as she could.

He wrapped his arms around her and gently stroked the back of her head.

Emira could sense the field of demons closing in around them, but still she wasn't afraid; she was safe in Elijah's arms. She knew he wouldn't let anything happen to her, and she believed in him—powerfully. His strength and tenderness made it easy for her. She could abide in his arms against this onslaught, as if in a sturdy lighthouse amid crashing waves.

Elijah slowly pulled away; he looked deep into her eyes and kissed her gently on her lips. He imagined in all of history, there had never been a kiss that meant so much. He knew it would be his last loving act in this world, and he was happy to have lived long enough to experience something truly divine.

"Elijah, your eyes!" Emira exclaimed.

Elijah could hear her shock. He could feel his eyes burning, but Emira had seen them do that before.

Elijah didn't understand. He touched his eyes, then looked at her blankly.

"They are glowing bright white!" she gasped.

It didn't matter to Elijah; his only focus was to make sure Emira would be safe after he was gone. All the tension left him. He could never have imagined dying a better death. He was truly happy.

"Run!" Elijah mouthed.

"Come with me!" she tried one more time; tears were again rolling down her face.

"I can't, but I can hold them off. Run *now*!" His face was uncompromising and his voice scolding.

As his father's men prepared to attack, Elijah gathered his composure and turned to meet them. His death might be certain, but his presence here tonight would be felt. He was ready.

# CHAPTER 103

"I WON'T LEAVE YOU!" The shrill voice echoing from behind him allowed a deep fear to crawl back into the depths of his soul.

"Please, Emira, I am not positive I can kill them all." Elijah's voice was shaky as he shouted over his shoulder.

He glanced at the tree line, hoping to see Khalid, before he turned back to Emira. He would give anything if his big bear of a friend was here to carry her away to safety.

"I'm not going anywhere." Her voice was soft but uncompromising. Elijah dropped his head; he knew they only had seconds. "So," she said, "what's it going to be?"

Elijah knew what she wanted. She wanted him to run away with her, but he couldn't. He would die anyway, and she would never be safe.

Elijah slowly raised his head and looked deep into her eyes. Tears were streaming from their corners. He stepped forward and wiped her tears away with his thumbs.

"Don't cry, please. I'm going to make sure you are safe. I'm going to kill them all."

Elijah whirled and grabbed a vampire's swinging sword hand

just before he would have been parted from his head. Holding the vampire's arm firmly with his left hand, he swung his short blade up and to the right, splitting the monster's head in two.

Elijah tossed his short blade into his left hand and pulled the vampire's sword loose with his right. He looked down at the dagger-like blade in his left hand and the short sword in his right.

He thought of Hassan. It had been ages since he had fought with sword and dagger. He thought about Hulagu and Ayda and how much each of them had taught him.

He realized now why it hadn't worked, why he had never been able to understand what they were trying to teach him. He had been a tree growing alone in the desert with no reason to live. All he had was the hate he clung to with such desperation. He hadn't been ready for what they wanted to teach him; he hadn't deserved it, not until now. Not until he had found his flower.

The vampire before him seemed to fall in slow motion, revealing a wave of immortals hurtling towards him. He glanced back at Emira once more and smiled. His heart was finally at peace; there was no more room left for hate or vengeance. Protecting Emira was all that mattered.

Once again it seemed as if everyone was moving in slow motion. His mind was clear. With just a few swings of his sword and a number of rips and jabs with his dagger, the surrounding vampires fell with ease.

The only dangers left were William and Solomon. Solomon backed up and threw his hands in the air as William clumsily pulled his sword. They were both staring with confusion at the fire in his eyes.

"What are you doing? What's wrong with your eyes?" William babbled as Elijah dropped both of his blades and continued forward.

"I'm coming for my sword," Elijah said. William's eyes widened as he looked down at the sword he was holding. Indeed, it was the sword of the Great Khan, the sword he had taken from Elijah, the sword Hassan had given to him. William smiled and slashed down at Elijah's neck. Elijah maneuvered out of the way with ease.

"Elijah, remember our brother, please," Solomon begged as William thrust his sword. Elijah quickly turned to the side to escape his blow, then grabbed William's extended arm with one hand and curled the other around the back of his neck, flipping him over his shoulder and onto the ground.

"Get up!" Elijah bellowed, and William quickly jumped to his feet, lunging forward with his sword extended, but Elijah spun out of the way and backhanded him hard across the jaw. William stumbled backwards but didn't fall.

Regaining his composure, William slashed at Elijah's neck. He jerked backward, barely avoiding the blow. Having anticipated Elijah's move, William immediately swung his sword back. Elijah quickly stepped forward and, with his right hand, he grabbed the back of William's sword hand. Holding it tight, Elijah hammered his left hand forward into William's elbow and watched the bones burst through the skin as the sword fell from William's grasp.

Elijah slowly reached down and picked up the Spartan sword. "I told you, Father, these things always seem to find their way into deserving hands." Elijah smiled as his father moaned and snapped his elbow back into place.

Elijah looked around for Solomon, but he was gone. "You're all alone, Father." William had crawled over to the old oak and propped himself up.

"Just get it over with," William groaned as Elijah approached. As he pressed the sword to his father's neck he began to feel awkward and uneasy. He felt something run from his eyes and nose, and when he touched it, his hand came away bloody. The blade in his hand began to feel like a lead weight. He couldn't hold it any longer; he was dying and he knew it.

"Run!" He turned and shouted to Emira as he fell to his knees. The smug grin returned to William's face as he picked up the sword and pressed it against Elijah's temple.

"They really do, don't they?" William's smile grew broad as he looked down at the sword in his hand. "Elijah, haven't you realized yet, you will never be better than me? The universe itself will not allow it," he boasted.

Elijah wasn't paying any attention; his focus was on Emira. "Run!" he tried to shout, but blood spewed from his mouth instead.

She wasn't running; their eyes locked while William raised the sword above his head.

"Don't worry, I will make it quick for both of you."

# CHAPTER 1104

KHALID SAW THE multitude of bodies scattered across the field. He was relieved when he saw Emira still alive and Elijah holding a sword to William's chest. He had actually done it.

Suddenly, the situation changed radically. He saw Elijah fall to his knees and William take his sword.

There was no time left. Khalid hoped his brothers would make it in time to help, but either way he had to act now or watch his friends die. He didn't hesitate. Stalking forward, he released a deep and vicious growl.

## CHAPTER 105

"GRRRR!" OUT OF the blackness behind him, Elijah heard and felt a deep, forbidding rumble, as if hell itself had burst open and was spilling out into the night. William froze. The hairs on the back of Elijah's neck stood on end as the stentorian, almost subsonic vibration behind him grew louder and closer. Glancing back, all he could see were two gleaming black specks sunk in the vast darkness.

Under the faint light of the moon a massive beast stepped forward. Elijah couldn't believe his eyes. It was the largest, most vicious-looking beast he could ever remember seeing, and it was growling thunder. The beast reminded him of the dogs he had seen on the Canary Islands off the coast of Africa, but this thing was much bigger.

It was the size of a small horse, and its muscles bulged in every direction. It was solid black and its jaws looked like they could tear even an immortal in half with one bite. Fearing the beast's intentions, Elijah rolled over onto his stomach, trying to crawl to Emira's side.

Elijah could feel William's sword in his back as the beast walked to Elijah's side and remained there. It looked at Elijah for a moment before raising its huge head and looking William directly in the eye. The beast was ferocious, but there was something very familiar about its eyes.

Elijah had heard of lycans, or werewolves, as they were called in the west, but he had never seen one. They were creatures of myth, said to be the rarest and most ancient of creatures, created by the spirit of the earth to protect mankind.

They were rumored to be vicious, and easily more powerful than the average immortal. The creature lowered its ears and growled fiercely at William; its teeth glimmered in the moonlight as its eyes began to glow bright red.

Heartened by the beast's presence. Elijah drew a deep breath. Surely William would not risk an attack now that he was faced by a beast clearly determined to protect him and Emira. Still, he knew better than to underestimate his father's stubbornness.

"One wolf, you think this changes anything?" William was trying to act strong, but Elijah could feel the blade twitching against his back; William was afraid.

Fearlessly, the beast took a huge stride towards William, who stood his ground. As if to settle this uneasy stalemate once and for all, the lycan threw his huge head to the sky and belted out a bone-shaking howl. One by one, deep, chilling howls came rolling down from the hills around them.

*He's not alone!* Elijah was elated when he heard at least three more. Now, William surely would know he was outmatched. Having attained what he came for, William turned and ran, disappearing back into the night from whence he came. Elijah wanted to give chase, but he couldn't even sit up.

Elijah suddenly heard thunder behind him. He turned his head to see a throng of beasts race past him, the big black one in the lead. They were going after William! Elijah hoped they would tear him to shreds.

# CHAPTER 106

EMIRA RAN TO Elijah's side as the beasts disappeared into the night. She rolled him over and cradled his head in her lap. Knowing what he had given up for her, she could think of no words that could convey what she wanted to say, so she just sat quietly, holding him.

Elijah was more than thankful to the lycan horde, but he would not trust Emira with anyone but Khalid. Elijah knew his fate; he could feel it sinking in as Mikal's dire warning kept ringing in his mind.

Thoughts of Khalid crossed his mind. He hoped the giant man was all right. He needed him to be here for Emira. Elijah's body ached from the inside out; he knew he had only minutes left.

He thought about William getting away with the rite and wondered what would become of the world. Would Emira be safe, with all that might happen after he was gone?

Emira studied Elijah's face and desperation gripped her. She could see his life diminishing. His strong, muscular features seemed to be shriveling into sharp edges. There was no color left in his face, and she could tell he wasn't breathing. He already looked more like a corpse than a man.

"Please, no! Don't leave me." Her voice rose with her fear. She clutched his hand again. Feeling it go limp, her heart sank as if to the bottom of a thousand oceans. With tears streaming down her face, she curled up next to his lifeless body and pulled his heavy arm across her chest.

She had been in that same position just last night. His strong arms pressing her tightly to his chest had given her such strength and an abiding sense of safety. But now, lying beneath the rain, there was no strength left in his lifeless body. She could no longer feel the comforting resonance of his strong heart beating against her back.

It was like a dream, a nightmare, and all she could do was cry. She was helpless. She looked on, unable to change the fate of the one she loved. She would watch him wither away to nothing, as would the love they had just discovered.

Elijah felt her soothing touch on his skin and was thankful for it.

*She's safe.* The knowledge warmed his soul as he drifted off into the afterlife, finally at peace.

# CHAPTER 107

A S EMIRA LAY there clutching Elijah's corpse, she blamed herself for everything that had happened.

He had sacrificed his life for her; she had to find a way to fix it. Tears continued to pour until Emira heard someone speak her name. Joy filled her heart as she looked down, expecting to see life flooding back into Elijah's body.

"I'm sorry for the way everything turned out." The voice was nearly a whisper.

Emira looked around to see where it was coming from, but saw nothing, only a serpent slithering its way up Elijah's leg. Emira pulled back and tried to pull Elijah's body away from it.

"There is no need to fear me, my dear. I am here to help. I can give him back to you, just as strong and willful as ever," the serpent hissed.

"Who are you? And what are you talking about?" Emira demanded.

"My name is Adol. Have you heard of me?"

"Yes, I have. You are evil and untrustworthy. You create the blood-letters," Emira accused.

"That I do, but only as pawns in this game of chess I have

played with my brothers for millennia now. We use different methods to inspire and motivate our game pieces, but in the end, is there really any difference? Your god uses you, just as I use my pieces on this game board of life. There are only two rules; we must keep our word, and we cannot directly use our powers against each other's pawns," the god continued.

"You are telling me this is all a game? That might be true for you and Mikal, but I know Odam is different. He seeks to help mankind. He even made that spell to give us a chance," Emira retorted with vigor and confidence.

"My girl, Odam is the one who started this game." Adol snorted with laughter. "He created the first immortals, the first pawns, the lycans, and from there it spiraled into this elaborate game of power and strategy."

"Let's say I believe you, and I let you bring him back, will he be the same as he was?"

"His body is old; he will have the same power and the same personality," Adol said.

"You will make him into a vampire!" Emira spat. "No, never! He would hate that."

"Elijah will be himself, inside and out. Whether there is goodness or evil in him, that will not change, I promise you. I can't force you, though, I just wanted to offer my help." Adol seemed to pause and think for a moment. "I will watch you until midnight tonight. If you change your mind, just find a place where we can be alone, and call on me.

"What would you demand in return?" Emira asked.

"Just a favor, a favor for a favor." Adol hissed and then slithered away just as Khalid approached.

Khalid could see Emira lying next to Elijah's lifeless body. He could hear her desperate cries and it broke his heart.

"Emira," he whispered as he ran his fingers through her hair. She was too upset to notice. "Emira." He spoke a little louder as he grabbed her under her arms and pulled her from beneath Elijah's dead arm.

"He's gone." She spoke quietly as Khalid held her up.

"I know. I'm sorry, but maybe now he has found peace." Khalid tried to comfort her. Emira pulled away and held her own weight. She looked up at Khalid sharply.

"Where were you?" Her tone and stare were accusations. "If you had been here, maybe things would have turned out differently." She had never spoken to Khalid that way before, but now she believed he deserved it.

"I'm sorry. I tried, but it wouldn't have made a difference. We would still have had to give up the ME to get you back. Elijah knew the consequences, and he was happy with his choice. He loved you Emira. No one could have kept him from doing what he did. Just try to remember it was a gift, freely given because of how much he loved you. He was a great man. I misjudged him." Khalid was speaking softly, trying to comfort himself as well as Emira. He was deeply regretful about how he had judged Elijah and hoped they could both learn to find some good in what had happened.

"I'm sorry. I know it's not your fault." Emira fell limp in Khalid's arms, weeping once again. Khalid himself was almost overcome with grief.

"It's okay. Come on. Let me take you back to the house so we can clean Elijah's body and bury him." Emira didn't say a word as Khalid lifted her off the ground and cradled her like a child. She saw a small group of men and women assembling behind Khalid.

"Khalid, we have to take you back now." Arhan's voice was soft and apologetic.

"I will come with you, but I must take her home and bury Elijah first." Khalid spoke with anger as he turned and looked at them all threateningly. They each stepped to the side as Khalid pushed past, carrying Emira home.

"Arhan, bring Elijah's body," Khalid commanded. Arhan slid his muscular arms beneath Elijah and lifted him effortlessly. He carried him to the large stone picnic table near the back door and gently laid him on his back. His body had withered completely; he looked like a thousand-year-old corpse. Khalid sat Emira down in a small chair beside the table. She just stared at the ground, expressionless.

"It just doesn't seem possible. I don't understand. He was so strong." Her voice was broken and her tears welled again.

"I know, I know. He was the strongest man I ever met." Khalid hugged her tightly. "You sit here next to Arhan." Khalid pulled a chair over and motioned Arhan to sit. "I'm going to get some towels and water so we can clean the body."

The council of immortals stood outside waiting while Khalid went into the house, filled a bucket with warm water, and collected a few towels. Walking back outside, he laid the bucket and the towels beside the stone table. Emira's expression was grim; she looked almost catatonic.

He wondered if she would ever recover. He thought about the judgment that was to come. He had never feared death until this moment, but he couldn't imagine leaving her alone now, when she needed him most.

Suddenly, the ground beneath Khalid's feet began to vibrate. He looked over at Emira and Arhan for confirmation, and saw they were also confused and concerned. A second later, the ground shook vigorously, as if a great earthquake had begun right beneath their feet. The earth roared like wicked laughter; it seemed the very ground beneath them might explode at any moment.

The sky above them turned dark and began to rumble savagely. Khalid could see Emira duck her head and cover her ears. Even the other council members seemed startled and nervous. Emira ran over to the table and braced Elijah's body so it wouldn't roll off the table.

As if out of nowhere, a huge man appeared before them. His skin was solid black. Emira stepped back towards Khalid.

*Odam?* Khalid couldn't believe his eyes. He hadn't seen Odam in hundreds of years. What was he doing here now?

"What are you doing here, old friend? Where have you been for so long?" Khalid's tone was harsh.

"I have been away for too long; you are correct. I am here now to give you my final instructions, and then I am going to try to convince my brothers to leave this place, and to leave you humans to yourselves. Our powers, of course, will still keep the balance, so the earth will remain as it is, as will your power and immortality." Odam's voice was loud but monotone.

"I don't understand." Khalid frowned.

"It is finally time for you to fulfill your true destiny, Khalid. With the ME in the hands of a blood-letter, there will be a war over all of creation, unless you keep her safe." Odam looked over at Emira and then back to Khalid. "If I can convince my brothers to leave this place, then you only have to deal with the immortals left behind. The earth needs its soldiers to protect her. Now is the time to rise up and kill every immortal blood-letter you can find!" Odam proclaimed.

"Khalid has betrayed you, Odam, and the council!" Ubaram interrupted in protest.

"I am Odam. Khalid is your leader; this is my decree!" Odam's voice thundered and Ubaram quickly bowed his head in submission.

"I am the breath of man. I carry him through his toils and struggles, his victories and defeats. I carry him from one brother's life to another brother's death. My power is neither life nor death, but will." Everything around them shook as his voice thundered down. "I need you now, Khalid. I need you to be strong if this world is to survive. You will now be my will upon this earth," Odam proclaimed.

"I don't understand, strong enough for what purpose?" Khalid could barely hear his own voice.

"To end it; to end it all." Odam bellowed. "The war of the immortals has just begun, and you can't let the vampires get their hands on *The Key!* Otherwise, there will be no stopping them," he said. "The blood-letter William could gain godlike power."

Odam paused for a moment and looked around at the immortals arrayed before him. "That is what is at stake. If you let them get this girl, William will become absolute ruler of this world in our absence." Odam's words were full of certainty.

"We will protect her; you have my word." Khalid spoke boldly.

"Now I bid you farewell; one day we will meet again. I will do my best to deal with the gods. I believe I can convince my brothers. You just make sure no others are created." Odam warned.

"Do me one favor before you go!" Emira shouted. Odam turned to the girl and looked at her for a few moments.

"What is it you wish of me?" He asked.

"Revive my friend, please." Emira turned and placed her hands on the concrete slab where Elijah lay. Odam walked over and looked down at Elijah's decayed corpse.

"So this one finally met his end, did he?" Emira could hear hints of satisfaction in Odam's voice.

"Please, we need him. I need him." Emira begged.

"I am sorry, but I cannot revive this man; he is not worthy. I have watched him cause much pain and suffering over the years; he is volatile, arrogant, and stubborn," Odam declared.

"Odam, please, he was instrumental in saving Emira from

the vampires today. Maybe he was bad, but he has changed," Khalid cried

"I am sorry, but a few good deeds do not atone for centuries of slaughter." Odam stated with absolute conviction.

"But—" Khalid was cut off.

"That is my final answer. Keep her safe, or this world will come to an end," Odam warned again.

"Elijah protects me. He has shown you he would die to protect me. That is what's important, right?" Emira begged with renewed intensity.

"I cannot depend on this man to protect *The Key*; one *Key* already died under his protection. He is simply not worth the effort to revive him," Odam stated. There was a blast of thunder, and he was gone.

Emira leaned over Elijah, and her tears fell on his shriveled corpse. Khalid stepped close and put his arms around her.

"I am so sorry," he said. Emira turned and wrapped her arms around his waist. She was dead on the inside.

"What did he mean that Elijah already let one *Key* die?" Emira asked, teary-eyed.

"I truly am not sure," Khalid replied.

# EPILOGUE

EMIRA SAT ALONE on a stool next to Elijah's corpse; Khalid had just gone into the house, and Adol's words played continuously on a reel in her mind. She couldn't imagine striking a deal with the devil of gods, but she also couldn't imagine living without Elijah. She stood up and leaned over the concrete slab.

"I'm sorry Elijah," she said as she kissed his forehead. "Adol, if you can hear me, I… I want your help." Emira stuttered getting the dangerous words out of her mouth.

Immediately, a snake slithered out from under the concrete table and transformed into a giant man with ivory skin and intricate carvings covering his entire body.

Emira's mouth dropped wide open. He was not at all what she had imagined; he was like a giant work of art.

"If I do this for you, you will owe me a favor." Adol's gray eyes narrowed as he stepped forward and gripped Emira's hand. "Are you sure this is what you want? You will have to do whatever I ask; the deal will be binding. You will have no way out." Adol stroked her hand as he warned of the consequences of her decision.

"What is it you want?" Emira asked, her mind racing.

*She is The Key, the only one who can read the rite.* Elijah's words swirled round and round in her mind. *That has to be what he wants,* she thought. She paused to considered the dire consequences of her actions, if she truly was *The Key,* and if Adol could force her to read the ritual.

However, in this moment, nothing mattered as much as having Elijah back. A world without him in it would be a travesty. Besides, she believed Elijah deserved to live, regardless of what Odam had said. Her hate burned deep for the god of her uncle as she recalled how quickly and how harshly he had judged the man she loved.

*If bringing Elijah back causes a reordering of the heavenly powers, then so be it,* she decided.

"What I want from you, my girl, is for another day." Adol smiled, hinting at emotion for the first time, although his gray eyes were impossible to read.

"I'm not an idiot. I know you want me to read that stupid ritual," Emira snatched her hand away from the giant god. "So you can inherit the power Odam locked away and use it to rule the heavens."

Adol smiled once more.

"You are definitely on the right track." Even Adol's whispers gently shook the ground beneath her feet. His power was obvious and immense.

Emira walked to the table and looked down at Elijah's shriveled corpse. "Where is he right now?"

"Don't worry about him. He is at peace, far away from the worries of this world," Adol admitted.

"I know Elijah, and he doesn't want peace, not until he has had his revenge, delivered his justice." Emira ran her fingers through his hair. She thought about their last kiss, and how he had given up his quest, the passion that had driven him for nearly a millennium, just to make sure she was safe. If she could, she knew she must give him back the opportunity she had taken away.

"Can you bring him back just as he was?" she asked again, as tears streaked down her face and onto Elijah's corpse.

"He will be the same person; he will have the same memories and emotions, but he won't be the same. He will be vampire. His strength and will come from within him, and from his age; those will not be affected. He will have a nearly unquenchable thirst for human blood; that will be the difference." Adol walked to the other side of the table and looked down at Elijah's corpse, then he looked up and wiped a tear from Emira's face.

"I can fix this," he said. "I just need your sworn promise."

Emira looked at Adol and then at Elijah. She thought he might well hate her for forcing him to become that which he despised.

"You will empower him fully, and, no matter what, you will never withdraw it. You will never betray him," Emira demanded.

"I will, and you will not be harmed either, as long as you keep your word. You have my word. I will empower him to his own end, no matter what that might be. He will be just like his father, except he will have no master. He will be free to follow his own will," Adol agreed.

"Then do it," Emira commanded.

"He will be an immortal like no other; he will be free." Adol's eyes widened as if he were in awe. "Here." Adol pulled an ancient-looking blade out of nowhere and handed it to Emira.

"What do you want me to do with this?" She asked.

"To make it binding, the agreement must be sealed in blood. If this is your wish, then make a deep cut in your hand, and it will be done."

Without hesitation, Emira wrapped her hand around the blade of the knife and squeezed hard as she pulled back on the handle. Blood quickly began to flow between her fingers and drip to the ground.

"It is done." Adol rumbled.

"What about Elijah? You haven't brought him back."

"I will, but you would be advised to leave first." Adol said. "He is going to be very, very hungry, and if his feelings for you are strong, it will be even harder for him to resist ripping open your throat."

"Just do it!" Emira shouted.

"As you wish." Adol spoke slowly and then vanished. A moment later he was back with a young girl in his arms.

"What are you doing?" Emira asked, her voice rising with tension.

"I can't create life, but once it's inside him, I will be able to manipulate it." Adol explained as he opened Elijah's mouth and slit the girl's throat with his fingernail. He held her over him, allowing the blood to flow into Elijah's mouth. After the draining blood had slowed to a drip, Adol tossed the body aside. "You better stand back," he said.

Emira took a few steps back.

Adol leaned over Elijah's corpse, placing one hand on his head and one on his chest. In just moments the decayed flesh began to come to life. Elijah's bones and muscles grew thick and strong.

"He will wake soon, and you need to be gone," Adol warned.

"I stay," she demanded.

"I need you alive, so go—now!" Adol's voice thundered.

"That will make us even, then. My departure must be considered my favor to you, and our agreement will be complete," Emira smirked.

Adol stood motionless. Emira could see his frustration as he disappeared once again.

"Huuuuu." Elijah took a deep breath and sat up. He turned

toward Emira and looked at her in disbelief. As the shock slowly melted from his face, a warm smile took its place and he pushed himself from the concrete slab and gathered her in his arms. "What happened?" he asked.

"I don't know," she whispered, feeling the tears of joy streak her face.

Elijah kissed her lips and then nestled her close. For a moment he knew nothing but warmth and beauty.

Then he noticed her pulsing jugular and something snapped. A burning hunger burst inside him, an uncontrollable thirst for blood. He pushed her back.

"Something is wrong," he said, breathing heavily. "You need to get out of here," he gritted as he closed his eyes and turned his head aside.

"No, Elijah. It will be okay," Emira cried as she stepped forward.

"*NOW!*" he roared as his head shot up, revealing searing blue eyes and razor-sharp fangs.

www.ingramcontent.com/pod-product-compliance
Lightning Source LLC
Chambersburg PA
CBHW061029030726
47504CB00002B/310

* 9 7 8 0 9 9 1 5 6 1 7 0 4 *